Dear Reader,

The first man I ever fell in love with was a cowboy. I was five and he was nineteen, and I followed him everywhere. It was probably a case of imprinting—like a duck. To this day, men in Wranglers and cowboy hats make my heart beat faster.

But it isn't only their physical appearance that appeals. Mostly it's the code they live by. The cowboy's code stresses independence and self-reliance, yet also demands generosity and caring. It asks a man to be both tough and gentle, reliable and spontaneous. Above all, it requires that he be honorable.

Luke and Noah and Taggart are all those things. I fell in love with each of them in turn as I wrote their stories. I hope, reading them, that you do, too.

Anne McAllister

ANNE MCALLISTER

CODE OF THE WEST:

The Cowboy's Code

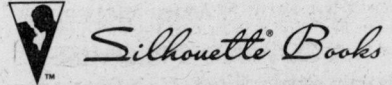

Silhouette Books

Published by Silhouette Books

America's Publisher of Contemporary Romance

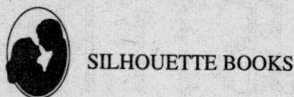 **SILHOUETTE BOOKS**

ISBN 0-373-20189-3

by Request

CODE OF THE WEST: THE COWBOY'S CODE

Copyright © 2001 by Harlequin Books S.A.

The publisher acknowledges the copyright holder of the individual works as follows:

COWBOYS DON'T QUIT
Copyright © 1995 by Barbara Schenck

COWBOYS DON'T STAY
Copyright © 1995 by Barbara Schenck

THE COWBOY AND THE KID
Copyright © 1996 by Barbara Schenck

Visit Silhouette at www.eHarlequin.com

Printed in U.S.A.

CONTENTS

COWBOYS DON'T QUIT

One

He was dreaming again.

The same dream. Always the same. They were bodysurfing near the pier at Manhattan Beach, he and Keith—laughing, joking, competing as always for the biggest wave, the steepest drop, the longest ride.

They were showing off for Keith's fans on the pier, all of them watching, waving, smiling.

He saw Jillian, Keith's fiancée, there, braced against the railing, her long dark hair tangling across her face in the wind as she waved to Keith, then looked out to sea and pointed.

They both looked back toward where she was indicating. The swell was already noticeable, building now, moving toward them.

"Wave of the day!" Keith yelled, grinning and moving into position, beginning to stroke toward shore.

Luke watched Keith go, then he moved too, slower, as

he always was in the water, but still in time. He caught the momentum, merging with the force of the wave, rising on its crest to see the water and the foam and the beach spread out before him. He caught a glimpse of Jillian leaning over the railing, watching intently. He spied Keith just ahead, already into the fall.

And then he fell, too, as the wave crested, curving under, dropping him headlong into the backwater. It pounded down on top of him, pressing him into the ocean floor even as it dragged him along. He felt a thump. His body collided with Keith's. Arms and legs tangled in the power of the wave. They struggled, shifted, separated. He felt Keith's fingers grab for him. They clutched, touched, clung, oddly frantic. And then they slipped away.

Away...

He opened his mouth to call. *Keith!*

But the water choked him. Gagged him. Pressed down upon him, swirling and pounding, grinding him into the sand, crushing his lungs, burning his throat.... Then for a moment, blessed air. And just as suddenly the wet suffocation was back, choking him, covering his nose....

Luke jerked awake. Hank, the old herding dog, was licking his face.

"Damn." He shuddered and pushed her away. "Hell of a way to say good mornin'," he grumbled, but he knew it wasn't Hank's fault. It was the dream.

Always and, it seemed, forever—the dream. And that wasn't even the way it had happened, for God's sake.

It—Keith's death.

Even now, almost two years later, it was hard to think of Keith Mallory as dead. Intense, dynamic, irrepressible Keith—mover and shaker, dreamer and doer, one of America's best-loved actors, not to mention Luke's own best friend—had always had more to live for, more to give than anyone he knew.

Luke's fists clenched futilely against the lingering feel of Keith's fingers slipping out of his grasp. He drew a ragged breath.

In reality he'd had no chance to come that close.

He hadn't even been in the water. He'd been standing high and dry on the riverbank, too far away to help, yet too near not to realize what was happening.

Luke sat up on his cot now, shivering not so much from the cold as from the memory. He dragged in another breath of the crisp Colorado mountain air and tried to shake off the shivers. But even though it was already July, at close to nine thousand feet it never got very warm until the sun was up, and what memories didn't accomplish, the cool morning temperature did.

He pulled his knees up to his chest and wrapped his arms around them, his body trembling in a now-familiar cold sweat. He rubbed a hand across his wet face, tasting salt amid the dog slobber. Tears. He rested his head against his bent knees and tried to steady his breathing.

Keith. Oh, God, Keith, I'm sorry. It should have been me.

The dog nudged his shoulder and tried to lick him again. Luke looped an arm around her neck and rubbed his face against her fur. Then he scrubbed a hand across his eyes and hauled himself to his feet. There would be no sleeping now, no point in even trying.

Not that he wanted to. Not when he dreamed.

He could tell from the faint light filtering through the window of the rough log cabin that it wasn't quite dawn. The sky to the east was still more dark gray than rose. But there was nothing to be gained by staying in bed; he would just lie there remembering what he would give his soul to forget.

He picked up the coffeepot, let himself out into the chill mountain air and headed toward the spring. He filled the pot, then carried it back to the cabin, dumped in some coffee and started a fire on the small propane stove.

He made himself concentrate on each task as he performed it. Whatever part of his mind he didn't keep firmly focused on what he was doing would be on the dream or, worse, on the memories that caused it.

He rubbed his fingers together. He couldn't feel the clutch of Keith's fingers anymore. Sometimes the sensation lasted for hours. Not today, thank God.

While the coffee was heating, he scrubbed his face with some of the water he'd brought up the night before, then dragged a comb through his shaggy dark hair. He could tell by feel that the next time he went into town he'd better stop by Bernie's and get a haircut. Not that he'd be going anytime soon. Lots of camp men these days came down off the summer range every week or so, but they had friends, family, people to see, mail to pick up, a life to keep in touch with in town.

Luke didn't. Nor did he want any. He set his hat on his head and tugged down the brim, then went back to the stove.

The coffee was hot. He poured himself a mugful and stood staring out the small window, making himself think about what he needed to do that day. Bring cattle up out of the creek bottom—that was a given. They were like magnets, those cows. You barely got them up to the head of the draw and left them, when they drifted right back down again. Or got spooked and ran back. He needed to circle up the mountain and check on the cattle near the national-forest land, making sure the gates were closed. Hikers didn't seem to realize all the work they caused when they didn't leave gates the way they found them. If even one gate had been left open, he'd have his day's work cut out for him.

In the early morning light he could look down across the meadow and see three of his horses already lurking by the quaky fence, waiting for him to holler them down and grain them. He didn't even need to holler anymore. He'd been doing it for more than a year now—long enough that they knew what to expect.

He took another swallow of coffee, then set his cup down and got out food for the dogs. There were two others besides Hank—a scruffy-looking catch dog called Muff and another Border collie named Tommy. They brushed against his legs as he poured their food out for them. Hank nudged his hand, her pointy noise wet and cold against his fingers. Luke rubbed her under the chin.

The panic was gone now. The pressure had eased on his lungs as the dream faded, and sunrise brought light, clarity and color to the mountain meadow he called home.

Breathing more steadily now, Luke finished his cup of coffee. He made and ate a quick breakfast, then set to work.

Some days entailed more work than others. Luke liked the work. He sought it, needed it, created it. Today, because of the dream, he made even more than there was.

He moved twenty head of cattle out of the creek bottom, doctored some foot rot and rode the fence along the national-forest line. The gates were all closed, but someone had cut the wire to get through where there wasn't one.

He rounded up a dozen cattle and brought them back down, fixed the fence, then circled through a stand of aspen toward the creek. And found one of his young bulls caught in the middle of a willow patch.

Bulls weren't the easiest critters to deal with at the best

of times, and when they'd been stuck as long as this bull had likely been, their tempers weren't exactly sweet. This fellow was no exception.

Luke was tempted to leave him. Nobody was looking over his shoulder, and it was his bull. But the bull couldn't do his job unless Luke did his. More than that, though, Luke knew a dreamless sleep came only when he was so dead tired he couldn't move.

He laid a loop over the bull's head, alternately dragging on the rope and urging the animal forward, while Hank and Tommy nipped and prodded. He was doing his whooping and hollering on foot, not on horseback, when the bull finally broke free and rewarded him with a kick at his ribs.

He missed. But that's when Luke discovered the bull had foot rot.

"Son of a gun," he muttered, taking off his hat to wipe a hand through sweat dampened hair. "Must be my lucky day."

He was dirty and sweaty, tired and sore by the time he rode back over the rise that looked down on his camp. The bull might've missed Luke's ribs with that first kick, but he hadn't missed his shin later when Luke was maneuvering his horse in close enough to give the animal an injection.

Luke figured he'd be hobbling tomorrow. He didn't care. Physical pain wouldn't keep him awake or make him dream.

Tonight he'd earned his sleep, and he thought he just might get it, too.

Until he saw someone sitting by his cabin door.

Nobody he'd invited, that was damn certain. Since he'd moved up the mountain a year ago last spring, Luke hadn't encouraged visitors. Jimmy, his hand, who was renting Luke's ranch house, came up whenever Luke asked him to help move cattle or to bring salt, and now and then he brought Luke provisions or a coffee cake or some cookies his wife, Annette, had made. But Jimmy had just been up three days ago. And Luke's only other visitor was his old schoolmate Linda Gutierrez's son, Paco.

"You don't want him around, you send him away," Linda had told him from the first.

But Luke knew Paco's dad had died three years ago, and he remembered all too well how he'd felt when his own dad had died. He'd been older than Paco when it happened—sixteen. Paco was only eight and needier even than he had been.

Luke hadn't had the heart to send the boy away.

Besides, talking with Paco was a form of penance. All the kid ever wanted to do was hear about Keith. He probably knew by heart every movie Keith Mallory had made, and he took great joy in asking Luke about the ones he'd worked on.

Luke wondered when he'd realize that it was his fault the boy's hero was dead.

He sat up a little straighter in the saddle now, trying to guess his visitor's identity. Whoever it was saw him and got up, beginning to move toward him now.

It was a woman.

A tall and slender woman in jeans that hugged curves no cowboy'd ever have. Long brown hair tangled across her face in the evening breeze. Then the breeze lifted the swath of hair and Luke felt as if the bull had kicked him right in the gut.

God, no! It couldn't be.

He shut his eyes, begged and pleaded with the Almighty. Then he opened them again, still praying.

To no avail.

It was Jillian. Jillian Crane.

Luke wished the earth would open and swallow him up.

No such luck.

He slowed his horse, tempted to turn tail and head right back up the mountain, knowing damned well he would have if she hadn't seen him. But she had, so he had no choice but to continue down.

He didn't know what the hell she was doing here. Couldn't begin to imagine. They hadn't seen each other since the day of Keith's funeral, almost two years ago.

They hadn't spoken even then.

They hadn't needed to.

Jill had said everything there was to say the afternoon Keith died.

Luke could remember it as clearly as if it had been yesterday. It had haunted him so often that it might as well have been....

They'd been two weeks into a new movie, a tough-guy, mountain-man script with lots of the action-adventure stuff that was Keith's forte and his stunt-double Luke's bread and butter. It was grueling, strenuous and more than a little dangerous—exactly the sort of thing they both loved.

They'd been filming for fourteen days straight from a gritty little town on the Salmon River in Idaho, and by the end of the second week in October they were as gritty, earthy and wild looking as the landscape.

It was still warm during the days, but chilly after the sun went down, and every night after they finished, he and Keith and some of the rest of the crew would warm their insides in the local bar.

They were a few beers into the warming process, throwing darts and arguing about which of them was the better shot—and hence the better man—when Luke stepped up to take his toss.

Suddenly the door opened...and there she was.

Jillian.

His dart sailed over the top of the board.

If anyone noticed, it wasn't Keith.

"Hey," Keith had shouted, a sudden, broad grin lighting his unshaven face. "My lady's come!" And he knocked over a bar stool in his haste to get to her.

Luke didn't move. He stood rooted to the spot, watching as Keith wrapped Jill in a bear hug, then turned, grinning, his arm looped over her shoulders, and faced the rest of them.

"Look who's here," he said unnecessarily.

"Bring 'er on over," one of the sound men had called out. "Plenty of room, ain't that right, Luke?"

For a moment, Luke didn't speak. Couldn't. He wasn't prepared. *So, get prepared,* he commanded himself. He drew a deep, steadying breath, met Keith's grin, then let his eyes settle on Jill. "That's right," he said.

Keith just shook his head. "Not on your life. Come on, sweetheart." He started to draw Jill with him toward the door, then stopped and kissed her slow and hard, surfacing only long enough to glance over his shoulder at them and say, "Find your own women to keep you warm." Then he dragged her off to his room.

Their room, Luke corrected himself.

The one right on the other side of the wall from his.

Not that he went back to his. He had no intention of lying there in his cold, solitary bed and thinking about Keith making love to Jill at that very moment on the other side of a few inches of plaster.

Because that's what Keith would be doing.

It's what Luke would be doing if Jill were his. But she wasn't. Would never be.

A man didn't poach on his best friend's girl.

A man got drunk instead.

He didn't go back to his room until after two the next morning. He stayed out as long as the bars stayed open. But even when he got back, drunk and dead tired, he still didn't sleep.

He lay there listening for the slightest noise, the softest murmur, the faintest rustling sound from the bed in the next room. He heard nothing. It didn't matter; his imagination was enough. He finished his bottle of whiskey only an hour before his alarm went off in the morning.

He made it to the set on time, but his bloodshot eyes and haggard face were a dead giveaway.

"Little too much celebrating?" Keith was in high good humor as he teased Luke about his hangover.

And why wouldn't he be? Luke thought savagely. He barely grunted a reply.

"Oughta get yourself a lady like mine," Keith told him cheerfully. "You wouldn't be out runnin' around if you had yourself a Jill."

For an instant Luke's eyes met Jill's. At once she looked away.

"Oh, for heaven's sake, Keith. Leave him alone," she said irritably, taking his hand. "Luke doesn't want an old stick-in-the-mud like me."

"He'd better not. You're mine." Keith grinned at her and punched Luke lightly on the arm. "C'mon. Grab some coffee and let's get this show on the road."

They were set up to shoot the scene where Keith's character, a renegade cowboy, escaped from a band of Indian pursuers, hurtling down a draw to where he'd left his canoe. Then, under a barrage of arrows, he was supposed to shove off, jump into the canoe and paddle into the roiling river while the white water swept him out of sight.

"We've got it almost all rigged," Carl Oakes, the stunt

coordinator, said to Luke when he and Keith found him on the riverbank. "Plenty of safety lines, so if things look grim, bail out."

Luke nodded. He swallowed, studying the tumbling white water, trying to psyche himself up. His head pounded, and his stomach was roiling worse than the river.

"I want to do it," Keith said suddenly.

Luke jerked his head around to see the determined set of his friend's jaw.

Carl rolled his eyes. "Don't be an idiot. That's what Luke's here for. He's the stuntman. You're the star."

Keith nodded. "Exactly. That's the point." And Luke could see him getting psyched up even as he spoke. "It's me that people want to see do it."

"You just want Jill to see you do it," Carl said, with a wink at Luke.

Luke didn't say anything.

Keith grinned. "Well, that, too."

"Garrison won't let you," Carl predicted. "No way he's going to let you."

But surprisingly, Garrison, the director, was willing to listen to Keith's argument. He even agreed that shooting Keith in close-up as he scrambled into the canoe, then panning wide as he moved downstream, was a good idea.

"No break, huh? Makes sense," he said, a speculative smile forming. "It's not too big a risk, is it?" He looked at Carl for confirmation.

Keith scoffed. "Carl's more careful than my mother. Aren'tcha, Carl?"

Carl scowled and muttered under his breath. But Keith kept talking and Garrison kept listening, while Luke stood by, wishing he was a million miles away, and didn't say a word.

He knew what was going to happen. He'd seen it before.

It wasn't just showing off for Jill, though Luke knew—and Keith knew—that was part of it. It was also that Keith was a fanatic about realism. If anything death-defying needed to be done for one of his parts, he wanted to do it. Carl always had the devil's own time arguing him out of it.

He was doing his best this time.

Finally Keith played his final card. "It will be a better movie. I can do it. I need to do it." He faced Garrison squarely. "I'll take full responsibility."

Garrison beamed. "Well, in that case..."

Carl muttered, but Garrison was convinced.

Jill wasn't, Luke could tell. "Are you sure about this?" she asked, her gray eyes looked worriedly into Keith's.

"'Course I'm sure." He brushed her lips with his. "Piece o' cake," he added. He took the flotation vest and began to put it on beneath his buckskin shirt.

Luke watched for a moment, felt his fists clench, then deliberately loosened them. He turned to help Carl get the canoe ready, then waited while Carl saw that the last of the safety lines were rigged.

Jill left Keith and followed Carl. "Are you sure there are enough? Is he safe?"

"As safe as I can make him," Carl said grimly.

Keith laughed and came after her, then kissed her again. "Don't worry about me. I'm the bread and butter around here. They won't let me drown!"

"But—"

"It's all right, Jilly," he insisted. "Better me than Luke here." He slanted a grin in Luke's direction. "He was partying a little too much last night."

"I was not!"

"Besides—" Keith grinned "—don't you know, cowboys can't swim!"

"I can so," Luke retorted.

"Not like I can. Who was California all-state breast-stroke champ in high school?"

Luke managed a smile at that. "*Breast* stroke?" He waggled his eyebrows. "You never told me that had anything to do with swimming."

Keith laughed easily. "Hey, not in front of my lady." He touched Jill's cheek. "Relax, hon, I'll be fine. Besides, it'll be a dynamite shot, you'll see. And everybody will know that it's really me."

"They won't care."

"But I care."

Luke saw their gazes catch and lock.

Finally Jill tore her eyes away from Keith and found Luke's, her gaze beseeching. "Can't you stop him?"

Can't you stop him?

He'd asked himself that time and again.

Could he have?

He didn't know. Maybe—if he'd argued harder. Maybe if he had, he would have won. God knew he should have tried. The fact was, he hadn't.

He'd kept his mouth shut and let Keith do the gag himself.

He'd have done it, pounding headache and roiling stomach and all, if Keith hadn't stepped in.

It was his job. But Keith was right about one thing: he wasn't a great swimmer. Not anywhere near as good as Keith. But if he did it right, he knew he wouldn't have to swim. He only had to launch the canoe, escape from the Indians who were shooting arrows at him and navigate the white water until he was around the bend in the river, where Carl's men were standing by to fish him out.

But Keith had pulled rank. "I'm the boss, remember," he said, then grinned. "C'mon, Carl, let's do it!"

Luke helped finish rigging the safety lines, then tossed a

neon-colored volleyball into the current half a dozen times so they could figure out the best angles. Then it was Keith's turn.

"Outta my way, man," Keith said. He winked at Jill and headed up the draw, leaving Luke standing beside her on the riverbank. She glanced at Luke, then turned her gaze back to the river.

So did Luke. He edged away.

The scene went like clockwork—Keith's mad scramble down the draw, shoving off the canoe and leaping into it, his desperate paddling as the Indians swarmed after him, only to halt at the river's edge as the canoe shot away into the surging water, past the first set of rocks, over the rapids, downriver.

And then, suddenly, the canoe slewed sideways against the rocks. It plunged, tipped and flipped Keith into the water.

"Keith!" Jill swallowed her scream, pressing her hand to her mouth, watching frantically, waiting for him to surface. And when he didn't immediately, she turned to Luke, horrified, looking to him for help.

Luke shook his head and took a step back. "He'll be fine," he said gruffly. "He's got a vest. He'll be up in a sec. Just got to get his bearings."

This was Keith, after all. Keith, the all-state swimmer. Keith the champ. Keith who could do damn near everything Luke could do in the way of stunts—and when it came to water, could do them better. He was only showing off, trying to prove that it was a good thing he was doing it, not Luke.

"Don't worry," he said to Jill.

But when seconds turned into a minute, then two, and there was still no sign of Keith's dark head, his own determined calm disintegrated. Panic bubbled up.

He started toward the river, first walking, then running, then wading frantically out into the water, with Jill stumbling along behind him.

"Keith! Damn it, Keith!" He stumbled through the water, lost his footing, fell, scrambled up again. "Keith!"

Then Carl was beside him, too, looking feverishly around, muttering. "Damn him. If this is a joke..."

Luke knew what he meant. It wouldn't have been beyond him. He looked up onto the shore, hoping now that it was. Hoping to see Keith, irrepressible as ever, sitting on a rock laughing at them.

He saw instead Jill's white, stricken face. He turned back to the river and plunged in.

He didn't find Keith.

Carl didn't find Keith.

Neither did the grip downstream who pulled out the canoe half an hour later. Nor any of the hundreds of searchers who scoured the river for the rest of the day and evening.

They didn't find his body until the following morning, a mile downriver.

Luke had to go and identify him.

"We know who it is," the coroner apologized. "It's just a technicality."

It wasn't a technicality to Luke, not when he had to stand there and stare down into the dark, still, silent face of his friend. His ears rang. His throat closed. He felt himself start to shake.

"One of his boots was badly scraped," the coroner was saying matter-of-factly as he consulted the report. "We figure that's what held him down. It must have got stuck between two submerged rocks and he couldn't get out."

Luke wasn't looking at the boot. He was looking at the bloody, raw tips of Keith's fingers—mute testimony to his friend's desperate, futile struggle to free himself.

But if seeing Keith was hard, being the one to tell Jillian what she already knew was worse.

And worst of all was hearing from her lips what he already knew himself.

She didn't say anything for a moment, just stared into the distance. And then, in a low, toneless voice, she spoke. "He was doing your job," she said, and her gaze shifted so that she looked squarely at him, her eyes brimming with pain and unshed tears. "You were supposed to be out there, not him."

She wasn't telling him anything he hadn't already told himself. And all the guilt he'd had over the feelings he'd tried so long to hide was nothing compared to this.

No, they hadn't spoken at Keith's funeral.

What else had there been to say?

What was there to say now? Luke wondered as he rode slowly down toward his camp.

He tugged off his hat and raked a hand through damp hair, trying to muster what strength he had left. God knew he'd need it.

She was every bit as beautiful and as desirable as she'd ever been. And she had every right to hate his guts.

He rode up almost to where she stood, but he didn't dismount. It wasn't polite not to. He knew that. He also knew he needed every advantage he could get. "Jillian." His voice sounded rusty to his ears.

She looked up at him, and he feared for a moment that she might manage a smile. He was grateful when her lips stopped short of it.

"Luke."

He swallowed, waiting, expecting her to say why she'd come, but she didn't. She just looked at him. He felt like pond scum. Like cow dung. So he did what he'd always done when he'd been around her before—he resorted to sarcasm.

"Don't tell me," he said gruffly, "you were in the neighborhood."

Then he turned his horse and swung off, managing to keep his back to her the whole time. He walked his horse toward the pasture where he kept his mounts, hoping against hope that she would somehow vanish if he pretended she wasn't there.

She followed him. "I've been looking for you."

He didn't ask why. Instead he got a comb out of the saddlebag, loosened the cinch from his horse, then eased off the saddle and put it over the fence. He moved with the same focused deliberation he used when he was trying to forget the dream. The same deliberation he used to remind himself that this woman was off-limits. He laid the saddle blanket over the saddle, then took off the bridle, put on a halter and began to brush down his horse.

Jill was so close he could almost feel the heat of her breath against his sweat-soaked shirt. He inched away.

"You haven't been exactly easy to find."

"Didn't intend to be." He didn't look at her. He kept currying the horse, as if he did it every night. He reckoned the animal must be amazed at the attention.

"No one knew where you went."

"Somebody did," he pointed out. "You're here."

"A last shot. And it was pure luck."

"Is that what it is?" he said bitterly.

"I think so." Her voice was quiet.

"How were you so lucky?" He twisted the word. He couldn't help it.

"I decided to come back to where you and Keith met in the first place. And, well, I ran into a friend of yours."

Luke had thought his friends would have known better than to betray his whereabouts. "Who?"

"Paco."

Luke smothered a groan. "I might've known."

"He's a lovely little boy," Jill said quickly, defensively almost.

"He makes Machiavelli look like Little Bo-Peep."

She ventured a laugh and tossed a lock of hair away from her face. "He's delightful. A regular charmer." She was smiling, but as Luke turned, her smile faded. "He knows every movie Keith ever made."

His jaw tightened. "I know." He brushed past her and opened the gate so the horse could go into the pasture. Then he replaced the rungs of the gate before he turned back to ask roughly, "So, why were you looking? What do you want?"

"To...apologize."

"*Apologize?*" He stared at her, dumbfounded.

She nodded. "Apologize," she repeated firmly. "For what I said to you—to you...that day. The day I...the day you—"

"I know which day!" Did she think he'd ever forget?

"And I know I just made it worse for you. I wanted to say I'm sorry. I was...overwrought."

"You were right."

"No."

He jammed his hands into his pockets and stared out into the distance. "Yes. If I'd been doing my job, Keith wouldn't be dead."

"Keith liked to do his own stunts. It was his choice."

"That's no excuse. I should've told him—"

"Telling Keith never did any good at all, and you know it. Keith could talk his way around anyone. Even you," she added, giving him a level look. "You'd have had to knock him down and tie him up to have kept him out of that canoe.''

''Then I should have,'' Luke said stubbornly. He kicked at the dirt with the toe of his scuffed boot. ''Look,'' he said finally, ''It was nice of you to drop by and apologize....'' He still couldn't quite say the word with equanimity. ''I appreciate it. Now it's gettin' late. It's gonna be dark before long and if you're gonna get down to the road before nightfall, you'd better get movin'.''

''Luke—''

But he didn't want to hear any more. *Couldn't* listen to any more. He and Jillian Crane had never talked to each other. They didn't need to start now.

''Come on. I'll see you down.'' He whistled at the horses and they trotted his way, the bay gelding eagerly nosing his shirt pocket for the sugar he knew Luke kept there.

Aware that she was watching, he frowned and pushed the bay's head away, got nosed again and finally gave in and fed him a sugar cube. Then he slipped the halter over his head and led him out of the pasture.

''Shut the gate,'' he said over his shoulder and moved to saddle the horse.

She did. ''Am I forgiven?''

He kept moving. ''Of course.''

''I didn't mean to hurt you. I—''

Luke wheeled around. ''Look, what you said, I deserved. If you want me to forgive you, fine. You're forgiven. But it doesn't change a damn thing!''

''Because you haven't forgiven yourself,'' she said quietly.

''No, I haven't. You're right about that.'' His hands clenched against the saddle. He bent his head. He would never be able to forgive himself as long as he lived.

''You ought to, Luke,'' she said gently.

"I don't think so."

"Yes, you should. And you should stop hiding out up here and—"

"I'm not hiding out!"

"No one knew where you were."

"Paco did, obviously. So do most of the people in town."

"But they wouldn't tell me. Did you ask them not to?"

He shrugged irritably. "Didn't want to be bothered. Not that I reckon a lot of people would want to know," he added gruffly.

"I did. Carl would."

"No." Next to Jill, the last person he wanted to see was Carl, the man who had hired Luke in the first place and who had come to be the closest thing to a father Luke had had in years. He'd done a lot of growing up under Carl's watchful, yet tolerant eye.

He didn't want to see the look in Carl's eyes now.

"Really, Luke—"

"No! And you'd damned well better not tell him where I am. Now come on. It's gettin' dark. You don't want to be trekking down the mountain in the dark."

"I could stay."

"The hell you could!" He looked at her, furious.

"We shared a house...before."

Luke's jaw tightened and his fury grew as he remembered those two weekends when Keith had sent him with Jill up to his house in Big Bear in the hopes that the paparazzi would follow them and give him some space.

"A little bit of obscurity, privacy, heaven," Keith had said when he'd asked Luke to do it.

Heaven, yes. But in its own way, hell, too. Luke remembered only too well what had happened the last time they were there—those few brief moments when desire had defeated him, when he'd forgotten who she was, who he was, how wrong anything between them would be.

Anger and guilt swamped him even now. "Is that what this is all about? You looking to pick up where we left off, maybe? Are you horny, honey?"

She slapped his face.

They stared at each other. Then Luke raised a hand to touch his stinging cheek, while she pressed her fingers against her mouth and looked at him, stricken. "I'm sorry," she whispered.

He turned away. "You shouldn't be. You should have done it then."

And he strode quickly down to where she'd left her horse. It was Jimmy Kline's sorrel. He wondered how she'd managed that. But then Jillian had always had a way about her, a way that had made most of the world fall at her feet—especially, he thought savagely, grown men who should damn well have known better.

"How'd you get Kline's horse?" he demanded.

"Paco introduced us. They were a little less eager to let me know where you were," she admitted. "But Paco convinced them."

"I'll bet," he said grimly. Well, the deed was done. Now he just wanted her gone. "At least you knew enough to loosen the cinch," he grunted.

"Jimmy told me to."

"Good ol' Jimmy," he said under his breath. He turned to her. "Get on." He swung easily into the bay's saddle. "Let's go." He started down the trail without looking back, wanting to get far enough ahead so they wouldn't have to talk.

But Jill caught up with him. "I didn't just come to apologize. And I didn't come for what else you implied," she said flatly. "I came because I need your help. I'm working on a book. A biography. Of Keith."

He didn't even look at her. He just kept riding, giving no sign that he'd even heard, wishing he hadn't. It didn't stop her.

"I've been working on it for the past year," she continued. "I've got almost all the interviewing done. I've talked to everyone who ever meant anything to Keith. Teachers, friends, relatives, directors, producers, other actors. Everyone, that is, except..." She didn't have to finish.

"No." *God, no.*

"I know you think it would be painful to talk about it," she said urgently. "All right, it *is* painful. But it also helps, Luke, believe me." She urged the sorrel forward until she rode beside him. "I didn't want to do it, either. But it gave me some perspective."

"I've got all the perspective I need." It was over. Past. And he couldn't talk about it. Couldn't relive it. Especially not with her. He'd never survive.

He urged his horse on, trotting now, keeping far enough ahead of her all the way down the road so that she would have had to shout for him to hear. Finally they reached the next gate. "Just follow the trail on down. Another half mile and you'll see the ranch house. You're almost there." He turned his horse.

"Luke, listen—"

"No. Goodbye, Jill." His voice was hard and flat. He didn't look back.

Two

Hell, Luke thought as he flung himself onto his narrow cot. Who needed dreams to wake him quivering and shaking? Who needed dreams to make him ache?

Not him. Hell, no.

Tonight he had reality to do the trick.

All the damned work he'd done all day, all the wood he'd chopped when he'd got back up the mountain, all the shirts he scrubbed threadbare on the old washboard well into the night hadn't banished reality one bit.

He only had to turn his head to see out the window to the tree where she'd tied her horse. Even in the shadowy moonlight, he only had to glance toward the pasture. He could see the stump where she'd stood. He only had to shut his eyes and in his mind he could see his cabin. But now when he saw the front steps, she was standing there.

Jillian.

Jillian Crane.

God, he thought as he stared up at the rough-hewn ceiling, why Jill? Of all the women in the world, why her?

For almost two years he hadn't seen her. He'd figured he wouldn't have to see her ever again. He'd counted it one of his very few blessings.

And now, out of the blue, she was here. Right here. On his mountain.

Standing mere inches from him. So close he could have touched her. So close her breath had actually touched him.

Damn it to hell.

And she'd come to apologize to him!

Apologize! When God knew he ought to have been on his knees apologizing to her.

Instead he'd done his best to insult her, to remind her of the one thing he should have pretended to forget—the day he had kissed her.

The day he'd discovered that, for all that she was his best friend's fiancée, he didn't have the self-control he ought to have. For a few brief moments he'd taken her for himself!

He'd had no right.

She was Keith's from the start. Luke hadn't even been around when Keith met her. He'd broken his leg during a chase scene toward the end of the filming of *Tiger's Dreams,* a movie they were working on in Spain. And as soon as he was able, Luke had flown back to California to recuperate.

Keith had gone on to London with the rest of the crew to finish up some interiors in the studio there. Near the end of filming, two days before he was due to come home, an American magazine writer named Jillian Crane had gone to London to interview him for an in-depth profile.

Luke never knew exactly what had happened at that interview. It was enough that Keith hadn't come back to California with the rest of the crew. Instead he'd flown to the Caribbean for "a little R and R" and a lot more in-depth discussion with Jillian Crane.

When he finally did come back to Los Angeles three weeks later, the article was finished; Jill wasn't.

She and Keith were a pair.

The first time Luke saw her was the day she and Keith had got back to L.A. He'd been staying at Keith's house because his own apartment had too many steps for a man just getting used to his walking cast.

He'd been limping around the kidney-shaped pool, when suddenly Keith had appeared in the doorway.

"Hey, Luke! You can walk again! So, c'mere. Want you to meet my lady."

"Your...lady?" He had never heard Keith call any woman that before. He glanced up, curious, to see a serious, dark-haired beauty looking at him. His heart skipped a beat. He took a step, slipped in a puddle and landed on his rear end.

They both rushed to his aid. Keith was laughing and grumbling. "Knocked you right on your can, did she? I'm not surprised."

"Are you all right?" the woman asked. She was leaning over him, patting him, her dark hair tickling against his bare chest.

"I'm fine," Luke snapped, brushing them both off, mortified by his clumsiness, which was a direct result of his instant reaction to Keith's "lady."

He still was mortified every time he remembered what had happened that day. But in retrospect, he supposed his falling was the best thing that could have happened. It had prompted him to shove Jill away then. And that had set the tone of his relationship with her ever since.

She was Keith's lady, so Luke steered as clear of her as

he could. It wasn't easy. Keith didn't drop his friends when he found a woman. Instead, he tried to get everyone together. For Luke it didn't work. He told himself that she had no affect on him or on his life at all. It wasn't true, of course. He couldn't look at her without feeling a renewed surge of attraction. And it didn't take long to figure out that the attraction was more than physical. He liked Jill Crane.

He liked the way she listened when people talked, liked her no-nonsense approach to Keith's very crazy, fast-lane life. He told himself she was stodgy, that after Jill's advent into his life, Keith changed. He became quieter, more introspective.

"Sane," Carl had said, laughing.

Probably. There had never been anything very sane about the things Luke and Keith did together. They went skydiving, shark hunting, motorcycle racing, and did a dozen other things, each more crazy and daring than the last. They were stubborn, competitive and tough as nails.

"Tryers," Keith called them. "Two of a kind."

But Jill brought out a side of Keith Luke really didn't know.

"A kinder, gentler Keith," Luke remembered scoffing when Keith had declined to go out bar hopping with him and another friend one night. "Man, has she got you tied down."

But Keith had just grinned and tugged Jill into his lap, shrugging equably. "Eat your heart out, chum," was all he'd said.

He never knew that there were times when Luke had. Luke had put up a good front. He'd told himself, Keith—hell, the whole world—that he didn't need sweetness and light and a gentle woman like Jill. As for the gentler side of himself, he wasn't sure he had one.

It was a damn sight easier to tell himself that if he wanted to steer clear of her.

And he did. He had...until that last afternoon at Big Bear.

They'd spent the weekend together, just he and Jill. It had been all Keith's fault, but he wanted a little time "out of the fishbowl," as he called it. It had worked once before when Luke had decoyed the press away, pretending to be Keith. He'd hated doing it, but he could understand why Keith asked him to. Fame wasn't always easy, and Keith went out of his way for his fans almost every day. He needed a little break.

So when Keith asked, Luke had gone. He'd argued that he could decoy them alone, but Keith had disagreed.

"You have to take Jill. If she isn't there, they won't believe you're me."

And so the two of them went together. Jill did her best to be pleasant and cheerful and polite. Luke did his best to be surly and uncommunicative. He didn't really want to be, but it seemed the smartest—and safest—way to spend a weekend with her.

But spending forty-eight hours in her company was an exercise in frustration beyond belief. Not only because he found her physically attractive, but because she was a nice person, a caring person. If he let her, she'd bring out the same good qualities in him that she brought out in Keith. Luke didn't dare. Because if he did, she'd bring out something else, too.

Finally, late Sunday afternoon, as they were lying beside the pool, he decided he just might make it through. There were only a few more hours to endure, when Jill glanced up from her book and said, "Don't look now, but there's a photographer trying to get a shot over the fence. Probably looking for a real hot picture.'' She grinned conspiratorially at Luke, then blew him a kiss.

A weekend's worth of frustration boiled over.

''Then let's give him something to really look at,'' he growled. And before he had time for second thoughts, he swung himself over by her chaise longue and kissed her hard on the mouth.

He'd meant it as a gesture. Nothing more, nothing less.

The photographer wanted to see some hot stuff? Well, fine, Luke would show him!

But he was the one who'd been shown.

He and, he supposed, Jill.

He touched his lips to hers, and what began as a kiss ended as a conflagration. Searing in intensity, burning in desperation. Mad and crazy and foolhardy, it endured and deepened, and finally shook him to the depths of his soul.

God knew where it would have ended if Jill hadn't finally pulled back, pressing her hand against her mouth and looking up at him with wide, frightened eyes.

''Keith,'' she whispered, horrified.

Luke's jaw locked. An eternity passed. Then he muttered an expletive under his breath and dove into the blessedly cold water of the pool. But he'd never been able to wash away the guilt.

She was back.

Luke couldn't believe it.

He'd spent the entire day doing his best to blot out the memory of Jillian Crane sitting on his doorstep just the night before, and he came over the rise that evening and damned if she wasn't sitting there again.

His horse, sensing sudden tension in the hand that held the reins, tossed his head and sidestepped.

"It's all right," Luke said automatically, reaching out to pat the horse's neck.

But it wasn't. It wasn't all right at all.

She'd seen him and was getting to her feet. She lifted a hand, but then dropped it and stood waiting, feet slightly apart. She looked like Annie Oakley ready to take on the bad guys at high noon.

And he was definitely one of the bad guys.

He should have realized that brushing her off yesterday had been too easy. This was Jill Crane he was dealing with. She might have been Keith's fiancée, but she was still a competent, diligent professional writer, an award-winning personality profiler.

He knew she didn't leave any stone unturned when it came to getting her story. Jill went after people like one of those old-time sheriffs who always got his man.

But she damned well wasn't getting him.

Nothing said he had to talk to her. And nothing on earth would get him to.

Once—*once*—he'd succumbed to her in a moment of weakness. It wasn't happening again.

As far as Jillian Crane and Lucas Tanner were concerned, *nothing* was happening again.

It was hard enough to live with the past if he just managed to leave it there. He was damned if he was going to rake it all up again. Least of all with her.

He scowled fiercely at her as he rode in.

"Well, here I am again," she said in a singsong, self-mocking tone.

"Why?"

"You know why. The book. It's important—to me, to Carl, to Keith's friends and to his fans. And whether either of us likes it or not, Luke, you're part of it. So—" she shrugged "—I guess I hoped you'd thought about it and changed your mind."

"All the thinking in the world isn't going to change my mind. I told you. No."

And he'd keep saying no until kingdom come if that's what it took. He swung down out of the saddle and faced her head-on. "Believe it. There's nothing you can do or say that will make any difference."

"You owe it to Keith."

It was like a knife in the heart.

He'd thought that nothing could touch him, that he was impervious, that he was prepared for any argument, could turn his back on any plea.

He wasn't prepared for that.

He swallowed a curse. He turned away, his fury making his fingers fumble as he tried to loosen the cinch. "Damn you. Keith wouldn't have asked that."

"Probably not. But then, Keith's not here to ask it, is he?"

God, it wasn't enough that she thrust the knife in. Now she had to twist it.

He spun around. "Damn it! How low are you gonna go?"

She winced and paled, but stood her ground, looking at him defiantly. "As low as I have to, I guess."

All the four-letter words he could think of tumbled around in his head. He yanked the saddle off, opened the gate and slapped the horse's rump so that it trotted into the pasture.

"Is this your revenge?" he asked finally.

"Revenge?" She frowned briefly, then shook her head. "Believe it or not, Luke, I'm not trying to hurt you."

He snorted. No, he didn't believe it. Why should he?

She had a right to revenge, even if he wouldn't have

expected it of her. But then, up until their kiss, he'd never given her much credit for passion, either.

Obviously Lucas Tanner had a lot to learn about women.

Would Keith have wanted him to cooperate?

Probably, he admitted. Keith was a star, eager for recognition. He relished the limelight.

He'd have preferred to have the limelight and a good long life, of course. But going out in the spectacular way he had would have appealed to his sense of drama. Afterward, though, he would want a good accounting.

Jill would give him a good accounting.

"You got all those other people. You don't need me," Luke argued.

"You were closer to him than anyone else. You were his best friend."

"Some friend," Luke muttered. He sighed and rubbed the back of his neck. "What do I have to do?"

"Talk to me about how you two met. Tell me about your relationship, the good things and the bad, what Keith meant to you."

"Nothing much, huh?" he said ironically.

"I know it will be hard. But there were good times, Luke. A lot of them." She looked at him beseechingly. "It's a chance to remember them."

"That's supposed to make me feel better? How about thinking about all the good times we could have had if I'd done my job?" He spun away from her and started walking toward the cabin, the saddle in his arms.

She came after him. "I told you, it wasn't your fault. But we can talk about that, too, if you want."

He spun around and glowered at her. "I damned well do not want!"

She took a step back, then said quietly, "It might help."

"Let's get one thing straight right off. If I talk to you

for your book, I'm talkin' just for your book. I'm not talkin' to ease my pain.''

''Because you want to wallow in it?''

''Go to hell!'' He started to turn away again.

''I've been there,'' she said quietly.

They stared at each other. All the pain, all the memories, everything he never wanted to think about again hung there between them.

Luke dragged a palm down his face. ''How long will it take?''

''It depends.''

''On what?''

''On you. On how much you're willing to tell me and how long it takes you to get to it.''

He started walking again. ''I'm not willing to tell you anything and you know it.''

''Then on how well you cooperate unwillingly.'' She was walking alongside him, and the wind carried the scent of something faintly flowery that he knew would be haunting him tonight.

He put the saddle in the shed, then headed toward the cabin. But when he got there, he didn't open the door. He stopped on the narrow front porch and folded his arms across his chest. He wasn't inviting her in. She'd invaded his mountain. She wasn't invading his home.

''So ask,'' he said.

She blinked. ''Not tonight. I don't want to just get started and have to stop. I'll come back tomorrow.''

''No.''

She looked taken aback.

''I'm workin' tomorrow,'' he explained, moderating his tone.

''I'll come along.''

''No!'' She much for moderation.

"It would be easiest. I—"

"I said no. You want me to talk, I'll talk. But you aren't going to follow me around."

"Then I'll be here when you get back tomorrow night."

"No. I'll come down. I'll meet you at the Klines' after I finish up here."

"It will be almost dark. You said—"

"I'll meet you at the Klines'. Tomorrow night. Take it or leave it." *Leave it,* he prayed. *Leave it.*

Jill met his gaze, then nodded. "The Klines'," she agreed.

He ground his teeth. "Be there by seven."

"I'm staying there."

"What?" How the hell had she wangled that? Did she know the house was his, that Jimmy and Annette were just renting it?

"Paco arranged it."

"That manipulating little son of a—"

"You like him."

"Like I like poison ivy," Luke grumbled.

Jill shook her head. She was smiling slightly. "He showed me the Porsche you carved for him. And the animals."

"Hell." The kid had no sense, no sense at all. Luke had figured the boy might show his mother the half-dozen wooden toys he'd made him. He didn't expect him to show the whole damn world. He let out an explosive breath. "Is there anything he didn't show you? Or tell you?"

"I don't know," Jill said gravely. "I'll ask him."

Luke muttered under his breath, then jammed his hands into his pockets. "I don't know what time I'll finish. I'll be down when I get done."

"I'll make us dinner."

"I'll eat on the way down. Go on now, or it'll be dark."

He turned and stalked toward where she'd left the horse. He untied the reins and slapped them into her hand.

"Is this a hint, Lucas?"

He scowled. "What do you think?"

She stood there with the reins in her hand, then she looked at him. He held himself still and met her gaze. But it seemed to take forever until she was finally in the saddle again.

"I'll see you tomorrow then," she said quietly.

He wished to God he could say, *Not if I see you first.*

Luke reckoned that being stuck in a blizzard might be excuse enough not to have to go down the mountain the following night. Or being eaten by a swarm of deerflies. Or dying in a forest fire. Or getting mauled by a bear.

Naturally, he wasn't so lucky. He survived the day intact, the weather turned warm, almost balmy, and the sky was a cloudless blue when he got back to the cabin shortly before six.

He took his own sweet time washing off in the creek, but finally he had no choice. He had to put on a clean shirt, comb his hair, slap his hat on his head, saddle a fresh horse and make his way down to the ranch house.

He might not know Jillian well, but he knew her well enough to be sure that she'd come after him if he didn't.

And while he was there he had a few things to say to Jimmy. There was no point in talking to Annette.

She'd had a crush on him since she was seven. He reckoned it was his good fortune—and hers—that she'd outgrown it enough so that when Jimmy Kline got old enough to ask her to marry him, she agreed instead of waiting for Luke.

She'd have waited forever before he got around to asking; probably she knew it.

When he reached the ranch house, he found Jimmy in the barn. The younger man looked up and grinned nervously. "You ain't mad, are you?"

"Whatever gave you that idea?" Luke's studied mildness made Jimmy wince.

He raked a hand through his thatch of red hair. "I told Annette we didn't have no business lettin' Jill stay here. I said it was up to you, it bein' your ranch an' all. But she'd already told Jill she could 'cause she was a friend of yours. Figured you'd be glad, she said. I guess you ain't." He'd figured out that much, at least.

Luke shrugged. He could think of several pithy things to say, all of which would be in vain. Jimmy understood—or thought he did. And Annette never would.

"Don't matter," he said now.

"It ain't entirely Annette's fault," Jimmy confessed after a moment. "I kinda liked the idea of havin' her here right now, too. Y'know, Annette's gettin' pretty big. She's due this month. And she was almost a month early when she had Jimmy."

Luke hadn't been there when eighteen-month-old Jimmy, Jr. was born, so he didn't remember that. But he could attest to the truth of Jimmy's earlier statement. Last time he'd seen Annette, she'd looked like a barn moving sideways.

It would be better to have someone on hand to take her to the hospital, in case Annette went into labor while Jimmy was out on the range. Even if that someone was Jill Crane.

"I see what you mean," he said.

Jimmy looked enormously relieved. "I'll take care of your horse," he offered.

"Jill in the house?"

"Ready and waitin'. We'll keep outta your way."

Luke would have rather had them in his way, but he

didn't say so. He left the horse for Jimmy to deal with and headed toward the house.

Annette had the door open the minute his boot hit the first step. "Luke!" She practically grabbed his arm to draw him in. "You came! I was really scared you'd be mad at me 'cause you're so—so kind of touchy…about…well, you know what about. But I guess you really want to talk to Jill, huh?"

Under the barrage of her enthusiasm, Luke didn't reply. Over Annette's shoulder he saw Jill sitting on the sofa, giving Jimmy, Jr. a bottle. She looked up when he came into the room. "He's almost asleep. I'm sorry. Do you mind waiting?"

He shook his head, mute, his gaze caught by the sight of her with the baby in her arms. He'd never thought about Jill with children before. She looked right at home. He jerked his hat off and crushed the brim in his fingers.

"Sit down," Annette said. "Sit down." Then she giggled and put her hand over her mouth. "Gosh, I'm dumb, tellin' you to sit down in your own house."

A tiny frown appeared on Jill's face, and he guessed that answered his question about whether or not she knew who owned the ranch. Well, if it made her uncomfortable, too bad. He hadn't invited her, and maybe she'd leave all that much sooner.

He said nothing, just sat down, balancing the hat on his thighs.

Annette waddled between him and Jill. "Can I bring you some coffee? And brownies? I made brownies today. And I got some butterscotch bars left, too. I made those Tuesday. Would you rather have those?"

"No, thanks. I ate on the way down."

"Oh, but—"

"I'm fine," he said firmly.

Jill stood up, smiling at the child in her arms, then looked over at Annette. "He's asleep," she said softly. "I'll just go put him in his crib."

"I don't know what I'd be doin' without her," Annette said to Luke as Jill carried the small, limp body of her son up the stairs to the bedroom. "I can't hardly carry him anymore 'cause of this watermelon here." She giggled and patted her stomach. "Jill's doin' everything."

Luke nodded absently. He wasn't looking at Annette's stomach; he was looking at the stairs. Though Jill had already disappeared into the bedroom, he could still see her as she'd looked carrying the little boy up them. She'd looked so natural. Hell, she'd have probably had one of her own by now, if only...

He let out a harsh exhalation of breath.

"Somethin' the matter?" Annette asked worriedly.

Luke shook his head. But he was almost grateful when, a moment later, Jill returned. She was carrying with her a loose-leaf notebook, a pen and a small tape recorder. "Where do you want to work?"

Luke glanced at Annette.

"I'll be quiet as a mouse," she promised.

Jill smiled at the younger woman. "I don't think that will work very well," she said apologetically. "Having someone listening tends to make the person I'm talking with uncomfortable."

"Not me," Luke said. No matter what Annette said about being quiet, he knew it was impossible. And the more she talked, the less he'd have to.

"And it makes me a little uncomfortable, too," Jill went on smoothly. "So I think we'll go for a walk."

"Oh," Annette said, crestfallen.

"Oh," said Luke. Hell.

Jill pulled on a sweater and went to the door, then looked back at him. Reluctantly, he followed her.

"Maybe you'll have a brownie when you get back?" Annette called after him.

Luke grunted a noncommittal response and shut the door.

"She's very fond of you," Jill said as they stepped off the porch.

"She used to be my sister-in-law."

Jill gaped. She dropped her pen and had to scramble for it. He reached down to get it for her and nearly bumped heads with her.

"I didn't realize you were ever…married," she said.

"I wasn't. My older brother was married to her sister when they were little more than kids. It didn't work out," he added after a moment.

Another disaster that could be laid at his door. If he hadn't been such a damned hothead after his old man died, lashing out at an unfair world and carrying a chip the size of the whole damned state of Colorado on his shoulder, always getting into trouble and expecting his brother to bail him out, Tanner might have been home the night that Clare had needed him, the night their son was born—and died.

He sighed and tugged his hat down.

"I'm sorry," Jill said gently.

Luke shrugged. "They're both doin' all right now."

That was his only consolation—knowing that, though the youthful marriage had collapsed after less than a year, Clare had now been happily married for nearly twelve years to a local doctor, and Tanner had finally met and married the right woman for him.

Luke didn't know much about his new sister-in-law, Maggie, but she sure seemed to have made a difference in his brother's life.

"Old Sobersides," Luke had called his older brother,

Robert, whom all the world but Maggie called Tanner. And the Old Sobersides appellation had come only if Luke was feeling charitable.

Usually he'd just called Tanner "The Grouch."

But Tanner wasn't grouchy these days. Ever since the wedding, he'd been smiling. And his smile had been especially broad in the last photo Maggie had sent Luke— one in which Tanner was holding their new son, Jared.

And damned if that thought didn't bring him right back to babies.

"Let's get on with this," he said harshly. "I haven't got all night."

"Is there a place we can go and sit down so I can write, or do you want me to tape while we walk and talk?"

Luke shrugged. "Doesn't matter. You're the biographer, not me." But he was shifting from one foot to the other as he said it, and apparently Jill noticed.

"We'll tape," she said. "And walk." She left the notebook sitting by the gate and turned on the tape recorder. It was tiny enough that she could hold it in her palm.

Luke looked at it warily. "That what you used on Keith?"

"A similar one, yes. But I took notes, too, because we were just sitting talking."

"For *three weeks?*"

She flushed. "At the interview. The three weeks was vacation."

"Right. I forgot."

Damn, what was he doing? He didn't care what they'd been doing down in the Caribbean. It wasn't any of his business. He needed to get out of here before he said something else stupid. "First question?" he prompted.

"Why don't you tell me about how you two met."

"That isn't a question."

"It's a request."

"You know all that," he protested.

"Not really. I know you were a cowboy around here and he met you when he was doing a movie. I don't know exactly how it happened."

No, probably she didn't. There was no reason why Keith would have told her. It hadn't changed anything much—at the time, anyway—for Keith.

It had changed Luke's whole life.

"I was workin' at Mike Sutter's spread across the valley," he said reluctantly, "and Keith's bunch was there making *Renegade's Moon.*"

"So it was almost seven years ago?"

"Yeah. They were shooting a scene, and one of their cameramen was wavin' his arms around, and he spooked some cattle. I headed 'em off and turned 'em before they ran the damn fool down."

"He must have been grateful."

"I guess. Babbled all over me. Heck, what was I supposed to do, let 'em trample him? It turned out Carl was watching and he needed somebody to do the same thing in the movie. So he asked me."

"And that's when you were hired?"

Luke shook his head. "I told him I already had a job."

He could still remember Carl looking at him dumbfounded when he'd said that. "He sorta drew himself up and tried to loom over me, asking, 'And you'd rather herd cows than work in the movies?' I said, 'Well, it's my job. I can't just leave my boss in the lurch,' and he said, 'And who is this boss who inspires such undying loyalty?' So I told him, and he went to Mike and told him to fire me."

"You're kidding."

"Nope. You know Carl. He doesn't believe in no. Mike said the hell he would. But then Carl explained what he wanted and Mike said it was all right with him, so I did it.''

''Were you scared?''

''I didn't know what to expect. Turned out it wasn't any big deal, really. Hell, I did it damn near every day of the week. But afterward they were all runnin' around, slappin' me on the back and saying, 'You're some horsebackin' fool! Man, how'd you learn to do that?''''

''How did you?''

Luke shrugged. ''Grew up doin' it. My old man was a cowboy. My brothers are cowboys.''

''I don't know anything about your family,'' Jill said, considering him thoughtfully. ''Do you realize you've never even mentioned them to me? Do your brothers work around here?''

''No.'' He didn't want to talk about them, or about anything else that was personal. ''I thought we were talkin' about Keith.''

''And we can't discuss anything else?''

''I didn't come down here to talk about anything else.''

She gave a small snort of impatience, then shrugged. ''Fine. So, you had your one day of glory. Did you meet Keith then?''

''Nope. Did that the next day. Carl asked me to come back. He wondered if I could fall off.''

''He wanted you to fall off a horse?''

Luke nodded. ''He said, 'We'll pay you $400.' I thought he was nuts. 'Four hundred dollars?' I said. Hell, first time anybody ever offered to pay me for what I'd been doin' for nothin' for years!'' He couldn't help grinning at the memory of his own astonishment.

''So I said sure, why not? Next day, when I showed up, Brent Hubbard—you know Brent, one of the stuntmen?'' He looked at her and when she nodded, he continued,

"Well, he asked me if I wanted some pads. I didn't know what he meant. 'Pads?' I asked him, 'What for?' 'Hip, knee, wrist, elbow, tailbone,' he said, and looked at me like I ought to know what he was talking about. But I didn't, and when I just stared at him, he told me to take down my pants."

Jill's eyes widened, and Luke flushed, realizing that she'd think he was an idiot for sure if he told her what he'd thought at first when Brent had said that!

"Anyway," he hurried on, "I found out what pads were when they put 'em on me. And I wore 'em while I did the riding and the falling. I was done before noon and I figured I'd better get movin' or Mike was gonna think I'd gone and quit on him. But Carl called me over and that's when I met Keith."

He could remember it as clearly as if it were yesterday.

"I recognized him," Luke admitted, "but it was like meetin' somebody whose name you've forgotten. I was saying, 'Hey, how are ya?' like I knew him because his face was familiar, but I didn't have a clue who he was."

Jill smiled. "Did he know that?"

"Of course. Later, he used to tell me he'd rescued me from a life of cultural ignorance." Luke grinned at the memory, and Jill grinned, too.

"Anyhow," he said abruptly, turning his head away from that grin, "that's how I met Keith. Carl thought I resembled him, and he wanted Keith to see what he thought. He should've known better. Keith didn't care how much I looked like him or didn't. He just wanted me to teach him everything crazy I knew how to do."

"I'll bet he did," Jill said softly.

Their eyes met again, and hers had the same gentle, wistful expression that Luke remembered seeing sometimes when he'd caught her watching Keith. The same slightly dazed look he'd seen in them the moment he'd kissed her, before she'd realized what they were doing.

His jaw tightened. He jerked his eyes away and started walking again rapidly. "I did his stunt work for the rest of the movie. Then he asked me to go back to California with him to work on his next one. And I figured, why the hell not? So I went."

"Was it a big change?"

He frowned. "From cowboying? Hell, yes. Cowboying, I did whatever needed to be done. Saw it and did it. Out there I always had somebody figurin' out what I was supposed to be doing. How fast I was supposed to be going. Which way to turn my head so's I'd look pretty for a camera. Or so's Keith would look pretty," he corrected. His gaze narrowed again at a sudden realization. "How come we're talkin' about me again, not Keith?"

"We're talking about both of you," Jill said patiently. "About the relationship between you. Relationships are complex."

"Not ours. It was simple. Keith Mallory was my friend. The best damn friend I ever had." He looked at her bleakly. "And I as good as killed him."

Jill's fingers clutched his arm hard through his thin cotton shirt. "Stop saying that. It isn't true."

"Isn't it?" He gave a harsh laugh. "Well, I guess that's debatable," he said bitterly, staring off into the distance. Then his gaze shifted and came back to meet hers. He swallowed. "But you can't tell me that once I—we—didn't betray him."

Three

——

"**I** know."

Luke didn't know what he'd been hoping. Maybe that she'd deny it, tell him he was wrong, that he'd been imagining things, thinking things that weren't true and never had been.

She didn't. She met his gaze squarely, her gray eyes dark now, yet oddly luminous and shining with moisture. Tears? Ah, God, no. He looked at her, anguished.

"You didn't want me to agree with you?" she asked him softly.

He kicked at a stone in the field. "No, damn it, I didn't."

"But it's true." She stared out across the valley. There was a small cluster of lights where Bluff Springs was and dotted across the far side of the valley were the isolated lights of ranch houses.

"It shouldn't have been," he said hollowly.

"No."

He toed a clump of grass this time. "You should've stopped me."

"Yes."

"Why didn't you?"

She shook her head. In the deepening twilight he could make out a tear as it trickled down her cheek. She didn't wipe it away. She just stared resolutely out across the valley. "I don't know," she said.

"You didn't even like me."

"I tried. When did you ever give me any reason to? From the day I showed up, you acted like I was contaminated or something."

"I never—"

"You were sarcastic and gruff, and every time I walked into the room, you left."

How could he explain what he'd felt from the first moment he'd seen her? How could he possibly tell her that just being around her made him feel awkward and unpolished, like the dumb, tongue-tied cowboy he was?

And the fact that Keith was clearly different when he was with her, calmer and more focused—a *gentleman,* for God's sake—didn't help matters, either.

"I never disliked you," he insisted. "I just— Hell, I kissed you, didn't I?"

"But why? Why did you?"

He stuffed his hands into his pockets and shrugged. "You were there."

"And Keith wasn't."

"No, that's not why, damn it! I wasn't doing it to try to beat out Keith!"

"Then why?"

He jerked off his hat and rubbed a hand through his hair, then shook his head. He couldn't begin to explain the combination of frustration and anger and hunger that had been building in him for so long. He knew better, damn it. He just—just...

"Because you were horny, honey?" she said lightly, mocking the words he'd said to her the day before.

Luke scowled and jammed his hat back on his head. "Yeah," he muttered. "I probably was."

"And I was handy."

His jaw tightened. He nodded curtly.

"Any woman would have done?"

"That's right." The look he gave her dared her to argue. She didn't, and somehow that annoyed him even further.

"So, what was your excuse?" he demanded. "Why did you respond? You did, you know," he added, in case she wanted to deny it.

She didn't answer immediately. She seemed to be actually considering the question. Then she shook her head, a bewildered look on her face. "I'm not sure."

"You're not sure?" he said sarcastically.

"I don't know."

He turned away. "Well, when you figure it out, let me know."

"I will."

He shook his head. "You know, you are really a piece of work, lady."

"An observation not to be taken as a compliment?"

He turned and caught a wry smile on her mouth. That almost-smile did something to his insides, brought back the very same feeling that had welled up within him that afternoon when he had succumbed to frustration, to temptation—to her.

He jerked his gaze away, angry with himself. "Take it any way you like," he growled, kneading tight muscles in the back of his neck. "I can't do this," he said abruptly.

"Can't do what?"

"This. Talk. Soul search." He twisted the words as he said them.

"You brought it up."

"I shouldn't have."

"If it needed to be said—"

"It didn't."

"Fine, let's talk about Keith."

"No. I told you, I can't. If you really need me to, give me some tapes and your tape recorder. I'll tell what I know into the tapes."

"I have to ask—"

"Tapes," he insisted. "Tapes or nothing. Look," he argued when she didn't reply, "it'll be better for you. If I do tapes, you don't have to hang around here waiting. Leave your address with Annette. I'll bring 'em down when I'm done and she can mail them to you."

"How do I know you won't just head back up into the hills and forget you ever saw me?"

"I wish to God I could."

"Luke…"

"I'll do it," he promised her. "I owe it to Keith."

"I didn't mean—"

"No. You were right. And I'll pay what I owe. But, for God's sake, let me pay it my way."

She opened her mouth to speak again, but he forestalled her. "Please."

His fingers curled into fists. He stared resolutely out across the now-dark valley. He couldn't look at her. He knew what he'd see—that look of wide-eyed confusion mingling with anticipation that he remembered all too well. The look she'd had when he'd kissed her.

"I'll do tapes," he said again. It was his last offer.

Jill sighed. "All right."

* * *

Inarticulate didn't begin to describe him.

Tongue-tied would have been a compliment.

Why he had ever thought talking on tape would be easy, Luke didn't know. It wasn't.

He started, stopped, mumbled, erased, cursed, muttered, started—and stopped—again. And again.

He'd practically flunked speech in high school. What had he been thinking of, for Pete's sake?

He'd been thinking of avoiding Jill.

It was as simple as that. But in fact, he didn't seem to be able to avoid her at all.

Oh, personally she might be back in New York, but in his mind—his damned, irritating, contrary mind—she was alive and well in those half-dozen little plastic cassettes that sat on his shelf and mocked him day after day, night after night.

When he couldn't just sit down and mindlessly rattle things off the way he'd hoped to, he thought if he prepared, then just spouted the words into the recorder, he could get enough distance from the topic—and from the woman—to do it.

So he spent his days when he was out checking the cattle and riding fence thinking about what he wanted to say, then scribbling notes in a pocket-size notebook.

But it didn't take him long to realize that writing down notes just meant he spent all day, every day, thinking about *not* thinking about her.

And thinking about Keith.

For almost two years he'd done his best not to think about either of them. With Keith it had simply been too painful at first. And with Jill...it had seemed far smarter not to.

He'd survived by focusing on the present, on this cow and that calf, on this fence and that piece of wire. He had managed to hang onto his sanity—just—by deliberately not thinking about the last seven years of his life.

But once he started to do what he'd told Jillian he would do, the memories just kept welling up, even though he couldn't seem to talk about them.

And with them came a whole roller coaster's worth of emotions. Ever since Keith's death Luke had been plagued by one in particular—guilt. But now, as he let his mind play back over the time he'd been Keith's friend, he found that there was a lot more to it. He was, by turns, sad and happy, angry and amused, delighted and distraught as he remembered the years he'd spent in the charmed world of Keith Mallory, God's gift to film, fans and friends.

And he found, oddly, that though he couldn't talk to the tape without feeling like a gold-plated fool, he had plenty to say to Keith.

"This is all your fault," Luke told his friend. He shoved himself further up against the tree trunk he was sitting in front of and rubbed Hank's back. Then he tossed a stone into the swift current of the river. "If you hadn't come up here making your damned movies, none of this would have happened."

It was midafternoon. The day was warm, working its way toward downright hot, and he'd spent the morning moving a couple bunches of cattle to new pastures. He had some more to move later, but cattle weren't fools. They moved easier when it was cooler, and Luke didn't mind waiting and shading up a bit while he ate a sandwich and drank some juice.

As he sat there with the dogs at his feet, he remembered the last time he'd sat under this tree. That afternoon almost two years ago, right before they'd started shooting up on the Salmon.

He and Keith had decided to take the long way around.

It was the first time in over a year that they'd gone off, just the two of them, to raise a little hell and have a good time.

It had been Keith's idea; he'd suggested it right after the weekend Luke and Jill had spent at Big bear. Jill had left to do a series of interviews in the East, and Keith had found himself with time on his hands.

"Let's do it," he'd said. "I won't be able to once I'm an old married man." He'd given Luke a lascivious wink. "Not that I'll be complaining."

And Luke, who was doing his best to forget kissing Jill, hadn't quite been able to look Keith in the eye. But the notion of just the two of them roughnecking around sounded good. "Whatever you want," he'd said gruffly.

They'd set off without any particular aim other than to go somewhere they could hang out where no one would recognize Keith or, if they did, wouldn't bother him.

The only place Luke could think of was his old stomping grounds.

"They'll let you alone," he'd promised. And he'd seen to it that they had. The cattle had already been brought down by the time he and Keith arrived, so the cabin wasn't being used and old Mick Cardenal, who owned the place then, had been happy to let Luke and Keith use it.

It was too early for hunting season, but they rode and loafed and fished. Luke taught Keith how to tie flies. Neither of them shaved. Both of them drank a lot of beer.

"When I die," Keith had said sleepily one afternoon, lying under this very tree, "I hope heaven turns out to be southwestern Colorado."

"What makes you think you're going to heaven?" Luke had said.

Keith had opened one eye halfway. "Because I have always led a pure, unblemished, undefiled existence. Why else?"

Luke had tossed a rock at him. And they'd both burst out laughing....

Now, two years later, Luke lay staring up through those same branches at another cloud-dotted Colorado sky.

"So, is it?" he asked Keith softly. "Is heaven like southwestern Colorado?"

"Who you talkin' to?" asked a childish voice behind him. Luke jerked up to see Paco standing there, holding the reins of Jimmy Kline's smallest horse. "You talkin' to God?"

Luke sat up straight, flushing. "What're you doing up here?" he demanded.

The boy shrugged narrow shoulders. "Running away from home."

"How come?"

"Too many girls." Paco wrinkled his nose. "Mama yells and Nelida bosses and Elena tags along all the time." Nelida was his older sister and Elena the younger. Luke didn't know them well, only enough to be glad he'd had brothers. "Can I live with you?"

"No."

"Why not? You got room. I could help you with the cattle. I'm a good rider. An' I can cook. Scrambled eggs. Toast. Bacon. I help Mama in the mornings in the café. Or I did," he added with a frown, "until Nelida bossed me out."

"Why'd she boss you out?" Luke asked, trying not to smile.

Paco took his question as an invitation to stay. He tied the horse and began balancing on a fallen log. "'Cause she's dumb. She says I broke the toaster, but I didn't. I fixed it."

"Does it work?"

"It would if she'd let me finish." Paco reached the end

of the log and turned around and walked carefully back again. Hank followed him. Paco jumped off, picked up a rock and hurled it into the river. "I hate her. How come you were talkin' to God?"

Luke had hoped Paco'd forgotten that. Fat chance. He shrugged his back against the tree. "I was just muttering."

Paco threw another rock, then walked to the edge of the bluff overlooking the river so he could see where it hit.

"Get away from there," Luke said. "You could damned well fall in."

"You'd save me," Paco said.

Luke snorted. "I'd wave adios, *chico*. Get back now."

Paco made a face, but he went back to the log and started balancing again. "So how come?" he persisted.

Luke sighed. "'Cause I got a woman bossin' me around, too."

"Jill."

Luke blinked. "How do you know?"

"She told you to make tapes about Keith."

"How do you know?" Luke demanded again.

"She told me."

Had she told the whole damned world before she left?

"How many you done?"

"None. Zero. Zip. *Nada.*"

Paco's eyes widened. "She's gonna be mad."

"I'll do 'em," Luke said gruffly. "It isn't exactly a piece of cake, talking into a machine."

"Talk to me."

Luke grunted. But it wasn't a totally stupid idea. In fact, it was a whole lot better than doing it by himself. He could answer Paco's questions. And Paco wasn't likely to ask anything he wouldn't be willing to answer. "Okay," he said.

"So, I can live with you." Paco beamed.

"I didn't say that!"

"But if we're gonna talk—"

"It doesn't take all day. Your mother needs you. You help her with breakfast."

"I'll help you. Please." Paco's dark eyes were beseeching.

Luke looked away. He picked up a rock and flung it savagely into the river. He ground his teeth.

"Remember in *The Thunder Rolls*," Paco said, citing one of Keith's best known movies, "where that kid, Jeremy, wants to stay with Keith on the boat—"

"It's not the same. It was a movie, for cripe's sake."

Paco cocked his head. "So it can't be true?"

"It can be," Luke admitted after a long moment. But he didn't want it to be. He threw another rock. And another. "Your mother won't let you," he said finally, hopefully, after a long moment.

"I'll ask her." Paco grinned.

She said yes.

"For three days," Paco told him the next afternoon. He looked disappointed as he reported the time limit that his mother had put on his stay with Luke. But then he brightened. "Maybe I can talk her into longer. I could break another toaster."

"Not in this life," Luke warned.

He was sitting on the steps of the cabin in the cool shadow of the evening, whittling a piece of soft pine. He tried not to show the dismay he felt. It had nothing to do with the kid personally, but Paco'd never believe that. Luke gouged his knife into the soft wood.

The boy scowled as he clumped up the steps carrying his sleeping bag. "You could at least say, 'We'll see,'" he grumbled.

''We'll see,'' Luke said dutifully.

Paco looked back at him over his shoulder. ''You're just sayin' that.''

Luke winked. ''We'll see.''

Paco grinned. ''I'll get a tape and we can start.''

It had sounded like a good idea yesterday. But now, faced with the prospect, he didn't want to do it anymore than he ever had.

''C'mon. It'll be fun,'' Paco said. ''I wanna know everything.''

It wasn't fun. And Paco did damn near want to know everything. But having the kid ask him questions was easier than doing it on his own.

He reiterated for the tape the stuff he'd told Jill about how he and Keith had met. Then he told Paco about the first movie in which he'd actually doubled for Keith, about some of the stunts he'd done, which Keith had argued he ought to be doing himself. Luke talked his way through the movies they'd made in Portugal and India, in L.A. and New York, in Alaska and Tanzania. He talked about the good times. And talking about them to someone who was all eager ears and eyes was bittersweet.

It was so easy to remember how much fun it had been, how charmed Keith's life had seemed.

And, of course, how tragically it had ended.

He talked until long after the sun had set. He sat there on the porch as the temperature dipped, and Paco sat huddled and wrapped in a sleeping bag, asking questions. Overhead a three-quarter moon slowly rose to hang like a single silvery beam in a star-studded, navy-velvet sky. And still he talked.

He didn't see any of it. Not the child, not the sky, not the moon nor the stars.

He was seeing Keith—Keith laughing when the horse

had bucked him off in Portugal, Keith waving his arms as the elephant's trunk curled around him and lifted him off the ground in India. He was remembering the way Keith had given him a thumb's-up sign after a rough-and-tumble bar fight in L.A., and the way he'd ridden a borrowed skateboard, standing on his hands, as they'd swooped through New York's Central Park. He was envisioning Keith, grinning like a fool through an ice-crusted mustache as he'd ridden behind a dogsled in Alaska, and a few months later, staring dreamily off into the sunrise on the Indian Ocean, his hand on the tiller of a traditional Arab dhow.

He remembered the utter stillness of the man and the moment.

And then Keith had looked over at Luke and smiled a crooked smile. "Who'd've thought a kid from Oxnard would ever come this far?" he'd said softly.

Or a boy from Bluff Springs, Colorado.

And who'd have thought that eight months later Keith would be dead, and that Luke would be back in Bluff Springs now?

He cleared his throat and jerked himself out of his reverie. "Do you know what a dhow is?" he asked Paco.

The boy didn't reply.

Luke looked around. Paco had been wrapped in his sleeping bag and was sitting behind him on the narrow porch, leaning against the wall of the house as he listened. He was still wrapped in the sleeping bag, still leaning against the wall, but he wasn't sitting any longer. He'd tipped sideways. His head was cradled in the crook of his arm, his lips were slightly parted, his eyes shut.

Luke studied him silently for a moment, then reached out and shut off the recorder. "That boring, was it?" he asked quietly.

Paco made a soft, whuffling sound. Luke set down his

knife and the wood he'd been whittling. He got to his feet and brushed the wood shavings off his jeans. Bending down, he slipped his hands beneath the sleeping child and lifted him easily in his arms. Then he nudged open the door with his toe and carried Paco into the cabin.

He couldn't remember ever holding or carrying a child before. His own younger brother, Noah, was so close to his age that Luke had never carried him and, as an adult, he'd only been friends with guys like Keith, as childless as himself, and Carl, a widower whose children were grown.

It was a strange feeling.

The boy's warm, trusting weight felt oddly comforting as he crossed the room and settled Paco on one of the narrow bunks. He tucked the sleeping bag around him, then stepped back and stared down at the slumbering child, feeling an unwelcome, unaccustomed envy of those men to whom the weight of a child was commonplace.

He'd never felt such an envy before. Had never *wanted* to feel it.

Still didn't, he reminded himself sharply. He didn't want to be responsible for other people. He wasn't good at it. Fatherhood, like marriage, wasn't for the likes of him.

He did his penance. He made the tapes. It was easier—as he'd suspected—to do them with Paco's help. He liked talking to the boy, liked answering the boy's questions, telling him stories, making him smile.

But it was harder than he'd dreamed for exactly the same reason.

Because of Paco, Luke spent every day, all day in the presence of childish innocence and trusting naiveté that enchanted and pained him at the same time. With unfailing good cheer and eager curiosity, Paco, astride Jimmy Kline's gentle mare, followed him like a shadow everywhere he went. He held the wire while Luke stapled it. He chivied cattle out of the willows while Luke did the same. He even wanted Luke to teach him how to give an ornery old bull an antibiotic injection.

"You don't have to learn that," Luke said.

"I want to do what you do."

And so he did. And in doing so, Paco treated Luke to three days' worth of a view of the world unhampered by cynicism, by the constant plague of "what ifs" and "might have beens." There was none of that as far as Paco was concerned. He saw the world—the mountains, the trees, the cattle, the people—and it was good.

Luke didn't understand it. The kid had lost his father, for heaven's sake. He had a mother who was coping with three small children, struggling and just barely succeeding to make ends meet. His biggest hero was a man who'd died in his prime. He had to know that the world wasn't a carefree place!

But if he did, the knowledge didn't seem to dull Paco's enthusiasm.

He met every morning with a smile and Luke's cynicism with a shrug. And without seeming to try, he was worming his way under the cowboy's thick hide.

Pretty soon, Luke thought grimly the last afternoon of Paco's visit, the kid would have him whistling while they worked. He was already making Luke think about what it would be like to have children of his own.

It was a relief when Thursday night came and he could send Paco home.

"You sure there's nothin' you forgot to say?" Paco asked hopefully while Luke saddled the sorrel for him.

"I'm sure."

Paco came to stand beside him. "What about when you

guys climbed that monument in New York? You didn't tell me much about that.''

When he and Keith had scaled the Soldiers' and Sailors' Monument on Riverside Drive, Paco meant. Something Luke was relatively certain Paco's mother wouldn't want her law-abiding son hearing more about. ''I told you enough,'' he said gruffly.

''How 'bout when you climbed those cliffs in Aca...'' Paco's brow wrinkled as he tried to remember ''...Aca-fulco?''

''Acapulco. And you heard enough about that, too.'' Luke tightened the cinch and tucked the sack of tapes in the saddlebag.

''What about the catacombs, then?''

''I thought you were asleep when I talked about that!''

Paco shook his head. ''Are there really passages under New York City?'' He was looking wide-eyed and eager, ready for a story.

Luke grunted. He'd said enough on the tape about the time he and Keith had sneaked down beneath the campus of CCNY and did a bit of underground exploring while they were there shooting a movie. He didn't suppose Paco would be going to New York any time soon, but he didn't think Linda would thank him for giving the kid ideas about that, either.

''Enough,'' he said. ''Go get your sleeping bag and I'll tie it on.''

Paco went, grumbling. ''You're just tryin' to get rid of me,'' he said when he came back.

''Yep.'' Luke lashed the sleeping bag onto the back of the saddle, then nodded at Paco, waiting for him to get on.

Paco stalled. ''Don'tcha get lonely up here?''

''No.''

''Never?''

"Never," he lied. "Come on. Get on and get moving. You'll be down at Jimmy's before dark. He'll run you into town. Ask him to mail the tapes to Jill while he's there, okay?"

Paco looked doubtful.

"Just do it," Luke said, giving the boy an impatient look that finally had Paco scrambling up into the saddle.

"If you say so."

"I say so." Luke dug in the pocket of his vest. "Here." He handed Paco two small figures he'd carved. A man and a boy, each on horseback. Paco's eyes lit up as he examined them. Then he lifted his gaze to meet Luke's.

Luke shrugged. "It's you and Keith."

Paco looked at them more closely. He shook his head. "Nope. It's me and you."

He didn't wait to watch Paco head down the hill. As soon as the boy started, Luke turned on his heel and strode toward the cabin. He went in and shut the door.

He was alone.

He sank down onto his bunk and sucked in the silence. This was what he wanted—space, quiet, solitude. He didn't need Paco. He didn't need anyone. It was far better like this, to be accountable to no one, beholden to no one. Alone.

He lay down on his bunk and stared at the wooden ceiling over his head, then turned his head and looked at the stripped-down bunk where Paco had slept the past three nights. It looked unusually bare.

"Better this way," Luke said aloud.

The kid was gone. The debt was paid.

He breathed deeply and let the air out slowly. He was free.

He got up off the bed and started to make himself some

dinner, trying to get back to normal, to think about tomorrow, about the cattle, about what needed to be done.

He wondered what Jill would think when she heard the tapes. He wondered especially what she would think of the last few minutes. He'd debated a long time about them. Finally he'd decided that he owed her.

He hadn't been able to forget the way she'd looked at him when they'd talked about why he'd kissed her. He'd tried to put it out of his mind. He couldn't. He could still see the pain and bewilderment in those wide gray eyes. He'd already caused her more than enough pain. That little bit, at least, he could erase.

He knew he wouldn't have had the guts to say it even then if Jill were anywhere around. But she was safely back in New York.

So last night, after Paco was asleep, Luke had taken the final tape back outside. He'd sat on the steps in the dark and turned the recorder on. It whirred almost imperceptibly in the silence for several moments before he began.

"That's pretty much it," he'd said finally. "That's Keith the way I remember him. The way I want to remember him, at least." He paused and stared out into the darkness. "There will never be another like him. I owe him the best years of my life."

Hank came and laid her head on his knee. He scratched her behind her ears, swallowed and went on, wishing his voice didn't sound quite so ragged. "I'm sorry that things turned out the way they did. Believe me, nobody can possibly be sorrier than I am." Another pause. Longer than the first. *Say it, damn it. You owe her.* "And I'm sorry I treated you the way I did, too." This time he jammed his finger on the pause button.

Damn, this was difficult. He took a deep breath. And another. Then he turned the recorder on again. "It wasn't because I didn't like you," he said. His fingers tightened in Hank's soft fur. "It was because I did."

He stopped and considered erasing that, then let it alone. He owed her that much honesty.

"That's why I kissed you, too. I just wanted you to know." He stopped then. There, that was enough. Wasn't it? No, it wasn't, and he knew it. He didn't just owe her for the kiss. He owed her for what he'd said to her the last time he'd seen her, too.

He cleared his throat, then paid his debt in full. "What I said to you the other day...it was a lie. I didn't want just any woman. I wanted you."

Four

He had the sun in the morning and the moon at night—and sixteen-hundred head of cattle, give or take a few, to look after every hour in between.

It was what he wanted, Luke reminded himself. Work, and lots of it. And no human beings depending on him.

He threw himself into it with renewed determination.

Any cowboy worthy of the name knew that the better part of moving cattle where you wanted them to go was letting them think the destination was their own idea. A buckaroo with brains just sat back and let them go, ambling along behind them, hedging up alongside only when they begin to drift. He damn sure didn't push them.

Luke did. He didn't seem to be able to leave well enough alone. He didn't seem to be able not to make work out of what should've been as natural as breathing.

It was because he didn't have Paco there, plaguing him

with an incessant barrage of questions. It was because just loafing along gave him too damn much time to think.

He didn't want to think.

So he made work. He moved cattle. He checked gates. He rode fence. He cut quakies and dragged them back to the wrangle pasture so he could replace some of the rotted rails in his corral fence.

He liked to tell himself that it helped. It didn't. Not really. Not much.

He was grateful—and he was damned sure the cows were—when he actually did have some real work that kept him on his toes. He never thought he'd be glad to see one of his better bulls develop a stifle injury, but bringing the ill-tempered beast down to the corral where he could give him cortisone and then keep an eye on him was at least a challenge.

And once he got the bull in the corral, it took every bit of his concentration to get the animal more or less immobilized by roping him and tying him between two trees so he could dismount and try to get close enough to give him the shot.

The bull twisted and kicked, catching one of Luke's shins right above the boot with a well-aimed hoof.

"Sheee—!"

"Are you all right?"

The question came out of nowhere. Luke's head snapped around.

Jill was climbing over the aspen fence and coming toward him.

He hopped up and down, clutching his leg, furious at the sight of her. "What in the sam hill are you doin' here? You're supposed to be in New York!"

"No."

"You said you were going back to New York!" Outrage mixed with pain.

"I never said that, you just said I *could*."

Which was true, he realized. Damn it all. "Get out of here!" he snapped. "What're you coming in here for?"

"He hurt you."

"He doesn't like people on foot."

"Then why were you?"

"Because I had to doctor him, and the damned horse has too much sense to get close enough." He rubbed his shin once more, then turned away and swung up into the saddle, ignoring her once he saw that she had climbed back over the fence.

He tried to pretend he was consumed with untying the bull. He could've gotten killed for all the attention he was paying.

God in heaven, what was she doing here?

Had she listened to the tapes?

Of course she'd listened to the tapes. She'd heard it all—including what he'd never have said unless he'd been certain she was two-thirds of the way across the country!

And now she'd come to…come to what?

With jerky, angry movements, he set the bull free, opened the gate and rode out of the pasture. "Shut the gate," he said tersely.

She did.

"I sent the tapes down. You got what you wanted," he said gruffly.

"Yes. Thank you." She walked over to the sorrel that she'd tied to a tree. She undid the reins and climbed into the saddle, then rode up next to Luke and sat there quietly, watching. Waiting.

She'd wait a hell of a long time before she heard him say anything as foolish as he'd said on that tape!

"Then you got what you came for. So why aren't you gone?"

"Because I like it here?" she ventured, giving him a smile that made his insides clench.

Deliberately he turned away from her and touched his heels to the sides of his buckskin, heading down the mountainside toward the cabin at a fast walk.

Jill followed.

He ignored her all the way down. He unsaddled his horse and turned him out, then limped toward the house, still without speaking. Jill kept right on coming.

When he got to the door he turned around. "Go home."

"No."

He ground his teeth. "What are you trying to do to me?"

"Talk to you. Get you to talk to me."

"I did my talking on the tape." And a damned fool he'd been to do it, too.

"You liked me." She said the words softly, wonderingly almost.

He scowled. "So?"

She smiled again. "I never guessed."

"You weren't supposed to."

"Why not?"

Was she dim, for heaven's sake? "Because, damn it, you were Keith's girl!"

"You...wanted me...all along?" She said that wonderingly, too, flushing after she said it, her eyes only connecting with his for a fleeting instant before looking away.

"Apparently," he said bitterly. "A man isn't answerable for his hormones."

"Is that all it was?"

"What do you want? A testimonial to your undying charms?" he snarled. "You want me to say I took one look and you knocked me on my ass? Fine. You did."

Her eyes widened then as if he'd shocked her. He hoped to God he had.

"Lust," he said succinctly. "I was horny, just like you said."

"But—"

"For you, okay? Not just any woman. I admit it. But it was wrong. And once it got the better of me, and I kissed you, and that was wrong, too!"

"Was it?"

Luke felt as if he could have heard a nickel drop in New York City. He swallowed, nonplussed, dazed, as if he'd just taken an unexpected uppercut to the jaw.

"Of course it was," he snapped when his wits returned. "We both know that."

She sighed. "Yes."

But she didn't say it firmly. His eyes narrowed and he looked at her closely. "What're you playin' at, Jillian?"

"Nothing. You're right. It was a mistake. And...thank you for telling me."

"Well, I didn't want you thinkin' I thought you were just a piece of..." He stopped, unable to even finish the sentence without offending her. And himself.

He jammed his fists into the pockets of his jeans and rocked back on the heels of his boots.

She nodded slightly. "Thank you," she said again.

"You're welcome." *Now, go,* he urged her silently. *Get on your horse and go!*

She didn't. She ran her tongue over her lips, chewed briefly on the bottom one as she stared down at her boots. Then she lifted her gaze again. "I have a confession to make, too."

He just looked at her. He couldn't imagine that it was anything he wanted to hear, but he knew she wouldn't damned well leave until she'd said it.

He didn't reply at all, just waited. Far overhead he could hear the faint roar of a jet on its way to Denver. Close by he could hear a magpie in one of the trees, scolding.

"I liked it."

His mind went blank.

"I liked your kiss," she said when he didn't respond. Her voice was low, but firm. Her eyes met his, frank and guileless.

His teeth came together with a snap. "Is that supposed to make me feel better?"

She took a step back. "Obviously, whether it was intended to or not, it doesn't."

"Smart lady."

"Am I?" she said almost bemusedly. "If I was, I don't think I'd be up here now."

"So why are you?"

"Because I admired your honesty. Because I felt I owed a similar honesty to you."

"Yeah, well, you've paid up, thanks very much, so you can go away now."

She didn't. She stayed right where she was and tilted her head as she looked at him. "So…was this honesty of yours a one-time deal, then?"

"What's that supposed to mean?"

"You're acting like you hate me. Again."

He shrugged irritably. "Force of habit?" he offered finally, reluctantly, embarrassed.

She laughed. "See if you can break it."

He shook his head quickly.

"Scared?" She gave him a mocking look.

He felt a muscle tick in his jaw. "What do you want, Jill?"

She hesitated, then shrugged and gave him a faint, almost-wistful smile. "I want you to kiss me."

He stared at her, certain he hadn't heard correctly. But she was just standing there, waiting, and then he was certain that he had.

"God Almighty, woman, how can you want that? I *killed* your fiancé!"

Jill said something rude and succinct and wholly out of character. He looked at her, shocked, and she stuck out her jaw as if defying him to make something of it. "I mean it, Lucas. And you know it, too. Keith died, but you're the one who's not living. You've shut yourself off completely up here like a hermit."

"I'm fine."

"You deserve more."

"I have what I want."

"How do you know?"

He yanked his hat off and rubbed a hand through his hair. "I know."

"Then why won't you kiss me? Are you afraid you might like it?"

"I know damned well I'd like it!"

"Well, then..."

"I can't!" Not and be certain that he could stop, that he could control the need that had been building in him practically since the moment he'd laid eyes on Jillian Crane. Not and be sure he wouldn't betray Keith even further.

"You can't?" The look she gave him would have undermined the resolution of a hundred stalwart men.

Luke steeled himself against it, against her. "No."

"Well, then—" she gave a tiny shrug and a shake of her head "—I guess I'll just have to kiss you."

"Don't! Jill, you can't—!" He took a step back, then another.

It was no use. She kissed him.

Luke was not unaccustomed to having women take the

initiative. There was a certain breed of women who preyed on men who did dangerous stuff for a living, especially lean, good-looking ones with heavenly blue eyes and a devilish smile. He'd met his fair share during the years he'd spent cowboying, but they were a mere handful compared to the legions he met once he started doubling for Keith.

Being kissed was nothing new to Lucas Tanner. He'd always been able to handle it. He'd always been able to handle *them.* He never, *ever,* felt out of control.

There was always a first time.

This was it.

The moment Jill's lips touched his, the instant he felt her hands slid up the thin cotton sleeves of his shirt, felt her fingers grip the muscles of his upper arms, the second the fullness of her breasts brushed against the wall of his chest, he lost it. Totally.

Willpower? He acted like he'd never heard of it.

Common sense? An entirely foreign term.

He only had one thought: Jill.

She consumed him the way a fire consumes a forest. If their first kiss had kindled his desire, this one sent him down in flames. All the best intentions in the world seemed powerless against it. Against her.

Maybe it was because he'd been resisting so hard. Maybe it was because he had wanted her for so long. There was no way he could even think about it rationally. He could only feel.

And what he felt was good.

It felt good the way her lips touched, then tasted his. It felt good to respond, to let his tongue tangle with hers, to make her, in turn, respond to him.

It felt good. It was good; but it wasn't good enough.

Luke needed more than her mouth on his. He needed his hands beneath the soft cotton of her blouse, sliding up on the petal-soft warmth of her back. He needed his knee nudging between hers, so that his thigh pressed into the juncture of her legs. He needed to feel the soft pressure of her leg against the arousal that strained against the denim of his jeans.

He needed Jill.

He didn't know which of them moved first. He didn't know who took the lead up the steps into the cabin, who opened the door, who kicked it closed after them. He didn't know whose fumbling fingers worked loose the buttons most quickly or whose fevered hands were fastest at skinning off the jeans they wore.

He'd never in his life felt this sense of desperation, of urgency. He didn't even stop to shed his boots. His jeans tangled in them and tripped him when he tried to bear her back onto the bed.

Gravity came to his rescue, and they ended up there anyway, their arms locked around each other, their mouths still nipping, seeking, tasting. But even the nips and the tastes and the delicious friction of flesh on flesh weren't enough. The hunger was unquenchable.

Luke had seen Jill in a bathing suit countless times. He remembered well the gentle curve of her hips as she walked down the beach. He recalled the swell of her breasts as she lay flat on the lounge and tanned. He'd spent more hours than he wanted to think about fantasizing just how those curves and swells would look if the bathing suit wasn't there.

And now he knew. He saw. He touched. With trembling fingers he traced the shape of her breasts, he teased them to peaks of arousal and felt her writhe between his legs.

"Luke! Oh!" And then she touched him, too. She brushed her hands down across the soft dark whorls of hair on his chest, then let them follow the trail that arrowed down his abdomen to his groin. She touched him there.

He groaned. Her name was a plea on his lips. He moved aside the vee of her legs and touched the center of her. She shut her eyes and arched her back. Her breathing became quick and shallow, as quick and shallow as his. The need surged inside him, thrummed through his blood, rushing, clamoring. He couldn't wait any longer. He'd been waiting years.

"Jill! I need— I've got to—"

She nodded frantically and drew him down to her, brought him into her. "Yesss! Oh, Luke, yes."

Yes. That's what it was. *Yes.* An affirmation. A connection. A tie to another human being. Not just any human being. Jill.

Jill, whom he had watched from afar. Jill, whom he had kept at a distance. Jill, whose smiles and understanding and faith had always been just out of reach.

But now, right now, she was his.

She was warm and sweet and slick, and she welcomed him eagerly. She smiled at him. She stroked his face and touched his lips, fitted her body to his. And in her arms Luke found heaven. Or at least he did until his passion ebbed and sanity returned.

And then he felt like hell for what he'd done.

He'd taken Keith's woman.

The one thing he'd sworn he would never do. The one thing he had managed *not* to do even when he'd wanted to. The one last shred of self-respect that he'd clung to— even when all the rest had deserted him—abandoned him now.

He rolled away from her, anguished and ashamed, and shoved himself off the bed. He yanked up his shorts and jeans, his fingers fumbling in his haste. He couldn't look at her. Couldn't even look down at himself.

"Luke?" Her voice was soft, questioning, worried.

And like a wounded animal, he lashed out. "Satisfied?" he asked her. "Is that what you wanted? How do I compare?"

She looked at him, stricken.

He spun away, unable to face the anguish on her face. She didn't say anything for what seemed like an eternity. He turned away.

He heard the cot creak as she sat up. She made no move to cover herself as she got off the bed. He didn't look at her, anyway. He stared out the window, his jaw clenched tight, his hands fisted inside the pockets of his jeans, as she picked up her clothes and put them on.

"Compared to Keith, you mean?" she said when at last she was dressed. She walked to the door and opened it, then looked back over her shoulder at him. "Compared to Keith, you're an ass."

It wasn't anything he didn't call himself. In fact, he called himself that and other things several thousand times worse over the next three days.

His anger was almost savage. He took an axe and practically mowed down an entire stand of quaking aspens. When he finished, exhausted and drenched with sweat, he rationalized that he had enough to replace the wrangle-pasture fence. He knew damned well he had enough to fence a quarter of Colorado, but he pretended he didn't.

It was really just a way to work off the fury and the pain he felt. Fury at himself for what seemed the ultimate betrayal of Keith's friendship. Pain at having to turn his back on what had been the most beautiful experience of his life.

When he dared remember the way he'd felt in her arms,

the way she'd felt in his, the way she'd given herself so completely, so selflessly to him, he ached all over again.

But even as he recalled the sweet fulfillment of that brief connection, he knew he had had no right to pursue her. He'd always known it.

And yet he'd taken her. Taken her sweetness and her love, and then lashed out at her, blamed her for giving him what he'd wanted.

Oh, yes. He was an ass.

"You're lookin' kinda peaked. Cows been keepin' you up late?" Jimmy grinned down at him from the back of his big buckskin gelding.

Luke straightened up from the posthole he'd been digging and wiped a hand across his stubbled jaw. "They keep me busy." And if they weren't the reason he hadn't been sleeping this past week, he damned well wasn't telling Jimmy so.

"Brought the salt up." Jimmy jerked his head at the packhorse trailing behind him on which he had loaded five fifty-pound bags of salt. "Thought I'd better get on it now. Don't want to be out of shoutin' distance much longer. Annette's already big as Riley's barn and she's swellin' some. She's gotta stay off her feet till her time comes. And when it does, I better be there."

"Leave the salt. I'll put it out when I'm finished here," Luke said as he bent to the hole again.

"Naw, it's okay. She won't need me today. She'll be fine. Besides, Jill's with her—"

"What?" Luke's head jerked around.

Jimmy nodded cheerfully. "It's workin' out swell. She likes the peace and quiet, says she can get a lot of writing done. I don't see how, myself. She's always cookin' and

bakin' and running to help out when Annette needs something. She even keeps an eye on Jimmy, Jr.''

Luke rubbed a hand across his mouth, then spat out the
dirt he'd managed to get in it. "Good for her."

"Er, it...ain't a problem is it, her stayin'?" Jimmy
asked, apparently struck suddenly by the notion that Luke,
as his boss and the owner of the ranch, might have something to say about it.

"I'm just surprised." He'd thought she'd be on the first
plane out, desperate to put as many miles between herself
and Lucas Tanner as she could manage.

"She's a trooper. Works like a Trojan. Wouldn't have
figured it, a fast-lane lady like her. But she doesn't seem
that way at all. She's just like regular folks. But then, I
reckon you already know that."

Luke grunted. He didn't need her virtues extolled.

"Reckon she'd make a good wife. Wonder somebody
don't snap her up."

"Keith was going to," Luke reminded him harshly.

A frown flickered across Jimmy's lean face as he reflected on that. "Yeah, right." He scratched his head.
"Don't suppose you could maybe double for him with Jill,
too?"

Luke slammed the shovel into an aspen branch so hard
that the wood snapped. "Go put out the damned salt!"

He got most of the row of postholes finished, moved the
bull out of the pasture, driving him back up the mountain
so he could earn his keep with the cows, and moved a
dozen or so cattle out of the creek bottom. He lost a calf
that had fallen into the swift current of the river and, wet
and cursing his bad luck, finally got back to the cabin after
five.

Jimmy's horse was standing in front of it, reins hanging
down.

Luke was surprised he'd stayed around. With Annette so close to her due date, he'd figured Jimmy'd hightail it home as soon as he finished. He dismounted, unsaddled and turned his horse out, expecting Jimmy to come out of the cabin when he saw Luke was back. He didn't.

It wasn't that uncommon for Jimmy to leave his horse untied to graze, but it was wholly unlike him not to loosen the cinch and let the buckskin have a breather.

Luke caught up the reins and rubbed the horse's neck. "Hey, fella, where's Jim?"

The horse stood placidly under his touch. He rubbed a hand down its side. The big gelding looked as if he'd been standing awhile. The sweat was already dry on his neck.

"Jim? Hey, Jimmy?" Luke gave a shout, then strode up to the cabin and poked his head in. Jimmy wasn't there. Luke muttered under his breath.

He changed quickly into dry clothes, saddled a fresh horse for himself and one for Jimmy, turned the buckskin out in the pasture and headed up the mountain.

It took him over an hour, and he was well beyond the third salt lick, when he finally heard a faint reply to one of his yells.

"Here!" came a voice rough with pain. "Up here."

Luke spurred his horse up the hill. He could see Jimmy lying beside an outcrop of rocks, his hat off, his red hair disheveled, his face white with pain. His right leg lay crookedly and he winced as he tried to lift himself onto his elbows when Luke rode up. The packhorse was at the far end of the alpine meadow, still half-loaded with salt.

"Rattler spooked m'horses," Jimmy said. "They both ran off. Packer didn't get too far. I broke m'leg, Luke," he said miserably. "Mighta done my wrist, too."

Luke swung down and crouched beside him, running his

hands lightly down Jimmy's leg. He could feel the displacement. It sent shivers down his spine.

"I'll try to bring the truck up."

Jimmy shook his head. "Help me on the horse."

"You can't—"

"Lemme try. At least lemme try. Give me a hand up."

Luke straightened. Jimmy held out a hand. Luke shook his head. "Let me lift you from behind. Your back okay?"

"Think so." Jimmy gritted his teeth as Luke came around and slipped his hands beneath his arms, then slowly and carefully began to raise him.

"Oh, hell—" Jimmy's breath whistled out as he bit off an expletive. Sweat broke out on his face.

"You gonna faint?"

"No." The answer came through clenched teeth. "Get me over to the damn horse."

Luke remembered the white-hot pain when he'd broken his leg in Spain. He could see it searing Jimmy now. He admired Jimmy's courage, admired his grit and determination. "Here now. You're up. Okay?"

Jimmy looked as if he was going to faint. "'Kay," he said numbly.

Luke swung back into the saddle. "All set?"

Jimmy, pale as death, gave a jerky nod of his head.

It was past dark when they got down to where the rutted trail down the mountain reached the narrow dirt lane. "I'll ride on ahead," Luke said, "and bring back the truck. You just keep comin'. Okay?"

Jimmy hadn't said a word all the way down the mountain, but it was too dark for Luke to see a nod, so he managed a "yes." Then, with supreme effort, he added, "Don't upset Annette."

Luke didn't have to. He could tell she was a wreck the moment he saw her face in the window, peering out anxiously, when he rode in. At first she'd looked relieved to see a rider. Then she opened the door, saw Luke, and the color drained from her face.

"What happened? Where is he?"

"He's okay. He broke his leg, that's all. He's coming. I'm taking the truck." He dismounted.

Annette was halfway down the steps. "I'm coming, too."

Luke took in her barnlike figure and the fact that she couldn't walk, only waddle. "The hell you are."

"He's my—"

"No."

"What's wrong?" Jill appeared suddenly, silhouetted in the doorway. When she saw Luke, her expression grew grim. She turned away from him, asking Annette, "What's the matter? What happened to Jim?"

"Broke his leg. Luke's going to get him in the truck. I want to go with him."

"Luke can bring him down better alone. Come on." Jill hurried down the steps and took Annette's arm. "You call the doctor. That way he'll be expecting Jimmy at the hospital."

Luke sent a silent blessing her way, grateful for her calm common sense and for the fact that she was already leading Annette back into the house. He followed them in and snagged the truck keys off the hook by the door. "I'll be back as soon as I can."

"Hurry," Annette urged him.

He started to reach out a hand to get Jill's attention, then dropped it. "Thanks," he said.

She ignored him completely.

He met Jimmy halfway, got him down off the horse and stretched out in the bed of the truck. Then he tied the horse onto the back and drove slowly down the lane toward the ranch house. Jimmy was holding his own when they got there. He slid forward on the truck bed until he sat on the gate. Annette was waiting on the porch.

"Oh my God," she said when she saw him. He looked paler than ever in the cold glare of the light atop the post near the house. He took hold of Luke's arm and tried to stand. He went down like a ton of bricks.

"Jimmy!" Annette shrieked.

Jimmy, Jr., sucking his thumb in the refuge of Jill's arms, started to cry.

Luke cursed under his breath. "He only fainted."

"Jimmy!" Annette was frantic now.

"He'll be all right," Jill said soothingly as Luke dragged Jimmy's inert body onto the truck bed again. "It's better that he's fainted. He won't feel the pain."

"But—" Annette was trying to clamber onto the back of the truck with him, pushing her way past Luke.

"Damn it. Get out of here!" Luke snapped.

Jill gave him a disapproving look and tried to catch Annette by the arm. "Let Luke take him. You shouldn't even be up, let alone exerting like this. You don't want to have this baby right now, do you?"

"I won't. Let me go! He needs me!"

"Ma-ma!" Jimmy, Jr. wailed in Jill's arms as his mother tried to push Jill away.

Luke let go of Jimmy and grabbed her by her shoulders. "Stop it. He doesn't need you now. Your baby's the one who needs you."

Annette stared at him, white-faced and shaking.

He scooped her up bodily and lifted her out of the truck, then set her on her feet, holding her steady. "All the way down the mountain, he worried about you. You and the baby. That was what mattered to him. Not himself. Understand? So you're not doin' anything that will jeopardize that baby.''

"That's right," Jill put in, surprising him. "Let Luke take him, Annette. You come and lie down. You'll be of more use to him later."

Annette looked from Jill to Luke to the still body of her husband in the back of the truck. Silent tears ran down her face.

Jill slipped an arm around her and pulled her away from Luke. He let her go. "Shh," Jill said. "It's all right."

"I'm so bad at this," Annette said, her voice wobbling. "I'm supposed to be brave. Jimmy says ranchers' wives are brave."

"Has Jimmy ever been a rancher's wife?" Jill asked archly, and Luke couldn't help swallowing a smile.

Annette blinked. "What?"

"Never mind," Jill said. She gave Annette a squeeze. "You're doing fine. All you have to be is Annette. That's enough. Come on, now." She drew her toward the house. "Luke will call when he has news." She gave him a look that said he'd better.

"Soon as I know," he promised.

Annette hesitated. "I want—"

"Damn it!" Luke exploded. "I'm his boss. He got hurt working for me. I'll see to this. What if you go into labor? Jimmy said you've been having problems. What if you lose that baby?"

She looked at him, shocked.

"It could happen," he said ruthlessly. "Do you want to go through the rest of your life thinking you killed your kid?"

"Luke!" Jill's voice was furious.

But he was beyond caring. He glared at Annette now, wracked with his own guilt over Keith, over Tanner and

Clare's baby, damned if he was going to let anyone else make a foolish choice.

Annette shrank back from his anger, seeking comfort along with her son in Jill's arms. "You'll call?"

"I said I would." Luke promised again, then met Jill's reproachful gaze. "Keep her here." Then he turned on his heel and headed for the truck.

Five

There were plenty of advantages to living in rural America. One of them was that the doctor you were taking your hired man to might be your brother-in-law by marriage. The disadvantage was that he might also be the man your ex-sister-in-law had married after divorcing your own brother.

Still, regardless of family complications, Russ Moberly would do his best, Luke knew.

He just had to get back from Durango.

"What the hell's he in Durango for?" Luke demanded when the starched white brigade met him at the door, loaded Jimmy onto a gurney and trundled him into the emergency room, transferred him to the X-ray table and left Luke to sit. And sit.

"He went to a golf tournament and banquet," the nurse on duty told him apologetically. Her name was Lucy Campbell and she'd been a couple of years ahead of him in high school. She'd been almost as reckless as he'd been in those days. Now she wore a wedding ring, and he could see photos of a trio of little girls tacked to the bulletin board behind her desk.

"And he didn't leave anyone to cover?"

"Dr. Milliken is here. But there was an accident on the highway just this side of the pass. He's operating right now." Lucy grimaced. "Then he's got another one. After that, it's Jimmy's turn. Don't worry."

He worried anyway. Not about Jimmy, but about Annette. He could still see her white-faced panic. He debated the merit of calling. He didn't have anything to report, after all. But he thought she'd probably worry more if he didn't.

Jill answered the phone. "How is he?"

"Doc's not here. At least Russ isn't. The doc who's covering for him is workin' on somebody else."

"So I can't tell her anything?"

"You can tell her not to worry. Hell, it's just a broken leg."

"Another time she might find that comforting. Right now she's been depending on him, looking to him for strength, and he fainted right in front of her."

"Not on purpose!"

"I know that," Jill said, "but she's emotional. It's the pregnancy. She can't help it."

"Well, make her help it, damn it!"

"By bullying her into it the way you do?"

"I never claimed to be a nice guy."

"What, and lie?"

Luke's teeth snapped shut. He deserved it; he knew it, but it didn't make it any easier to take. Out of the corner of his eye he caught sight of movement down toward the operating room.

"Gotta go," he said. "I'll be in touch when something happens."

Nothing did for hours. It was well past two in the morning when, almost simultaneously, Doc Milliken finished with his second accident victim and was able to deal with Jimmy and Russ Moberly shouldered his way through the door and tossed his jacket on the counter.

"Golf banquet?" Luke said to him.

Russ flushed. "Once a year. And they're tearing up the pass. Let's have a look at you," he said, turning to Jimmy.

At last things began to happen. It was a nasty break. It would need surgery. On that both Doc Milliken and Russ agreed. The wrist was broken, too, but not as badly.

"We'll just cast it," Russ said.

"It's my ropin' hand," Jimmy muttered, then moaned as they settled him back onto the gurney to move him to the operating room. "Call Annette," he instructed Luke as the doors opened and then began to swing shut behind him. "Tell her I'm fine."

But when Luke rounded the corner into Admitting to use the telephone, he found Jill.

"I thought I told you not to bring Annette down! Take her home! Damn it, you get her down here, all riled up, and what do you think she's going to do?"

"Have the baby."

"Damn right. So—"

"Too late. She's having it."

He blanched. "The baby? She's havin' the baby? *Now?*"

"They've taken her down to be prepped."

"She can't!"

"I'm sure when you're God you'll do a better job of arranging the universe. In the meantime," Jill said acidly, "even without your permission, Annette is having the baby."

"Jimmy's just gone into surgery," he argued, not that it made a damn bit of difference.

"I'll tell her."

"But—"

But Jill had turned her back on him to talk to the admitting clerk, another woman he'd gone to high school with. Jill finished giving the clerk—Nancy, he remembered her name was—the information that Annette must have given her on the way into town. She didn't look at Luke again. He might as well have vanished right off the face of the earth as far as she was concerned.

It might not have been a bad idea from his point of view, either.

He felt like a man standing in the eye of a storm. He didn't connect with reality again until he noticed that Jill had finished and was heading down a corridor.

"Hey!" he called after her.

Nancy, the clerk, glared at him. "For heaven's sake, Luke! This is a hospital!"

"Sorry," he muttered. He strode down the hall after Jill.

Nancy leapt out of her chair and went after him. "That's maternity! Only fathers are allowed. You can't go down there!"

He glanced back. "You gonna stop me?"

He caught up with Jill as she reached the labor room. "I want to tell her myself. It was what I told her I'd do."

Jill looked at him, then nodded and stepped out of the way. "By all means."

The minute he stepped into the room he had second thoughts.

Annette was lying half propped up in a hospital bed, her hair as woolly and wild as a sheep at the end of a long, cold winter. Her face was colorless except for a high flush along her cheekbones, and her eyes were huge and smudged.

''Jimmy?'' she asked, her fingers white as they clutched the bed rail.

''In surgery.''

''Is he in a coma?''

''Of course not.'' Then he remembered that the last time she'd seen her husband, he'd been out cold. He rested his palms on the rail at the foot of her bed. ''He came around before I even got him to the hospital. Really, Annette, he's— Are *you* all right?''

The last burst from him because as he was speaking she began to shift uncomfortably. Her hands went to her abdomen, her lips tightened into a thin line, her whole body grew tense.

Jill brushed past him and leaned over her. ''Relax, Annie. Breathe slowly. Deeply. Easy now. Easy.''

Luke, who in his time had delivered his fair share of calves, found that watching human labor wasn't nearly as sanguine an experience.

Annette tried to take a deep breath. It had a ragged edge and with it came a small moan.

''Steady,'' Jill said softly. ''You're doing fine. Just fine.''

Sweat beaded on Luke's upper lip. ''Are you sure?''

Jill shot him a hard glare. ''If you're going to say things like that, get out of here.''

''I was only asking,'' he protested. ''Maybe I should get a nurse.''

''The nurse is just outside. She's got another mother to attend to. Here, give me a hand.''

He blanched. ''I deliver calves, not babies.''

''Not that kind of help,'' Jill said impatiently. ''We have a doctor for that. I mean help her breathe. Rub her back.''

''You want me to...rub her back?''

"Purely platonically," Jill said, giving him a hard look. "Don't worry. You'll be quite safe."

Then Annette began to have another contraction and Jill turned abruptly away, giving Annette all her attention, urging the woman to match her breathing. The contraction passed. Annette rolled onto her side. Jill reached over the bed rail and rubbed her back.

Luke watched. He saw her hands move in slow, even, rhythmic strokes over Annette's back, and he remembered the way those same hands had touched him. His eyes traced the profile of her bent head, the fall of her hair as it curved behind her ear, saw the tip of her tongue jut out for just a moment and run across her upper lip. And he remembered the way her hair had brushed against his chest, the way her tongue had touched his lips, had tangled with his tongue.

His fingers clenched around the bed rail. He stifled a groan.

Jill slanted him a glance.

"Here it comes again," Annette said, and he saw her try not to tense as the contraction overtook her.

"Doing fine," Jill murmured, still rubbing. "Just fine."

"I'll do it," Luke said suddenly, needing to do something.

Jill looked doubtful, but he stepped forward, and she moved aside and let him take over. He rubbed Annette's back, and it was purely platonic. But he couldn't help what his mind was thinking. In his mind the skin he touched and stroked and kneaded was Jill's. Annette let out a sigh of something—relief, bliss, momentary freedom from pain? Luke didn't know. What his mind heard was the eager whimper that Jill had made when she was loving him, being loved by him. He flicked a glance in her direction.

She was watching his hands. Her breathing was shallow. Her lips were slightly parted and seemed to tremble.

"I gotta go," he said abruptly, and he jerked his hands away from Annette and took off out of the room without looking back.

"What happened? Is he...all right?" Annette asked.

There was a second's pause. Then he heard Jill answer, "I think he went to check on Jimmy."

He'd totally forgotten about Jimmy. But it seemed a good idea—and a way of salvaging his sanity. For the next hour he shuttled back and forth between maternity and surgery. There was no way he was going to start touching Annette again, not when all he could think about was touching Jill in entirely more intimate ways. Finally Jimmy was out of the operating room and in recovery. Annette seemed to relax more after that, and Jill favored him with a fleeting look of approval.

Around five in the morning, Jimmy recovered from the anesthetic and the tables turned. One of the nurses, thinking she was being helpful, told him that Annette was in labor, and at once Jimmy tried to get up to go help her.

"The hell you are," Luke exclaimed. "You're staying right here."

"But she needs me! She's counting on me. It's my kid!"

"She's got Jill. They're doing fine."

"You sure?" Jimmy sagged back against the bed. "Thank God for Jill," he murmured. He shut his eyes for a moment, then looked at Luke once more. "Go see how they're doing, will you?"

So for the next hour and a half, Luke went back and forth bearing reports the other way.

Annette moved into transition finally, needing to pant, becoming frantic and clinging to Jill's hand, squeezing it so fiercely Luke thought the bones would break.

But Jill never faltered. She brushed Annette's hair away from her face, blotted her cheeks and forehead with a cool damp cloth, all the while keeping up the soft words of encouragement that Annette needed to steady her breathing.

"Time to move to the delivery room," Annette's doctor decided at last.

He asked Jill to come along. "She'll do better if you're there," he said. Then he turned to Luke. "Guess you might as well come, too, if you're reporting back to Dad."

"Me?" Luke gulped. "But I—"

Annette's gaze fastened on him. "Please. For Jimmy."

He wanted nothing more than to back right out of the room and keep on going. He was nailed to the floor by Annette's beseeching blue eyes. He gave one small, jerky nod of his head. She beamed. Then the beam turned to a grimace, and she clutched Jill's hand.

"Oh, God! I need to...I need to push."

"Let's go," the doctor said.

Luke thought that cows had it better. No one told them they had to move right when they were in the throes of delivery. No one hustled them from bed to gurney to delivery table while they agonized. But then, no cow, to his knowledge, had ever had Jill to help her through it. And Jill was an asset, no doubt about it.

She steadied Annette by her mere presence. She spoke calmly and soothingly all the while the doctor and nurses did their bit. She kept Annette focused, stroked her cheek, brushed her hair out of her face, let her fingers be mashed by Annette's desperate ones.

Luke watched. And felt as useless and out of place as a steer in a pen full of heifers. He wasn't sure exactly when the faint, queasy feeling and the perception that things were getting stuffy turned into something a little more pressing. One minute he was standing there, watching as Annette strained to push with the contraction, and the next he felt a rushing sound in his ears and he took a desperate step back toward the wall.

"Oh, hell," he heard the doc mutter. "Get him outta here."

And the next thing he knew he was out in the corridor, sitting in a chair with Jill pushing his head down between his knees.

"Deep breath," she said. "Now another."

He dragged in the air, felt himself shudder, heard the rushing sound in his ears fade gradually. He stared down at the linoleum between the blue gauze sanitary shoes they'd made him put on over his mud-caked boots. In the distance he heard a baby crying.

"All right now?" Jill asked, and he managed a nod, embarrassed to death.

"I'll just go back in then. See if we've got a girl or a boy making all that racket."

She was long gone before Luke realized that the baby crying must be Annette's. He lifted his head slowly and slumped back against the chair, closing his eyes. God, what a jerk he was.

He could hear people talking and moving around inside the delivery room. Above them all, he could hear a baby. Furious and indignant. But alive. Thank God for that.

He took another deep breath, then two. He needed to go back in—if they would let him. He needed to get all the particulars and go tell Jimmy. But he could well imagine the reception he'd get. Luke Tanner damned near fainting at the sight of a baby being born? Hell, he'd never live it down.

Maybe if he waited, a nurse would come and tell him.

When the door opened finally, Luke straightened and looked up hopefully.

It was Jill. "Better now?" she asked.

He stood up quickly, his cheeks still burning. Immediately, he wished he hadn't; he was still dizzy and had to grab the doorjamb for support. Jill started to reach for him, then tucked her hand into the pocket of her slacks.

Luke swallowed and took a deep breath. "I'm fine. Just got a little light-headed, I guess. Must've been hungry or something."

She didn't call him a liar. She just nodded. Then she smiled. "It's a girl."

He'd forgotten about the baby. Now he grinned. "Sounds like a banshee."

Jill laughed. "She's a fighter. Annette will have her hands full, I'll bet." Her laughter faded and she smiled again, almost wistfully. "Lucky girl," Luke thought he heard her say. She looked away.

"I'll go tell Jimmy," he said.

"Come see the baby first. Then you'll be able to report firsthand." She opened the door to the delivery room and held it.

The nurses smiled. The doctor looked up from whatever messy business he was engaged in and grinned knowingly at him.

Luke shrugged sheepishly.

"Where'd you go?" Annette asked. She was pale but composed now as she lay on the delivery table looking up at him, her baby cradled in her arms.

Luke shrugged awkwardly, feeling heat creeping into his face. "I just…needed some air."

Annette's eyes widened. "You mean you had to… you…got sick?"

"I did not get sick!" he retorted, then grinned at the knowing looks. "Much."

Annette giggled. "Wait'll I tell Jimmy!"

"You do and you'll be living back in town," Luke threatened, but she just laughed again.

"You won't kick us out," she told him confidently.

"Yeah, well, not if you keep quiet about it," he said gruffly, then edged closer to get a look at the baby. "Not bad," he said. "Little more wrinkled and redder'n a calf, but—"

"Lucas Tanner! She's beautiful," Annette protested, hugging her sleeping daughter close.

"Whatever you say. Got a name yet?"

"Jimmy and I are going to have to talk about it," Annette said, then her eyes widened and she levered herself up slightly. "How *is* Jimmy?"

"Doing fine. And probably antsy as hell waiting for news."

"Go then," she urged him. "Tell him she's seven pounds eleven ounces, twenty inches long, has lots of beautiful brown hair, lovely blue eyes, and she's absolutely gorgeous."

"She is? Er, yes, ma'am." Luke gave her a grin and a wink and started for the door.

Jill was standing in front of it. She looked tired and disheveled and more beautiful than ever.

And, God help him, even now he wanted her.

Their eyes met, and he knew she didn't want him—or anything to do with him.

Taking a deep breath, Luke brushed past.

The sun was already well above the mountaintops by the time he'd talked to Jimmy, relayed all the messages about his new daughter and reassured him that Annette was doing fine. He was just heading out to be the first customer in Paco's mother's café when he looked up to see Jill coming out of Annette's room.

"Everything okay?"

She nodded. "She's sleeping. So's the baby."

"So's Jimmy."

"Good," she said. She looked as if she might go past him.

"You okay?" he asked her.

"I'm fine." She gave him a wan smile. He shifted awkwardly from one foot to the other, wondering what else to say. Jill leaned back against the wall and shut her eyes briefly.

"You must be beat."

She opened her eyes and rubbed the back of her neck. "First delivery I've ever been through. Takes a lot out of you even when you aren't the one doing the work."

"You were pretty impressive. You got her through it."

"She needed me to."

"You're calm in a crisis."

"Not always," she said, and he knew they were both remembering Keith's death. It was always there between them.

He set his hat on his head and tugged it down. "I gotta go. There's a ton of work to be done."

She hesitated, then said, "I'm going to get breakfast at Linda's. Do you want to come?"

He wanted to; he didn't dare. And thank heaven this time his stomach didn't growl and betray him. "Naw," he said, even as he realized what it must have cost her to invite him. His mouth twisted. "Thanks anyway. Maybe some other time."

Jill didn't answer. She started toward the door.

"Jill."

She turned halfway around.

"About what I said the other day... I'm sorry."

* * *

Jimmy would have been irrigating in the morning in the south field. He would have been mowing hay in the north later that afternoon. He would have fit in fixing the gate by the Peelers' place somewhere in between. Luke didn't get down the mountain to work on the irrigation until past three.

First he had to feed the dogs and horses, haul the salt, check the cattle, move a bunch up out of the willows, doctor a calf that had pinkeye, shut a gate some hikers had left open and ride an extra two miles just to check another gate he was sure he'd have to open if they left it shut. They had. He did. So by the time he finally rode into the yard by the ranch house, it was already midafternoon.

Jill's rental car was parked by the kitchen, so she was back from the hospital. He didn't go into the house. He turned out his horse, then took the truck and headed for the fields.

Cy Nichols, his neighbor down the highway, was already there.

"Ran into Jill in the café this morning," he said, lifting his hat and running a hand through thin, gray hair. "She told me what happened. We figured we'd help out." He jerked his head toward the far side of the field, and for the first time Luke spotted a small form hunkered down alongside one of the ditches. Paco.

"He's a worker, that one," Cy said, blue eyes crinkling in his sun-weathered face. "He'll make a good hand."

"I expect he will. Much obliged to both of you."

Luke did the irrigating. Paco fetched and carried. Cy started the mowing. "That's enough for today," Luke said when Cy finished the first field. Then, stomach growling and back aching, he remembered the gate.

"Need a hand?" Cy asked.

Luke shook his head. "Thanks for all you've done."

Cy dismissed his afternoon's work with a wave of his hand. "We'll be back tomorrow." He ruffled Paco's hair. "Come on, boy, time we got you home for supper."

"Told ya I could help," Paco said to Luke out the open pickup window.

Luke gave him a tired grin. "I reckon you did."

He watched Cy's pickup disappear down the road in a cloud of dust. Then he straightened up, got in his own truck and headed for the gate.

It was past seven when he loaded his tools and drove back to the house.

He saw with surprise that Jill's car was still parked by the kitchen. He figured she'd have gone into town to see Annette and Jimmy and the baby.

He probably ought to drive in himself, but he was dirty and sweaty and hungry, and he hadn't slept in thirty-odd hours. He didn't think he had the strength to ride back up the mountain, clean up in the creek, ride back down and drive into town.

He could shower in the house. But doing that meant seeing Jill. He didn't do it.

He picked up his saddle and bridle, and was heading toward the corral when he heard a shout behind him.

"Hey, Luke!"

He turned to see Russ and Clare's eleven-year-old son, Dan, leaping off the porch and coming toward him.

"What're you doing out here?" he asked when the boy got close.

"Staying."

"Staying? Here? How come?"

"'Cause Mom went to California for a school-nurse conference and Dad had to go to Denver for some state meeting, so Aunt Annette said me an' Kevin could stay with her."

"Annette's in the hospital."

"Yup, I know. She had a girl. We saw it this morning when Mom took us and Jimmy, Jr. in."

"So Annette can't take care of you."

"I know. Jill is. She said it didn't matter, since she's got Jimmy, Jr. anyhow."

Luke tried to digest that. He'd thought Clare and Russ would be keeping Jimmy, Jr. not the other way around. "She's got all three of you?"

Another nod. "We're helping. I coulda helped you today with the irrigating, but you left so fast, we didn't even know you were here until you were halfway up the road. Can I help you tomorrow?"

Luke felt light-headed again. He dragged a hand across his face. "Sure. I guess."

"I'll be ready. Want some dinner?"

Luke blinked. "What?" he asked, but his stomach had heard this time, even if his mind was still sorting out the rest of what Dan had told him. It wasn't letting him turn down a meal again. It growled loudly.

Dan grinned. "We're finished, but there's lotsa leftovers. Jill said you could have some."

Did she? And what had prompted that?

"I don't think so," he said, and his stomach registered an immediate protest. He pressed a hand against it.

"You want me to tell her you're not hungry?"

Luke sighed. "Maybe I could go for a little something." But he took his time following Dan to the house, and all the way there he was certain he was making a mistake.

He was right.

It didn't matter that he knew she had every reason to hate him. It didn't matter that he hated himself. It didn't matter that she wasn't a bit glamorous or even convention-ally pretty as she stood at the sink washing the dishes, with

Jimmy, Jr. clinging to her jean-clad knees and Russ and Clare's younger boy, Kevin, revving Matchbox cars back and forth across the floor behind her.

He still couldn't take his eyes off her.

She, on the other hand, was apparently cured of any lingering interest in him. She barely flicked a glance his way, then shut off the water and picked up a towel to wipe her hands.

"You want something to eat? I'll reheat the stew," she said briskly. "And make some biscuits."

Luke bent the brim of his hat in his hands. "Don't go to any bother."

"No bother," Jill said flatly. She scooped the baby up with one arm and set him down to play with Kevin. Then she opened the refrigerator, ignoring him.

He deserved it. He knew that. It didn't help much.

"Er, reckon I oughta clean up a bit. You mind if I take a shower?"

Her gaze raked his dirty- and sweat-stained jeans and shirt, his grubby, unshaven jaw and disheveled hair. "It's your house. Anyway, I'd say the time would be well spent."

Luke flushed. He nodded his head jerkily and headed upstairs to the bathroom. Once there, he stripped quickly and submerged himself beneath a stream of hot running water. It was bliss. So much bliss that he almost fell asleep just standing there. Only when someone turned on the hot water downstairs and he got a sudden spurt of cold did he jerk himself awake and stumble out to dry off.

There was no sense putting his dirty clothes back on, since he kept most of his clothes here anyway. Tucking a towel around his waist, he made his way down the hall and into his bedroom.

He stopped dead and stared. One of Jill's blouses was

hung over the back of the rocking chair in front of the window. A pair of sandals poked out from beneath the bed. A suitcase was tucked beside the dresser. A hairbrush, some lipstick and a pair of earrings lay on top of it. Jill was living in his room.

Jill spent each night sleeping in his bed.

He ran his tongue over suddenly dry lips. His fingers clenched against folds of the towel around his waist. He looked at the bed and tried to imagine her there, her head on his pillow, her body curled beneath the quilt—the quilt that was the only thing he had left from his mother.

Deliberately, he turned away from the bed—from the thought. He fished a shirt off a hanger and pulled it on. He grabbed a pair of shorts and some jeans out of a drawer and pulled them on. He sat down on the edge of the bed to pull on his socks. When the mattress gave under his weight, he felt himself sag, too.

The day and the night and the day caught up with him. The trek down the hill with Jimmy, the night in the hospital, the surgery, the baby's birth, the cattle, the irrigation, the gate.

Jill.

He sighed. His fists tightened against the worn denim covering his thighs. He dropped his head back and stared at the ceiling. It wasn't the ceiling he saw. It was Jill.

He could hear her now, saying something to Kevin and Dan, then laughing at their reply. They laughed, too. He heard Jimmy, Jr.'s high-pitched giggle and remembered the way Jill had looked with Kevin playing underfoot and Jimmy, Jr. hanging onto her legs. Comfortable. In her element. Maternal. Gentle. At ease and capable with the children just as she had been with Annette last night. More examples of what a good mother she'd have been. If only…if only…

Once more it all came back to that.

There was no end to the memories, the might-have-beens. There never would be. He sank back on the bed and gave in—just for a moment—to the bone-wearying fatigue that overcame him.

Six

It was already light when he opened his eyes. For a long moment he didn't remember where he was. Then he did. And groaned.

He was lying on his bed—*Jill's* bed. He'd sat down to pull on his socks before going down to eat supper how many hours ago? He didn't even want to think.

It didn't matter. Supper was a dead issue. God, how could he have done that? And where had Jill slept since he'd taken her bed?

A glance around showed him that she hadn't shared it with him. There was only one dent from one body. He finished yanking on the socks he'd started with hours ago, then fumbled with the buttons of his shirt on the way to the bathroom. Then, combing his hair with his fingers, he hurried down the stairs.

"Good morning."

She was already up, sitting beside the high chair, feeding

Jimmy, Jr. some cereal. She was wearing the same jeans and shirt she'd been wearing the day before. He wondered if she'd gotten any sleep at all.

"Sorry," he muttered. "I didn't mean to crash like that."

"You'd been up a day and a night and a day."

"So had you."

"I caught forty winks yesterday when Jimmy, Jr. took a nap."

"That's a lot," Luke said sarcastically.

"I'm fine. Besides, it wouldn't have done me much good to go to bed. Jimmy's been fretful. He's teething."

"So you've been sitting up with him all night?"

"I was down on the couch at first. He woke up about four and I went up and gave him a bottle. We fell asleep in the rocker." She flushed slightly.

"In my—in *your*—room?" She'd sat there and watched him sleeping? "You should've kicked me out!"

"You were sleeping like the dead. Besides," she added, "it's really your room."

He figured she had realized that, but her saying it made him feel awkward just the same. "You've been using it. You should've woke me up. Or...you could've lain on the bed, too. It's big enough."

"Sleep with you? Hardly."

He scrubbed a hand down his face. "Aw, hell, Jill. I said I was sorry about that. I never meant... You gotta know I didn't mean...what I said." He looked at her beseechingly. She looked back at him, her expression noncommittal. "I was angry at myself," he said. "Not you."

She looked as if she might argue, then simply shrugged. "You're going to have to come to terms with it eventually, Luke."

"I have."

She just shook her head, then turned away from him and opened the refrigerator.

"There's hot cereal on the stove," she said. "I can make you eggs and bacon."

"Cereal's fine." He dished up a large bowlful, added milk and ate it while he stood at the sink. He put two pieces of bread in the toaster between spoonfuls and was glad when they popped up just as the cereal was done. He buttered them, then washed them down with a cup of coffee.

Jill finished feeding Jimmy, Jr. and got up.

Luke rinsed his dishes, set them on the counter and grabbed his hat from the chair where he'd left it the night before. "See you around," he said and opened the door. He got halfway down the steps and turned back. "I told Dan he could work with me this afternoon. I'm going up the mountain now. I'll be back down at dinnertime."

"It'll be ready."

"No," he said quickly. "I didn't mean that."

He fed the dogs and horses, then circled up the mountainside to check the cattle. Some needed moving, two needed doctoring. He brought a steer down to the pasture where he'd had the bull before. It had a long cut on its flank that he wanted to watch for infection. Doing only what needed to be done took him all morning.

He could have taken all day, but he knew that Dan would be waiting, and so would all of Jimmy's work. Still, it was nearly one-thirty by the time he got back down.

Jill came to the door as he stepped onto the porch. "Cy and Paco came by and got Dan. He said he'd wait for you to start the haying, but they'd be opening ditches in the west field."

"God bless him." Luke started toward the truck.

"Here." When he turned, she thrust a good-size sack

and a thermos in his direction. "I've made your lunch. You have to eat," she said almost gruffly.

He took them. "Thanks."

He ate in the truck on the way to the field. She'd packed him three roast-beef sandwiches, an apple, some carrot sticks and half a dozen chocolate-chip cookies still warm from the oven. Inside his lunch sack was another plastic bag filled with more cookies. On it she'd stuck a note: "To share with the rest of your crew."

Luke smiled, knowing how welcome they'd be.

He was right about that. Cy and Dan and Paco were more than willing to take a brief break while Luke took over the tractor. Then they all went back to work, the boys on the ditches, Cy and Luke on the mowing and raking, until suppertime, when Cy said he'd better get going because Mary would have his hide if he was late and her soufflé fell.

"Mary makes soufflés now?" Luke remembered Cy's good-natured wife as a top-notch meat-and-potatoes cook.

"Oh, sure. Gotta branch out now we're retired." Cy winked as he walked to his truck. "Keeps us young."

"You reckon wearing yourself out helping me keeps you young, too?" Luke asked.

"Of course." Cy climbed in and started the engine. "I'll see you tomorrow. Let's go, Paco!" he called to the boy, who was skipping rocks in the creek with Dan.

"Aw..." The reluctance in Paco's face was obvious.

"Let him stay for supper. I can bring him in later. Gotta run in and see Jimmy and Annette, anyhow."

Cy nodded. "He'd like that. I'll tell Linda."

"Thanks. And thanks for the help. Don't know how I'd manage without you."

Cy shrugged. "It's what friends are for." He gave a wave of his hand, and the truck rumbled off.

Jill had supper simmering on the back of the stove when

they got to the house, and it was served up on the table by the time they were washed and dried and ready to dig in and eat.

Luke didn't argue. He knew all about protesting too much.

He sat at the head of the table where she pointed. She sat at the foot, with Dan and Paco on one side and Kevin and Jimmy, Jr. in his high chair, on the other.

They talked and laughed, and Kevin spilled his milk. Paco said he didn't like green beans and Jill told him to eat three bites. Luke backed her up without even thinking about it until he'd done it.

Like she was the mother and he was the father. Like they were a family.

The sharp pain of realization bit him suddenly and without warning.

He didn't *want* a family. Even a pretend one. Even a temporary one.

He shoved his chair back and stood up.

"I got some things that need doin' in the barn. Send Paco out when you're finished and I'll run him into town when I stop at the hospital." He carried his dishes to the sink, dumped them in the dishpan, then pushed open the door. "Oh, and...thanks for supper."

He figured he'd give Paco half an hour or so, then head for the truck. The kid wouldn't keep him waiting much longer than that, and it would mean he wouldn't have to go back into the house looking for him.

He didn't. Paco was waiting. So were Jill and Dan and Kevin and Jimmy, Jr. The bigger boys were all sitting in the back. Jill had fastened Jimmy into a car seat in the cab. She was sitting next to the door.

"We're coming, too," she said.

Luke opened his mouth to argue with her, took one look

at all the boys' expectant faces and got in the truck. At least there was a toddler between them.

The baby had a name.

"Julie Elizabeth," Annette announced when they arrived en masse to see the sleeping, considerably less red and wrinkled baby.

"A big improvement," Luke said to the infant as he bent over her small bassinette and looked down at her. "You might get a date to the prom, after all."

"Luke!" Annette tossed a magazine at him.

"Hey," he grinned, fending it off. "It was a compliment."

She made a face at him. "Go bother Jimmy," she said. "Let us girls have a chat."

So Luke took the boys, minus Jimmy, Jr. who was sitting on Jill's lap, into the other wing of the hospital, where Jimmy was propped up in his hospital bed. The boys were suitably impressed with his cast, especially when he invited them to autograph it. But within minutes they grew bored.

"There's nothin' to do in here," Paco complained.

"You're telling me," Jimmy grumbled. "I want to go home."

"Go play catch on the lawn," Luke suggested. When they were gone, he asked, "When will they let you out?" It couldn't be soon enough as far as he was concerned.

"Day after tomorrow," Jimmy replied glumly. "They had to split the cast because of the swelling. Probably won't get to put another on until tomorrow night or Saturday morning. Then, man, I'm outta here." Jimmy stretched his hands over his head, then dropped them gingerly into his lap. His shoulders slumped. "But even then I'm not going to be good for much."

"We'll keep you busy," Luke promised.

"I can't ride. I can't rope. Hell, I can't even write my name. And I didn't get to help Annette with the delivery."

"They did all right without you."

"They did fine," Jimmy grumbled. "Women can always do it without us."

Luke grinned. "Not all of it."

A reluctant smile creased Jimmy's tanned face. "Well, yeah, there is that." Then the grin faded. "But I didn't mean that. I meant, bein' there. I wanted to be. It's—I dunno—part of bein' a dad."

"I wouldn't know." Luke paced over to the window, caught sight of the boys out on the lawn and abruptly turned away from them, too.

"You ain't gettin' any younger, Luke," Jimmy reminded him with more intuition than Luke would have given him credit for.

He didn't answer. He stuffed his hands into the pockets of his jeans and shifted from one boot to the other.

"Nice name, Julie," he said at last in an effort to distract Jimmy. "Named her after Julie Sutter, did you?" He grinned. Julie had been one of Jimmy's early steadies. She was married herself now and lived in Texas. "I'm surprised Annette let you."

"Wasn't after Julie. We wanted to name her after Jill, but we didn't want to confuse things, so we picked Julie instead. It's pretty close."

Luke stared at him. "After Jill? Confuse what?"

"Oh, we figured it might be awkward havin' two of 'em around. Not even a Junior, like our Jimmy is, you know?"

Luke didn't know. "What the hell are you talking about? Jill's not gonna be around. She's just here to work on her book."

"Yeah, but—"

"Then she's leaving! Going back to L.A. or New York

or wherever! Good grief.'' He muttered this last under his breath, trying to mollify his outburst somewhat as he paced around the small room. He stopped at the foot of the bed and fixed Jimmy with a hard, narrow gaze. "How come you thought she was staying?"

Jimmy just looked at him and shrugged.

He wondered if Jill knew they'd sort of named the baby after her. He didn't ask, but he slanted her several glances once they were all packed into the truck for the trip back to the ranch.

She was poking her head out the window, telling the boys to sit down and keep their hands in. They were waving to friends at the local spring-fed swimming pool as they passed on their way to drop Paco off at his house.

"Let's go swimming!" Dan yelled.

"Hey, let's!" Paco shouted, and Kevin added his cheers. Luke ignored them.

"Please!" Dan called. "How 'bout it, huh?"

"Please?" yelled Kevin and Paco.

Jimmy, Jr. yelled, too, and clapped his hands.

Luke drove on past, went all the way up the lane where Paco's house was and pulled up in front.

"Can we go tomorrow night?" Dan asked when Luke shut off the engine and they all climbed out.

"We've got haying to do."

"We can work late," Dan said. "It's Friday. The pool's open late. Please? We're comin' in anyway to see Annette and the baby. Besides, it'll feel good on our muscles. My dad says that soakin' in mineral water is good for your muscles." He gave Luke an ingenuous grin.

"Prescribes it, does he?" Luke grumbled.

Dan nodded eagerly. So did Kevin. And Paco.

Luke looked at Jill. She didn't say a word.

"We'll see," he said at last.

"Yea!" Kevin yelled. Then he looked at Luke, his expression slightly sheepishly, as he explained, "That's what Mama says right before she says yes."

Luke's muscles were definitely in need of a long, hot, mineral-water soak by seven-thirty the following evening. He'd wrestled enough cattle and horses and tractors and bales of hay that day to give him a personal interest in the well-being of each and every muscle he had. Still he was reluctant to stay at the house for supper, then afterward take the kids and Jill to the pool.

So why was he doing it?

Because he felt responsible, he told himself. Dan and Kevin might have been left with Jill, but they were left on his ranch, in his house. And he felt responsible for Jimmy, Jr. because Jimmy worked for him. And he felt responsible for Jill because...because...

For a man who didn't want any responsibilities, he sure had a hell of a lot of them right now. But they were temporary, he assured himself. On Monday Clare and Russ would be back. Annette and Jimmy would be home even sooner. Tomorrow morning. And Jill would leave. Soon.

One night wasn't going to kill him.

It might even be fun.

It might be too much fun. It might be too easy to enjoy it, to find himself wanting those responsibilities for himself, to find himself wanting to be part of a family.

He was afraid of all that when they parked in the swimming pool's parking lot, and Jill took Jimmy, Jr. with her into the women's dressing rooms to change while he took Dan and Kevin into the men's room with him.

Dan leapt into the pool at once, barely missing two other

boys who were playing water tag. Kevin stood on the side, then looked over his shoulder at Luke.

"It's okay," Luke said. "Go on."

"You come, too," Kevin said as his brother surfaced and splashed water at him.

"Later," Luke promised. He sat down on one of the lounges and dropped the towels in a heap.

"Come on, chicken," Dan called his brother. "Jump!"

Kevin sat down and dangled his feet in the pool.

Jill appeared just then, her tall slim figure as tempting as he remembered it, even though this time she was carrying Jimmy, Jr.

Luke remembered the last time he'd seen her in a bathing suit. The weekend at Big Bear. His jaw tightened.

"See?" she was saying to Jimmy, Jr. "There's Dan. Let's go in with him."

"'Nnn!" Jimmy, Jr. shrieked, slapping his hands against Jill's shoulders. "'Nnn!"

She put him down on the edge of the pool next to Kevin, then sat beside him briefly. "Ooh, it's warm," she said, flipping a quick smile over her shoulder at Luke. Then she slid off the side into the water and turned to take Jimmy, Jr. in her arms.

"Can I stand there?" Kevin asked her nervously.

"Not quite," Jill said. "Let's move down here." She edged away toward shallower water. Kevin went with her and slid carefully into the pool. Dan dove and plunged around them like a playful dolphin. Luke watched.

"Hey, Luke! C'mon in!" Dan urged.

"Yeah, c'mon!" Kevin called. He was jumping up and down, too, now, confidence growing.

"Naw." Luke shrugged. "I'm tired." He looked away, but in doing so caught Jill's eye. She was watching him, her expression concerned. His jaw locked and he deliberately looked the other way, then turned over and stretched out on the lounger, ignoring all of them.

"Lookit me, Jill! Lookit, Luke!" he heard Kevin shriek a few minutes later.

"No, look at me!" Dan yelled. "Jill, look! Luke! Watch!"

Luke heard Jill cheer, then laugh. "What a splash!"

He supposed both boys must have been doing cannon-balls by that time.

"Watch me now!" Kevin called. "Watch this!"

"Terrific!" Luke heard Jill say after another huge splash.

"Now me!" There was another shout, then another. And pretty soon it sounded as if half the kids in Bluff Springs were clamoring to have Jill watch them.

Luke rolled over finally, feeling guilty for turning all the responsibility over to her. He looked where she had been, then discovered that she had moved and was now standing in the pool almost at his feet. She still held Jimmy, Jr. in her arms, while she watched Dan and Kevin and half a dozen other kids as they took turns jumping. As she watched, she shifted the baby from one arm to the other, then after a few minutes, shifted him back again.

"I'll take him."

Her head jerked around. She looked up at him. "What? Oh—" she smiled at him "—thanks."

He hunkered down beside the pool and reached for the boy as Jill lifted him up. But the moment Jimmy felt himself being taken out of the pool, his face screwed up and he started to cry.

Jill laughed. "I guess he doesn't want to get out just yet." And she took him back and cradled him against her side. "I'll keep him awhile longer."

"He's too heavy for you."

Jill shrugged. Their gazes met. He saw gentleness in her

gaze. He saw understanding—understanding of feelings that, until this very moment, he hadn't even known he had.

He hadn't been in the water—except in his dreams—since Keith had died.

He sat down on the edge of the pool now and dangled his legs. The water was warm and soothing, just as Dan had promised. Still he felt reluctant. It was so easy to remember.

But Jill remembered, too. Slowly he pushed himself off the side and slid down into the pool until he stood next to her.

She smiled. *Don't,* he wanted to say.

He held out his arms. "Give him to me," he said, and he took Jimmy from her.

"Practicing, Luke?" He looked up to see Lucy Campbell from the hospital.

"Just helping out," he said.

"Fatherhood becomes you." She gave Jill a conspiratorial smile. Jill flashed Luke a half guilty, half worried look—a definitely apprehensive look. But before anything more could be said, Paco appeared.

"C'mon in!" Dan yelled.

Instead of running and doing just that, Paco squatted down on the edge of the pool and looked at Luke with dark, serious eyes. "I can't swim. Will you teach me?"

"Me?"

"You swam with Keith. You told me about bodysurfing. You said he was a champion."

"He was. I'm not."

"But you swam with him."

"Not in competitions."

Paco looked wistful. "I'd ask my dad, but I don't got a dad."

Oh, hell.

"Here," he said to Jill. "Hold Jimmy."

Luke wasn't much of a teacher, but Paco was determined. The trouble was, he was also obviously scared stiff. His lean young body went rigid in Luke's grasp. His fingers dug into Luke's arms. His breath came fast and shallow.

"Relax. You gotta relax," Luke said. "Here. I'll hold you. I got my hand under your belly. Feel it? Now stretch out and stroke forward. I'm not gonna let go. I promise."

"You s-sure?" Paco stuttered, trying to stroke, his movements jerky.

"I'm sure. Here, forget that. You gotta get used to the water a little. Come on, hang onto my back and I'll swim with you."

"Not where it's deep!"

"Not where it's deep," Luke promised. He took Paco onto his back and felt the boy's arms come around his neck like a death grip. "Loosen up a bit," he gasped. "You'll choke me."

"S-sorry." Paco loosened his grip fractionally. Luke began a slow, easy breaststroke, with Paco riding along.

"Can I ride? Can I?" Kevin yelled.

"Not now," Luke said. "You can already swim. Paco's just learning."

"I'll give Kev a ride," Dan said.

"And not drown him?"

Dan grinned. "Aw, shucks, how'd you guess?"

"I have brothers, too."

They shared a conspiratorial grin, then Dan promised, "I won't drown him. This time."

So he took Kevin on his back while Luke swam with Paco, and gradually, as they moved back and forth across the pool, the boy relaxed. He saw how much fun Dan and

Kevin were having and he started to smile, too. He even bounced up and down like Kevin did and waved at Jill.

Luke looked over as Jill waved back. Then she grasped Jimmy, Jr. by his arms and twirled him around in the water, smiling at the little boy's giggles, then lifted him high into the air and snuggled him against her. Over the top of his head, her eyes met Luke's.

And her gaze held so much of what he wanted and feared that he couldn't look for long.

But if he couldn't look at her, other men could—and did. Mike Sutter's nephew, Garrett, and one of Sutter's hands, Dave Cole, had come for an evening swim and a chance to check out the available girls. It didn't take them long to find Jill.

The next time Luke paddled back across the pool with Paco, Garrett was standing next to Jill, holding Jimmy for her. He had the beginnings of a wolfish grin on his face.

"'Sa matter?" Paco asked when Luke tensed beneath him.

"Nothing." Luke stroked closer. "Splash Jimmy," he said to Paco.

"Huh?" Paco looked at Jimmy, Jr. and then at Garrett holding the little boy and all the time easing closer to Jill.

"Oh!" Paco, no dummy, splashed. He made sure he wasn't hitting Jimmy nearly as much as he was hitting Garrett.

"Hey!" Garrett yelped, turning to see where the water was coming from.

"Sorry," Luke said and gave them a bland smile. Paco grinned fiendishly.

But it wasn't as easy to do a second time, when Dave Cole moved in as well.

"You want to watch it," Luke said to Jill with deliberate casualness later that night as he headed toward the door.

The boys had wanted him to stay the night in the house, but he had dogs and horses to feed. And it was the better part of common sense not to hang around Jill too much.

She was sitting cross-legged on the sofa, drying her hair with a towel, and she looked up at him. "What's that supposed to mean?"

He shifted from one foot to the other. "Garrett and Dave. You want to, uh, be careful not to...not to...encourage them."

Jill looked at him from beneath the curtain of her hair. Then she shook her head. "They're nice guys."

Luke grunted, trying not to look at her. He didn't need to. He could close his eyes and see her smiling up at Garrett, see her laughing at Dave's stupid jokes. His teeth came together with an audible snap.

Jill's eyes widened. "Why shouldn't I encourage them, Luke?"

"Keith—"

"Keith," she said firmly, "would want me to be happy. You, of all people, should know that."

He knew it. But damn it... "With Garrett Sutter?" He fairly spat the name. "Or Dave Cole?"

"So give me another suggestion."

He couldn't. He had no right.

Seven

He was certain that once he got Annette and Jimmy and the baby home from the hospital, things would get better. Which went to show how little he knew. He couldn't disappear up the mountain and pretend that they could cope without the steer, because it was obvious they couldn't.

Jimmy didn't have a walking cast, but at least he had a cast that wasn't split anymore. Still, he couldn't drive the tractor. Nor could he do the baling. He couldn't even hobble along and open the dams of the irrigation ditches.

"I can help. I'll ride," Jimmy said. But if his leg dangled down too long, the swelling became far too painful, and the effort it took for him to get up on a horse's back in the first place made it unreasonable.

At least everyone thought so but Jimmy. "I'm not an invalid!" he bellowed fifty times a day.

"Stuff a sock in it," Annette told him. "Here. Hold the baby while I hang out the wash."

So Jimmy held the baby, balancing her gingerly against the cast on his broken wrist, looking like he'd rather run in the other direction. But at least it liberated Jill to help Luke in the fields.

"I don't need your help," he told her the first day she showed up as he drove out on the tractor.

"That wasn't you calling around noon looking for a hand to help out with the baling?"

He scowled, lifted his hat and rubbed a hand through sweat-drenched hair. "Know a lot about baling, do you?"

"I grew up on a farm in Iowa."

He stared. "I didn't know that." He'd always thought her innate elegance came from a sophisticated background.

"You can take the girl out of the hayfield, but you can't make her totally forget it. Although I have to admit, I have four brothers who helped a lot more than I did. And it was in Iowa, so it might not be the same. But I think I could manage to be of some use if someone was willing to teach me." The look she gave him was a direct challenge.

"What about your book? Don't you have a book to write?"

"I'm almost finished. Want to read it?"

"No." He started the tractor engine again. "Come on. Get on."

"Ah." Cy grinned when they got there. "Now this sorta help is more like it."

Luke let her rake. She caught on to the tractor driving quickly. "It must be like riding a bike," she called as she drove past.

"Just don't grind the gears," he yelled back.

"No fear," she said, and promptly did.

Luke winced. He stripped off his shirt and wiped his face with it, then hung it on a fence post. "Come on, Cy. Let's get loading."

He reckoned if he worked her hard enough that would be the last he saw of her.

So the next day—and the next, and the next—he found her lots of work to do. Raking. Baling. Driving the bale mover. And every day she came back for more. And when she finished what he gave her, instead of retreating, exhausted, which she certainly had a right to do, she brought them food from the house, then went down and helped Paco with the ditches.

She worked long and hard and she helped a lot. Luke appreciated it, in spite of himself. He even managed to say so after she'd been working with him for more than a week.

It was almost suppertime that evening and they'd finished the haying at last.

He gave her a ride back to the house on the tractor, and when she got down, he said, "Thanks. You've been a good hand."

"Good farmer," she corrected with a smile, swiping her hair away from her face. She had taken to wearing a cowboy hat now, but it didn't quite tame the long strands. "I don't do horses."

"You ride."

"Like a sack of potatoes."

"I could teach y—" He stopped, aghast at what he had almost offered. "You do fine," he said gruffly. "Anyhow, you won't need to do horses in New York." And he started the tractor abruptly, heading it toward the shed.

Usually by the time he got in the house, Jill had grabbed a quick shower and was in the kitchen helping Annette get supper on the table.

But tonight she was nowhere to be seen. He didn't intend to notice. He certainly didn't comment. Not, at least, until Annette said, "Let's eat," and he discovered that it was only she and Jimmy and himself at the table, Jimmy, Jr. having already eaten and Julie sound asleep.

"Where's Jill?" he asked before he could stop himself.

"Got a hot date." Jimmy winked.

"She's going out to supper with Garrett," Annette announced with what seemed considerable relish.

Luke didn't say anything, just shrugged and sat down at the table and started dishing up.

It wasn't his business what she did. All the same, he couldn't stop himself from giving her a hard look when she came downstairs a few moments later, her long hair piled into an intricate knot on the top of her head, a few tendrils escaping to tickle her neck. Her lissome curves were no longer outlined in denim and chambray, but in coral-colored silk the likes of which Bluff Springs had never seen.

"Wooo-weee!" Jimmy whistled.

"Oh, envy," Annette murmured, shooting Luke a significant look.

He gritted his teeth, bent his head and sawed at his steak.

"Where'd you get that?" Annette asked.

"In New York."

Luke chomped down on a piece of steak. It figured. All that business about being an Iowa farm girl was obviously long forgotten.

"Reckon I better ask Garrett what his intentions are," Jimmy joked.

Luke ignored him. He wouldn't have looked up even when Garrett came to the door to get her, except Jimmy invited him in, then kidded him about going out with the second-most-beautiful woman in Colorado.

"I won't argue, only because Annette's a good friend," Garrett said, smiling at Jill in a way that said all too clearly who he really thought merited being number one. Luke's knife hit his plate with an extraordinarily loud smack.

Garrett glanced his way and his smile faded slightly. "I'm not poaching, am I? If you and Jill are—"

"We aren't," Luke said, and he shoved his chair backward so hard it tipped over. He ignored it on his way out.

Three days passed. Luke didn't go down to the ranch. No one came up. Cy had said he'd look in and take care of what he could, and since the haying was done, Luke felt justified in staying away.

At least he did until the evening of the third day, when he was sitting on the steps of his cabin, sipping an after-supper cup of coffee and whittling a coyote out of pine. He was appreciating the solitude and the serenity of his existence and determinedly not thinking about Jillian Crane and the effect she had on him. A glance down the mountain showed him a rider heading his way.

For a single instant, his heart leapt as he remembered Jill coming up before. But another long moment's scrutiny proved it wasn't Jill. It was a man. With two good legs. A man who sat a horse easily. Garrett?

Luke stood up, his fists curling lightly at his sides as he watched and waited. And then he saw who it was, his whole body relaxed and a grin spread across his face.

"Noah!" He came down the steps waving a hand at the rider, who waved right back and spurred his horse to move a little faster.

"Son of a gun, what're you doin' up here?" Luke demanded as his younger brother got within speaking distance. Rodeo bronc rider Noah Tanner didn't often make social calls as he moved relentlessly back and forth across western America in pursuit of the NFR gold.

"Just passin' through," Noah said now, swinging down

out of the saddle. "On my way to Washington, then thought I'd stop and see Tanner and his brood." He grinned. "Mag's p.g. again. Did you know?"

Luke shook his head.

"They're both happy as pigs in you-know-what. Anyhow, I was within twenty miles and, hell, I figured I hadn't seen you in a long time, so why not? Besides Tanner said—" He broke off suddenly.

"Tanner said what?"

"Nothin'."

"What'd Tanner say?" Luke thrust his face right into his brother's and was glad of his extra two inches.

"Said I should see if you were okay," Noah muttered. "He was worried."

"Of course I'm okay. Why shouldn't I be? Since when did you two start playing mother hen?"

"Reckon Tanner has a time or two," Noah reminded him.

"Yeah. But you?"

Noah rubbed the back of his neck. "You weren't doin' so good the last time I saw you."

Right after Luke had bought the ranch and moved back to Colorado, he meant. Right after he'd spent months on the road, trying to forget the past.

"You looked like you'd got stomped by Mr. T," Noah went on. He meant the bull, Luke knew, not the television actor.

"That was then. I'm fine now."

"If you say so," Noah agreed equably. He didn't look completely convinced, but he let it drop. "Got any coffee goin'?"

"I'll make some."

"Appreciate it," Noah said. He turned his horse out while Luke went back to the cabin. Then, carrying his saddle, Noah came in and sniffed appreciatively. "One good thing about you havin' been a Hollywood hotshot, you learned how to make interesting coffee."

"This is good, old-fashioned Colorado coffee."

Noah made a face. "Left that behind, too, did you?" He settled onto one of the narrow beds and grinned up at his brother. "Didn't leave Jill, though, I see."

"I didn't bring her here!"

If Noah was surprised at his vehemence, he didn't let it show. "That's what she said. Said she had to track you to the ends of the earth before she found you."

"She what?" Luke stared at him.

"Said she'd been all over God's green earth lookin' for you. Paris. London. Hawaii. Said she was always just a little too late. So she just wrote the book without you, then gave it one last shot." He cocked his head. "You didn't know?"

"Uh-uh." What would he have done if she'd found him while he was still running? What would he have done if he'd opened his hotel room door in Paris or London or Hawaii or any of the other places he'd tried to hide from himself and found Jill standing there?

Nothing more than he'd done already, he reminded himself savagely. He jerked up the coffeepot and began to pour.

"She's a looker, that Jill," Noah mused now, folding his hands across his trophy belt buckle and stretching out on the bed.

Luke got another mug down out of the cupboard. "How you doin' in the standings?"

"Tenth. Not as good as I'd like. Prob'ly not as bad as I deserve. I've had some lucky breaks, drew some good horses. Reckon I might make it to Vegas if things keep goin' my way. How come you're up here if she's down there?"

Luke expelled an irritated breath. "Why shouldn't I be? She's writing a book. I'm riding the range. I live up here. She's just staying down there."

"I don't think so," Noah said.

"What's that supposed to mean?"

"Means you're actin' just a little too snuffy, I'd say. Kinda like Tanner was before he reckoned he and Maggie could get hitched into the same harness and pull in the same direction without the world cavin' in."

"I'm not like Tanner," Luke said shortly. "He had a happy ending."

"You can, too, if you want one," Noah said. He sat up and leaned toward his brother. "It isn't impossible."

"You're turnin' into a hell of an optimist."

"Maybe. But it's true," Noah maintained. "Tanner'll tell you. You gotta go after what you want in life. You want Jill, go after her."

"I don't want Jill!"

"No?"

Luke turned his back and stared out the window. "Leave me alone."

"Ain't like you to be a quitter, Luke," Noah said quietly.

"You can't quit what you never started."

"Didn't you...start something?" Noah's words fell like stones into the silence. Luke wondered exactly how much he knew, how much Jill had told him.

Damn, had she spilled her guts to his brother? Luke went to stand in the doorway, his spine stiff, his knuckles tight on the door frame.

"You can't quit," Noah said to his back. "Cowboys don't."

He came, he flung his words of Western wisdom and, like he always did, Noah left.

His words, however, pricked at Luke at odd times during the next few days. He fought them off, ignored them.

There were such things as false starts, he told himself. He and Jill had had one of those. You weren't really quitting if you turned your back on those. You were just showing good sense. It was better this way—for both of them.

Besides, in time he would forget her. With Jimmy home and Annette getting her energy back, with Cy checking in every day and Clare calling to help out, Jill had probably already packed her bags and left for New York.

Maybe she'd left when he had, he thought.

Or maybe she was staying around—thinking about a relationship with Garrett Sutter.

"Damn it!" He had ridden right into an overhanging branch.

He shoved it away and rode around the tree, then turned his head as he caught sight of some movement just down the mountain through the trees.

At first he thought it was a wandering cow, though he hadn't seen one on the way up. Now he saw that it was a horse. One of Jimmy's horses. What the hell…?

Touching his heels lightly to his own horse, Luke headed down the slope after it. Surely, with a broken leg, Jimmy hadn't been stupid enough to come looking for him and get himself bucked off. Had he?

Luke caught the horse's reins and started down the mountain, looking.

He heard her before he saw her. *Jill.* Which didn't bring the relief that it should have. She was in the pasture where she'd found him when he'd been doctoring the bull, the one where he had the steer now, the one he'd told her to stay out of on foot.

Obviously she was on foot now.

But it wouldn't matter with the steer the way it would

have with the bull, and she didn't sound as if she'd been hurt, though she must have been tossed off.

By the time he reached the fence, he could see her clearly. She looked none the worse for wear as she backed toward him, edging over near the pile of quaky branches that he'd cut for the corral. She kept her eyes on the steer, which was still standing on the far side of the pasture in high grass, regarding her curiously.

"Stay there," she told him. "Just stay right where you are. Don't come any closer."

Luke sat silently on the horse and watched, his amusement growing as he did so. All too often around Jill, he had felt foolish, even when she hadn't meant to inspire any such feeling. It was comforting, since she clearly wasn't hurt, to have the tables turned for once.

He dismounted quietly, glad she was making so much noise she hadn't heard him. Then he eased his way over the fence, aiming to come up behind her.

"I mean it," Jill was saying to the steer, which had taken a step or two in her direction. "Don't come over here."

The steer, unused to being talked to in anything except four-letter installments dished out by irritated cowboys, looked at her as quizzically as a steer can manage to look.

Luke moved closer, still not speaking up, wondering what Jill would do if the steer decided to pursue his interest. He imagined her turning and running straight into his arms. He couldn't help it; he grinned.

She'd reached the pile of quaky branches now, and she picked up one of the short ones, waving it like an oversize baseball bat. "See this?" she said to the steer. "Want it right between the eyes? No, of course you don't. So just don't—"

But the steer did. He tossed his head and started toward her, first at a walk, then at a slightly faster gait.

"Don't!" Jill warned.

Luke, almost behind her left shoulder now, expected her to turn and run. She stood her ground and assumed a batting stance, for all the world as if she were Henry Aaron looking for his sixty-first.

The steer kept coming.

"Watch it!" Jill cried, stepping into her swing.

"For God's sa—"

She caught Luke on the follow-through—right between the eyes.

Not that he realized it at the time.

At the time all he saw was the swing...and stars.

The first thing he heard was Jill, half-hysterical, crying, "Luke! My God! Are you all right? Luke!"

He couldn't see her at all. The pain was blinding, but even if it hadn't been, his eyes were swollen shut.

"Oh God, I'm sorry! I'm sorry! Come on! We've got to get out of here. The bull's—"

"'S a steer," Luke mumbled.

"What?"

"'S not a bull," he managed to say, struggling to sit up with the aid of her arm behind his back. "'S a—"

"Steer? Why didn't you say so?" Abruptly she pulled her arm out and let him drop back onto the ground.

He groaned.

Immediately she was contrite. "I'm sorry. I still shouldn't have hit you. But if I'd known—" Accusation began to creep back into her voice.

"You made your point," Luke said gruffly. He tried to open one eye. He could barely manage to let a little light in. It hurt like hell.

"Can you stand up?"

He did, finally. His head felt as if it were going to come

off. He couldn't keep his balance without her holding him up. So much for having the advantage. He groaned again.

"Let's get you to the horses." She helped him slowly over to the fence. The steer, curious again, was practically breathing down their necks by the time they got there. Luke dreaded having to bend down and climb between the wires, with reason. He almost passed out by the time he got to the other side.

"Can you ride?" Jill asked.

"I can ride," he muttered.

She insisted on holding onto the reins of his horse in case it decided to go somewhere other than the cabin. Luke assured her that it wouldn't, but she was stubborn and he was in no shape to fight with her about it.

A tentative exploration with his fingers indicated that he had a lump the size of a goose egg between his eyes, and his nose was probably broken.

"Thanks," he said when they reached the cabin.

"You need to see a doctor," she said.

Luke couldn't imagine telling any doc in town what had happened to him. If his almost passing out in the delivery room was memorable, this ought to go down in Bluff Springs history as first-class folklore.

"No," he said. "I'm stayin' right here."

"But—"

"No," he said, and slid off the horse before she could argue further.

"Damn it, Luke. You need help."

"I need to be left alone." He could make out the cabin and moved toward it. "Turn out my horse and you'll have done your good deed for the day. Then go away."

"But—"

"Go on. You've got things to do, I'm sure." He turned back, not that he could really see her, but he could pretend.

"Why'd you come up here, anyway? Something wrong down at the ranch?"

"No. I came to tell you I was...leaving."

Still, the news shook him. He took a stumbling step backward, then steadied himself, trying to ignore the sudden hollowness inside.

She hesitated, but when he didn't say anything, she went on. "Annette and Jimmy are doing all right and I got the book finished. So, well, I figured it was time. I...have an assignment I've been thinking about taking." She sounded casual.

"Good for you." He stuffed his hands in his pockets. He was glad he couldn't see her now. He wished she couldn't see him. Hell of a way to remember him, looking like he had a piñata for a head.

"I...talked to Carl the other night," she said after a moment. "He has a job he thinks you might be interested in." There was an oddly breathless quality to her voice.

"No."

"It's a western. Right up your alley. Starts filming in the fall and—"

"I said *no*."

"Luke, you need—"

"I don't need anything, except to be left alone. No. Thank you." His fingers curled into fists. There was a hammer slamming against an anvil behind his eyes. He turned back toward the cabin, moving carefully, determined not to make a bigger fool of himself by tripping and falling on his face. "Goodbye."

Hank fussing at the door woke him. The other dogs whined, too. Luke felt like whining himself. It had taken him hours to go to sleep. He hadn't had any ice to put on his face, but he'd got water from the creek and used soaking compresses in an effort to get the swelling down. If it had worked, by the time he went to sleep the effect had been marginal.

His only consolation was that Jill was really gone. Finally he could begin to try to forget her. As he'd drifted off to sleep, the pain finally giving way to sweet oblivion, he'd allowed himself a sigh of something like relief.

But relief was short-lived. The dogs were going nuts.

"What the hell's the matter with you?" he snarled, hauling himself to a sitting position and fumbling to light the kerosene lantern.

Outside he heard a horse neigh and he cursed vehemently, certain that Jill had left the rungs of the fence down and the horses were off to the four corners of the earth.

Damn! He struggled to his feet as the dogs barking grew even more frenzied.

The door opened as he got the lantern lit.

Jill said, "I'm ba-a-a-ack."

Eight

"What the hell—?"

"You didn't imagine I'd leave you here alone, did you?" Jill asked. She came right up to him and studied his eyes in the golden light. He could barely make her out, even now. He gritted his teeth.

"I'd hoped," he muttered.

"Well, I wouldn't. You might have a concussion. You really should see a doctor."

"Don't start," he warned, "or I swear to God I'll throw you out right now."

"You and whose army?" And she took his arm and dragged him back toward the bed. "Lie down. I've brought some ice." She looked around. "I'll put it in a plastic bag and wrap it in a dish towel." She glanced about. "Good. You have dish towels."

"How uncivilized do you think I am?"

"Don't ask."

He heard her moving efficiently across the room, heard the clinking of the ice. Then she came over and sat on the bed. He edged away. Gingerly she laid the ice pack across his eyes and the bridge of his nose. He sucked in his breath.

"Hurts?"

Like hell. "I've had worse."

"I suppose you have." He could hear the smile in her voice. "Shh, now. Just try to sleep."

He couldn't possibly sleep. Not with her right next to him. What did she think, that pain deadened desire? She needed to think again. Still, when she didn't move about, just sat quietly beside him while the ice did its numbing best, he found himself relaxing without trying to.

"You said you were leaving," he murmured, fighting to stay conscious.

"I changed things around."

"What things?" Conversation would help, he decided. It would keep him from feeling quite so cozy.

"I arranged to keep the rental car, canceled my plane reservations and told Annette not to give someone else my bed." He could tell that she was smiling again.

He breathed more easily, not at the smile but at the idea that at least she planned to leave, to go back down to the ranch.

"Not that I expect I'll be using it, really," she went on, just as if she'd heard what he was thinking. "I'm staying with you."

"No. I told you no."

"Wanna fight about it?"

He groaned.

"I'm truly sorry about this, Luke."

"For smashing my handsome face?"

"Yes." And he could tell from her tone of voice that she actually meant it. He reached up a hand and pushed hers away, moving the ice pack off his eyes as he squinted up at her. It was a mistake.

She looked like an angel, her disheveled dark hair like a nimbus around her face, and all of her lit in the soft golden light of the lantern. It made him want her all over again.

A ragged sigh slipped from between his lips. Gently Jill replaced the ice pack. He felt something soft brush across his hair once, then again. Her fingers? Probably.

Her lips?

God, he had to stop thinking things like that!

"Go to sleep," she told him. "Don't worry. I'll take care of the horses and the dogs in the morning."

He should have protested. He should have told her he could manage, but God, it felt so good, despite the pain, just to give in this once.

Once wouldn't hurt, would it?

He could regain the ground he was losing tonight when he felt better tomorrow.

Couldn't he? *Couldn't he?*

When tomorrow came she wouldn't let him out of bed.

If he hadn't used a lot of choice, four-letter words when it came to preserving his modesty, she probably wouldn't have even given in to him on that.

She hovered all day—except when she was out feeding the horses or checking the cattle. He was glad when she left to do it. But once she had, he worried all the time she was gone.

What did she know about moving cattle? She might be a farm girl by birth, but, hell, this was the woman who couldn't tell a steer from a bull! She'd kill herself out there.

He tried not to fret about it. He didn't want her to think he was that worried. But when three hours passed and she hadn't reappeared, he couldn't pretend indifference any longer. He hauled himself out of bed and reached for his jeans.

The door opened. "What on earth are you doing?"

"I was, uh—" He couldn't even come up with a convincing lie. He sank back onto the bed, weak with relief. "Worried," he muttered. "About the cattle. Did everything go all right?"

She nodded. "Of course, I didn't really do anything spectacular. All the fence was intact, so I didn't even get to pretend I could mend it. I know I was supposed to get the cattle out of the creek bottom, and I tried. But they didn't want to listen, and they were bigger than I was, so I wasn't a huge success as far as that goes. But I did get the horses fed." She shrugged, grinning. "I might be a farmer, but I'll never make a cowboy."

"Doesn't matter, does it?" Luke said. He laid back on the bed, his head still pounding.

"Might." Jill's voice was soft.

He shot her a wary look. "Don't," he warned.

"Don't what?"

"Push."

"Is that what I'm doing?"

"Aren't you?"

She flushed and looked away.

"Uh-uh. So forget it. Forget me."

"I can't."

"I'm not worth it, damn it. Besides, once you had me, you wouldn't want me."

"How do you know?"

He never should've started this. He'd hoped that by spelling things out, confronting her, he'd get her to turn tail and run. He should've known she'd be like a grizzly when cornered, ready to do battle. Hell.

"Because," he said, his fingers curling into the bedroll, "I'm not Keith."

"No," she said. "You're not."

"I'm not cheerful and eager and a regular damned Boy Scout."

A hint of a smile touched her lips. "That's for sure."

The muscles in his jaw tightened. "I don't make the kind of money he did or have the fans he had or anything else."

"True."

"So what're you doin' here?" Even he could hear the anguish in his voice.

She smiled once more and lifted her shoulders in a gentle shrug. "Beats the heck out of me. I must be a glutton for punishment."

The next morning he awoke to find her lying on the other bed. It was still very early. He didn't need a watch to tell him that. He could see better this morning.

He wouldn't need Jill to do his work for him. He could send her home.

He rolled over onto his side and propped his head on his hand and looked at her. She was asleep.

He'd spent so much of the time he was with her either trying to ignore her or fighting with her, that he'd had damn few chances to simply savor the beauty and gentleness that was Jill. It wasn't in the best interests of his mental health to do so now. He knew it. But he didn't seem to be able to stop himself.

And hell, at least he'd have the memory. When he was a crotchety old codger still wrangling horses and punching cows, he could drag it out and look at it in his mind's eye again and again.

It was worth the risk.

She was lying on her back, one arm under her head, the

other clutching the blanket against her chest. He really couldn't see all that much of her, except her face. It was enough. His eyes traced the soft fullness of her cheeks, then leisurely moved down the stubborn line of her jaw. His gaze lingered first on the dark brown half-moons of her lashes, then dropped to her mouth. He remembered kissing that mouth. He could remember its taste. And the memory brought with it a need, surging up unbidden and unwanted inside him. Stifling a groan, he fought it off.

But whatever sound he didn't manage to stifle woke Jill. She stretched and rolled onto her side, opened her eyes and looked at him.

''Good morning.'' The softness of her voice sent a shiver down his spine.

''''Mornin'.'' His own voice sounded rusty. He rolled up to a sitting position, knowing full well the danger of lying there looking at Jill lying there looking at him.

She sat up just as quickly. ''I'll do it. You should stay in bed.''

He slanted her a grin. ''I appreciate the offer, but this is one thing you can't do for me.''

Jill blushed as he tugged on his jeans and ambled toward the door. ''You're all right?'' she called after him.

''Fine.'' He was, in fact, much better. Not that he looked it. His face looked worse than the time a bull had caught him with a flying hoof back in his rodeo days. Not surprising. That had been a glancing blow. This had been anything but. His one consolation was that having to look at him ought to turn off any lingering interest Jill might have.

But if it did, she didn't show it.

By the time he got back, she was up and dressed and had the coffee on. He could smell it the moment he opened the door. It set his stomach to growling and he pressed a hand against his belly. All of a sudden he was starving. He said so.

"I don't wonder," Jill said. "You didn't eat anything yesterday."

He couldn't remember much about yesterday. Only that she'd been here fussing over him, that she'd gone to check on the cattle, that he'd worried until she came back, that he'd tried to make her see sense and that she hadn't. Obviously, or she wouldn't still have been here.

"Sit down. I'll make you breakfast."

It was too early to argue with her. He sat down and let her make it. She'd come equipped, that was for sure. He usually got by on fruit and bread and cold, dry cereal out of the box. She came with eggs and milk and bacon.

By the time he'd put away three eggs, half a dozen strips of bacon, four pieces of bread that she toasted by holding them on a long fork over the burner on the stove, complete with some of Annette's homemade strawberry jam, his stomach thought he'd died and gone to heaven.

He couldn't have suppressed the sigh of contentment once he finished even if he'd tried. Hank slid her head onto his knee and looked hopefully for a scrap. There weren't any. He scratched her ears.

"Sorry, old girl. It was too good."

Jill smiled. "Thank you."

He looked up and met her gaze. Then he hauled himself to his feet and started toward the door. "Better get goin'," he said. "Thanks for breakfast. And for…you know…bothering." He set his hat on his head and opened the door.

"Can I come?" Jill said. "Just for today," she added even as the word *no* was forming on his lips.

He hesitated, then nodded. "For today," he agreed.

After all, he reasoned, he could hardly say no when she'd done so much for him. Besides, she was leaving. For good. Pretty soon memories would be the only thing he had.

Once, when he and Keith had been in Australia doing a movie, Luke had had the opportunity to spend the last evening he was there in a bar talking to an old Aborigine who had had a minor role in the film. The talk had ranged far and wide, covering the virtues of American versus Australian-rules football, the best points of American versus Australian saddles. And, of course, they'd spent considerable time debating—and sampling—a multitude of American and Australian beers.

But what stuck in Luke's mind now, five years later, was something the Australian had said about time. There was ordinary time, he'd told Luke, and there was ceremonial time. Dream time. A time that existed on another plane of reality altogether.

Then, muzzy-headed with beer and the fatigue that accompanied the end of the shoot, Luke had only had a vague sort of grasp of what he was talking about. It made a lot more sense to him as he spent this day with Jill. He didn't know if the Aborigine would agree that what they were sharing that day was dream time or not, but as far as Luke was concerned, it qualified.

The day was clear and cool when they set out. First they fed the horses, then saddled up two of them and headed out so that Jill could show Luke the reluctant cows she'd met the day before. Then he showed her how to convince them to move and left her to it.

"Aren't you going to help?" she asked him.

"If you need it."

She got a small, determined smile on her face. Then she

urged her horse forward. "Come on, cows," she said. "Move it."

Eventually they moved. She did surprisingly well. He smiled his approval. She smiled back. The day got a little warmer.

They made a circle to see to the cattle that she hadn't had a chance to check on the day before. Luke found one logy calf that he wanted to keep an eye on, so he drove it and its mother down to a lower pasture, the one where the steer that had been involved in his downfall still stood.

"This is the infirmary," Jill guessed.

"In a manner of speaking."

Jill shook her head and looked at him with a mixture of chagrin and pity. Then she rode up close and peered into his blackened eyes.

"They do give you a certain *je ne sais quoi*," she told him, with only the barest twitch of her lips.

"It's nice to know a woman who can defend herself," Luke replied soberly.

And once more they smiled, and the day warmed even more. If Luke sensed the danger in those smiles or in the warm feelings growing between them, he ignored it. He just soaked up the impressions and the memories, willing to let the present take care of itself.

Dream time.

Yes, that's what it was.

It could have been meteorological conditions, or it could have been the increasing heat between them, but at that moment there was a white flash, followed by a loud peal of thunder. Huge clouds rumbled over the mountains and rain started pouring down.

Brief thunderstorms were frequent in the late afternoon during the summer months. But this one was a gullywasher, with thunder rumbling, lightning streaking and rain coming down in buckets.

"Come on," Luke shouted, touching his heels to his horse. "We're close to the cabin. Let's go."

Of course, they were drenched by the time they got there. And if it was possible to be any wetter, they got that way by the time they unsaddled and turned out the horses. Then, laughing and gasping, they ran across the clearing and stumbled up the steps and into the cabin. Luke slammed the door and fell back against it.

In front of him, Jill stood still, her jeans and shirt plastered against her skin, outlining her willowy curves. She turned and he saw her lips trembling. Her teeth chattered.

"Are you cold?" he asked her. He was burning himself, hotter now than he had been all day.

"No, uh...yes," she said, crossing her arms and rubbing her hands against her soaked sleeves.

"You'd...better get out of those clothes."

Their eyes met. Everything that had been growing all day—all week—hell, forever, as far as Luke was concerned—seemed suddenly too strong to deny.

Dream time.

Just today. He wouldn't ask for more than today.

"Jill?" His voice was ragged. He swallowed hard. "Take them off."

Her gaze dropped. She lifted her hands, and her fingers began to fumble with the buttons of her shirt, but they trembled and she made little progress.

"Let me?"

Her hands fell away. She looked up again, and everything he'd ever wanted to see in her eyes was there. More than he deserved to see. More than he could accept. But he couldn't look away. Not now. Not today.

"Just once," he whispered.

She tipped her head. "What?"

He gave his a little shake. "Nothing." He laid his hands against her breasts and began to work the buttons of her shirt. "If you want to say no, say it now."

A faint smile lit her face. "I'm not going to say no, Luke." And then she raised her own hands and began to undo his shirt as well.

Her fingers brushing against his chest made him tremble. Her breath against his lips made his knees shake. Her mouth tracing the line of his jaw made him insane. He practically tore her shirt getting those buttons undone. But even when he got that done, it still clung wetly to her skin and he nearly had to peel it off her. He made quicker work of her bra, then bent his head and kissed the tip of each uplifted breast.

"Luke!" She shivered at the touch of his lips, which only made him want to kiss her more. And more.

Her hands moved to drag his shirt from his shoulders, and he stepped back long enough to allow her that, then wrapped his arms around her and hauled her close. It was good. Hell, it was wonderful.

It wasn't enough. Soggy denim stood between them and ecstasy. He moved impatiently to unfasten her jeans, even as she was doing the same to his. The wetness of the material prolonged the agony, yet somehow made the feel of her naked skin against his, when it finally happened, all that much better.

There were still boots. Luke didn't want to deal with boots. He wanted Jill now, all of her. But Jill had other ideas.

"Wait," she said. And she knelt in front of him, encouraging him to lift first one foot, then the other, so that she could tug off his boots. He did, bracing himself by holding onto her shoulders. His eyes fastened on her naked back, her curly, damp hair. He felt a surge of desire so strong it rocked him. And then she had his last boot off, had snaked his jeans away, too, and finally he was free.

Free to draw her down onto the bed and do the same to her, tugging her jeans and panties down her hips, then wiggling her free of both them and her boots so that she lay naked before him. Dream time. Heaven help him, yes.

She raised her arms to him, inviting him, and there wasn't the faintest possibility that he'd be able to say no. He'd lost whatever chance he had long before they'd started on each other's buttons, no matter what he said.

In dream time there was no past, there was no future, there was only now. And now was what Luke needed. The past hurt too much. The future was out of his reach. It didn't matter. For the moment he had everything.

He had Jill.

He lowered himself onto her, his hands stroking her soft damp skin, tangling in the wet curls of her hair. His lips brushed against her forehead, then nibbled at her brows, kissed her nose, then fastened at last on her mouth.

He intended to go slow, to savor, to prolong the joy and the excitement. But his will didn't get its way. The eager movement of Jill's body beneath his undid all his best intentions. It teased him and it coaxed him, and he was lost.

When her hands found him to bring him inside her, he had no power to resist. Nothing in him, not even his mind, at this point, wanted to resist. He only wanted her.

Dream time.

Yes, that's what it was. The one time when all was right with the world, when he was home and warm and safe and loved. When he was one with the woman who had somehow, from the first time he'd seen her, seemed an elemental part of his existence.

He didn't think about reality, didn't focus for once on

the thousand things, large and small, that would prevent such a union. He couldn't. He was a part of it, consumed by it, wholly centered on Jill, on loving her the way she ought to be loved.

Just once.

And he did. He could see it in her face as she tossed her head from side to side. He could feel it in the clutch of her fingers against his back. He could savor it in the swift clench of her body around him, in the lift of her hips, in the press of her knees against his hips and, finally, in the soft groan of his name as she touched her lips to his.

It was this last gentle whisper that shattered him. All vestiges of control deserted him. He was lost. He was loved.

Dream time. His time. Her time.

He felt her hand stroke his hair, then move down to feather lightly along his back. She pressed a kiss to his shoulder, then another to his jaw. He lifted his head and looked down at her. She smiled. It was a soft smile, a gentle smile, a loving smile. She lifted her other hand and laid it lightly on the side of his face.

"I love you," she whispered softly.

Dream time was over. Well over.

He rolled away from her, onto his back, and folded his arms beneath his head.

"When are you going back to California—or is it New York?" he asked. He didn't look at her. He tried to keep his voice neutral, to keep all the emotions he felt roiling inside him shut out. He opened his eyes, but he looked at the rough-hewn wooden ceiling; he didn't look at her.

She didn't answer at once. She shifted on the bed. He could almost feel her withdrawing, regrouping, then preparing to mount another attack.

Don't, he wanted to beg her. *It won't help. It won't do either of us any good at all.*

"Actually," she said at last and with just the tiniest edge to her voice, "it's Los Angeles this time. It's a magazine assignment."

"Another movie star?"

She nodded. "Damon Hunter."

Luke knew Damon Hunter vaguely. They had met at several parties. Keith had never done a picture with him, but often the roles Keith hadn't taken, Damon had. Now Damon was getting roles that once would have been Keith's. Would he get Keith's girlfriend, too?

Behind his head, Luke's fingers tightened into fists. Consciously he worked at relaxing them, and telling himself he didn't care if Damon did, telling himself that her words of love didn't mean anything.

"You'll like that," he said with as much indifference as he could manage. "It's right up your alley."

"What's that mean?" He could hear her trying to keep her voice level.

"The movie-star bit." His mouth twisted cynically. "Another Keith."

"There will never be another Keith," she said simply. "But yes, I'll enjoy it. I like doing interviews. I like people. I like finding out what makes them tick."

"Is that what you've been doing with me?"

Her mouth pulled tight for a moment. "You know it's not."

"Yeah." He did, but he didn't really want to deal with it even now. "What's so interesting about movie stars?"

Jill shrugged. "The fame angle, I guess. Fame puts tremendous burdens on people. Regular people tend to think it makes the famous ones different, but it doesn't. They still want happiness and love and good health, just like the rest of us.''

''And they have no more chance than we do of getting it,'' Luke said. ''Take Keith.''

''Keith loved his life,'' Jill said firmly. ''He wouldn't have changed it. He wouldn't have done anything differently.''

''He would have liked to have lived.''

''Of course. But he made his own life, lived it on his own terms. Even when it was hard, he never ran away from it,'' she added. ''And he never second-guessed himself.''

''He never had time.''

''Some of us have too much time.''

''I wish I didn't,'' Luke muttered.

''Come back to L.A. with me. Go see Carl. I told you he wants you for a movie he's going to be doing.''

''With who? Damon Hunter?''

''I don't know. It could be.''

''No way.'' Luke shook his head adamantly.

''So what are you going to do? Sit up here on this mountain and wallow in your misery for the rest of your life? I thought you had more guts than that.''

He looked at her, stung. ''Damn it, what do you want me to do?''

''I want you to say that what happened to Keith was a terrible thing, but that you're not going to let it be the end of your life, too. I want you to come back and go to work again, pick up your life.'' She faced him squarely, her gray eyes imploring him, challenging him. ''I want,'' she said softly, ''for you to admit you love me, too.''

Their eyes met. He saw urgency in hers, and support and something more.

Love? Promise? Faith in a future that he hadn't let himself believe in for years?

He didn't know. He didn't try to figure it out. He was afraid to.

Jill was right; he didn't have the guts. He could ride wild horses, jump off cliffs, wreck cars and walk away without a qualm. He couldn't do this.

As far as he was concerned, he had no right to the happiness that loving Jill would bring him.

"Luke?"

Slowly he let out a long breath, then shook his head. "I can't."

Nine

She left that evening after the weather cleared.

She didn't argue with him. She didn't berate him or harangue him. She didn't have to. He could see it in her eyes.

When he said, "I can't," the light simply went out of them. The color in her cheeks seemed to fade. Her mouth pressed into a thin line—not a hard line, just a sad one. She let out a slow breath, then turned away, dressing slowly, keeping her back to him, as if by doing so she could pretend he wasn't there.

He dressed, too, also without speaking. There wasn't really anything else to say until he stuffed his feet into his boots. Then he said, "I'll saddle your horse."

She nodded, her back still turned.

He let himself out into the cool evening air. It was that fresh, after-the-storm weather that washed the world clean and made everything look bright and new.

Luke didn't *feel* new. He felt a hundred years old. He

moved as if he were that old, too. He knew it was prolonging the inevitable. He knew he was a fool. He ought to be running to saddle her horse and get her on her way.

But everything he did seemed in slow motion. He felt numb. He caught her horse and even debated briefly about whether he ought to ride down with her. He decided against it.

He wanted it over, didn't he?

He got the horse saddled and bridled, then led it back to the cabin. Jill was waiting on the porch.

She had the clothes she'd brought packed in her saddlebags. He took them from her and slung them over the back of the horse and tied them on. Then he handed her the reins.

They faced each other. The wind lifted her hair, trailing strands across her cheek. Unconsciously she tucked them back behind her ear. Overhead Luke could hear a jay scolding. He could hear his own breath whistling lightly between barely parted lips.

He started to move them, to force "goodbye" past them with all the indifference he could manage.

But before he could, she took a step toward him. She lifted her hand and brushed light fingers over his battered forehead, then let them linger for just a moment on his cheek.

He held himself rigid. Then she leaned forward. Her lips brushed a fleeting kiss across his and just as quickly were gone again.

But not so quickly that his fists didn't clench at his sides. Not so quickly that he didn't have all he could do not to reach for her, not to grab her and hang on, not to take the kiss he really wanted.

He held himself tightly in check, stiff as a fence post, not even breathing, as she gave him one last, wistful smile. Then she turned and swung up into the saddle.

"Goodbye, Luke," she whispered.

And was it only the breeze or did he hear the whispered words *I love you*, as she rode away?

He didn't stay to watch her leave.

As she rode off, he turned and strode toward the shed. He moved quickly, grabbing his own saddle and tack, then whistling for his horses. He saddled the buckskin, his movements swift and jerky.

The horse whinnied and shifted, aware of Luke's agitation, unaware of what was causing it, yet becoming agitated himself as Luke swung into the saddle and kicked him into a trot up the mountainside.

He was a snuffy horse, big and strong and hard to control. Exactly the challenge Luke needed now. He would have liked to have galloped flat out. Too bad he had more sense. Otherwise he could have broken his fool neck and been done with all the pain. But like as not he'd have broken the horse's, too, so he didn't. He just rode. And rode. And rode.

He didn't let himself think about Jill riding down the mountain. He didn't let himself imagine her saying goodbye to Jimmy and Annette. He didn't envision her giving Jimmy, Jr. a bear hug and dropping a gentle kiss on baby Julie's head. He turned his mind away from the thought of her getting into her little red rental car and driving out onto the highway, heading for the airport, heading for the plane that would take her to Denver and then to Los Angeles.

Or he tried to stop thinking about her, anyway.

The ground was wet from all the rain. The branches that slapped him as he rode showered him again and again. And when he could ride no longer, he stopped by the trees where he and Keith had sat that autumn day almost two years ago.

He thought about things he wished he could change. He

thought about Keith. He thought about Jill. He scrubbed at his eyes with the back of his hand. Damn branches, shaking water down that way.

His horse shifted beneath him. He patted her neck. "Let's go then," he said, and tugged his hat down and rode west, down the mountain, into one of God's most spectacular sunsets.

If there was an irony to the way his life was turning out, he wasn't in the mood to appreciate it.

He'd lived in the cabin by himself for more than a year. It had never really bothered him before.

It was lonely now. He told himself that was nonsense. Mere days of Jill's presence could hardly have made that much difference.

But when he lit the lamp, the first sight that met his eyes was the bed where they'd made love. The sleeping bag was still rumpled. On the pillow, close together, were the depressions where two heads had lain. Muttering under his breath, Luke plumped the pillow and shook out the sleeping bag, then spread it out again.

There. Now it was as if she'd never been here.

Except there was a pile of paper sitting on the table.

He frowned. What the…?

He crossed the room and picked it up, and knew even as he did so exactly what he would find.

Luke's fingers clenched around the manuscript, then he dropped it and turned away. He didn't want to read it, damn it. She knew that.

So why had she…?

He muttered an expletive under his breath and banged back outside to sit on the steps. But there was no relief. It was there, taunting him, beckoning to him. He swatted a deerfly, then another. Slapping and muttering more, he banged back inside again.

And saw the manuscript.

He wasn't going to read it. He wasn't! His eyes hurt. His face was still swollen. Even if he wanted to—which he didn't—he was in no shape to read.

So he ignored it. He picked up the rope he'd been braiding before Jill had invaded his life. It seemed like aeons ago. He needed to get back to it, needed to get his bearings. He dropped down on the bed, tugged off his boots, stretched out, leaned against the wall and started to work once more on the rope.

But he could see the manuscript out of the corner of his eye even when he concentrated on the rope.

He looked away.

What had Jill used of what he'd given her? he wondered. Which, if any, of his stories had she told? What did she say about his friendship with Keith? What, if anything, had she said about what had existed between the three of them?

Damn it, nothing had existed.

She had said that, hadn't she?

He turned and looked at the manuscript, then turned away again and tried to concentrate on the rope. Usually he could braid automatically. Tonight he got knots. He cursed, started again, turned his head and looked at the manuscript once more.

Was Keith there between those pages? The Keith he remembered?

Was the Keith he remembered the same man that she knew?

"Aw, hell." He tossed the rope aside and stood up, got the manuscript and sat down with it on the bunk.

He shut his eyes. His fists, resting atop the paper, tightened briefly. Then he drew a breath, opened his eyes and moved his hands away.

He started to read.

He didn't really know what he expected. Something dry and two-dimensional, perhaps. Something sad and schmaltzy, maybe. Certainly a mere facsimile of the vital, vibrant man Keith Mallory had been.

It wasn't what he got. What he got was the Keith he knew and loved—his best friend of all time—and another Keith—*many* other Keiths—that he had never known at all.

From the start Luke and Keith had taken each other at face value. They had never poked and probed into each other's past. Keith had known of Luke's brothers. He had known Luke's parents were dead.

But Luke had never entertained him with stories of his growing-up years. He had never confessed the fear and pain he'd felt when his mother had died, when he was only five. He had never admitted the desperation, the panic he'd felt at sixteen when his father had been killed in a riding accident. He'd never talked about his subsequent scrapes and brushes with "authority," nor about the times his older brother had had to bail him out. He had certainly never told Keith about feeling responsible for his brother's marriage going wrong. What was past was past. He didn't talk about it.

And Keith had never really talked about his past, either.

So Luke had never known about Keith's parents. Keith had never mentioned them. Not to him, anyway.

But they were here because Jill knew about them. Probably, Luke realized, Keith hadn't opened up to her, either. Not at first. But Jill had persisted. She'd asked. She'd cared. Luke could see that right away. This was no dry, objective study. This was a labor of love.

And what she hadn't learned from Keith, she'd learned

after his death, by talking to those who'd known him as a child. She couldn't ask his mother, because she'd died when Keith was twenty-two.

But she had found his father, a hard-edged Los Angeles businessman with little time for anyone, a man who was in fact reluctant to admit that film idol Keith Mallory was his son.

"He lived a frivolous life," Ronald Mallory had told Jill in the brief interview he'd granted her.

But from the way Jill showed Keith—and the way Luke remembered him—his life was anything but frivolous. It was a celebration.

But it was a celebration, Luke discovered, that had grown out of confronting pain and moving beyond it. As he read of Keith's relationship with his parents, he understood him far better than he had when he was living with him day by day.

He met Keith the child, bright, yet shy, and almost pathetically eager to please. He saw Keith the only son, seeking his father's approval desperately, yet willing to fight that father whenever he felt his mother was threatened.

And threatened she'd apparently been—though that was something else Keith had never told Luke.

Luke was shaken by what he read. The Keith he'd known had seemed golden, blessed, the possessor of talent, looks, brains and charm. He had trouble imagining at first a Keith for whom things had sometimes been uncertain, bleak and even frightening.

But the more he read, the more it made sense. It clarified Keith's sometimes-desperate competitiveness. It made his sheer exuberance and childlike delight at simple joys much more understandable. It made his gentleness with women and children far clearer.

It made Luke pause for thought.

He thought he'd made pretty vast changes in his life with his move from rural Colorado to fast-lane L.A., but he saw that geography and lifestyle weren't the only sorts of changes a man could make.

He read on. He met Keith the brother. Another revelation. He'd never even known Keith had sisters. He had. Two of them, both younger.

Jill had found them. Maybe she'd even met them before Keith's death. Maybe Keith had shared them with her. In any case, both had related stories that showed Keith to be equally protective of them.

In subsequent chapters Luke met other Keiths—the schoolboy, the swimmer, the striver. Mischievous and competitive. Dogged and determined, yet always ready for a laugh. The coach's dream, the athlete who was always ready to go one better, to fight just a little harder, to take on one more challenge. These were Keiths he knew, and yet they, too, were clearer now.

And then there was the Keith who acted, the Keith who became all things in one man, who did whatever the script demanded. Luke knew him almost as well as he knew himself. But Jill had known him better. Better, probably, then Keith even knew himself.

Luke found the stories he'd told Jill. The catacombs story, the skateboard story, the ones that showed Keith off the set to be as zany and likable and charming as the scripts made him out to be in the roles he played.

They were exactly as he had told them—and yet, reading them, seeing them happening in his mind's eye as they had once happened in reality, Luke understood them better, too. They made him smile. They made his throat tighten and his eyes sting. He blinked a few times, then read on.

He met the Keith Jill knew.

The Keith he'd never known, for all that they had been best friends.

Jill's Keith was the man who'd stood behind the man the public met, the man who'd laughed and joked and roughnecked with Luke. This was the Keith who had lived with pain and uncertainty and fear. This was the Keith who knew his limitations all too well. Or feared he did.

He was afraid of marriage, Jill wrote. Luke stared at the words, astonished. He'd never heard Keith claim any such thing. But even as he read the words and doubted them, he sensed that they were true.

He remembered wondering over the almost two years Jill and Keith were an item why they didn't get married. He even remembered asking once or twice. Jokingly, of course. Not seriously. Certainly not as if he cared.

Both times Keith had brushed him off, had said something vague about doubting if Jill would have him, which at the time Luke had thought was the biggest crock in the world. But now, knowing what he knew, he supposed maybe Keith had meant what he'd said.

Certainly that was what he'd told Jill. His own parents' marriage had been so bad, he'd been terrified at the thought of trying it himself.

''You should have children,'' Jill wrote that she'd told him once when they were walking along the beach and a couple of little boys had nagged him into building a sand castle with them. He'd done it willingly, eagerly. ''Don't you want children?'' she had asked him.

Keith had said that he did. ''A lot. I love kids,'' he'd told her. ''They have such promise.''

Luke could remember him saying that, too.

''I'd like to have children, too,'' Jill had told Keith wistfully. ''With you,'' she'd added, in case he didn't get it.

''You mean marry me?'' Keith had asked her. There had

been what seemed an eternal pause, a pause long enough for Jill to wish she'd never made any hints at all, to wish that she were fifty feet underground or fifty states away, to regret her presumption a thousand times over.

And then he'd asked, "What if I'm like my old man?"

His hesitation hadn't had anything to do with her at all. She'd been amazed.

"You're not," she'd told him. But he'd looked doubtful. And finally she'd said, "I don't believe you are. Not for a minute." Then she'd looked him straight in the eyes and said, "I'm willing to risk it. I'm willing to do whatever it takes. Are you?"

And because he was Keith, and because he loved her, he'd said yes. He took the risk. He made up his mind to try.

That was the best part of Keith, Jill wrote at the very end of her book. *He was never afraid to put his hopes— his future—on the line.*

Keith Mallory died far too young. He died in an accident that needn't have happened, but he died in circumstances that he himself chose. He made his life, and himself, what he wanted them to be. He always tried to be the best Keith Mallory he could be. Ultimately, his legacy to us is not a list of films he made or the parts he played. His legacy is his life, the example he gave to those of us privileged to know him.

That night Luke had the dream again. They were body-surfing, he and Keith. Jill was standing on the pier, watching, waving, smiling, pointing out the wave of the day. They caught it, the two of them. It swept them high and fast, then flung them over. They crashed, struggled, tangled, parted, reached. Their fingers touched just for a moment. An instant, no more.

It was the same, except the end. This time Keith made it to shore.

It was Luke who slipped away....

"What happened to your face?"

Luke sat bolt upright, stunned and shaking. He stared around wildly, trying to get his bearings, still drowning, floundering up to find Paco standing at the end of his bunk.

The boy was looking at him, concerned. "Somebody hit your face? That why you were yelling?"

Luke lifted a hand and touched his face gently, wincing. He scowled. "Wasn't yelling," he muttered. He eyed Paco narrowly through the swelling. "What the hell are you doing here?"

"Was so yelling," Paco said stoutly. "Thought somebody was killin' you. It's why I came in. Jill sent me," he added.

Luke's head snapped up. "What?"

Paco shrugged narrow shoulders. "She said you needed help. She said to come."

"Well, you can just damn well go home again!" Luke hauled himself to his feet. The manuscript, which had been lying on his lap, cascaded to the floor, scattering papers all over. "Damn."

"What's that?" Paco said, bending to start picking all of it up.

"Jill's book."

The boy's eyes widened. "The one about Keith? Can I read it?"

"I don't know, can you?" Luke started to duck down to help Paco pick up papers, but his head hurt when he bent over. He straightened up again, grimacing.

Paco didn't notice. "I can try," he said eagerly as he

straightened the pages. "Will you help me with the words I don't know?"

"No." Luke turned away, raking a hand through his hair, then stopped and sighed. "Oh, hell, I guess."

Paco beamed. "Thanks. I'll finish picking this up while you make coffee. Then we can get to work. An' tonight I can read."

"I don't need—" *Any help,* Luke started to say, but he didn't finish, because the fact of the matter was, he did. Jill, damn her, was right. She knew him, like she'd known Keith, even better than he knew himself.

Until the swelling in his face went down, until he could see better, he *did* need someone. Even someone as little as Paco. Well, fine. He'd agree. As long as it wasn't her.

"Yeah, awright. Just lemme get some coffee and we'll go."

He turned his back on the boy and the manuscript, grabbing the pot and heading out the door. When he got back, having fetched the water and dunked his head in the creek, Paco was reading the book. He didn't even look up.

Luke made the coffee, then changed his shirt, dragged a comb through his hair and sort of made up his bunk. By the time he finished, the coffee was ready. He poured himself a mug, then glanced at Paco, still reading.

"Want some?" he asked.

Paco didn't even look up. Obviously Jill had captured another reader. Luke pulled a wry face and took a long, scalding swallow from the mug.

"She's gone then?" he asked, without even realizing he was going to.

"Huh?" Paco looked up as if he were coming back from a long way away, then realized what Luke was asking him. "Oh, Jill? Yeah, she left last night."

That surprised him. She'd only left him last night. "Planes go out that late now?"

Paco shook his head. "She drove to Albuquerque." He said this last as if it ought to have been obvious and bent his head over the book once more.

Luke supposed it was if he gave it any thought. She could hardly want to hang around. Hell, he couldn't blame her. He finished off his coffee and clanked the mug down into the dishpan. "Come on. Let's get going."

"Can't I just finish the first—"

"Later." And Luke strode out the door and clumped down the steps without looking back. Behind him he could hear Paco scrambling to catch up.

This morning's weather was clear and cool and fresh after yesterday afternoon's torrential downpour. The world looked bright and new. The first day of the rest of his life, as the cliché went....

The first day of the rest of his life without Jill.

It was what he wanted, damn it. It was what he deserved, wasn't it?

"'S a good book, I think," Paco was saying seriously as he rode up alongside. "So far, anyhow. I'm only on, like, page 20, 'cause you wouldn't let me go any further."

"You said you came to work."

"Yeah, well, I am," Paco replied. "But I like Jill's book. Did you like it, Luke?"

Luke grunted and touched his heels to his horse.

"I didn't know Keith had two sisters like I got," Paco went on, keeping up. "You didn't tell me that," he added accusingly.

"I didn't know."

"How come?"

Luke shrugged irritably. "Never came up. Come on. See

those cows down there in that willow thicket? Let's move 'em out."

The creek was still running high from the storm and Luke's horse stumbled, getting its footing as he maneuvered in close and began urging a bunch of cows back up the mountain. Paco's tongue poked out from between the thin line of his lips as he concentrated on doing the same. The cows moved with their customary reluctance, ambling up the slope, stopping to swat at flies, and then, when Luke whooped them on, finally moving again. He was willing to bet they'd be right back down there tomorrow.

The second day of the rest of his life.

He wheeled his horse around. "I'm going to look over in the meadow beyond the ridge, see if I can find the bull. You ride this bunch on up, okay?"

"By myself?" Paco looked doubtful and eager at the same time.

"If you think you can do it."

Paco's chin came up. "'Course I can do it."

Luke allowed himself a smile. "Good. When you've got 'em up, ride along that fence above the rise. I'll meet you by the pines near the river."

Paco nodded. "Sure. I brought some lunch in my saddlebags. My mom made us sandwiches an' sent apples, an' Annette stuck in a whole bunch of brownies and some cherry pie. We can eat up there, 'kay?"

Luke tugged on the brim of his hat. "Right. See you then."

It wasn't that he didn't want to spend time with Paco, it was just that right now it was too much. He was still raw from Jill, still trying to shake off a night spent reading about Keith—a Keith so real and so vital that it was inconceivable to think that he was dead.

But he was dead.

And for all that she had created a work of art in her manuscript, Jill's book couldn't change that.

He found the bull, his foot wedged between some rocks where the creek had overflowed. He was snorting and tugging and should have been happy when Luke showed up to get him out. Of course, if he was, he was in no mood to express his appreciation. In fact, he barely missed nailing Luke's ribs where they had finally begun feeling better.

"Ingrate," Luke called when the animal, freed finally, snorted and tossed his head, then trotted away. But the bull was easier to deal with than Paco talking incessantly about Keith. Luke lifted his hat and shoved a weary hand through sweat-dampened hair, then he settled his hat back on his head, turned his horse and started up the mountain.

Paco was already there, sitting by the stand of pines near the storm-swollen river. He was eating an apple and he had the rest of the food laid out on a flat rock, but he bounced to his feet when he saw Luke coming. "I got all the cows up," he announced. "An' I checked the fence. It's fine. An' the gate's shut."

Luke swung down off his horse. "Thanks." He ruffled a hand through Paco's short, dark hair. "You did good."

Paco grinned and grabbed some of the food. "Mom packed ham and cheese and peanut butter and jelly. Which do you want?"

Luke settled under the tree with a ham-and-cheese sandwich, an apple and two pieces of the cherry pie that Annette had made. Paco ate his apple and swung from the branches and asked Luke if Keith had ever swung out of trees the way Tarzan did. Then he ate a peanut-butter sandwich and balanced along the dead logs, hopping from one to another, his arms outstretched, and asked if Keith had ever tried tightrope walking. After he'd finished, he helped himself to the brownies and, with one in each hand and the remains of another in his mouth, he went to walk along the edge of the steep bluff above the surging river.

"Did Keith ever—"

"Get back from there," Luke snapped at him. But it was too late.

He'd barely spoken when Paco said, "Hey!" and tumbled over the edge of the bluff into the rampaging water below.

"Paco!" Luke shot to his feet, scrambling over a fallen log, tripping on a rock, lurching to stand at the crumbled edge of the bluff in time to see Paco's dark head disappear as he was carried downstream by the force of the water. "Paco!"

He stopped to think only one thing: *Paco couldn't swim.* Then he yanked off his boots and flung himself in. The icy, churning water closed over his head, dashing him hard against the rocks. He fought his way to the surface, scanning the river for any sign of the boy.

"Paco!" He screamed the boy's name and was rewarded by the briefest flick of an arm lifted in a wave—and then it was gone again.

He struck out for where it had been, swimming as desperately as he ever had, shoving himself away from rocks he scraped over, fighting for every bit of headway he could make.

"Try for the bank," he yelled. "Grab on to something!" But the sound of the river pouring over rocks swallowed his words, and he knew that chances were Paco never heard them.

Every few seconds he caught sight of the boy—an arm, his dark hair, once only a hand—and the terror he knew at the thought of Paco being pulled down, being caught, trapped the way Keith had been, went like a shaft right through him.

"Please, God, no!" he cried.

And then, thank God—for no one else could have done anything—Paco caught on to the face of a rock outcrop. His grip was tenuous as he fought the current. Luke could see him looking back, his face white and his dark eyes wide with panic.

"Hang on," he yelled.

And Paco did, for as long as he could. Then, right before Luke had him, just as his fingers touched him, Paco reached for him, lost his purchase on the rock and slipped away.

"No! Damn it! No!"

It was the nightmare come to life. The panic of losing Keith all over again.

Luke kicked and plunged back into the current, pushing himself, reaching...reaching...touching...grabbing—*a hand.*

He jerked it, pulled as hard as he could, sank under, fought his way up with one hand and his feet, never letting go of those small fingers with the other. *Come on. Come on.* And then the hand fastened hard on his, clawed its way up his arm and—

"Got you!" Luke said it through a mouthful of water, looked into Paco's terrified face and did his best to grin. They weren't through it yet. Not nearly.

The current had them again, sweeping them ever downward. The river had widened here, making it less fearsome in one respect, more so in another. There was less chance of them getting caught as Keith had between rocks, but it was farther to the safety of the shore.

"Hang onto my neck," he told Paco. "Don't fight it."

Paco's teeth were chattering. His fingers bit into Luke's arms, then got a stranglehold on his neck, almost choking him.

"Go easy," Luke said, and he could feel Paco trying,

but he knew it wasn't easy. Not for either of them. Slowly he fought his way toward the bank, and at last, he caught onto a rock.

"Here. Let go of me. Grab on here."

"No! I can't! I need—"

"Do it!" Luke commanded. He couldn't hang on much longer. The weight of the boy was pulling him back into the current. "Come on. Grab! Now!"

He reached back and pried the boy's fingers loose, put them on the rock. Paco clung to it, terrified.

"Pull yourself up."

"I c-can't." His teeth were chattering so badly he could hardly talk.

"You can," Luke insisted through his own clenched teeth. "You've got to. Keith would."

Paco looked over his shoulder. Their eyes met.

"Do it."

He gave the boy a shove with all the strength he had left. Paco made it up onto the rock.

It was the last thing Luke saw before the water closed over his head and he was swept away.

Ten

It was what he'd wanted, wasn't it?

To give up.

To let go.

To die…like Keith had.

He hadn't saved Keith, but he had saved Paco. The boy was tired, scared, shaken to the core, but he was safe. He would make himself do now whatever he thought Keith would do.

He'd make it.

Luke didn't have to.

He was tired, god-awful tired. He'd been tired so long he couldn't remember ever not being tired. The water didn't seem so cold now. Nor so frightening. It seemed almost friendly, sweeping him along, pulling him down.

It would be so easy to stop fighting it, to quit.

To die.

He'd toyed with death often enough over the past few

years that his life no longer passed before his eyes. He didn't see the things he'd done, the places he'd been. He'd seen them all before.

He saw instead the things he'd miss.

His mind filled with scenes of sunsets and sunrises, roundups and brandings, snowfalls and storms—all the things he loved that he'd never see again.

Was that what every man saw in his last moments?

Was that what Keith had seen?

Had Keith seen Jill?

Luke was seeing her now. His mind cleared of everything but the sight of her.

There was no river, no rocks, no roiling water. There was only Jill looking at him, a sad, wistful half smile on her face. He remembered that look, that smile. He'd seen them on her face the first time they'd made love, and the second.

He'd seen them again after she'd asked him to come with her, after he'd said, ''I can't.''

He hadn't understood what he was seeing then. Now he did. It was his future slipping away from him. The future he would miss if he quit.

Keith never quit.

Luke remembered his bloody, scraped fingertips. No, Keith hadn't quit. He'd fought with everything that was in him for his life, for his future, for his dreams.

''We're two of a kind,'' he remembered Keith saying once. He could almost feel Keith with him now, challenging him. *Go for it, man.*

Two of a kind?

God, yes!

The resolution he hadn't thought he had took hold, galvanizing him.

Yes! He owed it to Keith to keep fighting. He owed it

to Paco. He owed it to Noah, who'd told him so. He owed it to Jill, who'd believed in him. *He owed it to himself.* It was a strange thought, almost foreign. He'd denied it so long. He didn't deny it now.

He wanted the future. He wanted the hope, the dreams, the promise.

He wanted to share them with Jill.

He started struggling again, fighting his way up, looking desperately for the bank, for a rock, for anything to hang onto. Please God, he didn't want to die!

White water surged over him. He got a mouthful, then another...and another.

Jill!

He fought upward, struggled toward the bank, his lungs searing, his arms leaden, his body a sodden log.

Jill! I'm coming! Help me, Jill!

He used every ounce of strength he had, fighting and pushing until at last his fingers scrabbled against rock. He hauled himself up, shaking, gasping, then fell headlong against the cold, wet stone. His heart thundered and his head still pounded with the sound of the river inches away.

He was out. He was alive.

He had a future.

With Jill?

He prayed to God that he hadn't left it too late.

She was nowhere to be found.

She was gone. Not just gone from Colorado. Of course, he knew that. He knew she'd gone to L.A.

He left the next morning—hired Doug, another Sutter, to help out, accepted gratefully Cy's offer as well and caught the next plane to L.A. Urgent business, he told Annette and Jimmy. He didn't tell them what. A man had his pride, after all.

But she wasn't in L.A.

Or maybe she was, but he couldn't find her.

He used every connection he could think of to find out where the hotshot young actor Damon Hunter, the subject of her proposed interview, lived.

But when he got to Hunter's Malibu canyon hideaway, talked his way past first the gardener and then the maid and was finally allowed to see the movie star himself, she'd come and gone.

"She's a quick worker," Hunter told him with a grin.

"Was she going home from here? Did she say?"

Hunter shook his head. "She looked like she needed a vacation. She was pale, you know?"

Luke grunted. If she was, he'd probably made her that way. "Thanks," he said, and turned to go.

"She give you those shiners, man?" Hunter asked, still grinning.

Luke turned again, his teeth clenched. Hunter took a step back, holding up his hands as if to protect himself.

"Hey, man, I was only askin'. I just wouldn't want to get on the wrong side of anybody who could do that."

Luke was already on Jill's wrong side. But the shiners hadn't hurt nearly as badly as not being able to find her now did.

He called Annette and Jimmy to see how things were going, then told them he was flying to New York.

"Flying to New York? Now? One way? Gosh," Annette said, "I guess you really are rich."

Luke didn't feel very rich. He felt especially poor when he got there, went to the apartment building where she lived and found out she wasn't there, either, and no one would say where she was.

"You think I should tell you about my tenants, you got another think comin', fella," the building super said.

"I'm a friend."

"Ya don' look very friendly." The super studied Luke's face, which was still a mottled blend of purple, blue and ghastly green. "Ya can leave a message if ya want."

"I'll wait."

The man shrugged. "Suit yourself."

Luke waited. All day. All evening. Into the night. He sat on a small bench in the foyer and watched Jill's neighbors in the West Side, prewar building as they came and went. He waited in vain.

"Ya can't sit here all night," the super told him.

"You've got a 24-hour doorman," Luke said. "Why can't I?"

"Because I said so. Get a hotel room and come back in the morning."

"Will she be here in the morning?"

"Who knows?"

She didn't come back in the morning, nor in the afternoon, nor in the evening, nor at any time during the remainder of the week.

"Ya know what they say about gettin' a life?" the super said to Luke on the sixth day.

"Yeah." He didn't want to leave, but the super was right. And whether he wanted it anymore or not, he had a life. It was his ranch. His responsibilities. He couldn't depend on Jimmy and Doug and Cy indefinitely. He had to go back.

He scribbled his number on a piece of paper and held it out to the other man. "Listen. Will you call and tell me as soon as she comes home?"

"I can't do that."

"Please. All I want is a chance to talk to her."

"There's phones."

"She'd hang up on me. Please." Luke thrust out the paper once more.

The super hesitated. "How many days you been here? Six? Seven? You're some persistent fella, ain'tcha?"

"Some damn fool, actually. Will you?"

"Well..."

"Please." And this please was accompanied by a hundred-dollar bill.

The super grinned and scratched his head. "Well, when you put it that way..."

But when more than a month went by and he hadn't heard a word, he pretty much gave up on getting the call. He still phoned Carl every few days to find out if he'd heard anything and still got the same negative answer. But it was all he could think of doing.

It had taken all his courage to make that first call, and when he had, Carl hadn't been easy on him.

"Finished whining, have you? Stopped running?" he'd asked when he heard Luke's voice the first time.

It stung, but Luke knew he deserved it.

"Yeah, I am," he'd said. "I need to see Jill."

"Don't imagine she wants to see you."

"Did she say that?"

"Didn't have to. A guy only had to look at her. My God, man, don't you think she's been through enough?"

"I want to apologize. I want to..." He stopped. He couldn't tell Carl what he wanted. He couldn't tell anyone but Jill. And he intended to fly back out to New York or to L.A. or wherever he needed to in order to pick up her trail again once they'd gathered and shipped the cattle the first part of October. But that was two weeks away, and until then he had his hands full.

The range work all fell to Luke, but Jimmy was doing

the paperwork now, and that helped. Doug had gone back to college at the end of August, though Cy still came out every day to lend a hand. They were coping, but the next two weeks would be hectic. And thank God for that. He spent most nights lying awake staring at the ceiling of the cabin, remembering Jill lying beside him. At least he was distracted from similar memories most of the days.

He was so distracted he didn't even connect when he came in for supper that night and Annette told him that a man named Eddie had called.

"That the guy with the Saler bull for sale?"

"I don't think so. He said he's from New York City and—" Annette wrinkled her nose in puzzlement "—to tell you that your pigeon had landed."

"Boy, you didn't waste no time," Eddie, the super, said when Luke walked into the foyer of Jill's apartment building early the next morning. He was grinning from ear to ear. "You're looking' better. No more bruises."

Not on the outside, anyway. Luke had sat up all night on the red-eye flight, trying to think about what he would say, and now his mind was blank. "Is she still up there?"

"Less she went out the fire escape. Came in yesterday afternoon and hasn't been out yet."

Luke headed toward the elevator. "Thanks."

"Hey, I gotta tell her you're coming." The super gestured toward the in-house phone.

Luke looked at him imploringly. "Please." He started to dig into his pocket, but the super waved him on.

"Just you be nice to her or it'll be my job."

The question was would *she* be nice to *him?* Luke knew he had no right to expect it. If she shut the door in his face it would be no more than he deserved. He just hoped he could get the toe of his boot in before she did so.

She lived on the fifteenth floor. The elevator had fancy inlaid wood in the paneling. The foyer outside the six apartments was carpeted with thick, rose-colored plush to muffle sound. Still Luke could hear himself breathing, could hear his heart pounding. He wiped damp palms on his jeans, shut his eyes briefly, then opened them again and knocked on the door.

The door jerked open. "Cara, I'm fine, really, I—" Jill stopped dead. What little color there was in her cheeks drained totally away.

Luke managed what he hoped was a smile. "Hi."

He saw her swallow. Her fingers tightened into a fist. "Luke."

"Can I come in?"

She hesitated a moment, then stepped back and let him in. Then she shut the door, skirted quickly around him and led the way into a sun-drenched room with a view of the park. It was a warm room filled with furniture that wouldn't have looked out of place back in Colorado.

He noticed for the first time that she wasn't dressed— not in street clothes, anyway. She wore a robe, tied loosely around her middle, and her long hair hung down her back.

"Are you sick?" he demanded.

She turned and faced him, shaking her head. Her fingers gripped the back of an armchair so tightly that her knuckles were white. "I'm fine."

"You thought I was somebody else," he said. "Somebody who was worried about you."

She shrugged. "My neighbor across the way, Cara. She knew I came home last night and she— Never mind about me. What are you doing here?"

He wondered where to start. "I read your book," he said at last.

"Oh?" He could hear the caution in her voice, the wariness that she had every right to feel.

"It was great. I never...I never knew. About Keith, I mean, about his parents. He never said. He never told me any of it."

Jill lifted her shoulders. "I'm not surprised," she said softly. "I think I was the only one he ever told. I debated for a long time about putting it in the book. I wondered if it was disloyal."

"It's not. It makes him clear. It makes him whole. It makes sense out of a lot of things that I never really understood."

"Good." Their eyes met for a moment, then she looked away.

She might have been on vacation, but he thought she still looked tired. There were dark circles under her eyes and she looked as if she'd lost weight. She twisted her hands together, then glanced toward the door.

"Thank you for telling me." *And now, goodbye.* He could hear the words even if she didn't actually say them.

"That's not all," he said quickly. "It...it made me think. What you said...about Keith always trying to be the best Keith he could. That was true. He was. And he is..." he hesitated a second, then plunged on, "an example. But you know—" and here he managed a wry smile "—I've got a hell of a long way to go." He looked straight at her and gave her his heart. "I could use your help."

She didn't reply. She stood staring at him, absolutely mute, and he went on desperately, "I know I don't have any right to expect it. Reckon you have every reason to tell me to go to hell." He dug a toe of his boot into the rug underfoot, then slanted her a quick glance and saw her run her tongue over her lips.

"What sort of help?" she asked hollowly, when he'd almost given up hope that she'd ever speak again.

He ducked his head, unable to look at her straight on. He rubbed a hand against the back of his neck. "Love me," he said. It was barely more than a whisper. He didn't think she could have heard him, except he heard her suck in her breath.

"I need you to," he went on doggedly. "I know I said I didn't want this. I know I said I couldn't live with the guilt of having what should have been Keith's. But what you wrote—about Keith taking a chance on life, about him never quitting. Well, you were right. He hated quitters. I guess," he said, his mouth twisting in a ghost of a grin, "I didn't want him lookin' down at me and callin' me one."

"That's why, is it?" Jill said softly, but there was just the hint of a smile on her face.

Luke nodded. "That's why. And because I love you." And then he stared at her, stricken. "Oh, God in heaven, don't cry. Please don't."

But she was, and he stood there, dumb as a crutch, not having the faintest idea what to do to stop her.

He took a step toward her, then halted, but the tears kept on and he couldn't bear it. "Jeez, Jill, you gotta stop. Please. I'll leave. Look, I'll just get out and you won't have to see me ever again. I promise. I—" He turned and headed for the door.

"No!" She held out her arms to him, tears still rolling down her face. "No. Don't go. I never thought you'd come. Please don't go."

He didn't. He went instead straight into her arms. He put his arms around her as well, crushing her against him, savoring the sensation of her trembling body pressed against him, relishing the softness of her skin and the touch of her lips on his. He brushed his fingers through her hair and kissed away her tears.

"I don't want to make you cry," he murmured. "I've made your life miserable enough."

She shook her head, smiling at him, touching his cheek with her fingers, as if when he'd come, he'd brought the sun. And damned if the room didn't seem lighter now, but Luke figured it was on account of her smile.

"I never thought you'd come," she confessed again.

"I'm a hard-headed son-of-a-gun. Takes me awhile to smarten up. Nothing like almost losing your life to figure out what makes it worth saving."

She looked at him worriedly. "What do you mean?"

So he told her. She drew him down onto the sofa in the living room and he cuddled her next to him while he told her about reading the manuscript, about having it still echoing in his head when Paco had fallen in the river.

He told her about the struggle to get the boy, and he hurried his explanation along when he saw how worried she was that something dreadful had happened.

"But I got him out," he said. "I got sucked back in and I was ready to give up. Then I remembered Keith. And I remembered you...and suddenly the future started makin' a lot more sense."

"I'm glad," Jill whispered as she turned in his arms. "You don't know how glad."

He rested his forehead against hers and took a shaky breath. "You think maybe you could show me?"

She smiled. "I think maybe I could."

She did, and her loving was sweeter than he remembered. Her body was lusher than he remembered, even though she was willowy still. Her touch was gentle, her kisses achingly tender. And as he matched her, touch for touch, kiss for kiss, he found he matched her tears as well, and he didn't even flinch when she touched one with her thumb and brushed it softly away.

"I tried to find you," he told her afterward, when they lay in her bed curled in each other's arms. "I went to see Hunter in L.A. I came back here and bribed Eddie, the super. I called Carl so often he thought I was deranged."

"Did you?" She sounded delighted. "I had no idea." Her smile faded slightly. "After that last day I had no hopes left."

"Where did you go? After L.A., I mean?"

"A friend of mine has a place in the woods in British Columbia. I went there. I needed to put my head back together, to figure out how to get on with my life. I had things to cope with I hadn't counted on." She turned in his arms, looking away from him. He felt a moment's panic.

"Being alone, you mean?"

"No." She paused and looked back at him. "Having a child."

For a long moment her words held no meaning for him. A child? What child? He looked at her closely and, all at once, saw new meaning in the dark hollows under her eyes, in the tired, gaunt look on her face. He found new meaning in the slight differences he'd felt in her body when they'd made love.

"A child? *My child?*"

She nodded.

"You're having my child?"

"Are you angry?" she asked quickly.

"No. Of course not." He wasn't. He didn't know what he was except glad he was lying down. A child! He could scarcely believe it.

"Truly?" She laid a hand on his arm, still looking worried.

Luke smiled, shaking his head. "I'm not angry. I'm amazed. I never thought. When did you find out?"

"I knew that day."

His smile vanished. He stared. "The last day? The day we...made love?"

She nodded. "I'd been feeling sort of sick. I was late. I did one of those tests. It was positive."

He shoved himself up against the headboard and looked at her, anguished. "Why didn't you tell me?"

"How could I? You didn't want responsibility for anyone."

She didn't say the words accusingly, though he knew she had every right to feel that way. He rubbed a hand across his face.

"I'm sorry," he said hoarsely.

She touched her lips to his. "I'm not. You're here now. For all the right reasons."

"I might not have been," he argued, still stunned.

"Life isn't made of might haves, Luke. We both know that," she said softly. "Life is made of what actually happens. You're here. We love each other. That's what matters. Not all the things we should have done. Now is all we have. Now we go on from here."

He hesitated, almost afraid to ask. "Together?"

She kissed him. "Forever."

A shudder went through him. He drew her up against him and rubbed his forehead against her hair. "It sounds wonderful. Just keep reminding me, will you?"

"Every day," she promised, and bent her head, nestling it into the crook of his neck.

"Would you ever have told me?" he asked her when they'd made love once more. His mind was still trying to grapple with impending fatherhood.

He felt her shift against him. "Yes. After he was born."

She touched his cheek and dropped a kiss on his chin. "A boy needs a father."

Luke swallowed. "It's a boy?"

Jill lifted her head and looked into his eyes. She smiled at him. "That's what they say."

He was born in April. A dark-haired, blue-eyed promise of spring. A lusty, seven-pound-nine-ounce gift of new life. They named him Keith.

* * * * *

COWBOYS DON'T STAY

Prologue

"It's whiter'n a polar bear's insides out there," Noah Tanner said, squinting through the windshield. "Snow's so thick I can't see the damn road."

His callused fingers flexed on the steering wheel of the van he was driving, and not for the first time, he wished they were closer to home. Or to his brother's Wyoming ranch, which was where he was headed and which was a damn sight more cozy than the Colorado post-office box he was calling home these days. He put his foot down a little harder on the accelerator, hoping to get in a few more miles before the full brunt of the storm hit.

They'd been doing their best to outrun the storm since leaving Vegas yesterday evening. Taggart had bet him then that they'd beat it to Tanner's ranch near the Big Horns in Wyoming. Now Noah hoped to God he was right.

"I don't mind a white Christmas," Noah continued, "long as it waits awhile."

His traveling partner, Taggart Jones, grinned confidently. "It will. What snowstorm would dare fly in the face of two world champions?"

At that Noah grinned, too—a grin still three parts amazement to one part satisfaction that, when the NFR finals had ended the day before, they'd both come out on top. Taggart Jones had become the Professional Rodeo Cowboy Association's bull-riding champion of the year. And two time second-place finisher, Noah Tanner, was this time—finally, at last—the PRCA champion bronc rider.

"Reckon you're right," he said, flicking a glance down at the shiny new gold buckle holding up his Wranglers.

But as the snow continued to swirl thickly around the van and the lanes of the interstate disappeared beneath the accumulation, Noah turned his attention back to the road and didn't feel quite so sure.

"We'll be fine," Taggart said. "Gotta be. Becky's Christmas program is tomorrow morning and I told her I'd be there. So come hell or high water—or snowstorms—I'm gonna be."

"Course you are," Noah agreed. If anybody could get through, they could. In the years he'd been going down the road from one rodeo to the next, the cumulative hours he'd spent on Interstate 80 figured in the weeks, if not the months by now. He reckoned he ought to know it by heart.

"It's the first year she hasn't been with me in Vegas since she was born," Taggart went on glumly.

Noah knew that the one blight on Taggart's otherwise fantastic finals was the fact that his six-year-old daughter had missed it because she was in school full-time now.

"She's gonna be madder'n a bee-stung pony if she missed it and then I miss her Christmas program, too," Taggart said as he rubbed the back of his neck, then grinned wryly. "Promising in blood to be back in time for her program was the only way I could stop her sneaking off and hitching a ride down.''

Noah grinned, too, at the notion of a six-year-old enterprising enough to find her way from Montana to Las Vegas. Still, he'd known Becky Jones since she was hatched, and if anyone could do it, headstrong, tomboy Becky was the one.

''If we make Tan—um, Robert and Maggie's before dawn, you'll be there in time.''

Taggart's mouth quirked into a grin. ''Still can't get used to him bein' Robert. Hell, he was Tanner for years.''

He still was, in Noah's mind, though Noah was doing his best to remember his brother had another name. ''Since he met Maggie, he's Robert. Well broke and lovin' every minute of it. Shoulda heard him when I called to tell him I won. He was excited enough, but I think tellin' me about Jared sittin' his new pony excited him a damn sight more.'' Jared was Robert and Maggie's two-and-a-half-year-old son, and even though he had to share the limelight with twin brothers now, Jared was still quite definitely the apple of his father's eye.

''I can understand that,'' Taggart said. ''Seein' Becky be a snowman in the play tomorrow's gonna thrill the heck outa me.'' He stared out the windshield at the swirling snow and added reflectively, ''More'n winning did.''

And the damnedest thing was, Noah knew he was telling the truth.

''Reckon I must be missin' something,'' he said, then slanted Taggart a grin. ''I'm sure as hell gonna be out of place at Christmas this year—the lone bachelor. Good grief, Tan—I mean Robert and Maggie, have three little curtain climbers now, and Luke and Jill have one. Reckon I oughta find myself a woman and have one of my own?''

''Don't rush things,'' Taggart counseled. ''It ain't

healthy." His own grin was weary and more than a little sad. "I oughta know."

That was true enough. Seven years ago, Taggart had rushed things. He'd met a bright-eyed, big-city girl in a funky New York restaurant after the rodeo in Madison Square Garden and had swept her off her feet. Julie Westmore had never known a "real live cowboy before."

They'd had less than forty-eight hours together before Taggart had had to board a plane west. But in the time they did have, he'd fallen head over heels with an equally love-struck Julie. In the next three weeks he'd spent a fortune on long-distance phone calls—as many as it took to convince Julie to marry him.

In December she had. Ten months later she'd had Becky—and by Christmas she'd left them.

She hadn't had a clue about what marrying a rodeo cowboy entailed. She couldn't stand following her husband down the road, and she'd had no desire to wait at home with a baby while he made a living the only way he knew how.

"We have nothing in common!" she'd screamed at Taggart the night after he got back from the National Finals six years before. Noah, who'd retreated to the other bedroom, had heard her loud and clear—the same way he'd heard the door slam, the footsteps running down the stairs and the wail of two-month-old Becky, left in her father's arms.

"She'll be back," Taggart had said hollowly the next morning.

But she hadn't been. Julie had got a divorce without ever seeing either her husband or her daughter again.

"It's just as well," Taggart had said on one of the rare occasions when he even talked about Julie. He and Noah had been spending a few days at Taggart's parents' house

north of Bozeman last winter. It had been a snowy afternoon, with not much to do but loaf around the house and
drink beer and get under Mrs. Jones's feet. "Julie was right,
you know. We didn't belong together. Still—" and here
he'd paused and glanced back at his five-year-old daughter,
who was playing with her toy horses in the middle of the
living room floor "—I reckon it was worth it. She gave me
Becky."

"Becky's a goer," Noah said now, and he smiled at the
way Taggart's pained smile turned into a real one.

"She's some kid, all right. Chip off the old block." The
smile became a grin and he laughed as he looked over at
Noah. "Did I tell you she wants to ride bulls?"

Wind buffeted the van. In the rearview mirror, Noah
could see a semi looming through the worsening snow.
"You gonna let her?"

"Hell, no," Taggart said promptly. "I'm not having any
daughter of mine doin' anything that dangerous. She'd
break her fool neck."

Noah laughed. "What's sauce for the gander…"

Taggart shook his head. "Don't you believe it. She can
be a barrel racer if she wants to," he added magnani-
mously.

"Generous of you. Hell—" Noah glanced in the mirror
again and sucked in his breath "—he'd better slow down."

"Who?"

Noah jerked his head. "That truck. He isn't gonna try to
pass, is he?"

But clearly he was. And then he wasn't.

Trying to brake on the snow-covered road only made
things worse. The semi didn't slow down; it began to slide
sideways.

Noah saw it coming in the mirror. The side of the trailer,
as red and cheerful as Christmas, swung around and in slow
motion slid straight at them.

One

He wasn't dead.

At least that's what they told him.

They were probably right. Being dead, Noah figured, wouldn't hurt quite so much. Every bone, every muscle—hell, every hair on his head—hurt like sin.

He mustered all his strength and shifted his position in the bed about an inch. At least there was nothing wrong with his memory. He knew exactly what had happened. He could still see it in his mind's eye—the truck trailer slapping into the van like Ken Griffey, Jr., ripping into a fastball. Noah felt like the cover, torn right off the ball.

He couldn't believe he'd really ridden nine out of ten NFR broncs just last week. It didn't seem possible. At the moment lifting his head didn't seem possible.

At least he could breathe. He could remember a time—just *when* was a little hazy, though—when even getting air seemed an iffy proposition.

It was because of his collapsed lung, he remembered them telling him. And that was because of his four broken ribs. And they were the result of that trailer playing baseball with the van, whacking him and Taggart clear out of the park.

Where the hell was Taggart? Noah couldn't remember having seen him since the accident, not since the paramedics had arrived and removed his friend's unconscious body from the van.

And that had been...when? He didn't know. He didn't know where he was—some hospital in Laramie? Cheyenne?—or how long he'd been here. Hell, and he'd thought his memory was all right?

He didn't know anything!

"Taggart!" Noah struggled to sit up. All his muscles screamed.

"Here now. It's all right." The voice came from the left. It was soft, soothing. Gentle. Female. "It's okay, Noah. It's okay."

At the sound of his name, Noah tried to turn his head. Other muscles protested. He groaned and his head fell back against the pillow.

"Your friend's all right. Take it easy," the voice said again, and a nurse came into his range of vision. A slender nurse in a starchy white uniform. A nurse with oddly familiar, wide green eyes and dark brown hair that was pulled back into a long braid. An even-longer braid than he remembered.

Noah stared, disbelieving.

"T-Tess?" It took him a minute to find enough air to form her name.

"Hello, Noah."

He smiled weakly and a little wryly. "What is this—déjà vu?"

A faint smile crossed her face. "Not quite." Her voice was soft, but her tone was neutral, professional. That wasn't the way it had been...how long ago? Seven years? Eight?

Even though, of course, it was how they had met. She'd been studying to become a nurse and was doing a practicum in the hospital where he ended up after getting hung up and kicked and concussed at the Laramie rodeo. He'd barely regained consciousness when his buddies had left him and headed down the road again. The next day, he'd been well enough to leave, but had had nowhere to go.

After a moment's indecision that was reflected clearly on her face, the dark-haired, starry-eyed nursing student he'd flirted with since they'd carried him into the hospital had agreed to take him home.

She wasn't the sort of girl he normally hung around with. The brash, eager "buckle bunnies" who generally followed him around were a far cry from the serious girl who had told him her name was Tess Montgomery.

Tess Montgomery had been thin and coltish, shy, yet surprisingly eager to please. She had also been the most beautiful girl he'd ever seen.

She still was. But there was no eagerness about her now, nor shyness, either—only a pleasant smile and cool, professional competence.

She was Tess Montgomery, R.N.—the first and last woman with whom he'd had what could even remotely be called "an affair." Tess Montgomery—one of the many women he'd loved and left. Tess Montgomery—the only woman who'd ever cried when he'd walked out the door.

God had one heck of a sense of humor, was all Noah could think.

What Tess thought, he didn't know. She was all business as she checked the tube in his chest that they'd put in when they'd reinflated his lung. When she was done, she listened with a stethoscope. He opened his mouth to say something.

She popped a thermometer in.

"Tess—"

"Shh." She moved to the foot of the bed and jotted something on his chart. He watched her. She used to smile at him, then, if he winked, look quickly away. Today there were no smiles—not after that first meant-to-be-reassuring one. He was just another patient now. In fact, it was probably worse. Maybe she hated him.

Naw, she couldn't. Could she? He wondered if he ought to ask. It didn't seem like the best place to start a conversation.

He shifted the thermometer. "Is Taggart...?"

"He's fine and he's right down the hall. Now hush." She went back to writing, ignoring him once more.

Noah scowled. "What's the matter with him?"

She glared. "He's doing fine," she repeated.

"He was unconscious!"

"Noah—"

"Tell me, damn it."

"I'll tell you," Tess said with exaggerated patience, "*if* you keep your mouth shut." And she closed her own mouth in a firm line, waiting until he slumped back against his pillows in acquiescence. Then she nodded, satisfied. "Your friend has a broken femur, two cracked ribs and a concussion. And yes, he stayed unconscious for most of yesterday, but he's awake now and quite coherent. More than you've been."

Noah frowned. How long had he been out of it, then? "When was it—th'accident, I mean?"

"Noah!"

"S'rry," he muttered around the thermometer, looking as abashed as he could.

At last she took pity on him. "The accident was yesterday afternoon. It's now almost 3:00 p.m. Tuesday."

He opened his mouth.

"And if you say another word, Noah, I will walk out of here and send Nurse Long Needle back in my place. And don't think I won't."

He hadn't known Tess long, but he'd known her well. She would do it. He fumed in silence while she took his blood pressure, shined a penlight into his eyes and shut it off again, then wrote some more. After about four hundred years, she took the thermometer out of his mouth.

"Nurse Long Needle?" He arched a sceptical brow.

"She's Cheyenne."

He didn't believe a word of it. "Behave, you mean?"

"Behave," Tess agreed.

Noah looked down at his aching body. His right shoulder and elbow were strapped against his torso. His ribs weren't taped, but they weren't exactly eager to go anywhere. He had a tube in his chest. His knee was immobilized in ice. There was an IV running from his left hand to a bag hanging by the bed. "I can't do anything else," he grumbled. "I want to see Taggart."

"By all means. Just hop right up and go down the hall. Room 218."

"Sarcasm, Tess?"

"Common sense, Noah."

He considered that, considered how far away the door was, considered how far away the floor was, for that matter. "You're probably right," he muttered after a moment. "So, when can I see him?"

"A day or so. Ask your doctor."

"Who *is* my doctor?" Hell, there was a whole world of stuff he didn't know.

"Dr. Alvarez for your lung. Dr. MacGuinness for your ribs and your knee and your elbow and shoulder."

"Do I have anything that isn't under a doctor's care?" he asked wryly.

Tess smiled. "Not much. You can have a pain pill if you want one. It's that time."

"Don't need one," he lied.

"Suit yourself." Tess started toward the door.

"Tess!" He levered himself up as far as he could.

She turned, one hand on the doorjamb. Her braid, he could see now, reached past the middle of her back. He remembered how her hair had looked fanned out against the white sheet. He remembered how soft it had felt to his touch. He swallowed.

"Are you...mad at me?"

She stared at him. "Mad?" Tess said. "No." She shook her head slowly. Her eyes met his for one long moment before her gaze flickered down briefly, then came up to meet his again. A faint smile touched the corners of her mouth. "Actually, Noah, I owe you a debt of gratitude."

There. She'd seen him—conscious and coherent this time—and she'd escaped unscathed. She'd even managed to be professional and polite.

It didn't matter that her hands were shaking as she walked down the hall to the nurse's station. It didn't matter that her breakfast was doing somersaults in her stomach and that there was a lump the size of a Rocky Mountain in her throat.

He didn't know that. And that was what mattered. That, and that she manage to keep her indifference firmly in place until Noah Tanner was once more out of her life.

"What's the matter?" Nita LongReach asked her. "You look like you've gone ten rounds with a ghost."

Tess shook her head and managed a wan smile. "Just hungry," she lied, knowing full well she'd upchuck if she even caught a whiff of a lunch tray right now. "I didn't eat lunch."

Nita grunted. "You work too hard."

"We all work too hard."

"But you more than most. You need a break. A vacation. A little joy in your life."

"I have a little joy in my life," Tess said. Her hands trembled less now. She wiped her palms surreptitiously on the sides of her white slacks.

"Besides Susannah," Nita said patiently. "You need more than a daughter and a job that takes all your time."

"Get a life, you mean?"

Nita grinned. "Get a man."

"No, thanks." Tess would have been far more emphatic if she thought Nita wouldn't accuse her of overreacting. She picked up a set of charts and riffled through them.

"Derek's interested." It hadn't gone unnoticed that earnest Derek Mallon, the new ob-gyn resident, seemed to be popping up everywhere Tess Montgomery went. "Either that or he's lost an awful lot of the time." Nita giggled. "Why else would he end up in orthopedics so often?"

"Maybe he's interested in you."

"I'm twenty years older than he is and fifty pounds heavier."

"Love is blind," Tess said blithely. It was also stupid, and dangerous to the heart, but she wasn't saying that.

"Well, if you don't want Derek, there're other fish in the sea. Want a cowboy?"

"*What?*" Tess almost dropped the charts in her hand.

Nita, noticing, looked speculative. "I'm not selling them, if that's what you're worried about. I just thought…what about either of those two rodeo cowboys? Handsome devils, both of 'em. They're a bit battered at the moment, but when the bruising fades…''

''No,'' Tess said flatly. ''I don't want a cowboy.'' Never again.

A debt of gratitude?

The words tumbled around in Noah's head, mocking him. What the hell did that mean?

Because he'd destroyed her childish fantasies? Because he'd loved her and left her? Because he'd squashed her young girl's dreams and taught her what men were really like?

Or was she just being sarcastic?

Probably. Without a doubt he deserved it.

He took the pain pill after all. And four hours later another. And then another.

They muddled his mind as much as they dulled his pain. He dozed and dreamed, and in his mind he saw a million horses, a million rides, a million miles of road…and a million memories of Tess.

''Do you take in strays?'' he'd asked her, only half-joking, the day he was to be discharged.

Her green eyes had widened perceptibly. She'd swallowed, then blinked. Then a shy smile had lit her face. ''I believe I could.''

So she had. He was broke and hungry, and his head still ached. She'd been kind, gentle, caring. She'd fussed over him with a tenderness he hadn't experienced since his mother had died, when he was four.

Maybe it was the care, maybe it was the concussion. Whatever the cause, she tapped a part of Noah that had lain dormant for so many years he'd totally forgotten it was there. He'd grown gentle, too, teasing her tenderly, smiling at her, laughing with her. Basking in the comfort of her concern.

He'd been on the road, without a family, for so long that all the TLC she was lavishing on him turned his head. It was wonderful. The picnics she took him on were fun. The hikes in the mountains and swims at the lake were fantastic.

But he wanted more. He was plagued with a young man's needs, a young man's lusts. And not too many days passed before Tess, overcoming her initial shyness, had satisfied them—had satisfied him.

For two weeks she welcomed him into her life, into her arms, into her bed. She gave him days of joy and nights of love.

Sometimes, lying next to her at night, he dreamed that he could have this paradise forever.

But in the clear light of day, he knew it couldn't last.

He was a rodeo bronc rider. A close-to-broke rodeo bronc rider. And the only way he could change that last fact was to get on down the road to more rodeos and leave Tess Montgomery behind.

Still, when his buddies came to pick him up on their way back to Cheyenne later that month, he'd felt a momentary pang. From the look on her face when he came out of the bedroom carrying his duffel bag and saddle, Tess felt more than that.

"You're leaving?" she'd said, her face going pale as she looked up from the dishes she was washing.

"Got to. They're waiting."

"I know, but—" she picked up a towel and dried her hands as she came toward him "—I thought… When will you be back?"

"Dunno." He shrugged and gave her his best rakish grin. "You know us rodeo cowboys. Always goin' down the road. Never stayin' in one place more than a night or two."

"You stayed here two weeks." She was looking like a wounded doe.

"'Cause I was hurt."

"And now you're well." He heard a faint bitterness in her voice as she turned away to stare out the window.

He dropped the duffel bag and saddle and jammed his hands into his pockets. "Now I'm well," he agreed. "Thanks to you," he added gently, wishing she would smile.

She didn't. Her fingers knotted in front of her.

He yanked a hand out of his pocket and touched her arm. She stiffened.

"Come on, Tess. Don't be like this. You knew I was goin'."

"Did I?" He heard the ache in her voice and tried to ignore it.

"Course you did. It's what I do, for Lord's sake. I got to. I never said I'd stay!"

She didn't look at him, didn't speak.

Outside Taggart yelled, "Hey, Noah, hurry it up!"

"See? I gotta…" He stared at her helplessly.

She shook him off. "Fine. Go." Noah saw a tear slip down her cheek, then another. She swiped them angrily away, then hugged her arms against her breasts. "They're waiting for you."

Damn it, he hated it when women cried! And over him! He couldn't believe it. He gripped her arm again, pulling her around, trying to make her face him. "Look, Tess. I didn't mean for this to happen. You know that. I never said…I never made any promises, did I? Did I?"

She looked at him then. It didn't help.

"I didn't," he reiterated desperately. "I can't. I got nothing to give you."

"Love."

Love? It couldn't be so simple. What about jobs? Money? Hopes? Dreams?

His hesitation was enough. Tess jerked out of his grasp and spun away from him. "Go on. Go away!"

But her misery was so clear he couldn't seem to move. "I can't... I need..."

"Well, I don't!" She jerked the door open and stood waiting, glaring at him. "I said go on!"

Noah's fingers clenched. His lips pressed into a tight line. "Fine," he said heavily after a moment. "I'm going." He yanked up the saddle and duffel bag and started past her. She was too close, too tempting. He leaned toward her and brushed a hard kiss across her lips, then turned once more on the top step. "I'll call you."

"No."

"I'll call you," he said firmly.

But he almost hadn't.

"Don't," Taggart had counseled. "It isn't fair. You don't want to keep her danglin', do you?"

A part of Noah did want to. The selfish part. The part that woke up several times a night after he'd left her, missing her. Longing for her laugh, for her smile, for the gentle way she touched him. The part that seemed always to be looking for her sweet, generous nature in every girl who flirted with him or teased him or knocked on his motel-room door.

But none of them was Tess. And Tess was the only one he hankered after. The only one he lay awake at night and wished for.

But Taggart was right. What could he offer her, besides the occasional night when he was passing through?

There was no point even thinking about it. Finally, in mid-September, he called her to tell her so.

"Noah?" she'd said when she heard his voice. "Oh, Noah!"

She sounded so pathetically happy to get his call, he'd felt like a heel for dragging it out this long. "Hi, Tess." He made himself sound cheerful, upbeat.

"Are you in town?"

"I'm in California. I been runnin' all over. You know what it's like."

"I guess," she said vaguely. "When are you coming?"

He took a deep breath. "I'm not."

"Not? At all?" Her voice was suddenly faint, as if he'd knocked the wind right out of her. All the eagerness he'd heard just moments before was gone.

He wanted desperately to put it back. He didn't dare. "Not at all," he said firmly. "I just…just didn't want to leave you wondering what had happened to me." He paused. "And I said I'd call so…here I am."

Over the wires he heard the long-distance hum. "Yes, well, thank you," she said finally, after so long a time he thought she might not still be there. She sounded very polite now. Very formal. "It was kind of you to let me know."

Kind? Not hardly. He wished he could think of something else to say, something that would make her feel better, make her know that this was for her own good, that she deserved a far better man than him. Somehow he didn't think she'd appreciate a testimonial.

"You…been all right?" he asked her at last.

"Fine," she said. "Just fine."

"Good. Good." He hesitated. "I, uh, gotta run. I'll see—" he paused awkwardly "—no, I guess I won't."

And he hadn't.

Until Tuesday.

"He's been asking for you," Nita told Tess two days later when she came back from her day off.

Tess didn't reply at once. She hung up her coat and shook the snowflakes from her hair, doing her best to feign indifference, though her heart had been beating faster for the past five days. She'd been desperate for a day off to regain her equilibrium, hoping it would be enough. It wasn't. Damn Noah Tanner for being able to affect her this way still. "Who's been asking?" she said finally, though she was sure she knew.

"The dark-haired cowboy with the to-die-for blue eyes. He's cuter than Derek, I'll give you that. Surely you've noticed."

"I can't say that I have," Tess lied. "How's Mrs. Forrest this morning?"

"Mrs. Forrest went home yesterday. Here. Breakfast just came up. Why don't you take around the trays. And—" Nita winked "—while you're at it, check out those eyes."

Tess grumbled, but took the cart full of trays. She knew all too well the mesmerizing power of Noah Tanner's blue eyes. She prayed they'd be closed—that he'd be asleep.

He wasn't.

"Hey, sunshine." He was still lying down, but he smiled at her when she appeared.

"Noah." She set his tray on the table.

"I figured maybe you were avoiding me, but Nita said you had the day off. I wanted to ask you, what's the debt of gratitude for?"

Oh, hell. He would remember that. "I was just glad you called that day," she said at last. "Put an end to it."

He looked at her closely. "I didn't want to give you false hopes."

"I appreciate it," she said dryly. At the time it had crushed her. When she had more perspective, she'd come to see he was right. She didn't want a man who didn't love her, who wouldn't be there for her.

"Figured you'd find a lot better man than me. Did you?"

Almost at the door, she turned to look at him. "Did I what?"

His blue eyes were boring into her. "Find a better man? Marry him?"

She hesitated. "I'm not married," she said at last.

Why the hell not?

If there was ever a woman who ought to be married, it was Tess Montgomery. Even a dyed-in-the-wool drifter—*especially* a dyed-in-the-wool drifter—like Noah Tanner could see that.

She was a nester, right down to her toes. Even in the slapped-together one-bedroom apartment where she'd been living, a place with as much inherent personality as a chicken coop, Tess Montgomery had created a home. And she'd wanted kids. She'd said so.

The men in Wyoming must be fools, Noah thought. Or eunuchs.

Or—*hadn't she married because of him?*

He shouldn't dare to think any such thing. And he didn't. Not really. Even he wasn't that cocky.

But Noah couldn't suppress a tiny grin as, deep down, some little-bitty part of him couldn't help wondering if it was so.

Taggart wasn't a fool. Or a eunuch.

And even though he was even more bruised and battered looking than Noah, not to mention tied to the bed with his right leg suspended in traction, when Noah finally got to visit his buddy, he found himself wishing Taggart wasn't quite so attractive to the opposite sex.

Or to Tess. Because he was, if that heart-stopping smile she was wearing when she came into Taggart's room was anything to go by.

"Good morning," she said in a cheerful tone Noah never heard when she came into his room.

And then she saw Noah sitting by the window and her smiled faded.

Taggart, who'd been complaining about hospitals and doctors and food and how he couldn't wait to get out of here, took one look at Tess and his face lit up. "Hey, my favorite nurse!" He tried to shove himself up farther in the bed.

Favorite nurse? What the hell did that mean?

"Don't do that," Tess said sharply to Taggart. "You'll hurt yourself. Here. Let me help you." She put an arm around his shoulders and settled him back against the pillows, then raised the head of the bed a foot or so. "How's that?"

"Great." Taggart gave her another grin and blew her a kiss. "You're my angel, aren't you, Tessie?"

Tessie? Noah's jaw clamped shut.

"This pretty lady is the only thing that makes bein' here tolerable," Taggart said. "She takes good care of me, don't you?"

"I try," Tess said with a demure smile. "What do you need?"

"You got any more of that orange juice?"

"Of course." And she vanished to get some.

"Wish they were all that sweet," Taggart said to Noah after she'd brought them each a glass, given Taggart a smile, Noah a nod, and left again.

"She's not that sweet to me," Noah grumbled.

Taggart lifted an eyebrow. "I thought all the girls fell at your feet."

"Not Tess. Not this time, anyhow."

"This time?"

"I was here before, remember? The time I got concussed ridin' Maverick's Dream."

Taggart blinked, then stared. "Tess is *her?* The one you…"

Noah gave a single affirmative jerk of his head. Then he reached over and picked up a copy of the football magazine on Taggart's bedside table, opening it and at least pretending to read.

"So are you still interested?" Taggart asked. He wasn't talking about football.

Noah kept his eyes on the magazine. "She was a nice girl."

"Still is."

Noah looked up and gave his friend a hard look. "Not one to be fooling around with," he said gruffly. "She deserves better."

Taggart grinned. "You are still interested."

"I'm not dead!"

"And thank God for that." Taggart smiled, then said reflectively, "When I came around, I didn't know what had happened to you."

"I saw you unconscious. I thought you'd bought the ranch. You looked like it," Noah answered, grateful for the change in subject.

"Bruised my pretty face," Taggart agreed. He grimaced and glanced at his leg. "And did this." They both stared in silent contemplation at the strapped-up, plaster-cast appendage.

"Good thing you aren't ridin' this week," Noah said. "You might've had to turn him out."

Taggart smiled, but the smile didn't quite reach his eyes. "Might've," he agreed. "My folks are on their way down with Becky. I didn't want 'em to bring her, told 'em it'd scare her, seein' me like this. But they said she'd be scared worse if they didn't.''

Noah hadn't thought about that, about what it meant to have someone depending on you to be well, to bring home the bacon. He'd called Tanner when he'd become coherent, long enough to tell his brother he'd been in a little accident and that he might not be there for a while. But Tanner had his own life, his own worries—a wife, three kids, a struggling ranch. He wasn't depending on Noah.

No one was.

And a good thing, too, he thought now.

"You'll be glad to see her," he said with as much cheerful determination as he could muster.

"Yeah." Taggart looked away and blinked rapidly. "I missed her damned Christmas program, though," he said roughly.

"She understands."

"I should've been there."

"We tried."

Taggart was staring out the window. "I'm gonna quit riding."

"What?" It was a good thing he was sitting down, Noah thought, or he'd have fallen right over.

"I'm retirin'. Stayin' home." Taggart spelled it out for him.

"You're just saying that 'cause you're hurt. When you feel better, you'll change your mind."

Taggart shook his head. "No. I won't."

"You can't quit," Noah said urgently. "What would you do? What *can* you do?" Riding bulls wasn't a stepping stone to a lot of other careers any more than riding broncs was.

"I'll think of something."

"You can't. You—"

"Shut up," Taggart said, as his gaze flicked suddenly from the window to a movement in the doorway. He straightened up against the pillows and pasted a smile on his face. "They're here."

And before Noah could ease his still-stiff body around, Taggart's parents appeared at his side, his gray-haired, tanned father smiling nervously, his thin, usually cheerful mother looking desperate as she focused on her son. A second later a small body brushed against Noah's arm. He turned his head to see Becky. He'd never seen Taggart's daughter less than irrepressible, but now she looked haunted, her eyes wide with worry as she stared at the man in the bed.

"D-Daddy?"

Taggart held out a hand to her. "It's okay, Beck. *I'm* okay."

For a moment she seemed to doubt him. But when he beckoned again, she flew at him, crying, scrabbling up onto the bed. Grimacing with pain and ignoring it at the same time, Taggart hauled his daughter up into his arms and hugged her tight.

"Oh, dear!"

Tess stood in the doorway, looking momentarily horrified at Becky's assault on the bed. Noah thought she was going to sweep the little girl out of Taggart's arms. Instead she scooped her up, shifted her around and settled her down gently once more so that Taggart could still hold her but she wouldn't hurt his leg.

"There." Tess's hand brushed lightly over the child's fair hair. "Better?" she asked gently.

Becky hugged her father, reached up and traced his bruised cheek lightly, then glanced once at Tess and nodded shyly. And Noah saw both of Taggart's parents begin to breathe again. Gaye, his mother, even smiled as she moved toward the bed to take his hand and drop a kiss on his hair.

Will Jones didn't move, but his smile broadened. "Thank God, son," he said, and Noah heard the emotion in his voice.

Watching them, Noah felt an ache inside that had nothing to do with his injuries. He looked away. "I'll see you around," he said as he got up.

At his words, Taggart's parents seemed to notice him all at once. "Oh, Noah!" Gaye said now. "Are you all right?"

"I'm fine," he said, edging toward the door.

"You poor thing. You look worse than Taggart."

Noah shook his head and kept moving.

"You don't have to go," Gaye protested.

"You visit with Taggart. That's what you came for."

"But—"

Tess stepped between them. "He really does need to rest," she said to Taggart's mother. "He's been up far too long." And she stayed between them until Noah was out of the room.

"Thanks."

She hesitated. "Don't you like them?"

"Of course I like them. They're Taggart's parents."

"Then why…?"

Noah cast around for words to express feelings he didn't completely understand himself. "They aren't *my* parents," he said finally, after a moment.

She must have remembered that his parents were dead, for the smile she gave him was one of gentle sadness. "Come on," she said. "Let's get you back to bed."

It wasn't much. Just the barest hint of empathy. But even so, it was the only real hint he'd had so far that she still felt something for him.

He embroidered on it for hours. Days. He couldn't help himself. He was going stir-crazy, lying around the damned hospital. The hour he spent in physical therapy every day left him exhausted and shaking, but for the most part, hour by hour he felt stronger, healthier and as if the walls were closing in on him. The only way out was in his mind.

And the only thing on his mind was Tess.

"How come you haven't married?" he asked her one morning.

She was taking his blood pressure, but from the sudden color in her face, it was hers that ought to be checked. "None of your business."

"It could be."

"No." She brushed a lock of hair away from her face as she moved away.

He shoved himself up in the bed. "I'm not saying it is," Noah said conversationally. "I'm only sayin' it might be. If, for example, you were carryin' a torch for me."

"Carry a torch for you? Think again, cowboy!"

Noah grinned, then sobered. "It was good, Tess," he said quietly.

She was writing something on his chart. She didn't look up.

"You were good. Too good for me. You still singin' in the choir at church?" He remembered how amazed he'd been when she'd popped out of bed after the Saturday night they'd spent loving. He'd been even more amazed when she'd told him where she was going.

People he knew believed in God, all right. Some of them even went to church. But no one he knew went so far as to sing in a choir. He'd gone along and listened, enthralled at the pure, sweet sound of Tess's soprano solo. Later, when they'd curled together in bed, she'd sung once more, softly and sweetly, just for him. "Do you?" he persisted when she kept writing.

"Yes."

"Gonna sing at Christmas?"

She nodded.

"You're staying in Laramie then? Not goin' home?"

"This is my home." He knew her parents were dead, too, but he remembered she had a sister somewhere in Wyoming. "My family's here now," she told him. She finished making notes on his chart and started toward the door.

"Tess?"

She turned.

"Sing to me."

She fled.

Call it arrogance.

Call it cockiness.

It was, sure enough.

Call it wrong-headed and selfish. It was that, too. And the product of too much time spent wishful thinking. But Noah couldn't help it. He was convinced she still cared.

She might act calm and cool and professional. She might deny that he mattered to her at all. But if he didn't, why did she avoid him, ignore him, then blush like a schoolgirl when he reminded her of intimacies they'd shared?

She cared. And he wanted her to admit it. To him. To herself.

That was probably why he kissed her.

If there was any rational reason for it at all.

He sure to goodness didn't plan it. He'd been sitting there, staring at the same damn four walls all the next morning, contemplating how he could get the doc to release him and how he was then going to get to Tanner and Maggie's when he did, when Tess came to take him to physical therapy.

She was brisk and bossy, and she acted like he meant no more to her than old man Hardesty across the hall.

So he kissed her.

To make her angry? Probably. To make her respond? Definitely.

She was right there, holding him up, helping him move from the bed to the wheelchair. So close. So impersonal.

And so he kissed her.

It was a hungry kiss. A demanding kiss. A kiss that sought to resurrect memories that eight years had been doing their best to erase. And the moment that his lips touched hers, the eight years vanished just like that. It might have been yesterday. Hell, it felt like yesterday.

He'd kissed a lot of women in the past eight years. None of them kissed with the same sweet hunger as Tess Montgomery.

Until at least, she realized that she was kissing him back. Then she jerked away, her face scarlet, her breasts heaving beneath her starched white uniform. She gave him a shove that sent him flat on the bed.

"Damn you, Noah Tanner!" She spun around and fled from the room.

Noah, ribs aching, knee throbbing, shoulder pounding, lay back and touched his lips and grinned.

Two

"What do you mean, I can't come for Christmas?"

Robert Tanner rubbed the back of his neck and looked around the tiny hospital room as if he wished he were somewhere else—anywhere else. Noah knew how he felt. He felt that way himself—and the news his brother had just imparted didn't help matters a bit.

"They want you here," Tanner said helplessly.

Noah had been surprised and delighted when his older brother had walked into his room ten minutes earlier. Then, seeing some gaily wrapped Christmas packages, he'd been curious. Now he was just plain mad.

"But Taggart left. He left today!" Noah argued.

With Becky and his parents hovering in the background, Taggart had crutched his way in to say goodbye less than two hours ago. He'd even grinned and said, "Hey, it won't be long for you. Come on up to Montana when you can."

And now Tanner was telling Noah he wasn't going anywhere!

"Why can't I?" he demanded.

"Physical therapy on the knee, apparently. If you'd had surgery, they might've let you come. Given you a chance to mend a bit before they put you through the torture. But since you didn't..." Tanner didn't need to finish the sentence. "Three times a week for now, the doc said. And we can't get you here from there—it's a good seven hours one way. You know that."

"So I'm supposed to stay in the hospital?"

"They didn't say that," Tanner said in the same tone he used to soothe jittery horses. "You can leave tomorrow or the day after. Soon as you get the all clear on the lung."

Noah muttered under his breath and poked at the macaroni and cheese on his lunch tray. "Hell."

Tanner crushed his hat brim with his fingers. "Oh, I don't know. You might find it restful. A damn sight more restful than the ranch is gonna be. Wall-to-wall rug rats at our place." He tried to sound disgruntled, but didn't manage it.

"I was looking forward to it," Noah said gruffly. It was the truth. Christmas had come to seem a lot more like Christmas since Jared was born. Even when he was only a few months old, Jared had made Christmas special. Last year, when he was toddling around, shredding wrapping paper and gumming the wise men in the hearthside manger, his innocent, wide-eyed joy had made it even more so. And now that Tanner and Maggie had eleven-month-old Seth and Nick, and Luke and Jill had eight-month-old Keith, Noah thought things would be even better.

Probably they still would be. Without him.

"Hell," he said again.

"We'll miss you," Tanner offered lamely. "We're just

grateful you're alive,'' he added, and Noah saw a shudder run through his brother as he contemplated what could have happened. ''You're damn lucky.''

He didn't feel especially lucky. He still hurt. He hadn't even begun to let himself think about when he might be able to go down the road again. And now he couldn't even go to Tanner's for Christmas. Neither of them spoke for a long moment. It wasn't the holiday they'd counted on. It could have been much better.

It could have been much worse.

''I'm glad you came,'' Noah said at last, mustering all the good cheer he could.

''I'd have come first thing, but Jared had the flu and the twins were cuttin' teeth, and I couldn't leave Maggie to cope with all of it.''

''No. I knew you'd come if you could. You always do.''

If something ever needed to be done, Tanner did it. He had been the responsible brother from the very start—taking care, taking charge—far different from Noah and Luke, who were always ready to move on and never look around—or back.

Now Tanner reached over to the bedside table and picked up the gold buckle Noah had won at the NFR. He weighed it in his hand, then looked at his brother. ''I never did this.''

''I may never do it again.''

''Don't matter. You got nothin' left to prove. Took some grit. And I reckon gettin' healed will take some more grit.''

''Taggart says he's quitting.'' Noah still couldn't quite believe it.

''I'm not surprised.''

Noah blinked. ''How come? He's got grit, too. A hell of a lot of it. Had to have, takin' care of Becky.''

''Exactly. Kids have a way of makin' you look at the long haul. And makin' you want to stick around.''

"I wouldn't know."

Tanner smiled. "One day you will."

"Not likely," Noah said gruffly. "I'm not exactly dad material."

There was a sound from the doorway, like an indrawn breath, and he glanced up to see Tess.

It was the first he'd seen of her since he'd kissed her. She looked stricken and started to turn away.

"It's okay if you want the lunch tray," he called after her. He wanted to talk to her, but not now. Not in front of Tanner.

She turned. "No. Not if you're not finished," she said stiffly.

"I'm finished," he said. "Come meet my brother."

Tess hesitated.

Noah beckoned to her. "He looks mean, but he doesn't bite." He knew she was a damn sight more wary of him than of his brother, but after another moment, she came slowly into the room.

"This is Tann—I mean, Robert. The nicest one of us. This," he told Tanner, "is Tess."

There must have been something in his tone that made Tanner take a closer look. Since his marriage, Tanner had never noticed any woman other than Maggie, but he was definitely checking out Tess now.

She smiled a little self-consciously, then held out her hand. "I'm glad one of you is nice."

"You can count on it." Tanner flicked a glance at Noah. "Been givin' you trouble, has he? I'm not surprised. You just got to ignore him."

"I'm doing my best."

"Don't let him get to you," Tanner went on.

"I won't."

They didn't have to talk about him as if he wasn't even there. Goaded, Noah said, "I already did."

Tess's cheeks turned a faint pink, but she ignored him and reached for his tray.

"I kissed her."

Her faintly flushed cheeks turned crimson. She snatched his tray off the table and made for the door.

"And she kissed me back. Didn't you, Tess?" he called.

But Tess had disappeared, shoving the clattering meal cart down the hall like she was qualifying for the Indy 500.

Tanner watched her go, then turned back to regard his brother speculatively. "I think you're askin' for trouble."

"Already got it."

"Because you kissed her?"

Noah shrugged. "There's a little more to it than that."

"Figured there might be." Tanner waited in case Noah decided to enlighten him.

Noah ran his tongue over his lips. "Years back we— well, we…" *We what? Slept together? Made love? Had an affair?*

How did you describe what had gone on between them for those two brief weeks? Noah plucked irritably at the blanket. "It's a hell of a mess."

"Seems like."

"Any brotherly advice?"

Tanner's eyes widened at the unlikely question. "Me? Sorry. I don't reckon the Tanner brothers are all that gifted when it comes to dealin' with women."

"Ain't that the truth?"

Tanner stood staring at the door, lost in thought. "She's a mighty pretty lady, though." A slow smile spread across his face and he looked at his brother. "If you play your cards right, I reckon you just might find yourself a place to stay for Christmas."

Noah didn't think all the tricks in the book would get him that.

He was gone. At last.

Discharged at 10:40 this morning, while she hid in the nurses' lounge, cowering behind a cup of decaf and a Danish and letting Nita see him into the wheelchair and out the door.

So she was a chicken. Nobody ever said she had to be brave. She simply had to survive.

And she would. Now.

She hadn't been so sure after that kiss. The kiss had devastated her.

Damn Noah Tanner, anyway. How dared he catch her off guard like that? How dared he kiss her as if he had every right?

How dared she kiss him back?

Because God knew—and she knew—that she had. She had, for a few moments, opened to him like a parched flower that, after eight long years in the desert, at last was given rain. His kiss had come so unexpectedly, so astonishingly, that she hadn't thought; she had only reacted.

And the worst thing was it had felt so terribly, terribly right. As if all the years and all the pain had fallen away, leaving only the man.

She'd been telling herself that the only reason Noah had mattered so much was because he was the first man who'd taken the time to get behind the facade to the real Tess Montgomery. The first man to whom she'd uncovered her inner self.

A country girl who had grown up rambling the hills by herself, Tess had never been given to easy conversation or the best of social graces. She was quiet and self-contained, more given to spending time with animals than people. Not that she didn't like people; she did. She just didn't have a lot of experience with them.

Nursing had appealed to her from the time she was small. "Tessie's got a healin' touch," her father always used to say. And it was true. She could take a sick calf and make it well again. The rabbits they kept in the shed near the house died for her sister but thrived for her. And when her mother had suffered from cancer throughout most of Tess's teenage years, it was her ministrations that made Susannah Montgomery relax and smile.

Tess knew even before her mother died that nursing was what she would do, if the money was there for school. It almost wasn't. But she'd got through the first year and a half with her father's help before his horse stumbled in a prairie-dog hole and he was thrown and killed. That had happened a little more than a year before the summer she met Noah. She was on her own then, living in a tiny apartment not far from the campus, working two jobs to afford her last year of nurse's training. Her older sister, Nancy, had married and moved to Omaha the previous spring. Tess had a few friends at work and at school, but little time to go out with them. Mostly she was alone.

She didn't realize how alone, or how much she longed for someone to share things with, until that dark-haired, blue-eyed bronc rider charmed his way from his hospital bed into her life.

She'd never done anything like that before—taken a man home. Especially not to stay. She never would have dared take a man like Noah home with her if he was operating at full strength. But he wasn't. In fact, he seemed to need her.

Heaven knew she needed him.

She hadn't realized just how much. It could still make her cheeks warm and her insides lurch if she dwelt very long on how foolish and naive she'd been eight years ago. In a matter of only a few days, she'd shared everything with him—her life, her hopes, her fears, her dreams. Her body.

Even now she blushed at how eagerly she had shared the intimacies of the flesh with him. Noah Tanner knew more about her than anyone in the world.

When he'd left, a part of her had died.

It was her own fault, of course. She knew that. He'd made no promises. He'd been sweet, gentle, caring. He'd been by turns whimsical, serious and funny. He'd been her friend, her confidant, her lover. But he'd never intended it to be permanent.

She'd only prayed he would.

She should have known better. Noah Tanner was a rodeo cowboy. A man who made his living going from place to place. A man whose dreams lay just over the next hill. He couldn't stay. It wasn't who he was.

Still, fool that she was, she'd hoped. Even after the battered red pickup had come and borne him away. After all, hadn't he said he'd call? Didn't that mean something?

When a month passed, and then another, she'd begun to suspect it didn't. Even as she found things she desperately needed to share with him, she began to think she never could.

And then one bright September day, the phone rang.

She'd known his voice at once. They'd never talked on the phone, but she hadn't a doubt from the first tentative, slightly gruff, "Tess?" that it was him. She hadn't been able to contain her joy. Just as, seconds later, when he told her he wasn't coming back—ever—she hadn't been able to disguise her pain.

More foolishness.

But she'd made up her mind that she wasn't going to be

a fool any longer. She was going to grow up, become the woman she'd always wanted to become.

And for all intents and purposes, she had.

Until early last Monday morning, when Noah Tanner kissed her again.

She'd steered clear, stonewalled, resisted. And she'd almost made it.

And then, without warning, he'd given her a kiss, and her resolutions had gone up in flames. Her indifference had crumbled at her feet. Like it or not, she'd turned into the same besotted idiot she'd been all those years before.

Why?

Because no one had ever taken his place.

Not really. Not completely. Oh, there had been a few brief encounters. With Mark, the respiratory therapist. With Steven, the CPA. With Jon and Jeff and Warren, with whom she'd managed two dates apiece. But all the men in the last eight years of her life she could count on the fingers of one hand. And not one of them had really known her.

Not the way Noah had known her.

Nita was right. It was time she got a man in her life.

Noah was an expert on motels. He appreciated even heat, cable television, spotless sheets and personal coffee makers. He was glad to be near the ice machine, so he had only a few feet to walk to replenish the bags of ice he was still putting on his knee.

But all the warm air, ice bags, coffee and holiday television specials in the world didn't do the trick.

It was Christmas, damn it. He wanted to be where the kids would be romping and shouting, the logs would be crackling in the fireplace, where Christmas carols would be playing in the background and the smells of gingerbread and cinnamon would be teasing his every breath.

He didn't want absolute silence, even if it meant excellent soundproofing. He didn't want to smell disinfectant, no matter how clean it meant the bathroom was.

He wanted to go home.

He shoved himself up off the bed and hobbled to the window, opened the drapes and stared out into the heavy snowfall. If he were ten years younger, he'd grab his gear and head for the interstate, determined to hitch a ride and say the hell with physical therapy. But he wasn't.

He was almost thirty-four. He felt more like sixty. God knew he had more miles on him than most sixty-year-olds. And if God didn't know it, his bones, muscles and sinews did. If he wanted to ride broncs again he had to stay and do his three-times-a-week therapy. There was no choice.

Taggart wasn't riding again, he reminded himself. Yeah, but Taggart had a reason not to, and parents who would let him take his time finding his feet again.

Noah didn't. He had brothers, sure, but he didn't want to impose on them. If worse came to worst, he supposed he could cowboy for Tanner for a while. He might even be able to go out to California and visit Luke and Jill, or head up to the range camp where Luke had holed up until Jill had flushed him out last year. But he couldn't stay there like his brother had.

He wouldn't last more than a week. Tanner and Luke were loners—strong, silent, solitary men. Noah needed people, excitement, challenge, not what he would get at the cabin—unrelenting solitude and the ongoing opportunity to face the flat, bleak nothing that was his future.

His future.

What future?

He looked at his pale face in the motel-room mirror. "And a very merry Christmas to you."

* * *

He lasted two days.

Two days of staring at four beige walls, one beige carpet, a beige-and-gray bedspread and reruns of every tear-jerking seasonal movie ever made. He called Tanner twice. The first evening he tried his best to sound both stoic and upbeat as he talked to his sister-in-law Maggie, too. The following night he spoke with Luke and Jill, as well. He hoped that just listening to them all—Tanner, Maggie, Luke, Jill and even Jared—would be enough or that it would make him glad he wasn't there.

By the time he hung up, he felt more lonely and bereft than ever. He got out the phone book and looked up Tess.

He didn't exactly intend to call her. He just wanted the number—to hang on to—whatever sense that made.

But then, as he watched the rest of *Miracle on 34th Street,* he found himself dialing her number before he stopped to think.

He got an answering machine.

"Hi," Tess's soft voice said, "Hope you're having a merry. Leave a message and we'll get back to you." There was none of the drill sergeant that he'd heard when she talked to him at the hospital. This was the warm Tess, the welcoming Tess. The Tess he remembered all too well. The machine beeped, waiting.

Noah hung up.

She was at work, of course. Or was she? Last week she'd had this day off. He sat hunched on the side of the bed, wondering where she was. Christmas shopping? Choir practice? *Out with another man?*

That idea stung. He slumped back against the headboard of the bed and contemplated his cool, beige surroundings. He remembered Tess's tiny apartment, painted a cozy buttercup yellow. Her furniture had been vintage garage sale, but she'd had a pile of colorful pillows on the sofa and cheerful travel posters on the wall. Her bedroom had been painted a soft blue with a double bed that sagged in the middle where they had rolled together every night.

They hadn't cared. They'd touched. Kissed. Loved.

Remembering, Noah shut his eyes and groaned.

He grabbed the remote control and clicked on the television, surfing through the channels, finding nothing to distract him. In his mind her soft voice played over and over again. *Hope you're having a merry.*

Yeah, he thought. *Right.*

He had to be at the hospital at one for physical therapy. The foot of snow that had fallen two days ago had been plowed aside, but as his taxi pulled up in front of the hospital, snow began to fall again.

He looked for her at the hospital. He saw Nita. She waved to him. He waved back, then crutched toward the physical-therapy room. He thought Tess might come in while he was waiting or while he was sweating and groaning through the weights and the bike and the stretching. He hoped she might come in after. He never saw her once.

On his way out, he stopped for a cup of coffee in the cafeteria, telling himself he needed the liquid refreshment. What he needed was a glimpse of Tess.

One of the other nurses from the orthopedic department smiled at him. Nita waved to him again as he hobbled back toward the lobby.

It was snowing harder now. The streets were thick with it as the cab took him back to his beige prison. He tried to steel himself to go in, but when the cab pulled up in front of the motel, he couldn't do it.

''Wait for me,'' he said.

He got his gear and checked out.

He didn't expect Tess to welcome him with open arms.

He knew better. But there had been something between them once—something he'd walked away from.

He wasn't asking for that back.

He was asking for a little friendship, a little understanding, a home just until Christmas was over. A few days. No more. Then he'd go back to the motel.

Then he could face the beige.

Her address wasn't the same as before. He didn't know what to expect this time, but was pleased to find that she lived on a street fairly near the university. It was in a neighborhood with trees and older homes and even the occasional picket fence, including one in front of hers. Exactly the sort of place he'd imagined her in.

Her particular house was a steep-roofed, white framed two-story with a huge fir tree in the front yard. The house looked solid and substantial and entirely too big and settled for one person. He wondered suddenly if she lived alone. She'd said her family was here now. He knew her parents were dead. Perhaps her sister and family had moved to Laramie? Would they welcome a stranger for Christmas?

Noah peered out the window, having second thoughts. Especially when he spotted a young girl in the front yard, rolling a ball to make a snowman. She had hair the color of Tess's and her cheeks were flushed from the cold. A niece? Probably. So the sister did live here.

"This *is* the right address?" the cab driver asked when Noah made no move to get out.

"Yeah. Yeah, I guess it is." He hesitated still, then thought about the beige walls again. Perhaps it would be better with her sister's family there; she'd be less likely to throw him out.

He paid the driver and got out of the cab, then stood holding his duffel bag in one hand and leaning on his crutches.

The girl in the yard was watching him. Close up, she looked even more like Tess. Beneath the wind flush on her cheeks, he could see Tess's freckles. Her nose was Tess's, too. Her hair was long and dark, just like Tess's had been when he'd first known her. Only her eyes were different. Tess's were a soft jade green. This girl's were a deep, dark blue. She didn't take them off him for a second.

"I'm looking for Tess Montgomery," he said finally. "Is she home?"

The girl shook her dark head. "Not yet," she said. "She'll...be home by three-thirty."

"Do you mind if I wait?"

She ran her tongue across her lips. "No," she said faintly. "You can wait," she said with a little more enthusiasm.

Noah slowly made his way through the snow and opened the gate. Seeing his awkwardness, she took his bag and set it on the front porch. He smiled. An ally.

She turned back to look at him again as he shut the gate, her scrutiny so intense it was a little unnerving.

"Nice snowman," he said.

"Thanks."

"I'd help but I'm...sort of laid up."

"Yes."

"I'm Noah Tanner," he said finally, realizing she had no idea.

"I know."

"You do?" Amazing. How many girls her age knew a world-champion bronc rider when they saw one? "Did Tess tell you about me?"

She nodded solemnly.

He grinned, pleased as punch. "You really know who I am?"

"You're my father," she said.

Three

He hadn't heard her right.

He *couldn't* have heard her right. "What did you say?"

"I said you're my…father." There was a faint hesitation, but no real question even now. He tightened his grip on the crutches.

"Your father?" How could he make it a question when she was looking at him with such wide-eyed sincerity. *How could he not?*

"I'm Susannah."

He couldn't even seem to get his tongue around her name.

"*Susannah!*" They both turned as Tess came running down the sidewalk, a panic-stricken look on her face.

Susannah beamed. "Mom! Look! Look who's here!"

Tess reached the gate and grabbed the pickets with both hands. Her eyes flicked from the beaming child to Noah. They stayed fastened on him. "What are you doing here?"

"Meeting my daughter?" He twisted the word. He couldn't help it.

There was a certain bitter irony to the whole situation that he was sure he would appreciate—given, perhaps, a hundred years. Right now he was having trouble believing it—believing her.

How could she not have told him he had a daughter, for God's sake?

Tess fumbled with the latch, then got it open. She crossed the yard to put her arm around Susannah. "Go put on the milk and we'll have some cocoa."

"But—"

"Go on. Now."

She sounded like a stern mother. Hell, Noah realized, she *was* a stern mother.

"But I want—" Susannah pleaded. When she got a look even sterner than the voice, she turned reluctantly and headed toward the door.

She'd barely gone ten feet when Tess rounded on Noah. "I don't know why you're here," she said in a furious undertone, "but I want you to leave. Now."

"No."

"You have no business here!"

"Apparently I have a daughter here."

She swallowed. "So?"

"So?" He positively gaped at her. "I find that out and you expect me to hop back in a cab and go away?"

"Yes." It was a hiss.

He shook his head. Slowly. Adamantly. "No."

"Damn it, Noah—"

"Damn it, Tess," he said mildly. "I'm not leaving. Unless," he added, "you want to tell me she's wrong. Is she?"

Tess hesitated, as if she'd love to say yes, then sighed.

"No. She's not. But it doesn't matter," she said, meeting his gaze defiantly.

"What the hell do you mean, it doesn't matter?"

"She doesn't need you. She's done just fine for almost eight years without you. She can keep doing fine without you."

"Why should she?"

"What?" Tess looked at him, aghast.

Noah stuck his chin out. "Why should she do without me now that I know about her?" He wasn't exactly sure what he was proposing. He just knew he had less reason than ever to walk away.

Tess's mouth opened and closed. "Because," she said finally, in the same fierce undertone, "our lives are fine the way they are. We don't need you coming in and disrupting things. Invading our lives and then, whenever it suits you, disappearing again."

"You think that's what I'll do?"

"It's what you did." And with that she turned her back and started for the door. "Go away, Noah," she said over her shoulder. "I don't want you here."

"I do." Susannah's clear childish voice rang out in the stillness. Both of them jerked around to see her standing in the doorway, watching them. "I want him," she said to her mother. "I asked for him."

He could see them silhouetted in the living-room window, mother and daughter—Tess with her shoulders hunched, Susannah, chin lifted. Their mouths were moving. Noah would have given his championship buckle to know what they were saying. Tess had made him wait outside.

"Stay here," she'd commanded as she moved to follow her daughter into the house. Then she'd turned back. "Or don't. That would be even better."

Wild horses couldn't have dragged him away. He ought, he supposed, to be giving those wild horses a run for their money, trying to see how fast he could leave. But he was rooted to the spot. Stunned. Amazed.

Enchanted.

That pixie-faced child with the deep blue eyes was *his?*

Suddenly the silhouettes disappeared from view. The door opened. Tess came out onto the porch. She drew a deep breath, then came down the steps, her hands tucked into the pockets of her jacket. She planted her feet firmly, then looked up at him, resigned.

"Don't tell me I was on her Christmas list," Noah said lightly.

"Worse. She didn't ask Santa to bring you. She asked God. You are," Tess said, her mouth twisting in grim humor, "the answer to a prayer."

Tess supposed she was becoming a fatalist. How else could she accept the disaster that had just befallen her? How else could she simply open the door to her house and let Noah walk in, then act as if she didn't mind?

She minded. She just knew she couldn't do anything about it.

When her daughter had looked up at her with eyes so like Noah's and said in an aching voice, "Just once, Mom. I wanted him here just once. So I asked God. I thought if He made it happen, you wouldn't care," how on earth could she send him away?

So it was God's fault. There was no other explanation. Maybe God thought Susannah needed to see her father. Maybe God thought Noah needed to meet Susannah.

Tess knew hers was not to reason why. Hers was simply to cope.

Oh, but God, it's so hard, she said to the Almighty, lifting her eyes to the ceiling as she hopped out of her uniform slacks. *And so unfair. What are You thinking of?*

She didn't know if she'd get an answer. But if He'd heard Susannah, He could jolly well listen to her, too.

From the kitchen downstairs she could hear the faint murmur of Susannah's childish voice regaling Noah with heaven-knew-what indiscretion while they drank cocoa.

Tess hadn't known what else to do with him when he'd followed her into the house, so she'd made them cocoa, then hovered, hawklike, moving between the stove and the table where Noah and Susannah sat. Ready to swoop down on any untoward comment either of them made.

But then Susannah had said, "You're going to spill cocoa on your uniform, Mom," and she'd had no choice but to retreat to the bedroom and change into jeans and a sweater.

She was still hopping around on one foot when she heard them come up the stairs, then pass her room on their way to Susannah's.

Oh, heavens! Tess dragged her navy sweatshirt over her head and stuffed her feet into a pair of loafers. Then she hurried after them.

It was too late.

An hour ago he'd been in a beige motel room. Now he was in a whole new world. Noah felt as if he'd fallen down a rabbit hole or as if a phantom bronc had dropped him on his head.

Was he really sitting in Tess's kitchen drinking cocoa with his *daughter?*

Was she really telling him about her second-grade teacher? About the presents the Secret Santas in their class-room had exchanged? What the hell were Secret Santas, anyway? She acted like he ought to know. He pretended that he did.

He didn't know if he said anything coherent at all. If he didn't, Susannah didn't seem to mind.

When they finished their cocoa, she looked at him shyly and asked, "Want to see how I knew it was you?"

He nodded dumbly and followed her up the stairs, perusing as much of Tess's house as he could on the way.

It wasn't large, but it was cozy, with the same homey atmosphere he remembered from her apartment eight years ago. The living room had a raised-hearth fireplace and two six-over-six windows that looked out over the snowy front yard. The sofa was covered in a muted plaid, and there was a rather worn armchair near the fireplace, an afghan tossed over the back. On the other side of the hearth sat a pressed-oak rocker, similar to one he remembered his mother having. The kitchen was painted white with dark green trim and had a green-and-white latticework wallpaper. Tess had arranged copper teakettles of all shapes and sizes on a shelf near the ceiling. As they went up the stairs, Noah saw a row of pictures of Susannah, from infancy to, he presumed, second grade.

The house was warm and welcoming, and none of it was beige. Noah liked that a lot.

He caught a glimpse of what must be Tess's bedroom as Susannah led him past. "This is mine," she said, pushing open the last door. "See?" She pointed toward her bedside table.

On it were three pictures. The first was a recent one of Susannah and Tess in a boat in the summertime, laughing as they looked at each other. Next to it was a slightly faded snapshot in a silver frame of a much-younger Noah and Tess, their arms around each other. He was smiling at the camera and Tess was smiling at him. Noah's attention was arrested for a moment by the innocence he saw in her face—an innocence no longer there.

He turned away and looked at the third picture. It was a photo of him. A fairly recent one, taken at a rodeo. He was sweaty and grinning and being presented with a buckle.

"It's from when you won Cheyenne," Susannah said.

He blinked, startled. "Cheyenne? Last summer?" He braced himself on one crutch and picked up the small framed picture to study it. Then he looked at Susannah. "You were there?"

"I asked Mom if we could go. I wanted to see who you were."

"Why didn't you… " *introduce yourself?* he wanted to ask. *Tell me who you were?* He shook his head, dazed.

"Mom didn't think we should bother you," Susannah said in a small voice.

"Not bother me?" He stared at her.

She gave an awkward shrug. "She was afraid you might not want to know me and I'd get hurt."

"She thought I wouldn't want to know my own daughter?"

"She said…well, she didn't think I should get my hopes up. But she took me. We watched. You were *amazing.*" Her eyes seemed to almost light up at the memory.

"But if you were there, why didn't you come back by the chutes?"

"Mom said it wouldn't be fair, surprising you like that. We saw you in the midway after and I was going to, but…"

"But what?"

"You were throwing baseballs and you won a stuffed cat," she said almost desperately. "You gave it to this red-haired lady with a little boy." She swallowed and looked up at him, her gaze haunted. "Is he…yours?"

"Susannah!" Tess appeared in the doorway. Her hair

was tousled, her sweatshirt askew. Her gaze went worriedly from Noah to her daughter and back again.

Noah glanced at her, then at Susannah. He shook his head. "No, he's not," he said, realizing what she'd thought. "That was Jared. My nephew."

Tanner and Maggie had brought the boys down for the last weekend of the Cheyenne rodeo. They'd been there to see him win, and afterward they'd gone down the midway. Noah's luck had held even there. He'd won a toy for Jared and, later on, two more for the twins, though Tanner had already taken them back to the motel for a nap. He'd been in his element that day, playing with the boys, having a ball. And his own daughter had been just feet away!

"Jared's your cousin," he told her as the realization hit him.

Susannah sighed with something that could have been relief. "I thought he was yours."

"I don't have any kids." He paused. "Except you."

Tess drew in a sharp breath. He gave her a defiant look, and set the picture down firmly on the table, positioning it so Susannah could see it first thing in the morning.

"Do you mind?" Susannah asked timidly. "Having me, I mean."

A man could drown in the pure, clear innocence of those eyes. Blue eyes. *His* eyes. Noah shook his head slowly. "No, Susannah. I don't mind at all."

In Tess's dreams, the three of them had sat around the kitchen table like this—as a family—sharing the day's happenings, planning the evening's events.

Sometimes, when Susannah was little, she had even pretended that Noah was there to share in feeding their daughter her mashed banana and tiny, cut-up bits of chicken. Tess would glance up and imagine what it would be like to have him smile at her when Susannah did something silly. She would think how she would feel if he put his arm around her and gave her a kiss as, together, they shared their delight in their growing daughter.

And now, against all odds—and against not only her wishes, but her better judgment—here he was.

Tess looked away. "Eat your carrots, Susannah," she said sharply.

Susannah scowled. "You know I hate them," she said. "Do you hate them?" she asked Noah.

He did. Tess remembered that. But tonight he shook his head. "Nope," he said, and stabbed three, sticking them into his mouth and chewing manfully. Tess couldn't help smiling just a little.

"Love 'em. Good casserole, too," he said when he'd swallowed.

"We were going to have leftover roast," she told him bluntly. "But there wasn't enough for three."

"Sorry." But he didn't sound repentant. "I like this. I don't get a lot of casseroles on the road. It's fast food and junk mostly. Or steak."

"I like steak," Susannah told him. "But Mom says it's too expensive."

"We can go to the store later," Noah offered. "I'll buy groceries."

"I have enough money," Tess told him flatly. "I don't need your help."

"It's not help. It's sharing. I'm not here to freeload. I never did. You know that."

She did. Even nearly broke eight years ago, Noah had done his best to pay his own way. "You don't have to," she said now.

"We'll split it," he said. "How's that?"

Knowing that more argument would be futile, Tess muttered agreement into her applesauce.

"Steak," Susannah said happily. "And then we can get the tree." She turned to Noah. "You can help us pick it."

Tess wanted to say no. She couldn't, and she knew it. But, God, she protested silently, how much it hurt to have your prayers answered when you'd stopped praying!

Tess fixed her daughter with a hard stare. "We're not going anywhere, Susannah Marie, unless you eat every one of those carrots."

Grumbling, Susannah did. Then Tess washed the dishes and Noah dried them. She didn't want him to do that, either. She wanted him to leave her in peace. But if she said so, he'd go into the living room with Susannah, and she wanted that least of all! So when he asked for a dish towel, she gave him one and tried not to brush against his shirt-sleeve with her elbow as she washed.

While they were doing the dishes, Susannah fed the cat. It was a long-haired, orange-marmalade tom that Susannah had found by the back door after a late-spring snowfall. They'd ignored it for several days, but it kept prowling around until finally Susannah prevailed upon Tess to let her feed it. Since then it had been part of their lives.

"What's its name?" Noah asked.

"Noah," Susannah replied, grinning.

Tess dropped a glass in the sink. "Damn!" Her face was burning as she tried to fish the broken glass out of the soapy water. She could feel his gaze on her.

"Noah?" He said his name with quiet speculation.

"I could call him something else while you're here," Susannah offered.

But Noah shook his head. He hunkered down carefully and scratched the cat behind the ears, then looked up at Susannah. "Did you name him after me?"

"Uh-huh," said Susannah.

At the same time, Tess blurted, "Not really."

"Because he was a stray," Susannah went on earnestly, while Tess wished the floor would open and swallow her up. "Mom said it was a good name because we couldn't count on him sticking around."

Noah's eyes turned to Tess. His smile faded.

Serves you right, Tess thought grimly as she dared to meet his gaze. In the stillness, Noah-the-cat purred madly and rubbed his head against Noah-the-cowboy's leg.

"But he's still here," Susannah said after a moment into the tense silence. "And it's been two years." Tess could almost see wheels turning in her daughter's head.

"Because he knows a pair of suckers when he sees them," Tess said flatly. "Right, cat?"

"Because he loves us," Susannah contradicted her stoutly. Her gaze went from the cat to her father.

Tess smothered a groan. She dropped the broken glass into the trash. "I think it's time we went looking for that tree."

Tess had a five-year-old Ford Bronco, a good snow car. Susannah climbed into the back. After stowing his crutches, Noah settled in front. Tess drove. No one spoke until they were inside the grocery store. Then Noah watched and listened as Tess and Susannah discussed the week's grocery purchases.

"What kind of cereal do you like?" Susannah asked him at one point "I like this—" she held up a colorful sugared variety "—but Mom says it isn't good for me. It has the same vitamins as the other stuff. I told her that, but she won't believe me. Do you believe me?"

"I didn't say it didn't have the same vitamins," Tess

said firmly. "I said it isn't as good for your teeth. Put it back, Suse."

Susannah looked at Noah beseechingly. Noah looked at her mother. It wasn't hard to read Tess's expression: *buck me on this and you're outa here.*

"It's a little too sweet," he told Susannah.

Her face fell. "But it's Christmas," she argued in a last-ditch effort.

"We don't get *everything* we want at Christmas," Tess said. "And you, young lady, have gotten quite enough." She turned then and pushed the cart briskly down the aisle.

Susannah hung back to walk with Noah. "She's not always this crabby," the little girl confided. "Usually she's pretty nice."

"Yeah," Noah said wistfully. "I know."

If he wasn't much use in the grocery store, he was even less so when it came to putting the bags in the car. By the time he navigated through the ever-deepening snow and stowed his crutches, then turned to help, Tess had the bags already loaded in the back and was waiting for him to get in.

Tess handled the Bronco easily through the accumulating snow. But as they slid when they came to a stoplight, Noah flinched, the memories of the trailer all too vivid.

Tess glanced over. "Sorry about that. Are you okay?" And for the first time he heard the soft note of concern in her voice that he remembered from eight years before.

"Yeah. Sure." He shrugged and tried to pretend his heart wasn't slamming against the wall of his chest. "Just a little skittish, I guess."

"Taggart said you saw it coming?"

"Uh-huh. Scared me sh—a lot."

Susannah leaned forward. "What scared you?"

"I was in a car accident. That's why I've got crutches."

Her eyes got big. "I thought you got that from riding a bronc. What happened?"

He told her briefly, glossing over the gorier bits as her eyes got wider and wider and her worried expression grew. Her lower lip trembled and she ran her tongue over it. "You're...you're not gonna die or anything, are you?"

"I'm not gonna die."

She seemed to breathe a little easier, but she still regarded him with obvious concern. Her hand crept up between the seats to clutch his. He turned farther around in the seat and gave her a smile.

"I'm fine, Susannah," he said again as Tess pulled the Bronco alongside a lot filled with Christmas trees. "I've never been better." And he was surprised to find that it was true. He'd stopped feeling sorry for himself somewhere around the time he'd discovered he was a father. He hadn't had a second to bemoan his fate since. Now he didn't want to.

He climbed out and leaned on his crutches, watching as Susannah, reassured, forgot all about him and ran into the forest of Christmas trees, scanning them for the perfect one.

Tess came around the car slowly, as if she expected him to jump down her throat the moment he got her alone.

Probably she did. And a part of him wanted to. Every time he stopped to think about Susannah, he wanted to rage at Tess. How could she have kept it from him? he demanded silently. Another part of him knew the fault was entirely his.

In any case, they could hardly discuss it now.

Noah drew a deep breath and let it out slowly. "She's beautiful," he said. They stood side by side, not touching. Noah could see Tess's hands jammed into the pockets of her down jacket. Snowflakes dusted her hair and turned to silver drops of moisture on her long dark lashes. Under the lights of the Christmas-tree lot, he could see the color in her cheeks, blurring her freckles into a rosy gold. Susannah wasn't the only one who was beautiful, he thought, tightening his own hands into fists as he resisted the urge to touch her.

Tess nodded, a faint smile lighting her face. "She is."

Susannah popped out from between two trees, waving wildly. "Come look at this one!"

"If it's hard for you to walk, you can wait in the car," Tess said.

One of Noah's crutches skidded on an icy patch. He didn't care. He wouldn't have missed this for the world.

"You're right, it's lovely," Tess was saying to Susannah when he finally reached them. It was an eight-foot tree, thick and well-formed and bushy. A perfect tree, as far as Noah could see. "But it's too big."

Susannah's face fell. "Why? Why is it too big?"

"We'd have to cut off three feet to get it on the table—"

"We don't need a table. Why can't we get a floor tree? We always have one of those little-bitty trees." Susannah looked up at her mother pleadingly.

Tess brushed a hand over Susannah's dark hair. "Little-bitty trees need families to love them, too."

Susannah's lower lip jutted out. "I know. But we've loved *lots* of little trees. Please, Mommy! Just this year?" She looked at her mother beseechingly, then turned to Noah. "Don't *you* think it's great?"

"It's great," Noah agreed.

Tess shot him a dirty look. "Suse, it's beautiful. I know that. But we can't af—" She stopped, biting off what she'd intended to say. "We just can't," she said flatly.

Susannah's small shoulders slumped. She kicked at the snow with the toe of one of her white, fur-topped boots. "I know," she mumbled.

Noah didn't have much trouble hearing what neither of them was saying: it was a great tree, but it was too expensive. But he knew Tess was damned if she was going to say that in front of him.

He could afford the tree—hell, this year he could afford a dozen tress—but he knew better than to offer. He glanced around for an alternative.

"*I'm* buying the tree," Tess said to him through gritted teeth in a tone pitched too softly for Susannah to hear.

"Fine, you buy the tree," Noah agreed. "What about that one?" He nodded toward an even taller tree that was full and bushy on one side, but had a rather obvious bare spot on the other. "It's not perfect," he said before Susannah could point that out, "but it's big. And if we put that side in the corner…" He deliberately didn't look at Tess.

He heard her draw a breath as if she might argue, but then she let it out again and didn't say a word.

Susannah, too, started to say something, then stopped. She approached the tree cautiously, as if getting too close might be a mistake. She wasn't smiling, but she did seem intrigued. Noah left Tess standing where she was and hobbled over to stand by Susannah. She was looking at the tree thoughtfully.

"You think they might sell it for less 'cause it's got this hole?" She slanted a glance up at him.

"I think they might. Want me to ask?"

She glanced over at her mother. Some imperceptible communication passed between mother and daughter. Then Susannah looked back up at him. "Yes."

Noah went to find the owner. He frankly didn't care if the guy wanted more—it was going to look like less, Tess was going to save face and Susannah was going to have her tree.

The owner, however, took one look at the tree and

agreed. "Be nice to give this one a good home," he said, as he carried it to the car for them. He even provided a couple of stout pieces of twine, which Noah used to lash it on top of the Bronco while Tess took out her billfold and paid.

Susannah bounced excitedly all the way home. "We got a floor tree! We got a floor tree!" she chanted over and over.

Tess didn't say a word. When they got to the house, Susannah helped her carry the tree into the house. Noah limped along behind on his crutches and hoped he'd done the right thing.

It didn't take long to find out. Once the tree was up and turned properly, its top nearly brushing the ceiling, Susannah's eyes sparkled and her smile seemed to cover her whole face. It didn't matter that there was a hole in the back. It didn't matter that the trunk was the slightest bit crooked.

"Come look, Mommy!" she yelled.

And when Tess came to the doorway from the kitchen, Susannah said, "Look! It's the biggest, most beautiful tree in the world!"

Tess looked at the tree, then at her daughter and, finally, at Noah. Did her gaze soften at all or was he dreaming it? "So it is," she said. "So it is."

Susannah didn't want to go to sleep. She wanted to decorate the tree.

"Tomorrow," Tess said firmly when the little girl was in pajamas and slippers and still pleading. She'd had enough for one day.

"All of us?" Susannah asked, her gaze flickering to Noah, who has been sitting at the kitchen table nursing a cup of coffee Tess had given him to drink while she supervised Susannah's getting ready for bed. She didn't need him hovering there, too.

"What?" Tess said, distracted even now by his presence.

"Can we all decorate it?" Susannah repeated. "You an' me an'..." Her voice faded as she looked hopefully at her father. It was as if she thought that once she shut her eyes, Noah would disappear.

Tess drew a deep breath and squelched the wish that he would. "Yes," she said, "all of us."

Susannah nodded. "That's all right then." She looked at Noah. "Will you tuck me in?"

Her request made him sit up straight, and Tess saw his fingers tighten on the coffee mug. "Tuck you in?" His gaze met Tess's. He looked apprehensive.

Good, she thought. She hoped he'd say no. He didn't.

"Sure," he said, and carefully pushed himself to his feet. "I'd like that."

Susannah beamed as he led the way into the hall and up the steps. She stopped at the doorway. "You, too, Mommy."

Tess hesitated. She didn't want to. Oh Lord, she didn't want to. It would be another dream laid low by reality— she and Noah together at their daughter's bedside.

But Susannah was waiting, and it was a ritual. Tess swallowed, then nodded her head.

Susannah beat them both to her room. She'd already scrambled into her bed, her small mouth curving into a satisfied smile as she looked from one parent to the other. Then she held out a hand to Noah. Awkwardly, he took it. She held out the other to her mother. Tess wrapped the small fingers in her own.

Susannah gave a satisfied sigh. "Good."

"Good night," Tess said firmly, and bent to drop a kiss on her daughter's mouth. Small, strong arms went around her neck, tugging her down so Susannah could give her a smacking kiss. "Night, Mommy." The look of pure, impish joy in her daughter's eyes made Tess's throat tighten.

"Sweet dreams, sweetheart," she whispered. *Don't let him hurt her,* she prayed. *Please don't let him hurt her.* Then she loosed her hand and stepped back as her daughter turned to Noah.

He looked as serious as she could ever remember seeing him. Tess wondered if he had any inkling what having a daughter meant. Did he even have a clue about the joys and the pains, the comforts and the responsibilities of parenting such a marvelous child?

Of course he didn't. He couldn't. He'd only known of her existence for a few short hours. He knew nothing about children at all.

But now that he knew about Susannah, what would he do?

An evening, a meal, a hunt for a Christmas tree were all well and good, but they meant nothing in the long run.

Of course, tomorrow he would still be here. He'd promised. So had she.

But after?

It didn't take a mind reader to know that Susannah wanted him forever.

Noah? Forever?

How likely was that?

Still, Tess's heart squeezed inside her chest when she saw him smile a little crookedly as he looked down at the little girl. "Night, Susannah," he said softly.

She took his hand again and tugged on it, pulling him toward her. He went down on one knee, oddly shy and rather clumsy, Tess thought, though it could have been because of his injuries.

He bent his head. And then he touched his lips to hers.

It was a sweet kiss. Gentle. Tender. A father's kiss.

Tess's eyes brimmed.

It was over in scant seconds. She saw a shudder ripple down Noah's spine as he drew back and started to stand. But Susannah's hand came up and held him still. Her fingers brushed against the day's growth of whiskers on his cheek, lingering for a moment. Then she smiled again. The look she gave Noah was one of such complete trust and childlike faith that Tess's heart wrenched in her chest.

"I knew you'd come," Susannah said.

Four

Neither of them spoke as they left Susannah's room. Neither said a word all the way back down the hall, down the stairs and into the living room. But both of them knew what was next.

It was the moment of reckoning—the first time in eight years that all the cards were on the table.

Noah thanked God at least he knew what game they were playing for a change, even though he still didn't have a clue where to begin. But if, as Susannah thought, God was involved in this, He'd provide the clues.

But He hadn't by the time they reached the living room, and there was nowhere else to go. God might be there, but He sure wasn't taking sides or directing the scene.

So it was up to him and Tess.

She stood in the doorway, looking at him with a gaze that combined apprehension and belligerence. With her feet slightly apart and her fingers curled at her sides, she reminded him of a mother bear ready to defend her cub.

And damn it all, a part of Noah wanted to attack her! He wanted to shake her and demand to know what she'd thought she was doing, keeping Susannah a secret from him all these years!

The saner, more rational part of him knew exactly what she'd been doing—showing good sense.

As much as it pained him to admit it even to himself—*especially* to himself—he knew exactly what had motivated her; and he knew she'd been right. He'd been no more ready to be a father eight years ago than he'd been to be a husband. He'd have made a mess of all three of their lives if she'd given him the chance.

He knew it. But knowing and accepting the truth of it didn't make it any easier to bear. He muttered an expletive under his breath.

"Well, too damn bad," Tess snapped, misunderstanding completely the source of his disgust. She slapped her hands on her hips. "I realize this isn't what you had in mind when you showed up on my doorstep. I suppose all you really wanted was a roll in the hay. Well, sorry, fella, you got a daughter instead."

"I don't—"

"A daughter doesn't exactly fit into your lifestyle, does she?" Tess went on without giving him a chance to protest. "Well, too bad, buddy boy. That's life!" Her eyes flashed. She glared. "And you have only yourself to blame. If you hadn't come nosing around, you wouldn't even know. God knows, I tried to keep it from you. I tried to protect you! And her," she added heavily after a moment.

All her flash and fire vanished as suddenly as it had come, leaving her burned out and weary looking. Tess sighed and rubbed a hand over her eyes, looking lonelier and sadder than Noah had ever seen her.

An odd, tight feeling grabbed at his chest. "You shouldn't have," he said gruffly. "Tried to protect me, I mean."

"You think it would have been better to have told you?" Her tone clearly told him she did not.

He shoved a hand through his hair, ruffling it. "I might've been worth somethin' to you. I could've helped you financially, at least."

"I didn't want your help. Not after—" She stopped.

"After what?"

"After your phone call. Surely you remember it? The one where you said, 'Oh, by the way, I'm never coming back'?"

"You knew? You knew then?"

"It had been two months!"

"I know! But I— Hell. You must've hated me."

"It would've been easier."

He looked at her closely. "Why didn't you just tell me? Blurt it out? I deserved it."

"Maybe. But we didn't."

He had the grace to flush. He stared at his boot tops, feeling lower than a cow pie, more incompetent than a newborn colt. "I could've helped," he said finally, desperately.

"I managed without your help." Her gaze flickered around their comfortable, albeit somewhat worn, surroundings, and she lifted her chin. "Susannah didn't do without anything important."

"Just her father."

"Damn you! You didn't want me! Why would you have wanted her?"

"I didn't mean it like that. I didn't, really. I'm sorry, Tess. It just...just came out." He moved toward her. When she backed up, he stopped where he was. "You're right. I can see she's fine. You've done fine. It's just that—" he sighed "—hell, I don't know. I never expected this."

In the Teflon days of his youth, his actions had never had consequences. At least, he hadn't thought so. Clearly he'd been wrong. Noah turned his back on her and limped to the far end of the room, needing air, space; feeling as if the walls were coming in on him. He muttered under his breath again, turned too quickly, tripped and almost fell.

"You ought to sit down," Tess said automatically.

"Before I fall down, you mean?" he said wryly.

She didn't smile, but her expression softened slightly. "Yes."

She was right. His leg was killing him. Leaning on the crutches for any length of time made his elbow and shoulder ache. Doing without them was dangerous as hell. So he sat. He slumped back against the couch and closed his eyes. He tried to think of what to say, what to do. All his mind could manage was replaying for the hundredth time the moment of revelation he'd had that afternoon. He could still see Susannah as she'd looked making the snowman when he'd arrived. Could still see the dark-haired, anonymous child he'd thought might be Tess's niece.

He shook his head, then opened his eyes. "That's why you were avoiding me all the time at the hospital."

She hesitated, then nodded.

"Would you ever have told me?"

"Maybe. Someday." She walked to the fireplace and picked up the glass snow globe on the mantel, staring into its swirling whiteness. "Susannah could have told you herself when she was grown—if she wanted to."

"Would you have told me in Cheyenne...if you hadn't seen me in the midway?"

Her knuckles whitened on the globe. ''She wanted to go. I didn't.''

''She told me that, too. Would you?'' he persisted

''I...I don't know.''

''You thought Maggie was my wife?''

Tess didn't reply. She was looking at the globe again, but he saw her nod almost imperceptibly.

''Was that the other reason you didn't say anything this past week?''

Another faint nod.

''You thought I'd be coming on to you if I was married?''

''I didn't think! I didn't want to think!'' She almost slammed the globe back on the mantel and spun to face him. ''I didn't let myself think,'' she amended flatly. ''I tried my best not to think about you at all.''

The silence that followed was broken only by the snap and crack of the fire. Noah-the-cat came into the living room and wound through Tess's ankles, purring. Noah could hear him clear across the room.

''Tess,'' he said quietly, ''you gotta know I didn't mean to hurt you. It isn't that I didn't want to come back. I did. But it wouldn't have worked. You know that. I couldn't stay. I just—just...would've left you again. And again.''

''I know. As you reminded me, you never made any promises.'' She shrugged. ''But I was young and foolish, and I simply couldn't keep from hoping.''

The look on her face sent a knife right through him.

''I was trying—this time—not to be old and foolish,'' she said quietly. ''For Susannah's sake mostly, but also for my own.''

''I won't hurt you again,'' he promised.

For a long moment Tess just looked at him. ''No. You

won't," she said. "Because I won't let you. But I can't prevent you from hurting Susannah."

"You can't think I'd do anything to hurt her!"

"I don't see how you can help it. I mean, here you are—" Tess's mouth twisted "—the answer to her prayer. And I know Suse well enough to know that it won't stop there. She'll be praying for you to stay. I know she will. And then what'll happen?"

I'll stay, Noah wanted to say. But he knew better than to promise such a thing. Hell, he hadn't stayed anywhere for longer than two weeks since he'd turned eighteen. He looked at Tess helplessly. "I don't know."

Tess sighed. She sagged into the lumpy armchair and hauled the cat up onto her lap. "I don't know, either," she said. She didn't look at him. Instead, she sat watching her fingers scratch behind the cat's ears.

A log shifted in the grate. The flames flickered, then ebbed to a low orange glow. Noah stared at it, then at Tess. He shoved his hands into the pockets of his jeans. Then he tipped his head back and shut his eyes.

If he'd given any thought to how he and Tess might spend their first evening together in over eight years, he'd thought in terms of a little apologizing, followed by a little cuddling, a little kissing and then—with the best of cowboy luck—a little making up for lost time.

He'd never, ever, imagined them sitting at opposite ends of the living room, each absorbed in thought, neither sure exactly how to deal with the other—or with the daughter who inextricably bound them.

"Is he still here?"

"Shh. Yes, of course he's still here."

"In your bedroom?"

"Shh. Yes, in my bedroom. It's where I put Uncle Philip and Aunt Nancy."

"Did you *sleep* with him?"

"Shh! No, I did not!"

"Oh."

Tess didn't have to shush her this time. All the eagerness, all the enthusiasm, all the awe and hope that Noah had heard in Susannah's voice died in that one small word.

Noah rolled carefully onto his side so he could see whatever was visible through the thin crack of light that shone from the hallway outside the room Tess had given him for the night. He had protested that he could sleep on the couch. He—unlike Susannah—had had no illusions that they might share Tess's bed.

"No," she'd said quite firmly. "I want you in there. It will keep you out of the way."

Put like that, how could he refuse?

Now he saw an eye pressed against the crack in the door. He winked at it.

"He's awake!" Susannah started to open the door.

It banged soundly shut again. "Enough," he heard Tess say fiercely. "You can not just barge in on company."

"He's not company. He's my father!" Susannah argued.

"He's still company," Tess said.

And damned well going to stay that way, Noah heard unspoken but all too loud and clear in Tess's tone.

Then her voice softened slightly. "He doesn't—I mean, no one likes being bothered when they just wake up, Suse."

"But—"

"You can see him when he gets up. Now leave him in peace and come eat your breakfast."

"But—" But Susannah, still managing feeble protests, was apparently hauled away.

Noah rolled onto his back, shoved himself up against the

headboard of Tess's bed and smiled. Why? Because he knew what she'd intended to say before she'd caught herself. *He doesn't like getting up in the morning. He's a grouch. A regular pain in the neck.*

And she would know. Oh yes, she would know. She'd teased him about it often enough. And she remembered, too. Even if she didn't want to.

Noah's smile widened.

Tess's bed was a full-size double, but just barely. It was not the sort of bed that gave the notion she spent much time in it—or did anything other than sleep when she was there. He wasn't surprised.

He *was* pleased, and that did surprise him.

He'd never given much thought to what the women he'd known had done when they weren't doing it with him. But he found he was gratified to discover that Tess, at least in her own bed, very likely hadn't been doing much of anything.

Her room was, in fact, only slightly less austere than a nun's room would be. A utilitarian, old oak dresser, chosen, he was sure, because of its functionality and not its antique value, stood against the far wall. There was a walk-in closet barely big enough for a child of Susannah's size to turn around in. And beside the bed, she had placed a small table on which there was a digital alarm clock, a rather battered paperback Tony Hillerman mystery and a framed snapshot of a somewhat-younger Susannah riding high on a playground swing, dark hair flying in the breeze. No pictures of him.

Curiously and unjustifiably, he felt nettled. Had he wanted her pining after him for eight years, for God's sake? He hadn't pined after her. Not after the first few months, anyway. Other than a momentary twinge every time he came close to Laramie, months would go by without him thinking of her.

He knew she'd remembered him every single day. And, he thought grimly, she hadn't needed a picture to do it.

Had she resented Susannah's entrance into her life? Certainly she hadn't wanted a baby. Not then, anyway. And certainly not under those circumstances. She'd been almost finished with her nurse's training when they'd met. She'd had grand notions of going on for an academic degree, perhaps even a master's, and then teaching.

Obviously she wasn't teaching. He wondered if she'd been able to realize any of her plans with a child to support.

Guilt washed over him once more. Damn it, she should have asked him for help!

Yeah, right, his more rational side responded. You were making such big bucks in those days. Eight years ago he'd barely been breaking even on the circuit. Gasoline and other traveling expenses, not to mention the fees he paid to compete, had eaten virtually all of his meager earnings.

Only in the last five years had he begun to see a bit of daylight in the profit department. If Tess had asked him for money in the early days, well, he'd have had to give up rodeoing, that was certain.

And then there would have been two of them who'd lost the chance to pursue their dreams.

The enormity of how much he owed her was borne in on him again.

Then, hearing Susannah's childish giggle downstairs, he realized that though he'd had his freedom, he'd lost something, too. And as much as he'd have liked to, he couldn't blame Tess for denying him. Not when he'd denied her first.

He sighed and hauled himself out of bed, pulling on a clean pair of jeans, then hobbling toward the bathroom to

...e. When he finished, he stood staring at his reflection ... the mirror, looking for signs of fatherhood, maturity, responsibility. It wasn't promising.

Susannah was sitting at the table, eating a bowl of oatmeal, and Tess was taking pieces of toast out of the toaster. Both of them looked up when he came into the kitchen. Susannah grinned. Tess turned away.

"I didn't think you were ever getting up. Did you see all the snow?" Susannah asked him, all eager enthusiasm. She shoved her chair back and went to the window, pointing. "Look."

Obediently Noah looked. There was at least a foot of snow on the ground and it was still coming down.

Susannah looked at him hopefully. "Want to help me make another snowman?"

"Noah's hurt," Tess said without turning around.

"I reckon I could manage a little helping," Noah said.

"After breakfast?"

"Libby's coming over to play after breakfast," Tess said. She was talking to the toast. "She and Jeff, so their mom can go do some Christmas shopping."

"They can help, too." Susannah shrugged her shoulders. "Libby's eight. She lives next door," she told Noah. "You don't care, do you? Her dad lets me do things with them sometimes," she added.

"I don't mind," he said. "That's fine. I'd like to meet her." *And her father,* he thought, feeling a vague resentment toward any man who habitually did things with his daughter.

Tess gave him an irritated look. He met it levelly. He knew she thought he was just saying what Susannah wanted to hear. Tess herself didn't want to hear that he actually was eager to meet Susannah's friend.

But he was. He was curious about a lot of things. Susannah's friend was simply one of them.

Tess set a plate of toast in front of him on the table. "Sit down and eat."

She looked tired, as if she hadn't slept any better than he had. He wanted to reach out and touch her, soothe her the way he knew he could. But he knew better.

Instead he nodded and sat down at the table across from Susannah. "Thanks."

"Then later we can decorate the tree," Susannah went on. If she was aware of the undercurrents in the room, she gave no sign. "Mommy makes cookies to hang on it," she told Noah. "Snowmen and Santas and angels and stuff. An' I've got the ornaments my aunt Nancy sends me. You wanta see 'em?" She was halfway out of her chair when Tess pressed a hand on her shoulder.

"Finish your breakfast. You can show him later."

"But—"

"You can show me later," Noah assured her around a mouthful of toast.

Susannah settled back in her chair. "'Cause you're gonna be here," she said with satisfaction.

They had barely finished breakfast when there was a knock on the door. Tess opened it, and a girl about Susannah's age came in.

"This is Libby," Susannah said. "This," she told Libby, "is Noah."

Libby blinked. "Noah? *The* Noah?" Obviously he'd been the topic of discussion in the past. Noah shifted uncomfortably under the girl's scrutiny. "Your...father?"

Susannah nodded, smiling all over her face. "My father."

Libby's eyes got saucer size as she stared at Noah. He smiled at her. Her eyes got even wider. She looked from

Susannah. "You did it," she said to her friend, her ~~an~~ awed, hushed whisper. "How?"

Susannah shrugged. "Dunno for sure. I was makin' a snowman an' a taxi brought him."

"Wow."

Tess clattered the cereal pot in the sink. "Oh, for heaven's sake. He was just getting out of the hospital and he needed someplace to go. Susannah, hurry up and finish your breakfast. Libby, where's Jeff?"

"He went to Mark's. Aren'tcha glad? I am. Mom says she'll be back by noon if you can stand me that long."

"We'll see," Tess said dryly.

Susannah slurped the milk out of her cereal bowl and carried it to the sink. "He's gonna help us with the snowman," she told Libby, tipping her head in Noah's direction. "But we gotta be careful of him 'cause, like Mom said, he just got out of the hospital and he's still sorta hurt."

Libby glanced shyly at Noah once more, then nodded.

Susannah hovered by his arm. "So will you be ready soon?" she asked.

"Don't pester," Tess said, trying to fish a piece of toast out of the toaster.

Susannah sighed, but then grabbed Libby's arm and hauled her toward the bedroom. "Come on," she said. As they disappeared, Noah heard her telling Libby, "Last night he helped us get a tree. An'," she added confidentially, "he slept in my mom's bed."

"Damn it!" Tess dropped the burned toast and popped blistered fingers into her mouth. She glared at Noah. "It's not funny!"

"Am I laughing?"

"You're smiling," she accused him.

"Sorry." He ran a hand down his face in an unsuccessful attempt to wipe off the grin. "C'mon, Tess," he said, pushing himself to his feet and moving back from the table. "You gotta admit there is a humorous element to it."

She turned away. "Maybe to you."

He hobbled over to her, cornering her between the refrigerator and the cabinets. "Hey," he said softly, touching her arm, turning her so that, even though she momentarily resisted, she finally faced him. "It's gonna be okay. She's not implying anything. At least I don't think she is—or not what you're thinking, anyway. Don't take everything so seriously. She's just a kid."

"She's *my* kid. And yours," she added grimly. "And she wants things she can't have!"

"So, she'll learn. We all do."

Tess tried to shrug away from him. "Easy for you to say. You're not going to be here to pick up the pieces."

"You think I'm going to stay around till Christmas, then just disappear?"

"You did before."

Her words stung, but he kept his face impassive. "I called."

"And said you weren't coming back."

"You could've told me."

"Why should I have when you clearly didn't want to be bothered?"

He pressed his lips together, but didn't answer. There was no answer, and they both knew it.

"Anyway, I didn't want you." She did push past him then, picking up the milk carton and opening the refrigerator door. "I still don't."

Her words hurt. And it didn't even help much to know she was lying. He wondered if she knew it. He wanted her to. "Don't you?" He challenged her softly, a brow arching as he looked at her. He remembered the kiss in the hospital and knew from the flame of color in her cheeks that she was remembering it, too.

Tess shut her eyes. He saw her fists clench at her sides. She drew a careful breath. "Don't do this," she said. The pain on her face was clear. "Please. Don't."

It was another one of her dreams—to stand in the window and watch Susannah and her father playing together in the snow.

Noah wasn't much good at rolling snowballs into body parts. Tess could tell that his ribs didn't like all that bending over. And his crutches didn't provide the best support on ice, either. Words of warning rose in her throat several times, but she wouldn't go to the door and say something. It was none of her business, after all.

Certainly Noah didn't move as easily as the girls did, but even when he wasn't helping, he stood watching Susannah and her friend as they labored, their cheeks turning bright red as they scampered around the small yard. He seemed enchanted, his gaze rapt as he leaned on his crutches, smiling, the ever-present wind tousling his dark hair and putting color back in his lean cheeks. He was still the handsomest man she'd ever seen.

Tess turned away. She was going to make cookie dough this morning, then chill it enough so they could cut out cookies this afternoon. She had no time to stand at the window gawking.

Somehow, she couldn't help herself. She was mixing sugar and eggs, flour and baking soda, butter and orange rind and mace. But she was moving back and forth from the table to the window as she did so. Checking on Susannah, she told herself. Keeping an eye on Libby, like a good baby-sitter should. What else?

She noticed that the girls were a little shy at first when

they discovered that Noah couldn't do much in the way of helping. They became rather self-conscious, slanting him wary glances, but not speaking to him.

But then, when the snowman was finished, they started throwing snowballs at it and at each other. It was only a matter of time until Libby's poor aim made Noah part of the action.

One moment he was standing there watching, and the next he got a fat, sloppy snowball square in the chest.

"Oh!" Susannah shrieked, clapping her hand over her mouth.

Both girls stopped dead and looked at him nervously.

They looked so terrified that Tess saw Noah grin. She remembered that grin—the hint that devilish mischief was about to befall someone. Slowly he scraped the snow off his jacket and began shaping it into a smaller, but still good-size, ball.

Neither girl moved. Then, taking careful aim, the grin spreading across his face as he did so, he threw the snowball at Susannah.

It hit her lightly on the top of her fuzzy pompom cap, and a cascade of wet snow dripped onto her lashes.

She giggled. She shook her head and wiped the snow off her face. Then, giving him a look filled with purely feminine wiles, she scooped up a ball of snow and flung it back.

The fight was on.

The odds were against him, and Tess was sure he knew it. Two bright-eyed, healthy, rambunctious grade-school girls were more than a match for a gimpy-legged, cracked-ribbed man, even one in his prime. But still, he gave, if not as good as he got, as good as he could. And Tess, because she was alone, was free to enjoy the spectacle. She rooted for the girls, giggling when one of them hit him on the back of the head with a large, fluffy ball that sent a cascade of snow down inside his jacket.

Tess laughed as she saw him squirm, then bend to scoop some more snow. He might have even held his own if his crutch hadn't slipped. But when he tried to catch himself, he twisted, skidded and landed flat on his back.

"Mom!"

"Ms. Montgom'ry!"

"Ma! Come quick!"

But they didn't have to say a word. Tess was already flying out the door.

She crouched beside him and lay a hand on his chest. "Don't move!"

Noah was struggling to get up. "I'm okay!"

"You're not. You could have broken—"

"I didn't break anything. I ride broncs for a living. I fall every day of my life." He looked equal parts irritated and mortified.

Tess didn't care. "Not on the ice. Not like this." She started patting him down, running her hands over him.

All of a sudden Noah sank back onto the ground and groaned.

"What is it?" she demanded.

Susannah and Libby looked immediately alarmed. "Did we kill him?"

"Of course not," Tess said sharply. But she was moving quickly as she unzipped his jacket and started unbuttoning his shirt. He could have reinjured his ribs. One of them could have repunctured his lung. Her hands pressed against his bare chest. "Where does it hurt?"

"Lower."

Her fingers moved down to the base of his rib cage. "There?"

"No."

They skimmed around toward his sides. ''Now?''

He shook his head. ''Hm-mm. Lower.'' She could feel his breath stirring her hair as she bent over him.

''Where?'' Her hands stilled momentarily. She raised her head to look at him.

He met her gaze, then dropped his in the general direction of the fly of his jeans.

Tess's face flamed. She sat back abruptly on her heels, put both hands against his chest and shoved him flat.

''Hey!''

''Mom!''

But Tess was already on her feet and heading back to the house as fast as she had come.

''Tess! I was kidding! Tess!''

She paused only long enough to scoop up a huge handful of snow. Her aim was better than the girls'. She got him square in the face!

The sound of the slamming door echoed all over Laramie. Noah reached up and wiped the remains of the snowball off his face. Susannah and Libby were staring at him, their jaws sagging, their eyes like dinner plates.

''She was kidding, too,'' Noah said to them as he struggled to get to his feet. His ribs hurt like hell. He knew Tess would tell him he deserved it. ''Give me a hand, Suse.''

The little girl reached out and, together, they got him to his feet. Both she and Libby brushed the snow off him, doing more smacking than dusting. Probably Tess would figure he deserved that, too.

''I don't think she was kidding. I think she was mad at you,'' Susannah told him solemnly when they'd finished. She looked worried. ''But I don't know why.'' She looked at him for an explanation.

He couldn't begin to give her one.

"Do you think she'll make you leave?" she asked a bit fearfully.

And Noah realized she was worried that he might. She couldn't possibly understand what was happening between him and Tess. She only knew that she—and her wish for her father—might end up a victim of their disharmony.

"No," Noah said firmly. "She won't make me leave."

"How do you know?"

"Because she's your mother and she wants the best for you." He was certain of that.

"But—"

"And I'll ask her not to."

Susannah swallowed. "Truly?"

Noah nodded.

"When?"

He contemplated the front door. In his ears he could still hear it slamming. In his mind's eye he could still see Tess's worried face as she bent over him, could still feel her hands on him, arousing him when he had no business being aroused, making him say things he had no right to say.

He knew he ought to give her time to cool off. But then he looked down into a pair of bright blue eyes, worried, waiting, hoping.

"Now," he said.

Five

——

"Tess?"

There was no answer. Noah left his boots in the entry hall, hung his jacket on one of the hooks just inside the front door and headed toward the kitchen. There was a bowl of dry ingredients for cookie dough on the table, a carton of eggs next to the bowl, a half-grated orange rind sitting on a plate. No Tess.

"Tess?" he called a little louder.

She didn't reply.

She wasn't in the living room or the tiny dining area. He hesitated, then started up the narrow stairs. She wasn't in her bedroom or the bathroom. A small sound came from Susannah's room, beyond the half-closed door. Noah went to the door and pushed it open. Tess stood with her back to him, her shoulders still hunched as she stared out the window toward the backyard.

"I'm sorry."

Her shoulders lifted in a stiff shrug. "Yeah, sure." Her voice wobbled, then cracked. She sounded as if she'd been crying. Something twisted deep in his gut. He came up behind her and would have touched her, except he was sure she would have flinched away.

"Come on, Tess. It was a joke. I—"

She whirled around to face him. He could see the track of a tear down her cheek. "It's always a joke with you, isn't it, Noah? Well, damn it, maybe I should laugh, but *I can't!*" She tried to spin away again, to duck past him and run out of the room. He grabbed her before she could.

"Aw, hell," he whispered, dragging her stiff, resisting body against his, holding her prisoner there. "I can't help it, Tess. I don't want to joke. I have to."

She continued to struggle for a moment, then sagged onto his chest. "What's that mean?" she muttered into the fabric of his shirt. Her question was equal parts caution and doubt.

He shrugged awkwardly. "It just…seems easier. I don't do too well at the deep stuff. Sayin' what I feel." Even this was hard. The words felt like lead he was hauling up all the way from his toes.

She backed up a fraction of an inch and lifted her gaze to connect with his. "You're saying it's a defense mechanism?"

He didn't know the term, but it sounded about right. "I guess." God, he was drowning in those green eyes of hers. He wanted her desperately; she had to know that. But he wanted her to know it was more than just desiring her body—because, damn it, it was.

"So try," she prompted. "Tell me…what are you feeling now?"

He scratched his ear, reluctant, but knowing she was waiting and that he owed her that much at least. "Incompetent.'' A corner of his mouth tilted wryly. ''Out of my depth. Horny?'' he added after a moment, then grimaced. ''See? It's always easier to talk about sex.''

Tess shook her head. ''For you. Not for me.''

''No. Probably not,'' he allowed. ''But then, you've always been a better person than me.''

''Don't say that.''

''It's true. Anyhow, I'm sorry for teasing you out there. You were worried and I appreciate it. I know you'd…rather not be.''

She looked at him almost shamefacedly for a moment, then glanced away.

''I want you to care,'' he said earnestly. And because he owed her complete honesty, he added, ''But I'm afraid of it, too.''

She looked at him then. ''Because it imposes obligations.'' She didn't make it a question.

He traced a circle with his tongue on the inside of his cheek and looked down at the toes of his boots. ''Yeah.''

''I'm not asking you for anything.''

''I know.''

She sighed. ''But Susannah is.''

''Not really. Well—'' he hesitated ''—she is sort of afraid you're gonna send me away.''

''As if I dared.''

''I told her you wouldn't.''

Tess gave him an arch look. ''How's that for confidence.''

''Not because of me,'' he said quickly. He loosed his hands from behind her and laid them on her shoulders. ''Because you love her.''

''More than anything in the world,'' Tess said fiercely. She stepped away from him and went to stare out the window.

"I know that," he said quietly. "She's a lucky kid."

Tess turned and met his gaze. They stared at each other.

Noah remembered the first time he'd looked deep into Tess Montgomery's eyes eight years before, he'd been young and stupid and out of his depth in the face of her passion and intelligence and hope and, yes, love. He'd taken them all as his due, barely even thinking about them—about her.

Now as he stepped forward, lifted a hand and, with a knuckle, grazed Tess's cheek lightly, he began to understand how much he had lost. Not just Susannah.

Her mother. Tess.

He swallowed hard against the lump in his throat, then ran his tongue lightly over his lips. "Thanks," he said softly.

She gave him a quizzical look.

"For still caring."

Her fingers knotted together. "I can't help it," she said.

It was only since Tanner had married Maggie that Noah had really begun to celebrate Christmas again. Until he'd started spending the holiday with them, the memories he'd stored up from his childhood—memories of cookie baking and house decorating and tree trimming and church going—had seemed locked away, frozen in the ice of a past too far removed to bring back.

To be honest, he hadn't *wanted* to bring them back. They hurt too much.

But the warmth and love he'd found in Tanner and Maggie's first Christmas together had begun melting the ice around those memories and washing away sharp edges of remembered pain. Each subsequent Christmas had freed them up a bit more.

But nothing had prepared Noah for the veritable flood of feelings and memories this Christmas brought him.

He went back outside, ostensibly to supervise the girls, but mostly to put some distance between himself and Tess. They weren't in the backyard where he'd left them, but he could hear girlish voices around front, so he limped that way.

"Look!" Susannah called to him. As he watched, she flopped backward and moved her arms up and down. Then she bounced to her feet and grinned at him. "See? We're angels!"

Snow angels. Noah's throat felt suddenly thick. He leaned on his crutches, grateful for their support.

Still grinning, dripping snow, Susannah hurried toward him, holding out her hand. "Come and make angels."

He didn't move. Couldn't.

"Or maybe you can't," she said, her face suddenly crumpling into a worried frown as she reached him. "Because of your leg?"

He gave himself a little shake. "It's all right."

"You don't have to fall over like we did," she said. "You could lie down careful like. Here. I'll help you." She took his hand.

Oh God. He swallowed painfully as he felt her mittened fingers wrap around his, and he allowed himself to be led. Susannah drew him with her to an pristine patch of untrampled snow next to the small angel she had made.

"Turn around," she directed.

He turned.

"Can you sit down?"

Awkwardly, he did. Then he stretched out full length in the cold snow and, as she watched him, moved his arms slowly up and down at his sides, making the wings. His eyes felt suddenly wet. From the cold, he assured himself.

Not because he was remembering another Christmas. Another pair of angels.

He'd been barely four that Christmas. And lonely, because that was the first year both his older brothers were in school all day. Even six-year-old Luke had left on the school bus each morning and didn't get home until it was nearly dark, so Noah spent the days by himself.

They didn't live in the city, but in an old, two-story tin-roofed ranch house on a remote Colorado mountainside, so he'd had no one to play with. No one to run and wrestle in the snow with. No one to throw snowballs with. Except his mother, who always had plenty of work to do—laundry, cleaning, cooking. Helping his father clean tack, mucking out the barn and doing something she called "book work" that was just columns of numbers to a four-year-old boy. It didn't look interesting at all. Certainly not as interesting as the snow that had begun to fall that morning right after his brothers had gone to school.

Noah had played outside by himself in it until his nose was frozen and his lips were blue. But playing alone was no fun.

"Come out," he'd begged his mother. "Just for a little while."

She'd hesitated, then looked at his pleading face and set aside the ledger with its columns of numbers that never added up the way she wanted them to. She came outside with him and threw snowballs and made a snowman and did all the rough-and-tumble things he did with his brothers. And then she walked over to the one area he hadn't run through, a space of pure, smooth, soft snow.

"Let's make angels," she'd said.

Noah had stared. "Angels?"

"Like this." Her dark hair had curled against her wind-reddened cheeks as she'd smiled down at him. "Watch."

Then, as he'd stared in openmouthed astonishment, his normally serious mother had toppled right over backward and flapped her arms. He'd never seen her do anything so amazing and he'd laughed.

She'd laughed, too. "Come and make an angel, Noah," she'd said as she got up carefully so as not to disturb the shape she'd made in the snow.

And he had. He'd flung himself backward the same way she had, and then, as she watched him, he'd moved his arms, feeling as if he were flying in slow motion through the soft, snowy drifts. And then she'd reached out and pulled him to his feet, then picked him up in her arms and snuggled him close.

"See?" she'd said, smiling and rubbing her nose against his cold cheek. "We're angels."

That was the last Christmas he'd had with his mother. Five months later she'd died in a car accident.

It was the first time he'd let himself think about snow angels in years.

Tess was making more cookies—gingerbread this time— when they came in. The house was filled with the smell of cinnamon and nutmeg, allspice and ginger. It made Noah's mouth water and his stomach growl. And like the snow angels, the memory of that smell made his throat tighten and something deep inside his chest begin once more to ache.

Still, he couldn't ache for long. Once she'd shed her jacket, mittens, hat and boots, Susannah was tugging his hand and looking up at him in bright anticipation. "All ready to make cookies?"

Tess, calm now, looked up and said, "Wash your hands," to Susannah and Libby and, Noah supposed, to him. "There are aprons in the drawer."

Before Noah knew it, he, Susannah and Libby were all wearing aprons. After he rolled out the dough, they cut out reindeer and Santas and Christmas trees and angels. Then Tess put the cookie sheets into the oven. In the background, songs from Christmases past played on the stereo. But little girls of Christmas present sang along off-key, and Noah, bemused, shared a grin over their heads with Tess.

It was the first genuine grin he'd seen on her face in eight years. The sight caused his heart to lurch oddly against the wall of his chest.

When they were almost finished, there was a knock on the back door. Tess opened it to a windblown-looking woman in her early thirties.

"Mom," Libby crowed, "did you see our angels in the yard?"

The woman nodded. "Hope she hasn't been too much trouble," she said to Tess. Then she saw Noah and her eyes widened. She looked at Tess for an introduction.

Tess hesitated, then said to Noah, "This is Janna. Janna, this is Noah."

She hesitated again, long enough for Susannah to add, "My dad."

Janna blinked, then mustered a polite smile and held out a hand. "How nice to meet you." There was a wealth of meaning in every word.

Noah smiled wryly as he shook her hand. "It's nice to meet you, too."

"Well," Janna said, clearly flustered. "I never expected…I mean, Tess didn't say you were coming."

"She didn't know," Susannah said matter-of-factly. "I prayed for him."

Janna couldn't seem to think of any response to that. She looked from father to daughter to mother, then at last at her own daughter before she finally decided on an appropriate response.

"Well, good," she said heartily. "Come on, Lib. Get your jacket so we can let Tess and Susannah and—and Noah have the rest of the afternoon to themselves."

Libby groaned. "Aw, Mom. I—"

"Now." Janna's tone brooked no argument. Libby sighed, climbed down off the chair and went to get her jacket. "Maybe I can come back later," she said to Susannah.

Janna chivied her daughter toward the door, shooting a glance back at Tess as she went. "Sorry," Noah heard her say under her breath. "You should have told me. I could have taken her with me."

"Nonsense. It was fine. This was just a fluke."

"He isn't here for Christmas?" Janna asked doubtfully.

"Yes, he is," Susannah said firmly, overhearing the conversation.

"Yes." Noah heard Tess agree. "But he's not staying."

Tess had grown up with the adage "Be careful what you pray for, for you will likely get it." She hadn't realized it applied to one's children's prayers, too. Surely she had never offered up such prayers herself, asking the Almighty for Noah to be a part of their Christmas celebration! Or if she had, it must have been years ago.

Shouldn't there be a statute of limitations on prayers? And shouldn't the one on those particular prayers have long ago run out?

It seemed not. And Tess couldn't help the bittersweet feelings that swept over her whenever she stepped back and allowed herself to acknowledge what was happening that afternoon.

They were making memories. The three of them this

time, instead of just two. Memories of snow angels and Christmas baking, of girlish giggles and hearty masculine laughter, of smiles and snowball fights, of tickling and teasing.

It was as if a scene by Norman Rockwell had somehow made it into a Norman Mailer book. Or, if her life wasn't quite that gritty, Tess hedged, at least into a book with a somewhat-harder edge. She reminded herself that it was no more than she'd told Janna it was—a fluke. A brief flash of something special—like those two weeks she and Noah had spent together eight years before. It wouldn't last.

She tried to resist. But Tess had never been a Scrooge. She couldn't say, "Bah, humbug," even when it was clearly in the best interests of her own emotional well-being to do so. No, not her. She was a sap. Altogether too willing to let herself be swept up in the spirit of the season—peace on earth and goodwill to men. Even to the one man she had the most to fear from.

"Just so you remember that," she muttered to herself as she carried a plateful of decorated cookies into the living room so Noah and Susannah could hang them on the tree.

"What?" Noah looked over at her.

She shook her head, unaware until that moment that she'd spoken aloud. "Nothing," she said.

He gave her a searching look, but when she determinedly shook her head again, he turned back to Susannah.

"You tie the loops," she was telling him, "after Mom threads 'em through."

"Loops? Thread? Seems like a lot of work to go through just to eat them," Noah said.

"We don't eat 'em, silly." Susannah giggled. "We hang 'em on the tree."

Noah feigned astonishment. "I've never heard of such a thing," he said.

And Susannah giggled again. "Show him, Mommy."

So Tess threaded a needle and made a hole through the top of each cookie. Then she cut the thread, and under Susannah's tutelage, Noah tied a loop through each one. Then Susannah took them and hung them on the tree. Except on the branches that were too high for her reach.

"See," Tess said as she struggled on tiptoe to put a silver-studded angel on one of the higher branches, "if we'd gotten a short tree, you'd be able to reach."

Susannah shook her head stubbornly. "I like this one. Noah can lift me up. Can't you?"

"Sure." He nodded and held out his arms.

"Your elbow!" Tess protested instinctively. "Your shoulder!"

But Noah lifted Susannah easily, and she turned her head, her dark hair brushing his cheek as she grinned at her mother. "See?" she said. Then she twisted to reach out and hang an angel on the tree. "Mommy, hand me another. Please?" she added when Tess gave her an arch look.

Tess handed her another. And then another, as Noah lifted her first on one side and then on the other until at last all the cookies were in place on the tree.

"There," Susannah said with a satisfied sigh. She gave Noah a hug and then wiggled to the floor. He let her down easily, but as he straightened, Tess saw him wince, then rub his elbow when he thought no one was looking.

Susannah took hold of his hand—as if she couldn't bear not to touch him, Tess realized with an aching feeling somewhere in her midsection. The little girl contemplated the tree with its tiny, colored lights reflected in the shiny icing on the cookies. Then she looked up at her father. "Isn't it beautiful?"

And he looked down at her. "Beautiful," he said softly,

and Tess was almost certain he wasn't talking about the tree.

"Did you ever have a tree this pretty before?" Susannah asked.

He shook his head.

"What was the prettiest tree you ever had?"

Noah shifted from one foot to the other. He looked almost at a loss for a moment, then slightly wistful. "Prob'ly the one we had when I was—when I was four," he said at last.

Susannah tugged his hand, pulling him toward the couch. "Tell me about it."

Tess could see his reluctance and felt an urge to jump in and save him, to tell Susannah to mind her own business. But then she thought, *It is her business. He's her father. She has a right to ask.*

Noah settled onto the couch, and Susannah tucked herself beneath his arm, snuggling against him. "Not much to tell," he said finally. "It was just a tree. My dad and my oldest brother cut it and—"

"They cut it?" Susannah was awed. "Really cut it?"

"It's what you do out there. We lived on a ranch. There were a lot of trees. We cut one every year."

"But if you did it every year, why was that one special?"

"Susannah," Tess warned softly. She couldn't help it.

Noah glanced up at her. "It's all right," he said. Then he looked back at Susannah. "It was the last year my mother was alive."

Susannah turned her head and looked up at him. "She died when you were just four?"

He nodded.

Her small hand crept onto his thigh and clasped his big one tightly. "You must've missed her just awful."

He looked down at their clasped hands and gave her a faint smile. "I did. I don't think I ever liked Christmas much after that," he said reflectively. "It seemed sort of hollow. As if the center was gone." Then he looked at her. "Until now."

Tess sucked in her breath.

"What was she like, my grandmother?" Susannah asked him.

"Your grandmother?" He looked puzzled, then the realization hit. "Oh, you mean my mother." There was another smile, this one bemused, almost. "Your grandmother." He repeated the words softly. "She would have liked you a lot."

It was surprisingly easy to talk about his mother then. Memories Noah had tucked away so many years ago that he couldn't believe they were still so close at hand came back unbidden. Maybe it was the season, maybe it was the mood, maybe it was the little girl sitting snugly against him, looking up at him with wide eyes, or maybe—just maybe— it was her mother, who hesitated, hovered, then came to sit in the old oak rocker by the sofa to listen to him.

Whatever it was, it made him open up the past in a way he'd never opened it up before. And if his voice got to sounding a little rusty, and once or twice he had to clear his throat, well, Susannah didn't seem to notice.

And Tess?

Tess didn't say a word, but he was aware every instant of her presence as she sat there, rocking slightly, listening to what he said.

He'd never told her any of this—had never really spoken of his family at all when he'd been with her eight years before. Then it hadn't mattered—or he'd thought it hadn't. Now he knew it did.

No matter how long he'd turned his back on those memories, they were still there. They still mattered. His mother, his father, his brothers—all of them mattered. Family mattered.

Were he and Tess and Susannah a family?

He flicked a glance in Tess's direction. He didn't imagine she'd think so. He suspected she'd deny it in a second.

But whether she wanted to admit it or not, Noah thought he could argue that they were. And they were making memories together this Christmas.

And next Christmas? What about that?

His arm tightened slightly around the narrow shoulders of his daughter. He dropped a kiss on the top of her dark hair. Next Christmas, too, he promised himself.

There was nothing that said he couldn't come back.

That evening he was on the sofa again, reading Susannah a story, while Tess was in the kitchen baking loaves of cranberry bread to give to the neighbors and to Susannah's teacher. When he heard a knock on the back door, Noah assumed it was Libby coming to play again. He heard Tess say something, and he sat up a little straighter when the voice he heard in reply was deep and undeniably masculine.

"Who's that?" he asked Susannah.

Before she could answer, Tess came into the living room, followed by a tall, lean man in a policeman's uniform. Susannah bounced up.

"Hi, Steve!"

"This is Steve Williams, Janna's husband," Tess said calmly, ignoring Noah's scowl. "He stopped to invite us over for dinner tomorrow. This is Susannah's father, Noah Tanner."

He could have stayed on the couch where he was; his bad knee gave him enough of an excuse. But for all that

Steve Williams had a wife, he was standing too damn close to Tess. And if that wasn't enough, the assessing look in his eyes had Noah hauling himself to his feet so he could meet the other man's gaze head-on.

Steve was an inch or so taller and broader shouldered than he was. Even so, Noah figured he could take him in a fight. Unconsciously he flexed his fingers, then curled them into fists. Tess saw the movement and stepped between them, giving him a hard look.

Noah took a deep breath and held out a hand. "Howdy."

Steve's handshake was as firm and no-nonsense as his gaze was unblinking. He dropped Noah's hand almost at once and turned back to Tess. "Janna and I thought, since you were with us last year and the year before, that it's become something of a tradition." He was looking at Tess, though it was clear enough to Noah who he was really talking to. "You're all welcome," he added almost reluctantly.

Tess hesitated.

"We'll be there," Noah said. And if he put just a little more emphasis on the *we* than was strictly necessary, well, he didn't think Steve Williams misunderstood. Their eyes met.

Steve nodded. "Five o'clock." He started for the door, then turned back. "We'll see you in the morning," he said to Susannah.

"Susannah is staying with them while I'm at work," Tess told Noah.

"I can watch her."

Noah saw Tess and Steve exchange glances. "We've already arranged…" Tess began, then stopped when she saw the sudden smile on Susannah's face begin to fade. "Well, I suppose. Are you sure?"

Noah bristled. "Of course I'm sure."

"What about your therapy?"

"It's only an hour. We'll work it out." He winked at Susannah. "Won't we?"

She nodded emphatically, the smile back in place.

Steve was looking sceptical. Tess was looking torn. Finally she sighed. "If you think you can manage."

"We can manage."

"Uh-huh," Susannah echoed. She smiled up at Noah, then leaned against him. He rested a hand on her shoulder and squeezed it lightly.

Steve hesitated, then said mildly, "Well, we'll be there if you wear out."

"I won't."

"It's a little longer than an eight-second ride," Steve pointed out smoothly.

Noah heard Tess suck in her breath. His own spine stiffened. "We'll see you tomorrow night."

Tess laid a hand on Steve's arm and seemed to steer him toward the door. "Five o'clock?"

Steve's gaze never left Noah's, but he allowed himself to be maneuvered back into the kitchen. "That's what Janna said."

Noah waited until Susannah was in bed before he tackled the issue. "Little bit of a watchdog, isn't he?"

Tess, busy wrapping loaves of bread in foil and putting ribbon and bows on them, didn't look up, but she didn't pretend not to know what he was talking about, either. "He and Janna are concerned."

"Janna didn't bite my wrist."

"She sent Steve," Tess said simply. She cut another piece of ribbon and put it around one of the loaves.

Noah shifted against the cabinet he was leaning on. "That's all it is?"

Her head came up abruptly and she gave him a hard look. "All what is?"

"He acts like he owns you."

"He's got a wife."

"That doesn't stop some men."

"It stops Steve. He's never looked at me twice. He's a friend, Noah. In fact, I think it would be fair to say that he and Janna are just about the best friends I've ever had. They've done a lot for Susannah and me since we moved next door. Not just baby-sitting, though heaven knows they've done plenty of that. When Susannah had pneumonia and I couldn't get off work everyday, Steve and Janna took care of her. When she broke her arm, Steve was the one who took her to the hospital. When she needed a 'dad' to go to a Brownies' dinner, he went. They've taken her with them when they've gone camping in the summer and skiing in the winter. I don't know what I would have done without them!" She stopped suddenly, apparently aware that her voice had risen and her fists were clenched.

"I see." He saw a lot more than he wanted to, in fact. Saw that there had been plenty of times when Tess hadn't coped as well as she wanted to give the impression that she had. That there were, whether she liked it or not, circumstances where just one parent wasn't quite enough. Mostly he saw that while he'd been oblivious to everyone's needs but his own, Steve and Janna Williams had been there for Tess and Susannah.

But I didn't know! he thought desperately. But he'd never wanted to know, either.

He'd never felt for any girl what he'd felt for Tess those two weeks they'd been together. It had seemed too serious, too real, too demanding for a man who was, he had to admit, little more than a boy deep down.

If he had stayed, he wouldn't have been much good to

her. He remembered his brother Tanner, who had married his high-school sweetheart, Clare, when he found out she was pregnant. Tanner had tried—hell, he'd done everything he could—to be a husband, a father-to-be and the sole guardian of his two younger brothers. It hadn't worked.

If Tanner couldn't do it, Noah knew there was no way he could have. He'd been wicked and wild and woolly in those days. Not much good even to himself.

And now?

"Don't you harass Steve tomorrow night," Tess said, her tone and her words jerking him back to the moment.

"I won't."

"I mean it." She was clearly unconvinced by his sudden acquiescence.

He shut his eyes briefly, considering Steve Williams, who was apparently a good husband, a good father. What was it Steve Williams had that he lacked?

Noah opened his eyes again and met hers. "I mean it, too," he said quietly. "I reckon I owe him a ton."

Six

He couldn't sleep. He lay in Tess's bed, tossing and turning, his mind tempted not by visions of seasonal sugarplums, but by photos of a little girl—and a bigger one—that danced through his head.

He'd asked for it, of course. He'd been thinking about all the things Steve Williams had shared with his daughter, and after Susannah had gone to bed, Noah had said to Tess, "Do you have pictures?"

She'd gone to the bookcase next to the fireplace, taken out half a dozen photo albums, and handed them to him. He'd sat on the sofa, turning the pages slowly, watching the years go past. In those few albums he'd caught a glimpse of Tess and Susannah's life for the last seven years. It had made him smile, made him laugh, made him ache.

Tess had left him to look at them alone, disappearing into the kitchen and rattling pots and pans.

"Who's this?" he'd called after her. "Where were you when this happened?"

And after she'd come back a few times to reply, she stayed, first standing beside the sofa, then perching on its arm, then finally sitting next to him and taking the albums in her lap. She'd answered his questions briefly at first. Then, as she looked over the pictures again, she smiled reminiscently and spoke at length.

He heard about holidays and vacations, about nursery school and class field trips and visits from the Easter Bunny. He heard about swimming classes and Brownie plays, horseback riding and Girl Scout Cookie sales.

Tess's voice had been soft and slightly husky. She didn't even try to hide the love and pride she felt. And sometimes, when she choked up a bit as she remembered a particular event, he'd wanted to reach for her hand or slip an arm behind her and pull her close.

He didn't, because he knew any such action would make her stiffen and pull away, and he didn't want to break the spell. So he'd stayed where he was—millimeters from her—until they'd closed the last page and sat silently, side by side, each caught in a tangled web of reflections. And then, just when he'd thought he might dare to turn and touch his lips to hers, Tess slapped her hands lightly on top of the last album and sprang to her feet.

"Well, there you have it," she said briskly. "Seven years in a nutshell. Now, if you don't mind, you're sitting on my resting place and I have to get up at 5:30...."

The moment lost, Noah hauled himself awkwardly to his feet. "I'll sleep out here."

"No. It's easier this way. Then I won't bother you when I leave for work."

He hadn't argued. And when she even declined his help

in making up the sofa into a bed, he'd gone meekly off to bed himself.

But not to sleep.

He'd been lying awake for hours, thinking about Susannah—and about Tess. About the years they'd had together.

Without him.

A jumble of images somersaulted in his mind, teasing him—a photo of a day-old infant in a pale pink sleeper looking cross-eyed at the camera; a half-dozen shots of a dark-haired toddler with toys and blocks, beside a wading pool or a Christmas tree; glimpses of mother and child at various ages and in various locations, laughing, giggling, mugging for the camera; and one separate section begun three years before, of Susannah smiling for school pictures.

But more than any of those, one particular image haunted him—a slightly blurred shot of Tess on the last page of an album, taken by Susannah. She'd been standing by the Ferris wheel on the midway at the rodeo in Cheyenne.

Had it been taken the day they'd seen him with Maggie?

When he saw it, he'd wanted to ask. He couldn't. Tess had shut the album abruptly, then stood up, effectively putting the past away.

But Noah couldn't.

He got up and, as quietly as he could, made his way out of the room and down the short hall to Susannah's bedroom. The door was slightly ajar and he pushed it open.

The blinds were only half-closed, admitting enough reflected light off the snow so that he could see his daughter snuggled against her pillows, one arm around a stuffed horse. His gaze flicked from Susannah to the pictures of him on her bedside table.

There were none in the photo albums—no sign of him during his daughter's first seven years. Because, of course, he hadn't been here.

But he had to admit that Tess hadn't shut him out of Susannah's life completely. On the contrary, she'd given her daughter as much of her father as she dared. He thanked her for that, even as he knew that it hadn't been enough for Susannah.

It wasn't enough for him, either. He wanted more—of both of them.

Gently he brushed his hand over Susannah's dark hair. She stirred slightly. ''M' Chris'mas,'' she muttered.

Noah's fingers touched her lips, then brushed her hair once more. ''Merry Christmas, sweetheart,'' he whispered. Then he limped out as silently as he'd come.

Downstairs, a soft glow beckoned. Tess had sent him off so she could sleep. So why was a light still on?

He made his way down the steps, and saw that the light came not from the reading lamp by the rocker, but from the Christmas tree. In the golden glow of the myriad tiny, colored lights, Noah could see Tess asleep on the couch.

He moved closer, drawn by the sight of her. She lay on her side, one hand tucked under her head, the other curled into the blanket, clutching it against her chest. Her lips were slightly parted, her hair loose and free against the pillow.

Only once before did he remember watching her sleep. It had been on the morning of the day he'd left, eight years ago. They had loved far into the night, eager and hungry for each other, giving and taking, touching and tasting, until at last, sated, they'd fallen asleep in each other's arms.

Tess had still been sleeping soundly when Noah awoke at the first hint of dawn. He'd lain there, savoring the warmth of her body next to his, already regretting that he wouldn't be enjoying that warmth the next time he went to bed. He'd turned his head and dropped a kiss on her hair, breathing deeply, savoring the soft, flowery scent of her, storing it away. Then he'd eased back, but only far enough to get a good look at her, to have another memory. He remembered thinking how beautiful she was.

He'd never told her that. Never told her, either, that those two weeks eight years ago had been the best two weeks of his life.

Why not?

Because if he had, he might've had second thoughts about what he was doing. And in those days, the only thing that kept him going was focusing on the next town, the next rodeo, the next ride. If he'd allowed himself to get sidetracked, he'd never have succeeded. He'd never have been champion of the world.

He'd have been a husband and a father instead.

A fair trade-off?

Not a fair question; he knew that even as he asked himself. There was no answer to the past. There was only the future.

A future with Tess?

Eight years ago he'd watched her sleep, then he'd taken a deep breath and turned away.

Now he came closer, bending down. She shifted and sighed, but didn't wake. Asleep, she hardly looked older than Susannah. But regardless of how she looked, she was a woman now.

She'd succeeded, too, probably even better than he had—though he certainly had more notoriety. She'd become a nurse. She'd become a mother. She'd raised, single-handedly and well, a beautiful child. His child.

He reached out a hand and touched Tess's hair, the way he had Susannah's. It wasn't enough. He knelt and dropped a kiss on her mouth. Her lips parted at his touch.

He wanted to touch them again. And again. Dropping his head, he rested his forehead lightly against hers. ''Thank you,'' he whispered.

She didn't stir.

Then he got slowly to his feet, adjusted the quilt around her shoulders and shut off the Christmas lights.

He didn't fall sleep until well past four.

"What's wrong?" Janna asked the minute she heard Tess's voice on the phone.

"Nothing," Tess said quickly. She shouldn't have called. Just because she was feeling jittery was no reason to bother Janna. "I just wanted to make sure you knew that Suse was staying with Noah today."

"Steve told me," Janna said. "Is it all right?"

"Of course," Tess said quickly. Too quickly.

"I'll keep an eye out," Janna offered. "I'll take her if you want."

"No. It's all right. I think he'll be fine with her. It's just that…just that—"

"Maybe you're worried he'll be too fine with her," Janna said with her usual perception. "And then where will you be?"

"Nowhere," Tess said firmly. "Susannah knows that. She has him for now. Not for always."

"Are you sure?"

"He hasn't given me any reason to think otherwise."

"What would you do if he did?"

Tess didn't want to think about that. "He won't," she said. "I've got to go. But, yes, keep an eye out, would you? Just in case…"

"No problem," Janna said. "I'm sure Libby will want to play with Susannah. He won't even know I'm checking."

"Good. He'll think I don't trust him otherwise."

"Do you?"

"Yes, oddly enough." With Susannah, at least. She had

GET 2

HOW TO GET YOUR
2 FREE BOOKS AND FREE GIFT!

1. Peel off the MIRA sticker on the front cover. Place it in the space provided at right. This automatically entitles you to receive two free books and an exciting mystery gift.

2. Send back this card and you'll get 2 "The Best of the Best™" novels. These books have a combined cover price of $11.00 or more in the U.S. and $13.00 or more in Canada, but they are yours to keep absolutely FREE!

3. There's no catch. You're under no obligation to buy anything. We charge nothing – ZERO – for your first shipment. And you don't have to make any minimum number of purchases – not even one!

4. We call this line "The Best of the Best" because each month you'll receive the best books by some of today's hottest authors. These authors show up time and time again on all the major bestseller lists and their books sell out as soon as they hit the stores. You'll like the convenience of getting them delivered to your home at our special discount prices . . . and you'll love your *Heart to Heart* subscriber newsletter featuring author news, horoscopes, recipes, book reviews and much more!

5. We hope that after receiving your free books you'll want to remain a subscriber. But the choice is yours – to continue or cancel, anytime at all! So why not take us up on our invitation, with no risk of any kind. You'll be glad you did!

6. And remember...we'll send you a mystery gift ABSOLUTELY FREE just for giving "The Best of the Best" a try.

SPECIAL FREE GIFT!

We'll send you a fabulous surprise gift, absolutely FREE, simply for accepting our no-risk offer!

Visit us online at
www.mirabooks.com

BOOKS FREE!

Hurry!

Return this card promptly to GET 2 FREE BOOKS & A FREE GIFT!

YES! Please send me the 2 FREE "The Best of the Best" novels and FREE gift for which I qualify. I understand that I am under no obligation to purchase anything further, as explained on the opposite page.

(P-BB3-01)

385 MDL C6PQ   **185 MDL C6PP**

| | | | | | | | | | | | | | | | | | | | |

NAME   (PLEASE PRINT CLEARLY)

ADDRESS

APT.#   CITY

STATE/PROV.   ZIP/POSTAL CODE

Offer limited to one per household and not valid to current subscribers of "The Best of the Best." All orders subject to approval. Books received may vary.

©1995 MIRA BOOKS

The Best of the Best™ — Here's How it Works:

Accepting your 2 free books and gift places you under no obligation to buy anything. You may keep the books and gift and return the shipping statement marked "cancel." If you do not cancel, about a month later we will send you 4 additional novels and bill you just $4.24 each in the U.S., or $4.74 each in Canada, plus 25¢ shipping & handling per book and applicable taxes if any.* That's the complete price and — compared to cover prices of $5.50 or more each in the U.S. and $6.50 or more each in Canada — it's quite a bargain! You may cancel at any time, but if you choose to continue, every month we'll send you 4 more books, which you may either purchase at the discount price or return to us and cancel your subscription.

*Terms and prices subject to change without notice. Sales tax applicable in N.Y. Canadian residents will be charged applicable provincial taxes and GST.

If offer card is missing write to: The Best of the Best,, 3010 Walden Ave., P.O. Box 1867, Buffalo, NY 14240-1867

BUSINESS REPLY MAIL

FIRST-CLASS MAIL PERMIT NO. 717 BUFFALO, NY

POSTAGE WILL BE PAID BY ADDRESSEE

**THE BEST OF THE BEST
3010 WALDEN AVE
PO BOX 1867
BUFFALO NY 14240-9952**

NO POSTAGE
NECESSARY
IF MAILED
IN THE
UNITED STATES

seen it in him from the very first, that intense concern about their daughter, that desire to keep her safe. He had the right instincts where fatherhood was concerned, Tess thought.

"I've got to go," she said again. There was absolutely no future in thinking things like that.

Someone was standing over him.

Noah could sense it at once, even without opening his eyes. The force of a stare, the shallow, quick intake of breath brought him through grogginess to full alert. How long had he been out? What horse had flattened him? His eyes snapped open.

"Good. You're awake."

Noah sagged back against the pillow, the rodeo arena of his dreams fading, the reality of Susannah staring him in the face.

"Morning," he mumbled, scrubbing a hand over his eyes, then squinting at her. "What time is it?"

"Seven," his daughter said cheerfully.

Noah stifled a groan. The last time he'd seen seven o'clock willingly, he had come at it from the other end.

"I brought you breakfast in bed."

"Breakfast? In bed?" He didn't think he'd ever had breakfast in bed in his life—not unless you counted potato chips and a six-pack of beer.

But Susannah was bending down and picking up the tray on the floor beside her. "It's not much. Cheerios and toast and orange juice. Mom won't let me use the stove unless she's here," she confided as she stood waiting expectantly for him to sit up.

Noah shoved himself up against the pillows. She settled the tray on his lap and handed him a napkin. He took it, then contemplated the very crisp toast and the slightly soggy cereal, and rubbed a hand across his whiskered jaw.

"Is it okay?" she asked nervously.

"It's wonderful," he told her. "No one has ever done this for me before."

"Never?" Her surprise showed. "Mom does it for me on my birthday every year. An' last year I did it for her on Mother's Day. I know it isn't Father's Day, but...you're prob'ly not gonna be here then," she said with determined indifference, and Noah felt a sudden twist in his gut at the assumption. "So I thought I'd do it now."

"It's the nicest thing you could have done."

Under Susannah's watchful eye, he ate every bite. Then, while she carried the dishes back down to the kitchen, Noah pulled on a clean pair of jeans and buttoned a blue plaid, flannel shirt across his chest. He was pulling on his boots when Susannah reappeared.

"What shall we do now?" she asked.

"How about you give me a hand making this bed," he said. "Then I'll help you with yours. And then, well...we'll see."

He'd expected Tess to leave him instructions, but apparently she hadn't. Still, his suggestion seemed to be the right one. "Mommy always says we have to get the house ready for Christmas, too," Susannah told him. "We can do it and surprise her."

So they made beds together. They did a load of laundry together. Then Noah washed the breakfast dishes while Susannah dried them. Afterward Susannah dusted the furniture and Noah vacuumed the carpet and swept the floors.

Then he said, "Coffee break," and made them both cups of cocoa, which he carried into the living room.

"Are you sure?" Susannah said doubtfully. "Mom doesn't let me drink out here."

"It's a special occasion," Noah decided. "We'll both be careful."

And they sat in the living room, side by side on the sofa, listening to a tape of holiday music that Noah put on. Susannah sipped her cocoa, then looked up at him and smiled shyly.

"I'm glad I asked God for you to come," she told him. "You're better'n a Barbie doll."

Noah was glad to hear that. He contemplated the clean house, the well-lit Christmas tree, the fire now crackling in the fireplace, the cat curled on the hearth rug, the small girl sitting next to him, and he felt a lump growing in his throat.

He said, "I'm glad you asked God, too."

If the day before had brought Noah all kinds of memories, today was a whole new experience.

He'd never been a parent before. Not really. The night he'd gone with Tess and Susannah to buy the tree, and yesterday, with Tess home to give orders and make decisions, didn't count. She'd been the parent then and he'd been hanging around.

Today, for the first time in his life, Noah felt the sense of being responsible for another person begin to settle in on him.

Susannah looked to him for answers, decisions, permission. He decided they'd clean the house. He decided they'd take a break. He decided they could drink cocoa in the living room.

It was heady stuff.

He felt benevolent and in charge when, shortly before noon, he let his daughter go out to play with Libby and her ten-year-old brother, Jeff.

"Half an hour," he said. "Then we'll go Christmas shopping."

He watched her trot down the steps, then he made himself a cup of coffee and settled down to read yesterday's paper and enjoy fatherhood.

Ten minutes later Jeff was banging on the back door. "Susannah's bleeding!"

What Noah said then was more instinctual than fatherly. He pushed past Jeff and hobbled, crutchless, out into the yard. She wasn't there! He spun around toward the boy. "Where is she? What happened?"

"Down the street in Radloffs' backyard. We were swingin' each other around and lettin' go and—"

"Show me!"

The wind cut through the thin flannel of his shirt as he limped hurriedly after Jeff. His leg ached and his teeth were chattering by the time Jeff turned into a driveway. Noah didn't notice anything but Susannah.

She was huddled on the ground, with Libby and two children Noah didn't know hovering around her. He pushed past them and crouched down as best he could.

His daughter looked up at him with an abraded cheek, a bloody nose, a split lip and one front tooth missing. Tears were drying on her cheeks, but he could see her striving to keep her voice from wobbling when she spoke. "I hit a tree."

Oh God, Noah thought. And the next thing he thought was, *Oh, Tess!*

He couldn't count how many times he'd scraped Taggart and dozens of other buddies up off the dirt in the arena when they'd been stomped by some of the rankest rough stock around. He did it as a matter of course and never batted an eye.

Now he couldn't move, couldn't think. He wanted Tess. He needed Tess!

A parent would know what to do!

And then he realized that he was the parent here. He swallowed his panic and tried to think.

Susannah wasn't dying. She was cut. She was bleeding. She was missing a tooth. "Is it just your face?" he asked her. "I mean, do you hurt anywhere else?"

She shook her head slightly, then grimaced. "Ow."

"How hard did you hit?" Did she have a concussion? He peered at her pupils. They looked all right. "Who are you?"

She giggled slightly. "You know that." She shot a glance at Libby and rolled her eyes.

"I do? That's right, I do," Noah said, snapping his fingers as if it had just come back to him. "You're Abigail."

Another giggle. "No, thilly. I'm Thuthannah."

Noah winced.

Susannah, hearing herself, giggled again. "Thuthannah," she repeated, carefully poking her tongue against her lip through the gap where her tooth had been.

So she didn't have a concussion. Just a new lisp, he thought grimly. And he was getting his wits back slowly—wit by wit, it seemed. "And you're five?" he persisted, just to make sure.

"Theven," she corrected.

"Right. Seven." He groped in his pocket for a handkerchief to hold to her nose. The blood seemed to be stopping anyway, probably because of the cold. "See if you can find her tooth," he said to the children. He remembered Deke Miller getting his front teeth hammered by a bull a few years back in Scottsdale. Someone with foresight had taken them along to the dentist, and he'd been able to save them.

They scurried over to the tree—all but Libby, who seemed more concerned about the rest of Susannah. She crouched down next to Noah. "We didn't mean to hurt her," she said earnestly. "We were just playing. Jeff and

Terry were swinging us. I went first. Then it was Susannah's turn. Is she going to be okay?'' Her eyes were wide and worried.

"She'll be fine,'' Noah promised. "Will it hurt if I pick you up, Susannah?''

"D-don't think tho.''

"Tell me if it does.'' He slid his arms under her and gritted his teeth, trying to get enough purchase in the snow-covered grass with his bad leg to stagger upright and not drop her. He stumbled slightly, but made it. Susannah wrapped her arms like iron bands around his neck.

"Got it!'' The boy called Terry came running, Susannah's tooth clutched tightly in his fist.

They made an odd procession along the sidewalk, Noah carrying Susannah, Libby and the other girl flanking him on either side, while Jeff ran ahead to open the door and Terry carried the tooth in his clenched fist.

The Williamses' door opened as he passed, and Janna flew out. "What happened? Is she all right? Shall I call Tess?''

"No,'' Noah said. "Don't call Tess.''

Not yet. Please God, don't let her see what a mess I've made of her daughter yet! He stumbled through the gate. Out of the corner of his eye, he could see Janna coming his way. "Go tell your mother she's okay,'' he told Libby. Then he carried Susannah into the house.

Jeff followed him. "Want me to call 911?''

"No.'' He set Susannah on the kitchen counter and grabbed a clean dishcloth, then dabbed at her nose and cheek, trying not to grimace and feel faint at the sight of all her blood.

God knew he'd seen plenty in his life. Why this should bother him so much he didn't know—unless it was because it was his daughter's.

"Who's your dentist?" he asked Susannah when he finished.

"Dr. Kincaid," Janna said, and he turned to find her standing right behind him. "I'll ca—I'll get you the number," she said.

The dentist's receptionist said to bring her right in. That was when Noah remembered he didn't have a car.

He borrowed Janna's. "I'll rent one," he promised, "as soon as we finish at the dentist's."

"Don't worry about it," she said, hovering over Susannah as Noah tucked her into the front seat of the car. "Are you sure you don't want me to call Tess? She'd come."

"No. I can handle it," Noah said. His knuckles were white on the steering wheel. He hoped he was telling her the truth.

At least Susannah wasn't crying for her mother. On the contrary, she wasn't crying at all. She sat stoically beside him and didn't say a word while he drove and tried to remember Janna's directions. Every few seconds he slanted a glance down at Susannah and winced at the scrape on her cheek, the blood drying beneath her nose and on her puffy lip.

What kind of father let his kid get smashed to bits the moment he let her out of his sight?

"Bring her right on back, Mr. Montgomery," the dentist's assistant said when he led Susannah into the office. With Susannah clutching his hand, he followed the woman to a room at the end of the hall. "Dr. Kincaid will be right in."

Noah alternated between hovering and pacing until the dentist arrived.

Dr. Kincaid was a short, cheerful man in his fifties. "Smile," he said to Susannah. Then, when she did, "Oh, my."

"We've got the tooth." Noah fished desperately in the pocket of his jeans.

"Open wide," Dr. Kincaid said, and with a gloved finger, he wiggled Susannah's other, intact front tooth.

"Here." Noah thrust the missing tooth at him.

"Give it to the tooth fairy."

"You can't save it?"

Dr. Kincaid glanced up and grinned. "No need. She's got a spare just waiting to come in."

"It was a…baby tooth?" Noah almost sagged with relief.

"Not that I would recommend such a drastic procedure for getting rid of your loose teeth every time, young lady," Dr. Kincaid said to Susannah.

She giggled.

"We'll take an X ray to be sure that everything's all right below the gum line. But judging from the looks of the one that's left, the one she knocked out was ready to go."

"Thank God."

Noah wasn't relishing explaining the split lip, bloody nose and scraped face to Tess. But not having to tell her that Susannah was going to go through life a snaggle-toothed wonder made things marginally better. He sagged into the chair and waited while Susannah sat stoically through the X ray. Then Dr. Kincaid cleaned her abrasions once more and bandaged the cut above her lip.

"I don't think she needs stitches," he said. "Just lots of TLC and plenty of soft food. She won't want to be chewing much for a day or so. Maybe you can talk your dad into a big dish of ice cream," he suggested to Susannah.

She looked hopefully at Noah.

He said, "I think that might be arranged."

The doctor helped her out of the chair, then ruffled her

hair and winked. "You tell your parents the tooth fairy better give you combat pay for that tooth."

Susannah grinned, then grimaced when the bandage above her lip pulled.

As they were going out the door, she looked up at Noah. "Do you know 'bout the tooth fairy?" she asked a little dubiously.

He smiled. "We've met a time or two."

She sighed. "Good."

They were heading back to Janna's car when Noah noticed that his hands were trembling. He stuffed them in his pockets. *She's all right,* he assured himself. *She's fine.* But it was all he could do not to scoop her up in his arms and just stand there, holding her, while he listened to her breathing. Did all fathers feel this way when bad things happened to their children or was it just the rookies?

"We'll pick up some ice cream on the way home," he promised as they got into the car.

Susannah looked disappointed. "Why can't we just get it when we go Chrithmuth thopping?"

He stared at her. "You want to go shopping?"

"I got to get a prethent for Mom. You thaid we would," she reminded him. "Thith morning."

"That was before you went head-on with a tree. You're sure you feel well enough?"

"Courth," Susannah said. She fastened her seat belt, then looked over at him. "I didn't cry in there at all. I wath tough, wathn't I, Noah? Brave, like you are when you get bucked off?"

Noah, about to back out of the parking place, stopped and looked at his small daughter. She was holding herself very still, her back straight, her hands clenched into tight little fists. Only her eyes wavered uncertainly as she looked at him.

A corner of his mouth tilted. He drew a finger along the curve of her jaw. "You were one tough hombre, Susannah."

Her gaze steadied. She managed a smile, a tiny one that didn't hurt. "Thath's all right, then."

Janna took them to get a rental car, and if she was dismayed at Noah taking Susannah, still bloody but unbowed, Christmas shopping, she didn't say so. She just asked, "We'll still see you for dinner at five?" when she dropped them off at the rental agency.

"We'll be there," Noah promised.

Shopping with Susannah was a painstaking process. For a man who could remember his own boyhood penchant for going through his meager allowance like it was water, watching his daughter comparison shop was something to behold. Obviously she'd got her frugal-consumer gene from her mother.

"I'm getting bubble bath. Mom likes bubble bath," Susannah told him when they'd shopped all the way up and down Third Street, after which she insisted he take her to one of the big discount stores. She was speaking slowly, avoiding the gap where her tooth had been, forming her words, especially the ones with S sounds, carefully. "The flowery ones."

"They had bubble bath in the last store."

"Yeah, but it's cheaper at the other place," she explained. "I only have six dollars and twenty-five cents. And I gotta buy you a present, too."

"No, you don't."

Susannah just looked at him. "I do."

It wasn't hard to figure out what to buy Susannah. The only thing she had eyes for was a bike. She didn't say anything when they wandered through the toy section, but her gaze lingered on a shiny red bicycle, and she ran her fingers over the handlebars as they went past.

"Libby has a bike like that," she said.

"Lucky girl," Noah replied. "Though I don't know how she'll ride it in the snow."

"It doesn't matter," Susannah said. "She'll ride it again in the spring." She got a sort of wistful, faraway look in her eyes, and it didn't take a mind reader to see what she was seeing—Libby racing past on her bright red bike, leaving Susannah standing on the curb, watching.

Not if he had anything to say about it!

She helped him pick out toys for Tanner and Maggie's three and Luke and Jill's little one. He bought bubble bath—the kind Susannah recommended—for both of his sisters-in-law. Then they went to a Western outfitter's store, and he bought a bridle for Tanner and a flashy rodeo shirt for Luke.

He didn't know what to get Tess.

"What do you think?" he asked Susannah. "What would your mother like?"

Susannah open her mouth, then seemed to think better of it. Her eyes got a soft, sad look in them as she just glanced at him and shook her head.

Nita LongReach was standing just outside the physical-therapy department when Noah and Susannah walked in. After one look at Susannah, she didn't even notice Noah. "I'll get her mother," she said.

"Don't," Noah said quickly. "She's all right."

Nita glanced at him and did a double-take. "My, aren't you a fast worker."

Noah flushed.

Susannah took his hand. "He's my dad."

Nita's eyes almost popped out of her head. Noah's face

burned hotter, but he made himself face her astonished stare.

Finally Nita got control of herself enough to press her lips together. She shook her head. "Oh, my," she said. "Oh, my!"

If she'd wanted to say more, she didn't get a chance, for the nurse from therapy called Noah's name and he went in, taking Susannah with him.

He rode the exercise bike. He lifted weights. He did the treadmill—all under Susannah's watchful eye. And all with the appropriate, macho bravado.

But when the therapist went to bend his knee, Noah's tough-guy image almost flew out the window.

Only the sight of his solemn-faced daughter watching him kept him swallowing his groans. Only the memory of her determined stoicism at the dentist's kept the involuntary tears that lined his eyelids unshed.

He was sweating and shaking when he was done.

"Best yet," the therapist said with an approving grin. "You'll have to bring her along every time."

Noah sagged onto the chair and grunted.

Susannah took a towel and gently wiped beads of sweat off his face. Her expression was serious as she studied him. "You were very brave."

Noah reached out a hand and touched her hair. Then a sound made him look up. Tess was standing in the doorway.

Seven

Obviously Nita had passed along word of their arrival. And if the look on Tess's face was anything to go by, she'd also given her a hint of what to expect.

Noah held his breath.

Tess crossed the room slowly, the only sign of her tension the clenching and unclenching of her fingers. Susannah turned to see who he was looking at, and for the first time, Tess saw her face. Noah tensed, waiting for the accusations to begin.

"Well," she said, letting out a long, slow breath, "at least you didn't break your nose."

Susannah grinned, displaying the gap where her tooth had been. "Th'other one wiggles, too," she said, demonstrating with her tongue.

"So it does," Tess said as she crouched down to Susannah's level to get a closer look.

"I took her to the dentist," Noah offered nervously, still

expecting the other shoe to drop. ''I took the tooth, too, but he said it was ready to come out.''

''It was.''

''I didn't mean—I never wanted—'' he began desperately.

Tess straightened and met his eyes. Her smile was gentle, almost rueful. ''Welcome,'' she said, ''to fatherhood.''

He wasn't sure that she didn't expect him to turn tail and run.

Three days ago, if someone had offered it to him, he was damned certain he would have. But now, he felt something inside him settle down and take root.

A sense of fatherhood? A notion of commitment to this child?

Yes.

And to her mother.

The thought came out of nowhere, unbidden, unheralded. And undeniable, for all he wasn't expecting it.

And to her mother? What did that mean?

It meant marry Tess.

Was that what he was thinking? The notion rocked him.

But yes, now that he considered it, that was exactly what he was thinking. Eight years ago he'd shoved away any thoughts of marriage without daring to take even a quick look. The very thought of tying himself to anyone or anything terrified him.

Not anymore.

On the contrary, it was attractive as hell. Hadn't he been moaning to Taggart the very day they'd been hit about being the lone bachelor among his brothers? Hadn't he been coveting their homes and their kids and their marital bliss?

Well, hell, he had a kid. He could have a home.

He could have Tess.

As if she was aware of what was going through his mind

at that very moment, he saw a flicker of apprehension cross Tess's face. She looked at him warily. "What?"

He shook his head quickly. He might know his mind at last, but he had enough sense not to spring a proposal on her in the middle of a waiting room.

"I was just thinking I like being a father," he said, when it was clear she was waiting for some sort of answer.

Susannah beamed.

Tess looked at him, then quickly away. "Yes, well... Christmas isn't over yet."

"I think I might like being a father for longer than Christmas."

Susannah's eyes widened. Her jaw dropped.

Tess's mouth pressed into a tight line. "Don't," she said softly, "make promises you won't keep."

Susannah, who'd had her prayers answered, and who had a scraped face and a tantalizing new gap in her grin, was the focus of everyone's attention at the Williamses' dinner. Everyone's attention, that is, except Noah's.

He didn't precisely ignore his daughter. But more than he watched Susannah, he watched Tess.

He watched her smiling as she helped Janna put the food on the table. He watched her bend and give Susannah a gentle kiss on the forehead in the one spot that hadn't been abraded by her collision with the tree. He watched her laughing at Jeff's retelling of Susannah's encounter with the tree—and it was funny, now that she was fine.

But Noah wasn't thinking about that. He was thinking that he wanted those smiles and those kisses and those gentle laughs to be for him.

And the only other thing he was aware of was that, while he was watching Tess, Steve watched him. Narrowly. Speculatively. Assessingly. Not saying much, just watching. Until supper was over, and Janna and Tess and the kids were cleaning up before they all went to a local nursing home to sing carols with Susannah and Libby's Brownie troop.

Then Steve pushed back his chair and said, "Speaking of hunting, you might like to take a look at my guns."

Noah, who knew a cue when he heard one, said, "I wouldn't mind," and followed Steve down the hall to a small den. Jeff hopped up and started to follow them.

"Not now," his father said.

"But—"

Steve stopped in the doorway and gave his son a stern look. "I said not now."

He was probably a good cop, Noah thought. He did authority well. Jeff obviously thought so. The boy sighed and slunk back toward the kitchen.

Steve ushered Noah into the den and shut the door. He went to the tall oak gun cabinet on the far side of the room, took out his key and opened it.

"I'd have let him stay," he said, not looking at Noah, "because I think it's important for a father to teach his son about guns. My father taught me. But..." He gave a slight shrug as his voice trailed off.

"But you wanted to talk about something other than guns."

Steve's eyes met Noah's. He didn't say anything for a moment. Then a corner of his mouth twisted wryly. "And you're going to say it's none of my business."

"Maybe."

"And maybe, in a strict sense, you'd be right," Steve said flatly. "But Tess has been our friend for three years. She's a good friend. We don't want her getting hurt."

"Neither do I."

They stared at each other, neither giving an inch, neither looking away. Finally Steve nodded, apparently satisfied that he'd made his point. He reached into the cabinet and took out a rifle. He put one foot on the seat of a high-back chair and cradled the rifle on his thigh. He ran his hand down the barrel lovingly, his head bent as he studied the stock. Then he lifted his gaze and met Noah's once more. "She's a beauty."

They weren't talking about guns. Noah nodded. "Yes."

"She deserves the best a man has got."

"I know."

"And that little gal—she's as precious to me as my own."

Noah inclined his head. "You've done good by 'em both. I appreciate that."

"Tess said you didn't know about Susannah." Steve balanced the gun in his hands for a long moment, then offered it to Noah.

He took it, letting it rest lightly in his palms, becoming accustomed to the weight. "No. But it's no excuse. I was young and dumb. I didn't think." He shrugged. "I should have known."

A fleeting, rueful smile crossed Steve's face. "I didn't, when Janna was pregnant. And I was with her every day."

Noah stared.

Steve nodded. "Reckon we both were a little too quick on the draw," he said ruefully. He ducked his head momentarily, rocked back on his heels and stuffed his hands in his back pockets. "She told me when she was three months along. And I married her."

"Just like that?"

The grin flickered again. "I had to undergo a bit of an attitude adjustment first. My old man helped. So did hers."

"You plannin' on helpin' me?"

"Do you need it?"

"Nope."

Steve smiled. "Then enough said."

He was watching her. Had been watching her all evening. So what was new about that? Tess thought irritably. He'd been watching her since the moment he opened his eyes and recognized the nurse standing over him.

This wasn't the same.

That had been flirting, teasing, a typical Noah Tanner approach to a woman he wanted to put the make on.

This was something else.

Or maybe she was hallucinating, wanting it to be something else. Because, God help her, she still wanted him. Even though she knew better, even though she knew he was as dependable as a snowman in springtime, she wanted him.

She'd tried not to, for goodness sake. She'd done her absolute best to hold him at arm's length ever since he'd dropped back into her life. But her absolute best didn't seem to be good enough. Not when Noah's deep blue eyes and all the matchmakers in Laramie, Wyoming, were working against her.

There was Susannah, of course. Even though her daughter hadn't actually said anything, Tess was no fool. She knew what Susannah wanted: her mother and her father together at last. So much so that she even gave up her chair next to Noah at the Williamses' dinner table, saying, "Can't I sit by Libby? Mom can sit here."

And damned if Janna didn't go along with it. Because, drat her, her neighbor seemed to be conspiring against her, too.

"He's all right," Janna had said, taking Tess aside when they'd come for dinner. "He handled that business with Susannah's tooth very well."

It was a high compliment from Janna, whose parenting instincts were finely tuned. "He's got what it takes."

Tess hadn't answered. Maybe he did have what it took to be a father; she didn't know. She didn't imagine she'd ever find out, even though Janna and even Steve seemed to think it was a good idea.

So did Nita, who had stopped her as they were leaving work that afternoon. "You're a dark horse," she'd teased. All the nurses had thought so, especially when Susannah didn't hesitate to reveal that Noah wasn't just any old patient who'd dropped in at Tess's house. "Who'd have thought you had a man like that on a string all these years?" Nita grinned.

"I didn't," Tess had protested.

But Nita had laughed. "Not much," she'd said. She meant the opposite.

Her view seemed to be the majority one at the Green Acres Rest Center, too. At least that was the impression Tess got when she and Janna took the girls' Brownie troop there that evening to sing carols.

"You don't have to come," she'd said to Noah firmly.

"I want to," he replied just as firmly.

"I'll come, too," Steve offered. And so they went.

Susannah might have looked like she'd gone ten rounds with the devil, but she sang like an angel. Tess would have beamed as proudly as she always did, if she hadn't been aware of Noah's eyes on her every minute. She wanted to tell him, "Watch the children, not me!" But she knew the guileless, innocent look she'd get if she did. So she suffered in silence. And grew more aware of him by the minute.

She wasn't the only one. Every single person she knew who listened to the Brownies sing that evening—Malcolm and Kenton and Buck, Addie Mae and Trudi, Joyce and Harriet and Sister Saint Joan, all the residents she and Susannah and the Brownie troop had visited during the year—enjoyed the program. But every one of them was far more interested in the man they didn't know, the one who, as Addie said, "had eyes only for Tess."

And when they found out who he was—because, of course, Susannah had to drag him from one to the other after they'd finished singing and say, "This is my father"—well, Tess could see the wheels turning in those elderly heads!

"Ah," they each said with a sigh, and looked him over with such intense interest that if she'd been Noah, she'd have wanted to crawl under a rock.

And then, as if their blatant speculation wasn't enough, each and every one of them shook his hand and said, "It's about time."

Noah seemed to take it all in stride. And Tess was the one who was squirming as his gaze never left her while he said to one and all, "You're right. It is."

And what, she'd like to know, was that supposed to mean?

Damn it, where was all that indifference she'd been so carefully cultivating since the moment Noah Tanner had reappeared in her life? What had happened to her stoic disinterest, her determinedly casual nonchalance in the face of anything he might do?

The longer he looked, the more she felt as if she was on fire.

"My goodness, Tess," Addie Mae said to her as they were leaving, "you have a regular holiday glow."

Which made it even worse.

She was glad that Susannah was almost asleep on her feet by the time they got home. It gave Tess an excuse to slip away from Noah's gaze. "I'll just help her get ready for bed,'' she said over her shoulder as she hustled her yawning daughter up the stairs.

Unfortunately for her, Susannah cooperated completely, and thirty seconds after her head hit the pillow, she was asleep. The only thing she said to her mother as she nestled beneath the quilt was, ''They liked him, didn't they?''

Tess nodded. She couldn't pretend not to know what Susannah meant.

Susannah smiled and hugged her stuffed bear against her chest. ''Good,'' she murmured, her eyes drifting shut. ''I thought they would.''

Tess stood looking down at her blissfully sleeping daughter, then reached out and smoothed a lock of hair away from her face. ''Don't want it,'' she whispered. ''Oh, darling, don't.''

It was vain advice and she knew it. But she had to say it because she knew all too well the pain of wanting what she couldn't have.

It was too much to hope that Noah would have taken himself off to bed by the time she got back downstairs. Instead, he was in the kitchen pouring out two cups of tea.

''Tea?'' Tess's eyes widened.

''Cowboys drink tea,'' he said defensively. ''My old man drank nothing else. My mother used to make it for us kids, too, sometimes, when we'd had a hard day. 'Cures what ails you,' she used to say.''

''And what is…ailing us?'' Tess asked cautiously.

He gave her a wry glance. ''I thought maybe seein' your daughter look like she'd plowed the north forty with her face would do it.''

''I told you, it happens. Stuff happens…to kids. You can't prevent it.'' But she took the tea gratefully when he held it out to her, curling her fingers around the cup, glad that she had it to hide behind. He was looking at her again.

"You were a lot nicer about it than you might've been."
As he spoke, he moved toward the door that led to the
living room, herding her before him, so that she found herself on the sofa without really understanding how she got
there. He sat down beside her. Close. Very close.

She took a hasty swallow and burned her tongue. "Is
that another way of implying you think I can be a bitch?"
she asked.

"Hell, no!" His look became as earnest as it was intense.
"How can you say that? My word, Tess, you're just about
the sweetest gal—you *are* the sweetest gal I've ever
known."

It was sweet talk, and she knew it. Sugar-coated words
designed to make her soften and smile and welcome him
with open arms.

And God help her, she wanted to do just that.

With everything in her she had been resisting him for so
long, fighting her attraction to him so hard, that she was
worn out. Her defenses were a shambles; the walls she'd
tried so desperately to build against him were rubble at her
feet. She had no strength left. And she wanted nothing more
than to stop fighting him. And herself.

She wanted to reach out. She wanted—fool that she
was—to love.

She wasn't quite a big enough fool to believe she'd get
it. Not love. Not from a footloose cowboy who, she knew
only too well, would be on the road again a few days hence.

But tonight—just tonight—with Noah; yes, she could
have that.

As long as she didn't expect undying promises, as long
as she knew exactly what she was getting—a night of
warmth and comfort, a night of sharing—it would be all
right. She would be safe.

Wouldn't she?

Tess didn't examine her reasoning too closely. It wouldn't stand up to scrutiny, as she well knew. But she also knew that she didn't have the energy to resist any longer. She had been without a man's touch—*this man's touch*—far too long. She was only human, after all. She had needs as much as anyone.

It was almost Christmas, so maybe her needs were nearer the surface than usual. Or maybe it was just that Noah was nearer than usual.

Whatever… When he took the cup from her fingers and set it on the coffee table out of the way, she didn't object. And when he set his own down, too, and laid his hands lightly on her arms, she didn't pull away. On the contrary, she found herself leaning into his touch, seeking it, seeking him.

She knew it was foolish. She knew that tomorrow she'd doubtless be sorry. But the light in his deep blue eyes drew her like a moth to a flame.

"Just tonight," she whispered. "Just tonight."

She didn't even think Noah heard. If he did, he paid no attention. As she spoke, his lips came down to swallow her words.

This kiss was different from the one he'd given her in the hospital. That had been a conquest—the kiss of a man with something to prove. This kiss was far gentler, far sweeter, far, far harder to resist.

Not that Tess was in any way resisting. She'd lost that battle. She wasn't even thinking about the war. Her only thoughts were of Noah and the moment. She wanted him— she *needed* him—now.

It was she who deepened the kiss, she who slipped her arms around him and tugged his shirttails out of his jeans. And as he shuddered at the feel of her hands against his heated skin, she smiled.

Yes. Yes. Just for tonight, she could have him.

Take it slow, Noah had told himself. *Go easy.* He hadn't counted on her sweeping him off his feet.

He'd been prepared to work this evening, to soothe and gentle Tess with the same patience his father had used on a skittish mare, to win her around.

But somewhere along the line, patience was no longer an issue, soothing and gentling were beside the point. He wasn't having to draw Tess along with him, he was having to put the brakes on!

If she kept on touching him the way she was, it was going to be over before they'd begun.

She'd touched him in the hospital. She'd held him and helped him and soaped him and washed him, and all the time, she'd treated him with the interest she might show a stick of wood. Her touch might have excited him then, if it hadn't so obviously done nothing for her.

Not so tonight. Not if the tremor in her fingers was anything to go by as they skimmed up beneath his shirt. And if it was affecting her, it was setting him on fire.

His ''go easy, take it slow'' took on an entirely different meaning once she'd unbuttoned his shirt and eased it off his shoulders, when her fingers began to work on his belt and her lips pressed another kiss on his. The merest brush of her fingers on the denim that covered him and he was in danger of burning right down to the ground!

Not that he was complaining. God, no. But—

''Tess! Wait!''

She stopped abruptly, her eyes wide and worried, her body suddenly stiff. ''What? What's wrong?''

''Nothing. Nothing's wrong. It's right.'' He smiled wryly and leaned toward her to kiss her eyelids. ''Too right.'' With trembling fingers, he worked with slow precision to undo the buttons of her blouse. ''I want you bad. But I want it to last. So easy does it, darlin'. We've got all night.''

Tess took a deep breath, and he saw a shudder run through her. Her lashes dropped for just a moment, then she nodded and a faintly wistful smile touched her lips. ''You're right,'' she said. ''We have all night.''

It wasn't enough. It would never be enough; she knew that. But she also knew it was all she was going to get. And so she did her best to simply immerse herself in the moment, to savor the smiles and the touches and the heat of his flesh against hers.

She would have tugged his jeans off right there on the sofa, but he wouldn't let her. ''No,'' he said in a ragged whisper. ''Not here.'' And he drew her to her feet and up the stairs.

She should have protested. She didn't want him making love to her in her bedroom. When the night was over, when Christmas had come and gone—and so had Noah—she didn't want to have to face the memory every day. But even so, she seemed powerless to resist. And when he ushered her into her room and eased the door shut behind them, she pulled back the covers and welcomed him into her arms.

It felt like coming home. She had forgotten how pleasurable the warm, solid weight of his body pressing into hers really was. No, that wasn't true. She'd never forgotten. She had only tried to.

There had been other men in her life in the eight years after Noah. There had been no other men in her bed.

She had tried to become interested in some of them: Mark the respiratory therapist and Steven, the CPA. She hadn't lacked for men who were interested in her. But none of them had attracted her in the least. Like Derek Mallon, they were pleasant and kind, but they weren't Noah.

Noah. After all these years. Tears pricked behind her eyelids as she felt the rough brush of his whiskers against her chin. Noah. A lump formed in her throat as his callused fingers caressed the smooth skin of her breasts. Noah. A fire rose within her as he moved to slip her jeans and panties down her hips.

Heaven help her, she still loved him.

And he was loving her. Not the way she loved him, but the only way he knew how. With his lips and his body, with the sure, gentle touch of his hands.

Tess gave herself over to it, allowing herself to relish what he could give, and giving to him in return. She had waited so long; she had so much to share. But she heeded his words and took her time.

They had all night.

She wouldn't think about the morning.

Noah hadn't been celibate since he'd made love with Tess. But he'd never had a woman who could hold a candle to her. No other woman had ever welcomed him into her bed, into her arms, into her body, the way Tess did. No other woman had made him feel so cherished, so valued, so loved.

He'd been a fool not to see it eight years before. But he wasn't a fool any longer. She was everything he wanted in a woman. And he set about with all the skill he possessed to show her.

It wasn't easy. He wanted her desperately. He made himself slow down. He shed his jeans and shorts and lay beside her on the bed. With his hand, he smoothed the curves of her body, then leaned in to touch his lips to hers. He made himself linger over her lips, her breasts, the smooth, shapely length of her legs. He savored the petal softness of her skin, so different from his own, taking his time, taking his pleasure—and hers—before at last his fingers found the center of her.

"Noah!" She stiffened and then melted at his touch.

"Mmm." He smiled, pressing a kiss to her lips as he slid between her thighs. "Not ready yet?"

"I'm ready!" Her legs came around him, drawing him in.

She was so tight and wet and warm that he very nearly lost it right then. Only the fact that she held perfectly still— held *him* perfectly still—saved him. He caught his breath. Then, when he dared, he at last began to move.

She tried to go easy. She tried to take it slow. But she'd waited so long—*years!*—for him. Her careful composure deserted her; her control snapped. She moved with him, at first as slowly as she was sure he wanted; but then, because she couldn't help it, the tempo picked up. She moved faster, harder, more desperately.

"Noah!" She gasped his name against his shoulder. Her fingernails dug into his back. Her body convulsed around him. She wept.

It wasn't slow. It wasn't easy. It shattered him. *She* shattered him. He tasted tears on her cheeks and didn't know whether they were hers or his own. Then he spent himself deep within her and sank exhausted, replete, content at last, into the cradle of her arms.

They'd had all night.

They'd loved—quickly and desperately, slowly and languorously, sweetly and playfully. And then, not long before morning, they'd slept.

Tess awoke by habit at a quarter to six. And thank heaven for the habit, she thought, because her alarm clock was still in the living room by the sofa, where she hadn't slept last night.

Slowly, carefully, she eased herself out of Noah's embrace. He muttered in his sleep and reached for her, hauling her back.

Just a minute. Just one more minute, she promised herself, snuggling once more into his arms.

She lay there, counting the seconds, sixty of them, as slowly as she dared, all the while memorizing the feel of the hard warmth of his body next to hers, the muscled weight of his arm wrapped around her, the soft whistle of his breath against her cheek. When she reached fifty, she turned her head and touched her lips to his, left them there, let them savor… *Fifty-seven, fifty-eight, fifty-nine.* Her hand slid up against the back of his neck, cupped it, drew him in. *Sixty.*

The night was over. The loving was over. The dream was over.

Tess sighed and slipped out of bed.

Eight

When he woke up, Tess wasn't there.

Noah reached for her instinctively, but the space where she had spent the last hours of the night curled next to him was already cold. Bright winter sun pouring through the window made him realize how late it was. Clearly she had already left for work, and he'd slept far too long.

Still he didn't get up immediately. He couldn't help lying there just a few minutes longer, luxuriating in the memory of Tess in his arms. Loving her was every bit as wonderful as he remembered. Her warmth, her eager responsiveness—everything about her made him lie there and smile.

He heard a rattling sound in the kitchen. Susannah, no doubt. Fixing him breakfast in bed again? He wouldn't have been surprised. Still, once was enough. It was his turn to do something special for her. He got up, stretched and grinned at the sore muscles, which were another reminder of the time spent loving Tess the night before.

Whistling, he went to take a shower.

He took Susannah out for breakfast. Her mouth wasn't nearly as tender as it had been the day before, so she tucked right into a plate of blueberry pancakes, grinning up at him between bites of pancake and swallows of milk. Noah downed an order of pancakes, two eggs, ham, toast, hash browns and coffee. It was more than he'd eaten in weeks. He felt better than he'd felt since the semi had slapped his van.

He was still whistling when they left the café.

He and Susannah finished the rest of her Christmas shopping before noon. They went home and wrapped the presents and put them under the tree. Then she went over to Janna's to take Libby the gift she'd bought for her that morning.

"Could she maybe stay with you for a while?" Noah asked Janna. "I've got a little more shopping to do."

Janna smiled. "Take your time."

It wouldn't take him long, Noah thought. But before he left, he had some phone calls to make. The first was to the doctor, who told him it was all right if he missed one therapy session. The second was to Taggart.

"Hey, buddy, how you doin'?" Taggart sounded just like his old self.

"Good." Noah leaned back against the sofa and stretched his feet out in front of him, crossing them at the ankles, looking at the photo of Tess and Susannah on the mantel. "I'm doin' good. Great, in fact."

"Ah." He could hear the smile in Taggart's voice. "Reckon you must've talk Tessie around then."

"Well, uh, sort of."

"Sort of? Doesn't sound like you."

"She had a...surprise for me."

"What sort of surprise?" Taggart asked cautiously.

Noah hesitated, then told his friend flat out, "We have a daughter."

He explained about Susannah, his words alternately hearty and halting, depending on whether he was talking about the beautiful child he was proud to call his own, or the two weeks that had led up to her conception.

Taggart listened without interrupting. When Noah finished at last, his friend only had two words to say. "Now what?"

"Now I'm gonna marry her, of course," Noah said. There wasn't any doubt in his mind.

It was a little more difficult to tell Tanner, whom he called next.

"Where the hell have you been?" Tanner demanded when he heard Noah's voice. "I've been calling your motel for three days. They said you'd checked out."

"I did."

"You did?" There was a low whistle. "You mean she really took you in? Son of a gun, I don't know how you do it," Tanner said after a moment. "Must be somethin' to have all that sex appeal."

Noah felt curiously nettled. "It isn't just sex appeal."

"Pardon me," Tanner said, amused. "Didn't mean to slight your intellectual allure."

"Maggie been teaching you new words?" Noah grumbled.

"Among other things," Tanner said with a certain amount of smugness. "Haven't you, babe?" he said, and Noah heard him give someone, presumably his long-suffering wife, a smacking kiss.

"Robert! Behave yourself!" Maggie said. But she was laughing and so was he, and Noah smiled, because in a few hours he knew he would be playing those kinds of games with Tess again. But first he had to fill the family in on the new additions. And now that the moment had come to do so, he couldn't find the words.

"What's her last name?" Tanner asked.

"Montgomery."

"And she's a nurse?"

"Uh-huh."

"Met her before, did you?"

"Yeah." Maybe if Tanner kept asking him questions, he'd find the words. How long would it take for his brother to ask, "Father any children with her?"

"Listen, Robert." Noah spoke his brother's name with a twist that was half-fond, half-wry. "Could I maybe talk to your wife?"

"Why?"

"Just let me talk to her."

"You shouldn't be asking what to get me for Christmas at this late date," Tanner teased. Then he sighed and there was another smacking kiss sound. A second later, Maggie's breathless voice said, "Noah, are you all right?"

"Fine. Really," he added, when the one word didn't sound very convincing. "Never been better, in fact."

"Truly? We were so worried. I'd have come with Robert when he came to visit you," Maggie assured him, "but the weather was pretty iffy right then and he didn't want to bring all the boys if there was a chance we might stall somewhere. We'll come as soon as Christmas is over, I promise. Maybe Luke and Jill can come, too. Will that be all right?"

"It'd be fine, Maggie, but I was wonderin' if maybe I could come and see you."

"But I thought the doctor said—"

"I've got to come back," he said quickly. "But he said

I could miss one session. We could leave here Christmas afternoon, spend the day after with you, then head back. What do you say?''

Maggie said, "We?"

Noah had always suspected his sister-in-law was pretty sharp.

"That'd be the girl I was tellin' you about," he heard Tanner tell his wife, apparently explaining the "we" on his behalf.

"Her name's Tess," Noah said, bowing to the inevitable.

"Oh, marvelous! And you're bringing her for Christmas? Even better." He could imagine her rubbing her hands together.

"That's not all he's bringing, I hope," Tanner said in the background. "Ask him what he's bringing me now that he's the cham-peen bronc rider in the world."

"Tell him," Noah said to Maggie, "that I'm bringing him a niece."

There was stunned silence on the other end of the line. It was the first time Noah ever remembered his sister-in-law being at a loss for words. "Noah?" she said after a long pause.

"Didn't hang up on you, did he?" Tanner asked.

Maggie didn't answer him. "Noah?" she said again. "Are you serious?"

"Her name's Susannah," he told her. "She's seven. She's beautiful, Mag. The most beautiful little girl in the whole damn world. You wouldn't believe…"

"Oh, Noah!" Her tone held a mixture of astonishment, love, pride and concern all at once.

"What's the matter with Noah?" Tanner wanted to know.

"Somethin' wrong with Noah?" he heard Luke ask.

"Tell 'em, Mag, will you?" Noah urged. "I…can't."

''But—''

''Please. I'll bring her. And Tess. We'll see you Christmas night.''

''I—''

''You're a jewel, Mag. Thanks.'' And he hung up.

A man who rode bucking broncs for a living couldn't be deemed a complete coward. But brave as he might be on the back of a horse, Noah didn't have the guts to tell Tanner about Susannah.

Maybe it was because of his brother's hasty, but determinedly responsible, first marriage on account of Clare's pregnancy, a far cry from his own less-than-chivalrous treatment of Tess. Maybe it was because his brother's son had died, while he, through no virtue of his own, was now unjustly rewarded with a lively, lovely daughter.

Whatever it was—guilt, immaturity, embarrassment, cowardice, all of the above—Noah couldn't face Tanner, even over the telephone. So he passed the buck to Maggie. She could do it with far more finesse than he could. And he'd be able to face his brothers better when they already knew.

''You haven't gone!'' Susannah opened the back door and stared at him.

''Uh, no. Not yet.'' Noah jerked back to the present. ''I was just…makin' a couple of calls first.'' He shoved away from the counter where he'd been standing. ''What are you doing back?''

Susannah flushed. ''I was just, uh, getting a game to play with Libby and Jeff.'' She started past him when the phone rang.

She picked it up. ''Hello?'' There was a pause. ''This is Susannah,'' she said, and Noah noticed how careful she was not to turn the *s*'s into *th*'s. He smiled.

Her eyes widened. "My uncle Robert?" She shot Noah a glance, then ran her tongue over her lips.

"What?" Noah straightened sharply. *That was Tanner on the phone?* He almost snatched the receiver out of her hand. Only a shred of common courtesy stopped him. That and the slow smile that he could see spreading over Susannah's face.

"I'm seven," she was saying now, apparently in response to one of Tanner's questions. "And a half." There was a pause. "April 12th."

Tanner must have asked when her birthday was. Noah's fingers itched to take the phone. Susannah was still smiling as she listened to whatever Tanner was saying.

"I know. My dad told me about them. We got presents for them." Tanner's boys, obviously. Susannah giggled. "I don't know if my mom will let me baby-sit yet."

Noah goggled at the thought.

"'Kay," Susannah was saying. "I'll see you tomorrow, Uncle Robert."

Noah expected her to hang up.

She said, "Hi, Uncle Luke."

So then he had to stand and tap his toes and shift from one foot to the other and wonder what Luke was saying to her. Whatever it was, it made her giggle and glance at him and then giggle again.

"Oh, no, he's really brave," she said at last, giving him another look. "You should see him when he goes to therapy. It hurts a lot, but he works really hard."

So Noah supposed that all his effort yesterday hadn't been totally in vain. He smiled at his daughter.

"He said I was brave, too," Susannah told Luke. "'Cause yesterday when he was baby-sitting me, I ran into a tree an' knocked out my tooth an' I didn't even cry...much.'' She paused. "No, he was careful,'' she said. "It was my fault.''

Noah scowled.

Susannah grinned at him. "Do you want to talk to him?'' she asked Luke. "Oh, okay. Yeah, I can hardly wait to meet you, too. Bye.''

She hung up and looked at Noah, starry-eyed. "That was my uncle Robert and my uncle Luke,'' she told him. "They said we're gonna see them tomorrow.''

He nodded, pleased now that Tanner had called, though a few minutes ago he'd done his share of worrying. He should have known his brothers would welcome a niece with open arms. They'd welcome Tess, too. And as far as what they might say to him privately, well, it was nothing he didn't deserve.

"I thought maybe we could drive up there tomorrow— after Santa comes,'' he added, in case Susannah was worried.

She didn't seem to be. "That'll be neat. An' then I'll get to see my cousins.'' She said the word with relish and grinned up at him again. "I always wanted a sister or brother,'' she confided. "But I don't care so much if I've got cousins.''

It was on the tip of his tongue to tell her that perhaps he and Tess would see what they could do about a brother or sister for her, too. But he thought it was something he'd better talk over with Tess first.

"I'm sure they'll be glad to have you, too,'' he said.

They were sitting side by side on the couch, their dark heads bent over a book that Susannah held across her knees, when Tess walked in the door. They looked up at her with identical smiles that made her heart turn over in her chest.

"Look, Mom! Noah's showin' me his scrapbook.''

A scrapbook of his rodeo days, Tess presumed. The chronicle of his travels down the road, culminating in the gold-buckle finals just over two weeks ago.

"Come see," Susannah commanded.

Noah flushed. "You don't have—"

But Tess slipped off her boots and hung up her coat, then said, "Let me see." It would be salutary, she told herself. It would remind her, in case she let her heart get in the way of her common sense, what really mattered to Noah Tanner. His scrapbook would point out very clearly who he really was.

So she got a considerable shock when she peered over Susannah's shoulder and found that she was looking at a childish drawing of a fat man in a red suit and a bunch of stick animals she supposed must be reindeer.

"Noah drew that," Susannah said, "when he was three."

"I wasn't much of an artist," he muttered. "Come on, Suse. We don't have to bore your mother with a bunch of old scribblings."

"I'm not bored," Tess said. Indeed, she was enthralled. "What is this?"

"It's Noah's scrapbook. I was tellin' you," Susannah said impatiently. "He made it with his mother when he was a little boy."

"We all did." Noah sounded almost defensive. The color in his cheeks was still high. "Me and Tan—I mean, Robert—and Luke. We put Christmas cards we liked in 'em, and drawings and letters to Santa. They were mostly Christmas books. But my mother put some snapshots in, too. After my dad died, we had to move, and my brother was, well, hurt, I guess. And angry. He was throwing everything out, and—" he shrugged "—the scrapbooks were about all that was left of when my mother was alive. So I saved 'em.''

The scrapbook Susannah held was rather shabby looking and water spotted, Tess noted now. There were two others on the coffee table, both equally worn.

''I had 'em stored at a friend's in Durango,'' Noah explained. ''I'd pretty much forgot about them until last Christmas, when I was at Tanner and Maggie's. An' damned if Tanner wasn't helping Jared make a scrapbook. He shrugged kinda awkward and said, 'I was thinkin' about the ones we made.' An' then he said, 'You were so young, you probably don't even remember.''' Noah grinned reminiscently. ''I didn't tell him I had them. I thought I'd give him his this Christmas. I picked 'em up on my way to Vegas for the finals, because I knew I was goin' to his place right after. I just remembered this afternoon that they were still in the van.''

''We went to the mechanic place—''

''Body shop,'' Noah explained.

''—And got 'em,'' Susannah finished. ''Come look,'' she invited again, and inched over so she was practically sitting in Noah's lap.

And Tess, in spite of her better judgment, was captivated by the chance to know the child Noah had been. She sat down.

He'd wanted to impress her. He'd wanted her to come home, take one look at him and remember the virile, eager man who'd made love to her the night before.

Instead she was seeing him as a three-year-old. Worse, a one-year-old.

It was bad enough having your daughter see a picture of you with your Christmas stocking and your diaper half falling down. It was downright mortifying to have the woman you'd made love to for hours take one look at the one-year-old Noah Tanner, smile, swallow a laugh and say, "What cute cheeks."

Noah didn't think he'd ever been so embarrassed in his life. He started to shut the scrapbook, but Tess and Susannah pulled it away from him. Then they sat there smiling and simpering at what a cute little boy he'd been, and what a jolly little snowman he'd drawn, and how handsome he and his big brothers had looked sitting in a row on the old runner sled in front of the house.

Finally, thank heavens, Susannah had seen enough. She wiggled and then bounced off the sofa and went to let the cat out. But even when Noah said, "You've seen all there is to see, believe me," Tess wasn't ready to relinquish the book.

"I thought Suse looked like me," she said wonderingly. "Except for the eyes, of course. They were always yours. But see how much she looks like Robert?"

"That's 'cause he was seven in that picture," Noah said. "Same as her." It was the last one in the book, the one with the three of them on the sled. It was the last Christmas his mother had been alive.

Tess shook her head. "It's not just the age. See? She has his jaw."

"Stubborn," Noah said. "Righteous. Determined."

Tess laughed. "How did you know?"

"I know Tanner."

"You told me he was the nice one of you three," she reminded him.

"He is." Noah reflected on the phone call Tanner had made. He'd probably been calling back to chew him out for not telling him about Susannah himself. But when she'd answered the phone, he'd completely charmed her instead.

"I think they're both nice," Susannah said as she came back into the room.

Tess frowned. "How do you know?"

"I talked to 'em on the phone. We're going there tomorrow."

Tess turned her frown in his direction.

"I just called them today to—to tell them about…you. Both of you," Noah said quickly. "And one thing led to another and, well, I know you've got Christmas and the day after off, and the doc said I can miss therapy once, so I thought it would be a good way to get the family together—"

"And I can see my cousins!" Susannah exclaimed.

"Are you sure—"

"Absolutely," Noah said. His gaze met hers. "They want you to come. *I* want you to come." His gaze beseeched her. He would have preferred to bring it up after everything was settled tonight. He should have realized that Susannah would take matters into her own hands.

Tess hesitated, then nodded slowly. It wasn't the enthusiastic response Noah had hoped for. But then he hadn't asked her the all-important question yet. And she obviously had no idea he was going to.

He swallowed a smile and allowed Tess her reluctance—for now.

It wasn't easy keeping a secret.

Right before dinner, when Noah was sitting on the living room rug with Susannah, helping her build a manger with Lincoln Logs, he'd glanced up to see Tess standing in the doorway to the kitchen, looking at them wistfully. He'd wanted to get up and go to her then. The ring was burning a hold in his pocket. But he wanted the time to be right. He wanted it to be just the two of them.

Then the phone rang and she went to answer it.

"It's for you," she called from the kitchen.

Tanner again? Noah wondered. Or Luke?

Tess didn't say. She barely looked at him when he came in to pick up the phone.

"Hey, Noah, is she as pretty as she sounds?" It was a rodeo buddy named Jim Jackson, a guy he and Taggart had traveled with on and off during the past year.

Noah grinned. "Prettier, if you want to know the truth."

"You always did land on your feet. Taggart told me where you were," Jim said. "Heard you almost bought the farm couple weeks back, you 'n' Taggart both. Tough luck. How ya doin' now?"

"Better," Noah said. He was watching Tess move around the kitchen, enjoying the sight of the inch or so of midriff he was able to glimpse when she stretched to get a bowl from the top shelf of the cupboard. "Much better."

"Reckon so, with a pretty lady to kiss it and make it well. Glad to hear it. So, when you gonna be ready to go?"

"Go?" Noah echoed. Hell, he hadn't even thought about that.

"Figured to head on down to Odessa for New Year's," Jim told him. "Good money down there. Might as well start off the year right. You game?"

"Not for Odessa. Not by a long shot. I'm stuck in Laramie for the time being, trying to get my knee back in shape." He told Jim about the thrice-weekly therapy sessions.

Jim whistled. "You gonna be up for Denver?"

"Don't know." He hadn't thought that far ahead.

"Don't know much, do you?" Jim was grinning; Noah could tell.

"No, but I'm learning," he said, still watching Tess move. God, she was lovely, even when she was setting the table and pretending to ignore him. Except he didn't want to be ignored. "Gotta go," he said. "You have a good Christmas." He hung up, stepped behind Tess, who stood at the counter dishing up potatoes, and dropped a kiss on the back of her neck.

She jumped. "Stop that!" She shot a worried glance toward the living room.

He scowled. "Hey, it was just a kiss. First chance I've had to do it today. You were gone when I woke up."

Tess's cheeks grew red. She rubbed the back of her neck and muttered something under her breath. Then she said, "Get washed up, both of you. It's time for dinner."

Susannah must have heard, because she appeared in the doorway. "I'm starving. Are you starving?" she asked Noah.

He looked at Tess, devouring her with his eyes. "You bet I am."

She blushed throughout the entire meal. She also avoided his gaze. Was she thinking about what they were going to do when the lights went off tonight? Was she as eager as he was? He hoped so.

"Stop wiggling in your chair, Susannah," Tess said sharply. "Christmas won't get here any faster if you do."

Susannah stuck out her lower lip and poked at the potatoes on her plate. "It takes forever," she complained. "It takes days and days, an' when it's finally Christmas Eve, it seems like the hours take days and days, too."

Noah, reaching into his pocket and touching the small velvet box with the ring he'd bought in it, knew exactly what she meant.

"When do we leave for church?" Susannah asked.

Tess glanced at her watch. "Forty-five minutes. Enough time for you to eat a good dinner and then help me with the dishes."

"You're coming, aren't you?" Susannah asked Noah. "I'm singing in the children's choir, then Mom's singing in the real one."

"I wouldn't miss it for the world."

They got to the church well before the candlelight service was to begin. It was the same small brick building Tess had brought him to eight years before. Then, they had come on a Sunday morning, on a day filled with bright summer sunlight. Tonight the sky was dark, with low, gray clouds, and all the color came from within. The stained-glass windows shone in jewel-like splendor as they headed up the walk toward the heavy double doors.

It had started to snow again, and for once the wind had stopped, so the flakes floated gently down, dusting the sidewalk and their jackets and coming to rest in lacy profusion on Susannah's dark hair. She was walking between them, holding Tess's hand in her right and Noah's in her left. Like a family, Noah thought, looking down and smiling at her. Susannah tipped her head back and caught snowflakes on her tongue.

He saw Tess give her a fleeting look of disapproval. But then she shrugged and smiled. "I can't say anything. I've done it myself," she admitted.

"When you were a kid?" Noah asked.

"Yes." She grinned. "And this morning."

He laughed out loud, and Susannah looked up at them both, surprised, and squeezed his hand harder.

As soon as they got inside the door, she shed her jacket and handed it to her mother, then darted toward the choir loft. All at once she stopped and turned back. "Where are you going to be sitting?" she asked Noah.

He looked at Tess for instructions. She hesitated, then pointed to one of the side pews toward the back of the church. "You can meet him here," she said.

When Susannah had vanished up the steps, she explained, "The children's choir will do the caroling before the service. Then they'll come down and the adult choir will sing. There's a place in the front for the kids who come without their families or whose parents are in the choir. Usually she sits there. But since you're here..." Her voice trailed off. She looked a little wary, a little worried.

"Oh, here you are, Tess!" A jovial older lady appeared at Tess's side. "We're just going over the offertory down the hall. Can you come?"

"Go ahead," Noah said. "I'll be right there."

Tess looked as if she might have wanted to say something else, then shrugged.

"We'll be waiting for you." He dropped a kiss on the end of her nose and saw the choir lady's eyes widen. Tess blushed, then turned and hustled her away.

There was something infinitely soothing and absolutely right about sitting in a pew in a candle-lit church on Christmas Eve and listening to the clear, high voices of the children's choir sing carols he remembered singing himself long ago. Last year he'd gone with Tanner and Maggie and Jared to the little country church closest to the ranch. Maggie had been enormously pregnant, and Tanner had been sweating about whether or not they would make it through the service before she gave birth. Noah had hassled him afterward about being such a worrywart.

"Yeah, well, you have a kid next Christmas and let's see how you do," Tanner had retorted.

Noah smiled. Little had they known, either of them...

The last of the carols died away. There was a bumping and thumping overhead, and then the sound of giggles and whispers as thirty or so pairs of feet clattered down the bare wooden stairs. Seconds later Susannah climbed over two couples sitting in the same pew and wedged herself next to Noah.

He slid his arm around her and she looked up at him. ''How'd we do?''

''You were wonderful.''

It was nothing but the truth. She was the most wonderful child he'd ever known. His nephews were pretty great, but there was no one on earth, in Noah's opinion, who could compare with this little girl.

She squeezed his hand for just a second, then pulled away and slipped down onto the kneeler, bending her head, closing her eyes and folding her hands. He watched while her lips moved in silent prayer.

Then she sat back again next to him. ''I was saying thank you,'' she told him, ''for you.''

Noah spent a good part of the service saying thank you, too.

You never had to put together horses.

It was one of the advantages of giving a pony for Christmas. There was no sprocket A to be connected to flange B. No doohickey G to be attached to thingamajig H. And no chain that slipped and slid no matter what you did.

Noah had disappeared into the basement as soon as they got home, so Tess got the job of urging Susannah off to bed. For once she didn't get any argument.

''The sooner I go to sleep, the sooner it's morning,'' Susannah had said as she'd climbed the stairs. ''I know. I know.'' Then she'd glanced back over her mother's shoulder, and her gaze lit on Noah. ''Maybe I won't get anything else,'' she said. ''Since I got what I wanted.'' But she didn't look too worried, and Tess just shook her head.

''Up the steps with you, young lady.''

''I'm going,'' Susannah grumbled, then once more she

turned back. ''Will you come and kiss me goodnight?'' she had called to Noah.

''I will.''

But in the meantime, he had to get started on the bike.

It would have been easier if he'd been able to get one already built—or even mostly assembled. But by Christmas Eve, as the sales clerk explained, all those had long since been sold. What Noah had was in a box, and when he spread it out on the basement floor, the only things immediately identifiable were the wheels, the handlebars, the chain and the pedals. It was going to be a long night.

Tess appeared at the top of the stairs. ''What are you...'' She stopped and stared. ''Oh, Noah. You shouldn't—''

He looked up from where he was squatting. ''Don't tell me I shouldn't have. That's pretty apparent,'' he said wryly. ''I hope you're mechanical, 'cause I'm sure as hell not. I can do a tractor if I have to, and a windmill in a pinch, but I'm a country boy, and this country boy doesn't know a thing about bikes.''

Tess shook her head, smiling, and started down the stairs. ''Go say good night to Susannah. She's waiting.''

He unfolded from the floor and started toward the steps, meeting her as she reached the bottom. He aimed a kiss at her, but she ducked past so fast he barely hit her ear.

''Go on,'' she urged him. ''You don't want her to come looking for you.''

Noah nodded. ''I'll be back.''

Susannah was tucked snugly into her bed, her hands folded on top of the quilt, when he appeared in the doorway. She smiled and lifted her arms toward him.

He bent down and gave her a hug. She wrapped her arms around his neck tightly, clinging for a long minute, then almost reluctantly she lay back down again. When he straightened, her fingers still clenched around his as she looked at him, her eyes as blue and serious as his own. "I love you."

Noah's throat tightened. He swallowed hard. "I love you, too, sweetheart." He bent and dropped a kiss on her lips, then brushed her hair back from her forehead. "You better go to sleep now or Santa won't come."

Susannah gave him a conspiratorial smile. "He always comes," she said confidently. "Even when I get up really early, he's always been here."

"Is that so? Well," Noah said, thinking of the disassembled bike scattered across the basement floor, "you might want to maybe sleep in and give him a little more time this year. He could be running a bit late."

"I'll try," Susannah promised, shutting her eyes.

Noah reached the door and turned out the light. "Merry Christmas, Suse," he said, glancing back at his daughter in the darkness.

She raised her head. "Good night, Daddy."

Daddy. She'd called him Daddy.

He didn't realize how much he'd wanted to hear it until at last the word had crossed her lips.

He hadn't disputed her calling him "Noah." He hadn't suggested anything else. He knew that fatherhood wasn't something taken lightly; it had to be earned. Not that he figured he'd done much in the way of earning it yet. But she was giving him a chance. If he'd worried at all that she might object to his marrying Tess and becoming a permanent part of their lives, that worry was assuaged. He dipped his hand into the pocket of his jeans and fingered the velvet box.

He was smiling all the way down the basement steps.

Tess put the bike together.

She was well on her way to accomplishing it by the time

he got back to the basement, the smile still on his face. He stared at the bike, then at her, in astonishment. ''How'd you do that?''

''I read the directions.''

''Yeah, but...'' He shook his head, dazed.

''Hand me the wrench,'' Tess said, jerking her chin toward one lying near his foot.

Noah handed it to her. She used it. ''Now the other one.'' He handed it over. She used it, too. She stood the bike up and checked the way the chain moved. It didn't slide; it didn't slip. Noah's brows lifted.

''Impressive,'' he murmured.

Tess colored. ''I hope you don't mind,'' she said quickly. ''I just thought I might help out a little while you were upstairs.''

''I don't mind,'' Noah said in his best magnanimous tone.

''I didn't mean to horn in,'' she apologized.

''No problem. No problem at all. Anytime you want to put a bike together, I won't stand in your way.''

She stood up quickly. ''You can finish.''

Pretty much all that was left to do was put on the seat and the pedals. He figured he could manage that. ''I bought a bottle of brandy when I was out today,'' he told her. ''It's in the bag on the counter. Why don't you go up and pour us each some while I finish down here?''

''Brandy?'' she said doubtfully.

''It's Christmas. We're celebrating.''

She looked a little wary and a little worried, but she nodded. ''All right.'' Still she shot him an apprehensive look over her shoulder as she went up the stairs.

It took him almost as much time to get the seat on and adjusted and the pedals moving smoothly as it had taken Tess to put together the rest of the bike. But finally he got it done and stood back to contemplate the job. For a rookie Santa, he hadn't done all that badly, although it was a good thing he'd had a Ms. Claus around to help him out. Otherwise he might have been at it all night.

Tess was sitting at the kitchen table with two snifters of brandy ready and waiting when he came up the stairs.

"You bought snifters, too," she said wonderingly. "I've never had brandy before."

He didn't make a habit of drinking it himself. But tonight was special. Besides, he'd never proposed marriage before, either.

He picked up one of the snifters, then reached out and took her by the arm, urging her to her feet. "Come on," he said and drew her with him into the living room.

The only lights came from the glowing fire in the fireplace and the tiny colored bulbs on the Christmas tree. Noah led Tess to the sofa. She sat down, clutching the snifter. He sat next to her, turned and faced her.

Her eyes were wide and luminous, her dark hair curling softly around her face. He wanted to bury his hands in it. He wanted to touch his lips to hers, to take her to the same magical place where they'd spent the night before.

And he would—just as soon as he said, "I have a present for you."

Tess blinked. "Present? Tonight? But I thought we'd open them in the morn—"

"Not this one," Noah said. He fished in his pocket, pulled out the tiny velvet box and opened it. A simply set diamond solitaire winked in the firelight. He picked it out of the box and held it out to Tess.

Her eyes got even wider. Her complexion seemed to pale. She looked at him with an expression he couldn't put a name to. "What is it?" Her voice sounded equal parts hoarse and incredulous.

He smiled. "An engagement ring. The wedding ring is upstairs in the bedroom." He took her hand to slip it on. Her fingers clenched into a fist.

"What's wrong? Don't you like it?"

"It—it's lovely." She seemed almost to choke on the words. She pulled her hand away, twisting her fingers together in her lap.

He snapped the box shut. "Tess? What's the matter with you? I'm asking you to marry me." He reached out and touched her chin, tipping her face up so he could look straight into her eyes.

She stared at him, stricken.

"Don't you want to marry me?"

Her fingers knotted even tighter. She shook her head and looked away. "No."

Nine

It wasn't fair.

How could he ask her to *marry* him? How could he take the one thing she'd wanted more than anything in the world and offer it to her for all the wrong reasons?

"What do you mean, no?"

It seemed like an age had passed since she'd said that one simple, yet monumentally difficult, word. In reality Tess supposed it hadn't been more than a few seconds, thirty at most. She looked up to see Noah gazing at her, his expression a mixture of astonishment and hurt.

Hurt?

No, not really, she assured herself. Not unless it was the sort of hurt that came with having one's charitable proposition turned down.

She drew a slow, careful breath, mustering calm, summoning strength. "I mean, thank you for the offer, but I don't want to marry you."

"Why not?"

Damn it! Couldn't he just leave it alone? What sort of man asked for an explanation when his proposal had been rejected?

"I don't love you."

She could tell from his expression that, of all the reasons she might have offered, that was one he hadn't expected. He looked as if she'd knocked the air right out of him. Something akin to a shudder ran through him. She saw his knuckles whiten as he gripped the velvet box, as if he would crush it in his hand.

"I see," he said.

He didn't—for which she was profoundly grateful.

"Thank you for the offer, of course," she said now, with as much lightness of tone as she could manage. "It's very kind of you, but—"

"*Kind?*" The word seemed to explode from him. "You think I'm offering to be kind?"

Tess gave a tiny, awkward shrug. "Well, I'm sure you have a variety of motives—"

He gaped at her. "You make it sound like I'm some criminal!"

She shook her head. "No." Though if the truth were known, he was murdering her heart. "I just...don't want to marry you—whatever your reasons. It wasn't what we agreed to."

"Agreed?" he echoed hollowly.

Tess stood up. "We agreed that you could stay until after Christmas. And that's it. Now, if you'll excuse me, I want to check on Susannah. If she's asleep, I can bring down the gifts from Santa. Then I want to go to bed. I'm really very tired." She fled up the stairs without waiting for a response.

* * *

She was afraid he'd left.

When she came back carrying gifts, after she'd made sure Susannah was asleep, he wasn't there. She thought he might have gone back down to the basement. She didn't want to look. She *didn't* look until more than an hour had passed, all the gifts had been set beneath the tree and she still hadn't heard a sound from down below. Finally she ventured to the top of the steps and peered down.

"Noah?" She said his name tentatively.

When she got no reply, she dared to creep down the steps. The bike was sitting there, ready to be put under the tree. Of Noah there was no sign. Tess looked all around the basement. She looked all around the house. Then she opened the front door.

There were recent footprints in the snow-covered steps. They led down the walk, out the gate and beyond.

He was gone.

And what was she supposed to tell Susannah in the morning? Not the truth, surely. Susannah, whose fondest unspoken wish had to be that her parents would get together, would never understand why Tess had said no.

"Damn you, Noah!" she raged in a ragged whisper. Noah-the-cat came to peer out the door from between her feet. He poked his nose out far enough to get snowflakes on his whiskers. Noah-the-cat came back in.

Tess watched him walk across to the hearth and turn around, then settle in on the rug. He yawned. He purred.

She started to cry.

She didn't even realize it at first. It was only when she felt something sliding down her cheek that she realized the unexpected wetness was tears. She swiped at them, irritated. She didn't want to cry. She'd shed enough tears over Noah Tanner years ago. She was past that, damn it. Past him!

But the tears wouldn't stop coming.

It was a quarter past two and she was huddled in a ball on the sofa bed when she heard the front door open, and a snow-dusted, dark shape came in. Tess couldn't help it; she breathed a sigh of relief. Not that he was safe—that went without question. Rather, that he was back, and now she wouldn't have to think of some lie to tell Susannah.

In the dim glow from the streetlight outside, she watched as he hung his jacket in the closet by the front door. She saw him lean against the wall and tug off his boots, then set them silently next to her shoes and Susannah's smaller ones. He stood there for a moment, looking down at them.

Then he gave his head a shake, scattering the snowflakes that had frosted his dark hair, and limped into the room.

Tess shut her eyes. The footsteps came closer, then stopped. She could feel him standing over her, staring down at her in the darkness. She didn't move, didn't breathe.

Finally she heard him sigh. The limping footsteps moved on.

If Susannah noticed that her mother seemed more tired than usual on Christmas morning, she didn't remark on it. If she noted that Noah's smiles didn't quite reach his eyes, she never said a word. She was thrilled with her bike, wanting to take it out in the nine inches of new snow and ride it.

"I can wear my new sweater and my new jacket," she told her mother.

"And shovel the walk with your new snow shovel so you can ride it," Noah said, which was the most light-hearted thing he'd managed to say all morning long.

"I didn't get a snow shovel, Daddy," Susannah retorted, giggling.

So he was still *Daddy* this morning, even if the word did

make Tess's already ivory complexion pale even more. Noah watched her reaction as she sat curled on the sofa amid the crumpled wrapping paper, sipping tea and holding the cat in her lap. She looked ill.

No worse than he felt.

Damn it, he still couldn't believe she'd said no!

It didn't make sense. Anyone could see it would be the best thing for everyone if they got married. Susannah would have both her parents. Tess wouldn't have to do everything alone anymore. And he would have the family he wanted, the family he'd begun to think he'd never have. And that didn't even take into account how good he and Tess were in bed together!

He didn't suppose she'd want him bringing that up.

She apparently didn't want him bringing up anything about last night, either. The only mention she made of it was just as Susannah came down to see what Santa had brought. Tess had still been on the sofa with the comforter tucked around her when Susannah had tugged Noah down the stairs. Her eyes had been like saucers when she'd caught sight of the bike. She'd looked from it to both her parents in mute astonishment.

"I never thought—!" she said at last. And then she was jabbering a mile a minute, talking about how wonderful it was.

She never heard Tess say to Noah in a low voice, "Thank you for coming back. It would have been hard to explain to her."

"Try explaining it to me sometime," he'd said harshly.

But she'd just shaken her head. "No."

And after that, she hadn't said another word. Now the gifts had been opened, the bike ridden in small circles in the living room, the new sweater and jacket tried on, the various and sundry other gifts they'd given each other exclaimed over. A breakfast of freshly baked cinnamon rolls and fruit cups had been eaten.

Susannah finished the last roll and wiped her mouth on her napkin. "When do we go to Uncle Robert's?"

Tess and Noah looked at each other. Then Tess looked away. "I don't know," she began, "if it's such a good idea—"

"They're expecting us," Noah cut in before she could worm her way out of it. Maybe it would be awkward; maybe he'd be sorry. Hell, he was already sorry. It couldn't get much worse. But Susannah had a right to get to know her uncles and aunts and cousins.

He saw Tess hesitate, saw Susannah, aware suddenly that something wasn't quite right, look at her mother beseechingly. Tess looked from her daughter to Noah and back again. Finally she sighed and shrugged. "Fine. We'll go."

"Uncle Robert says they've got horses," Susannah told her mother, as if she was an adult promising a child a treat. "You'll like that."

Tess gave her a reluctant smile. "Yes, I expect I will."

She obviously didn't expect to like much else. But she swallowed whatever other objections might have occurred to her and helped Susannah and Noah load the car.

"When're we gonna get there?" Susannah asked, bouncing on the back seat before they were barely out of Laramie.

"Don't start," Tess said.

It was a long drive, over six hours from door to door. Happily, Susannah was exhausted enough from the excitement of the holiday that she slept for a good part of the trip. Tess and Noah took turns sharing the driving. Tess did most of it because Noah's leg still bothered him. Not that he talked about it.

They drove the entire afternoon and, once Susannah was asleep, neither one of them said a word.

Susannah was in heaven. She had uncles who doted on her, aunts who chatted and laughed with her and little cousins who thought she was the best playmate in the world. She had a pony to ride, the grandson of the hired man to show her all the best hideouts in the barn and five eight-week-old golden-retriever puppies to entertain her.

Whether Noah and Tess were in hell or simply in purgatory depended on what was happening at any particular moment. Noah, seeing ever more clearly the happiness of his formerly lone wolf brothers as they hugged and teased their wives, ached at the thought of never having that kind of closeness with Tess and Susannah. Tess, seeing women she liked instinctively happily married to men so like Noah that she could scarcely believe it, was pierced by sadness that that joy would never be hers. Noah, watching Tanner roughhouse gently with his three sons until he felt Susannah's arms go around his waist and pull him into a rough-housing match of their own, hated knowing just how few chances he would have to show this little girl how much she meant to him. Tess, watching the quiet contentment and easy authority with which Tanner handled his brood, and the gentle awe with which Luke still treated his firstborn son, ached at the knowledge that Susannah would never experience such day-to-day joy with her father.

The old family albums Noah gave his brothers brought tears to their eyes.

"I thought they were lost years ago," Tanner said, shaking his head in disbelief. "Look, Mag!" He called his wife to come sit beside him and leaf through the pages. "This is the horse I was tellin' you about. And here's that old sled I wiped out on."

"Let's see," Maggie said eagerly.

And as she tucked herself in next to him, Tess felt a pang of envy at their closeness, at the past and the future they would share.

"My, you were a handsome devil even when you were five," she heard Jill tell Luke moments later.

"Me?" Luke flushed and ducked his head. Tess was amazed. She'd never imagined a fast-lane Hollywood stunt coordinator like Luke Tanner would have a bashful bone in his body. Apparently, where his wife's compliments were concerned, he did. She felt a little self-conscious overhearing, as if she was eavesdropping.

"They're still lovebirds," growled Everett Warren, the old cowboy who was Tanner's right-hand man.

"It's nice," Tess said, and tried to keep the envy out of her voice.

She had expected to feel awkward, to be treated coolly or at least sceptically by Tanner and Luke and their wives. She was welcomed with open arms.

"We were so worried when we thought Noah was going to be alone for the holidays," Maggie confided later.

They were sitting in the living room after a sumptuous dinner, she and Tess on the sofa, Jill, who was nursing baby Keith, in the rocker by the fireplace. Tess could hear Susannah and Jared giggling and talking upstairs. The twins, Nick and Seth, as alike as two peas with their dark hair and deep blue eyes and the promise of heart-stopping Tanner grins, were already sound asleep in their cribs.

The other Tanner brothers were in the kitchen doing dishes.

Tess had been amazed, but the other women seemed to take it as a matter of course when, after everyone helped clear the table, their husbands shooed them out of the kitchen.

"It's a tradition," Maggie explained. "The first year we were together, Robert said I did so much cooking and baking for the holidays that, just once, he wanted me to sit down and put my feet up. So that night he and Luke and Noah did the dishes. And then the next year I was nursing Jared when it came time to do the dishes—" she grinned "—not even on purpose. And so they did them again. And after, well, Robert said it was good for them, too. They rarely talk to each other. Christmas night they talk. And," she said cheerfully, "we can talk to you."

Tess gulped.

Jill smiled at her. "We don't do the third degree, so don't worry. We're just glad to all be together. And glad you're here, too."

"So am I," Tess said, and found it was the truth.

"A new tradition," Maggie said. "Every year we add a bride."

Tess bit her lip and looked away.

"Oh, heavens. I'm sorry," Maggie said quickly. "Me and my big mouth. And here I am, jumping the gun as usual. Robert says I take too much for granted. But if Noah doesn't come through and—"

"He has," Tess said softly, before Maggie could finish the warning. "I said no."

Both women looked at her, their eyes wide in the room's sudden silence. Upstairs, the childish laughter continued. The low sound of Noah and his brothers' voices coming from the kitchen rubbed against Tess's battered emotions. She pressed her lips together and shook her head mutely.

"You can't tell me you don't love him," Maggie said quietly after a moment.

Tess didn't dare try to tell her that. She might have been able to convince Noah, but she'd seen enough of his sisters-in-law in the few hours she'd been here to be sure she couldn't lie anywhere near well enough to convince them that she didn't love him.

"So what's the problem?" Jill asked, her expression serious, gentle, yet concerned when Tess didn't reply.

Tess shook her head again. "It wouldn't work," she said finally, when it became clear that they weren't going to take silence for an answer.

"You don't trust him?" Maggie said.

"Has he ever lied to you?" asked Jill.

"Maybe he has," Maggie reflected softly, staring into the fire. "Robert did a lot of lying—to me and to himself."

Jill smiled. "So did Luke, come to that."

They both looked at Tess sympathetically.

There was a sudden crash and a howl from upstairs.

"Uh-oh," Maggie said, jumping up to go see what had happened. "I knew it was too good to last."

"I like her," Luke said. He picked up a glass from the drainer and began to dry it.

"Me, too," Tanner said as he put away the ones Luke had already dried.

"She's the best little girl in the world," Noah agreed readily, his hands deep in soapy water.

"Not Susannah," Luke said. "We all know that goes without saying. I'm talking about Tess."

"Me, too," said Tanner.

Which Noah had suspected all along. But a little determined misunderstanding seemed like the better part of common sense. He'd hoped it would deflect their questions.

"When're you gonna marry her?" Tanner asked.

So much for the usefulness of being deliberately obtuse. Noah reached for another dirty plate and dunked it in the soapy water. "I'm not."

Both his brothers stopped dead and stared at him.

"The hell you say!" Tanner practically jumped down his throat.

"What the—!" Luke almost leapt right after him. Then he stopped and took a close look at his younger brother's face. "What happened? What's wrong?"

Both of them closed in on him then. Noah avoided their eyes, shaking his head, staring down at the water in the sink. "Nothin'," he mumbled.

Neither of his brothers spoke for a moment. They looked at each other. "Hang in there," Tanner finally said.

"Don't quit," Luke advised. A grin quirked the corner of his mouth for just a moment. "Remember? You told me, cowboys don't."

"Surprised you didn't hit me in the mouth," Noah muttered. God, he'd been an overbearing son-of-a-gun in those days. "Should've."

His brothers looked at each other again, then at him.

"If you come back without her in the spring," Tanner said, "maybe we will."

If threats would have got Tess to agree to marry him, Noah might have tried some. If pleading or cajoling would have worked, he'd have given that some thought, too. But if she didn't love him, what more was there to say? What good would it do?

And if, come spring, Tanner and Luke gave it to him on the chin, well, it was no more than he deserved. The thing was, Noah figured he'd deserved it more eight years ago. Back then he might have been able to do something about marrying Tess. Back then she had loved him.

But he'd had other goals, other dreams.

He'd loved her, too—at least as much as he'd been capable of loving anyone in those days. But more than a relationship, more than a marriage, he'd wanted to be the bronc-riding champion of the world.

And now he was.

He was proud of his gold buckle; he couldn't deny that. He was proud of his perseverance, his determination, his skill—all the things that had gone into making him number one.

But hearing everyone call him ''Champ'' for the year, as nice as it might be, was somehow far less appealing than hearing one little girl call him ''Daddy'' every day for the rest of his life.

But Tess didn't love him.

He didn't know if Susannah was simply exhausted from the excitement of the visit to Tanner and Maggie's or if she somehow sensed the mood of her parents as they headed back to Laramie the following afternoon. Whatever it was, the eager babble they'd listened to on the way up and the joyful noise they'd heard all the time she was with her cousins gave way to pensiveness when their time on the ranch had run out and they headed south once more.

Several times Noah thought she must be sleeping. But when he glanced over his shoulder, it was to find her staring out the window, a look of deep thoughtfulness on her face.

Tess wasn't talking much, either. She did sleep some, or at least pretended to. He hoped that, in her sleep, she would slip his way and rest her head against his arm, so that he could slide it around her and draw her close and feel the softness of her curls against his fingers as he drove. But she leaned toward the door, her head resting on the window, the cold glass obviously preferable to the warmth of his arm.

When it was her turn to drive, Noah debated doing a little sleeping and perhaps a little drifting himself. But though years of going down the road had taught him to sleep in a car at the drop of a hat, they'd also taught him that resting his head on Taggart Jones's shoulder wasn't the way to go. And the habit of leaning against the door was so deeply ingrained that he couldn't even fake sagging the other way. So he sat upright and silent all the way home.

Susannah was still asleep when Tess pulled into the driveway.

"I'll carry her in," Noah said.

"I can wake her up."

"No." He wanted to carry her, and he didn't give Tess a chance to argue. He got out and pulled the seat forward, then reached into the back to scoop his daughter up into his arms. It was an awkward angle. The movement hurt his still-somewhat-tender ribs, and the lifting put pressure on his knee that he was sure the doctor would frown on.

He didn't care. He wanted to hold Susannah in his arms. God only knew how many more times he'd be able to do it. He could stretch out his time with them for a few days longer. Maybe, if Tess allowed it, until the first of the year. But then their agreement would really have been pushed to the limit. His leg would be well enough—or it wouldn't, and he'd need surgery. But in any case, he'd be gone.

He hugged Susannah's slender form against his chest as he carried her into the house and up the stairs to her bedroom.

Tess followed, carrying her small duffel bag and two model horses that Susannah's cousins had given her for Christmas. "I'll get her into pajamas."

Noah settled the sleeping child on the bed and straightened. "Then I'll unload the car." Just like an old married couple, he thought as he went back outside.

An old married couple with no future. He found it hard to swallow past the lump in his throat.

He carried in the rest of their gear and then the presents

Tanner and Maggie and Luke and Jill had given them. In the last package was a small stack of photos that Jill had taken with an instant camera Maggie had given her. Photos of all of the Tanner cousins playing together in the snow; of Susannah, Jared, Keith, Seth and Nick all sitting in a row on a sled in a pose much like the one their fathers had been in thirty years before; of Noah and Luke and Tanner standing in front of the Christmas tree; of Jill and Maggie and Tess sitting together on the hearth, of Tanner and Maggie and the boys, of Luke and Jill and Keith.

Of Tess and Susannah and himself.

"Family groups," Maggie had said without a trace of irony. "We can start our own albums."

But, damn it, Noah wanted more than an album full of Christmas memories. He wanted Tess and Susannah all year.

"Daddy?" He heard Susannah calling him from the bedroom. She sounded scared.

He took the stairs two at a time. His leg hurt. He didn't care. "What is it? What's wrong?"

When he appeared in the doorway, the relief on her face was clear. "I—I thought you'd gone." Her voice wavered.

"I told her you were downstairs," Tess said defensively. Then she turned away, going to the closet to hang up one of Susannah's shirts.

"I was bringing in the presents," he said easily. "I'm not goin' anywhere. Not for a while," he went on, for both their benefits. "I've gotta get my leg sorted out first."

Susannah smiled and settled back against the pillows again. "Good."

Tess didn't say a word.

Not that many days passed until he got a medical all-clear. His leg was mending. "Quicker than we expected," the doctor told him. So he didn't have to go in anymore.

"You just keep working at it wherever you go," the therapist told him.

"And we'll be keeping an eye out for you," the doctor, a rodeo fan, promised. "You take it easy at first, but just go on the way you've been and you'll do fine."

And of course, because they were almost right down the hall from her, they shared the good news with Tess. They thought she'd be pleased.

She was. But not for the reason they suspected.

And when fate somehow decreed that Jim Jackson call that very night on his way to Denver for the stock show and rodeo, Tess said, "Oh, yes, he's all better. I'm sure he'll be ready to go."

So what was he supposed to say? *I'm not?*

"Reckoned you'd be gettin' antsy 'bout now," Jim said cheerfully to Noah when Tess handed him the phone. "I can pick you up on my way down if you want. You ain't too far outa my way."

Noah looked at Tess. She was looking at him. Waiting. Hoping?

He dragged in a harsh breath. Why postpone the inevitable? "All right," he said. "I'll look out for you about ten." He hung up and met Tess's gaze. "I'll be leaving in the morning."

She nodded. "It's about time."

"You're going? Away?" Susannah was standing in the kitchen, her fingers gripped around the back of a chair. Her voice sounded as hollow as his stomach felt. "For good?"

"Of course not," he said briskly. "Now that I know you're here, I'm not just vanishing forever. I'll be back."

"When?"

She would ask that.

He shrugged, turning to pour himself a cup of coffee, his fourth cup this morning, and it wasn't even eight o'clock. "I don't know. My life's not all that regular, you know?"

Of course she didn't know. How could she? She was seven years old. She'd never gone down the road in her life. "Sit down and eat your cereal," he said.

She sat, or rather slumped, in the chair. She didn't look at him.

He scanned the boxes on the top of the refrigerator. "What kind do you want?"

She shrugged and picked up her spoon and idly tapped it on the table. "I'm not hungry."

"You've got to eat breakfast. It's the most important meal of the day."

"Not if you throw it up." The spoon whacked the tabletop.

"You're not going to throw it up."

"I might."

Noah thought he might, too—the very thought of leaving was making him ill—but he wasn't going to admit it. "Don't say that. Here. Have some of these corn things."

Susannah made a gagging sound, but she didn't protest when he dumped some cereal into a bowl, sloshed milk on it and set it in front of her. She didn't eat it, either, though she did stir her spoon around in it so that within minutes it became a soggy, unappetizing mess.

"Did you get up to say good-bye to Mommy?"

"Yeah."

Tess had told him last night he didn't have to. She had to be on duty by seven and would be leaving at six-thirty.

"We'll say good-bye tonight," she'd told him briskly just before bedtime. "No sense in you getting up." And then she'd stuck out her hand, shaking his as if he were some vacuum-cleaner salesman she was glad to see hit the road.

Which wasn't that far from the truth, he reflected grimly.

He'd got up anyway. Hell, why not? He hadn't slept all night. He'd lain in her spartan room trying to memorize it all, just like he had last time, so he could take it with him, close his eyes and dream he was in her bed again—in her arms again, as he had been that single wonderful night. The night before reality had come crashing down on him.

He'd got up and come down while she was eating her piece of toast. But if he'd been hoping for a last-minute reprieve, he hadn't got it. She'd outdone herself with cheerful babble, telling him how nice it was that he had mended so well and so quickly, how much he must be looking forward to getting back on the road again, how important it was to do what a person loved to do.

"And you do love it," she'd said firmly.

He'd nodded his head. It was true.

"I love you, too," he'd said.

For an instant she'd looked almost stricken, then she'd turned and grabbed her coat. "I'm going to be late," she said, and without another word, she'd vanished out the door.

He'd stood watching her go, feeling helpless. As helpless as he felt now, watching Susannah muck about miserably with her cereal.

"I've gotta get my gear," he said after a moment, when he couldn't bear watching her any longer. And without another word he bolted out of the kitchen and up the stairs. He'd already packed his duffel bag. He'd borrowed Tanner's old association saddle when they were there for Christmas. His had needed a bit of work after the crash. He lugged them both downstairs now.

Susannah was sitting on the rocker in the living room.

The Christmas tree was gone now. The manger scene that had been on the mantel had been put away. So had the brass candlesticks and the nutcracker that Tess's sister Nancy had brought them from Austria. The room was back to its everyday self.

Life was getting back to its everyday routine—Tess off to work, Susannah to school and Noah going down the road.

"Will you write me?" Susannah asked him.

"Sure."

"Will you call?"

He hesitated. Could he stand the pain of pretending indifference every time he got Tess on the phone?

Susannah noticed his reluctance at once. Her face fell. "It's okay," she said. "You don't have to."

"I want to!" Noah protested. "I love you."

Susannah didn't say anything to that. She just looked at him. Disbelieving? He hoped not, but he didn't know.

There was a beep of a horn outside. "That's Janna," he said. "You've got to go."

Susannah stood up. In one hand she clutched the top of a crumpled paper lunch sack. In the other she carried her backpack. She looked up at him, then ran her tongue over her lips. The lower one quivered. Suddenly she dropped both the sack and the backpack and launched herself at him, grabbing him around the waist.

Noah pulled her up, hugging her against his chest, choking from the tight feeling just beneath the warmth where her small body touched his heart. She kissed him, a great smacking kiss, a desperate kiss. And the one he gave her in return was no less intense.

There was another insistent beep.

"You gotta go," Noah said hoarsely, drawing in one last breath of soft, little-girl scent. And then he set her down.

They looked at each other.

A single tear slid down Susannah's cheek. "I love you," she told him.

"I love you, too," he told her.

"Both of you," he added quietly to himself after she had gone. "More than anything else in the world."

"Figured you'd come," Jim said as he bustled past Noah into the living room and grabbed the saddle sitting by the rocker. "Said to Mike I reckoned you'd be about stir-crazy by now. Hell, you been in one place more'n a month!"

Noah picked up his duffel bag and carried it out. Jim had the back of his pickup open and was tossing the saddle in by the time he got there. He already had his own gear and Mike Hansen's in there, along with their saddles and rigging bags, a couple of sleeping bags, a camp stove and a pair of the biggest speakers Noah had ever seen.

"Pile on in," Mike said, shoving over.

Noah looked over his shoulder at Tess's house. His gaze flicked from the snowman in the front yard—a new one he and Susannah had built just yesterday to replace the one she'd been building the day he'd first learned he had a daughter—to the upstairs window above the front porch, the one in Tess's room—the room where he had lain alone and lonely, the room where he had known a night of perfect love.

"What'sa matter?" Jim asked. "Forget somethin'? Well, if you have, you better think of it right quick 'cause we're movin' out." A wide grin split his face and he rubbed his hands together. "A new year, a new race, a new chance to have it all."

"All?" Noah echoed hollowly, still looking at the house.

Jim and Mike both focused on his gold belt buckle.

"Well, hell, you've already had it, I reckon," Jim said,

''but there's plenty of us still hungry. Ain'tcha hungry no more, Noah?''

"Course he is," Mike answered for him. "Noah's always hungry. It's what makes him so damn good. He never quits goin' after the gold.''

"'Cause he loves it, don'tcha, Noah?" Jim said. "Loves the challenge. Like you always said—more'n anything else in the world.''

There was no Noah in the kitchen. No Noah in the hall.

No Noah sitting in the rocker with his sock-clad feet resting on the hearth, the way he'd been just yesterday.

No Noah anywhere in the house at all.

He was gone. Down the road again, just the way she'd always known he would. Just the way she wanted it.

Or at least she'd thought it was. Until today.

And if she'd hoped that her misgivings would vanish when she opened the front door after work that afternoon, she was disappointed.

She was the only one home.

It was no big surprise. She knew that Susannah had a Brownie meeting after school and that Janna was going to take the girls by Green Acres for a visit afterward. So Susannah would be home by five-thirty. That was only two hours away.

Tess kicked off her shoes, shrugged out of her coat and looked around. She should be relishing the quiet. The peace. Having the place to herself again.

She wasn't.

Because she missed him. Loved him.

She'd driven him away. Now she wanted him back.

"How perverse is that?" she asked Noah-the-cat as she bent down and scratched him under the chin.

He rubbed his head against her leg and purred.

Tess sighed and got to her feet again, then climbed the stairs slowly, unbuttoning the white uniform tunic as she went, peeling it off as she entered the bedroom.

"Well, if you're beginnin' as you mean to go on, we've got a hell of a start."

She almost jumped out of her skin. "Noah!"

He was leaning against the brass headboard of her bed, shirtless, his arms folded behind his head. A slow smile crept across his face as he looked her up and down.

Tess's face flamed. Clutching the tunic in front of her, she glared at him. "I thought you left. You said you were leaving!"

"Nope."

"But—"

"Was goin' to," Noah said. "Then I got to thinking. Somethin' Jim said about why I was good at bronc riding. He said I worked so damned hard at it 'cause I loved it more than I loved anything else." He gave a small shrug. "Yeah, well, it *was* true. It isn't anymore."

Tess stared at him.

"I know you don't believe me," he went on. "You think I'm only sayin' it on account of Susannah. But that isn't true, either. I love Susannah. No question about it. But that's father-daughter stuff. It isn't close to the way I love you, and I'm damned well gonna prove it to you." Now he was almost glaring at her, as if daring her to challenge him.

She ran her tongue over her lips. "Are you?" she said softly. "And how are you going to do that?"

"Perseverance. You aren't gonna be able to get rid of me."

"No?"

He shook his head. "Nope." He moved his head so she could see his hands.

She gaped.

Noah grinned at her. "I figured handcuffin' myself to the bedpost was a pretty good way to start."

It was perhaps not his most-well-thought-out scheme, but it did seem to be getting her attention. Noah was grateful for that. Steve had thought he was nuts when he'd banged on the door this morning asking to borrow a pair of handcuffs once he'd sent Jim and Mike on their way. Maybe it was nuts, but desperate times called for desperate measures. And it was the only thing he could think of to do.

Tess stared, and then she laughed and—damn it to hell— were those tears running down her cheeks? "You're crazy, you know that?" she said finally.

"About you," Noah said earnestly. He leaned as far toward her as he was able. "I'm no good at sweet talk. But I never lied to you, Tess. Not then. Not now. You are the best thing that ever happened to me. I should've seen it years ago. I was too young and too dumb."

"You weren't ready for marriage," Tess murmured.

"Not then. I am now. I'll do the best I can for you— always. Do you believe me?"

Slowly she nodded her head. "I believe you, Noah."

From her purse she pulled out a rumpled copy of *ProRodeo Sports News*. It was folded open to the coming rodeo listings. "I was coming to Denver next weekend after you."

Now it was Noah's turn to stare. "You were? You changed your mind?"

"When you said you loved me, I was afraid to trust you," she admitted. "But then I got to realizing what you told me is true—you don't lie. You've never lied to me, never promised something that you didn't mean. Maggie and Jill said Robert and Luke lied to them and lied to themselves about their feelings. You never have. When you didn't love me, you never told me you did—''

"That's me," Noah said with a snort of self-disgust, "honest as hell."

"I'm glad," Tess told him. "Because when you tell me you love me, well, I do believe it."

And then she crossed the room, bent over and touched her lips to his.

He tried to reach for her. He was stuck fast. "Unlock me," he said against her lips.

"What?" She kept on nibbling, teasing.

Noah struggled against his bonds. "Unfasten the cuffs. The key fell down behind the bed."

"Mmm." Tess smiled and kept on kissing him. She settled onto the bed and ran her hands lightly down his chest.

He shivered at her touch. His hands tightened on the brass. "Tesssssss!"

She unfastened the fly of his jeans, easing down the zipper, then tugging the denim down his legs. His briefs quickly followed them.

"Tess!"

She grinned. "This is fun."

"I'll show you fun!" His hips lifted right off the mattress as she ran her hands lightly up the insides of his thighs. He sucked in a sharp breath. "Damn, Tess!"

The grin widened. "Lots of fun."

"For you, maybe," he growled.

She pulled back and looked at him with wide-eyed innocence. "You're not having fun?"

He groaned. "C'mon, Tess."

"I will," she said saucily. "Don't rush me."

But damned if she wasn't rushing him! The things she was doing were driving him wild. Feather-light touches that made him ache. Gentle nips that left him breathless. Warm breath that nearly sent him spinning out of control.

"You want me to suffer," he moaned. "That's why you're doing this."

She settled back on her heels. "Is it? I thought it was because I loved you, too."

He stilled completely, his gaze fixed on her. "Do you mean that?" he asked hoarsely.

She tipped her head. "Do you honestly think I'd be doing this if I didn't?"

Slowly, solemnly, he shook his head. No, there was no way on earth Tess Montgomery would be this intimate with a man unless he meant more to her than any man in the world.

Noah's head dropped back against the pillow. He grinned all over his face. "In that case, sweetheart, go right ahead."

It was interesting, actually, making love with your hands cuffed to a bedpost. He'd sure as hell never done it before.

He wasn't sure he wanted to do it again any time soon.

He didn't mind giving her the control, he just wanted to use his hands. He wanted to touch her, tease her, caress her, bring her to the fever pitch she brought him to before finally unlocking the cuffs and setting him free.

When at last she did, he entered her with one swift, shattering movement. But what he lacked in finesse, he more than made up for in urgency. And he wasn't too worried that Tess would complain. She was exploding in his arms at the very same time.

After, when she lay curled against his chest and he had his arms wrapped around her, he started thinking of other ways he could make love to her—with her—now that he had the time, and the future, to try them all. He smiled in anticipation.

"You know what you told Susannah," he said softly, his

lips against her hair, "about how cowboys always move on?"

Tess lifted her head and nodded slowly.

"Well, it ain't so." He touched his lips to hers. "Not always. Not when they smarten up, anyway." He grinned. "This cowboy's here to stay."

Epilogue

One year later

It was, just as Tanner had said last year, "wall-to-wall rug rats" again this Christmas at the Three Bar C ranch. But this year Noah was here to see it—he and Tess and Susannah, a family at last. Noah surveyed the chaos in the living room with a smile on his face.

Seth and Nick, approaching the terrible twos, were shredding bags of discarded wrapping paper, their presents paling in the light of such great sport. Keith was sitting in the middle of the floor sucking his thumb and contemplating a Keith-size rolling horsey that Jared was pushing around and around, making race-car noises.

Susannah, God bless her, was curled in the corner of the sofa, absorbed in a stack of *Black Stallion* books her aunt Maggie and uncle Robert had given her. It was the first time she'd settled down in the house since Noah and Tess had taken her out to the barn that morning to show her the two-year-old black gelding who'd been waiting just for her. She'd been stunned. Amazed.

"He's beautiful," she'd cried. "Better than even my bike." And they hadn't been able to get her into the house until Noah had gone out and dragged her in when dinner was on the table.

An angry wail from upstairs reminded Noah that there was even one more rug rat this time around—a girl, Katharine Elizabeth, called Katie, born to Luke and Jill in August.

"Reinforcements," Susannah had called her only girl cousin, and she'd breathed a deep sigh of relief. The news of Katie's arrival hadn't stopped her from pestering her parents, however.

"I really could use a sister," she'd told Noah and Tess on more than one occasion after their marriage last February. "Or even a brother," she'd allowed, though she'd wrinkled her nose as she said it. "You know, it isn't good for a girl to be an only child."

They'd smiled then, but they hadn't committed themselves.

Now, of course, with Tess waddling around as big as Tanner's old red barn, neither of them had to say a word.

God, she was beautiful, Noah thought as he studied Tess's freckled cheeks, which had turned rosy in the heat of the room. He smiled just looking at her. Her curves were so different now that she was full with his child. He'd loved to touch her when she was lithe and lissome, but no more than he delighted in running his hands over her now. It was all he could do not to walk right out into the living room and—

"Hey!" Tanner's voice broke into his reverie. "If you figure standin' over there by the door and lookin' the other way is gonna keep you from having to dry your share of these dishes, buster, you're dead wrong.''

Noah turned just in time to catch the snap of a damp dish towel against the seat of his jeans. ''Hey, yourself! I was just thinking.''

Tanner saw what—or who—his brother was looking at and gave him a knowing grin. ''Sure you were. Reckon Tess is gettin' sort of tomatolike in that red dress,'' he added cheerfully.

''She is not!''

At the ferocity of Noah's tone, Tanner broke up, laughing.

Luke, elbow deep in soapsuds, joined in. ''God, you're easy to tease,'' he said as Noah bristled.

''Just like old times,'' Tanner agreed. He turned to Luke. ''You remember when he was nuts about that mangy ol' yellow dog?''

Noah was across the kitchen in a tenth of a second flat, ready to commit mayhem. ''That dog was not...!''

But Tanner was grinning his head off again. So was Luke.

''Aw, hell,'' Noah muttered.

Tanner poked him in the ribs. ''It was the prettiest damn dog in Colorado,'' he admitted, thirty years too late.

''It was,'' Noah agreed gruffly.

''And Tess is one heck of a tomato,'' Tanner said. He aimed an appreciative glance in her direction.

''Sure is,'' Luke said. ''You're damned lucky to have her.''

''I know it,'' Noah said softly. He told himself that every day of his life.

''Reckon we're all lucky,'' Tanner said, catching sight of his own lovely Maggie just coming down the stairs.

''Uh-huh,'' Luke said. He wiped his hands on the legs

of his jeans and turned to stand shoulder to shoulder with his brothers as they all three contemplated the women—and the children—who had brought such joy into their lives. "Damn lucky."

And Noah, remembering Susannah's prayer last Christmas, sent one of thanksgiving in the same direction now. Then he swallowed against the lump in his throat.

"Nope," he said, with a catch in his voice that his brothers politely—and uncharacteristically—ignored. "We've been way more than lucky. We've been blessed."

* * * * *

THE COWBOY
AND THE KID

For Grace Green
who knows about heroes called Taggart

For Nan Welch
who makes third grade
at least as much fun as work

And most especially for Brett Leffew
who makes riding a bull look easy
and doing research a joy
This one's for you

One

Having a father was a big responsibility.

Becky Jones knew that better than almost anyone. She'd been taking care of her own father by herself—except for now and then, when Grandma and Grandpa and her dad's best friend, Noah, lent a hand—since she was two months old, and she'd be eight in October. That was a long while.

Taggart—that was his name—was a pretty low-maintenance dad most of the time. He was thirty-two years old and in good health except for the pins in his knee and the occasional twinge left over from his bull-riding days. He didn't yell a lot or smoke or spit or chew—which was better than most of the dads she knew. He took off his boots when he came in the house; he washed the dishes almost every night; he kept his room pretty neat and he let her make a mess in hers.

Also, he'd been around since she was born, and that was a big plus as far as Becky was concerned.

It was certainly more than her best friend, Susannah, could say. Susannah's dad, Noah, hadn't even known he had a daughter until almost two years ago!

That seemed pretty careless to Becky, but she could hardly talk since her own mother didn't get any prizes in the responsibility department. She'd got fed up and left Becky and her dad more than seven years ago and had never come back.

At least once he knew Susannah existed, Noah Tanner had stuck around. He was even married to Susannah's mother now. Susannah said he and Tess, her mom, were in love. Becky guessed they must be because they'd had another baby—a boy called Clay—right after Christmas last year and were going to have another baby this November! Pretty soon Susannah would have lots of brothers and sisters to share the responsibility with. With *two* parents, you'd probably need that.

Becky, however, was on her own.

Until two years ago that hadn't been a problem. Before she started going to school full-time, Becky had gone down the road with Taggart from rodeo to rodeo, and she'd done a pretty good job taking care of him and keeping him out of trouble. Other cowboys got drunk and chased girls and raised heck, but not her dad.

"Taggart's getting pretty settled these days," her grandpa often said.

And her grandma always nodded and ruffled Becky's hair. "And we know why, don't we?" she would say, smiling at her granddaughter. "Because of you. You take such good care of your dad."

But she couldn't prevent the accident. She hadn't even been with him at the time.

She'd started first grade that fall and had stayed with her grandparents while Taggart had gone down the road without her. Becky thought that was dumb. She'd always learned a lot going down the road. Hadn't she learned to read by sounding out the letters on road signs? Couldn't she follow a map almost as good as he could? But arguing was useless. Sometimes her dad was as stubborn as the bulls he rode. She'd had to go to school anyway, and he'd traveled with Noah all that fall.

Noah hadn't been able to prevent the accident, either.

It had happened in December almost two years ago, right after the National Finals Rodeo. Becky remembered how mad she'd been because she couldn't even go to that— she'd *always* gone to the finals with him!

But he'd said, no, school was more important. Becky disagreed, and she'd intended to tell him in no uncertain terms— after she gave him a big hug.

On the day he was due to arrive she'd bounced out of bed early, wondering if maybe he was already waiting downstairs to surprise her. It would be just like him to get here early. She knew he missed her as much as she missed him. Besides, he was bringing her a big gold buckle this time because he was the new champion bull rider of the world! Naturally he'd be in a hurry for her to see it.

She'd rushed to pull on her jeans and shirt, buttoning it wrong and not even stopping to do it over, so eager was she to race down the stairs and leap into his arms.

He wasn't there. Only Grandma and Grandpa were in the kitchen, standing real stiff as they looked at her. Then Grandpa had come over and put his hands on her shoulders.

"There's been an accident, Beck," he told her in a low quiet voice, the one he used when he was gentling his horses. Becky thought he looked the way he had when the foal of his best mare, Cedar, died last spring. "A truck hit Noah's van in the snowstorm. Your dad's in the hospital in Laramie."

"Hospital?" Becky knew all about hospitals. That was where they'd taken her great-grandma before she'd died. It was where old Mr. Ennis had gone, too, and she remembered them burying him last Fourth of July. It was also where her friend Tuck McCall's mother had been. She was dead now, too.

Becky felt like the time Tuck had hit her in the stomach with his football. Only worse. A million, trillion times worse.

Her father wasn't dead, they told her. He was in a coma. That was like sleeping, Grandma said. Only sometimes, Tuck told her later—which nobody else would—you didn't wake up.

All the time her dad was in the coma, Becky had had that football feeling.

"He'll be all right, you'll see," her grandma had told her over and over. But Becky had seen the fear in her grandmother's eyes and knew Grandma had the football feeling, too.

The next afternoon they said he woke up. Becky wasn't sure she'd have believed it—even though her grandma was laughing and crying at the same time—except Grandma held the phone out so Becky could talk to him.

"D-Daddy?"

"Hey, Pard." He sounded awful, like he'd swallowed Grandpa's chew. But it was him; nobody else ever called her Pard.

She breathed again. "Daddy." The football feeling was gone. She felt like she could fly.

"Sorry I missed your program, Pard."

As if she cared about a dumb old Christmas program. "When are you comin' home, Daddy? Soon?"

"Soon."

"For Christmas?"

"You'd better believe it. They're not keepin' me one minute longer than they have to. You can come and get me, okay?"

"'Kay." She gripped the receiver tightly, the way she would hang on to his neck if he were here. She listened to him breathing. It was the best sound she'd ever heard.

"Love you, Pard," he said at last.

"Love you, too."

Her grandma took the phone back then. Becky ran out to the barn and climbed up on the top rail of Cedar's stall to press her face into the sorrel's mane. There, for the first time since she'd heard about the accident, Becky cried.

Sometimes, if she thought about it now, she could get scared all over again. She knew it had scared her dad, too. Once he got better, Taggart said he wasn't ever leaving her again. He and Noah decided that going down the road was just too hard on family men. They were both world champions. They'd proved all they needed to prove.

So they started a bull- and bronc-riding school. Grandpa had the stock, and Taggart and Noah had the know-how. Now, a year and a half later, it was up and running.

Noah and Tess and Susannah had just finished building a house down the road. Becky and Taggart had lived with Grandma and Grandpa while he and Noah got things going. But three months ago, Grandpa and Grandma had decided to try "city life" and bought a house in Bozeman, leaving Becky and her father on their own.

Most of the time they were fine, just the two of them.

But sometimes, lately she wasn't sure.

This past summer, for example, when they'd gone down to the rodeo in Cheyenne, and he'd been trying to win her a stuffed bear in the shooting gallery, he'd missed five times! Not because he wasn't a good shot. But because instead of looking at the target, he was busy watching some lady with tight jeans and long blond hair!

Becky's company hadn't been enough the day they went over to the rodeo in Missoula, either. He spent so much time talking to that barrel racer from Oregon that he didn't realize how much soda pop and candy Becky had eaten. She'd been sick all night.

She'd thought maybe he was just distracted when they were traveling. She knew her grandpa had an old saying, something about "keeping them down on the farm...." Becky assumed he meant the ranch, but lately even at the ranch things had been strange.

Like tonight when they were having dinner at Susannah's. Becky and Susannah were playing chopsticks on the piano, and she turned around to see if her dad had noticed how good she was getting. But instead of watching her, he'd been watching Noah kiss Tess. He'd had a funny look on his face, too.

"They're making up for lost time," Susannah explained. "Newlyweds do that." She'd giggled. Becky had, too. Taggart didn't even smile.

Becky left Susannah playing the piano and slid off the bench to go to where he stood propped against the windowsill. She leaned back against his legs and felt his fingers settle on her shoulders and tighten until they almost hurt. She reached a hand back and touched his. His grip eased and his fingers covered hers. His thumb rubbed the back of her hand.

Later that night when they were driving home, she had to ask him three times if she could drive the truck through the gate when he opened and closed it.

"Huh?" he said at last. Then, "Sure, if you want to." But it seemed to Becky as if he'd barely heard. He didn't even tell her what a good job she did when he got back in the truck. He didn't seem to notice at all.

"Are you missing Julie?" she asked him finally when he was tucking her into bed. Her mother, she meant. She never called her Mommy because no one else ever had.

He blinked, then frowned. "Missing Julie? Of course not. What the heck brought that on?"

Becky gave a tiny shrug and scrunched back into the pillow. "Dunno. I just…wondered."

He looked at her narrowly. Then he shrugged, too. "Don't be stupid." Then he ruffled her hair and dropped a kiss on her lips. "'Night, Pard."

Becky's arms came up and locked around his neck, tugging him down for another, harder kiss. "'Night," she said fiercely.

When he left, he winked at her, and she smiled, thinking she was imagining things and that everything was going to be all right.

But when she woke up a few hours later, she could hear the television on. Unless he was watching cartoons with her or videos of bull rides, Taggart almost never watched TV. Curious, Becky crept downstairs.

He was watching a movie. Not even a car-chase movie, which, as far as she knew, was the only kind he ever watched. On the screen she saw a man and a woman talking, arguing. Talking some more. And then, when the music got really soppy and the lady sniffled and wiped her eyes, they started smiling at each other. And then they were touching. And kissing. A whole lot of kissing.

Taggart flicked the remote. Becky figured he'd shut it off. She was wrong. He played it back and watched it again. And again.

For a long time, even after he shut it off, he didn't move. He just sat there, his hands in his lap, while Becky crouched on the steps, watching. At last, he got up—real slow, like when all his muscles hurt from bull-riding—and walked to the window. He stood with his hands tucked into his pockets staring out into the darkness.

Finally he turned, and Becky got a glimpse of his face for the first time. He looked like Tuck had hit him in the stomach with his football. Hard.

"What you need is a mother," Susannah said.

It was two mornings later, and they were walking up the road toward the gate where the school bus stopped. It was the first day of school, and, as a treat, Taggart had allowed her to spend the night with Susannah so they could walk to the bus together.

He seemed to remember that having a friend on the first day always helped, even if you'd been going to the same school your whole life. He was good about things like that, so Becky wanted things to be good for him, too.

But a *mother?* Becky looked at Susannah. "What for?"

"You *know* what for." Susannah gave her an impatient look and tossed her long dark hair. Susannah was a year older and she knew a lot. She rolled her eyes significantly.

"Oh," Becky said. "That."

Actually, she didn't know a lot about *that*. Not when it had to do with men and women, anyway.

She knew about bulls and cows. She'd seen artificial inseminations. It seemed like a good idea to her—less messy. She didn't know how her dad felt about it. She didn't think it was something she ought to ask.

"I'm not sure I want a mother."

"What's wrong with a mother?" Susannah sounded offended.

"I don't know. I haven't ever had one, have I? Well, not for long, anyway." Becky shifted her backpack from one shoulder to the other and scuffed the toes of her cowboy boots in the dirt.

"I guess not," Susannah said, contemplating Becky's mother's desertion. Then she said, "But you know mine. You like her, don't you?"

Becky nodded. Sometimes she envied Susannah her mother. It had been different when her grandmother was still around the house. But now that Grandma was in Bozeman, no one ever baked cookies or canned tomatoes or bought new barrettes for her hair.

Tess did all those things. She was also good with Band-Aids when you skinned your knee. Taggart believed in toughing it out—they didn't have a Band-Aid in their house. He wasn't much good at barrettes, either, though he could braid well enough.

It came from making bull ropes, he'd told her. Becky doubted if mothers learned to braid that way, but she didn't suppose it really mattered. And he did try.

"Well, then," Susannah went on, "you'll just have to get yours back."

Becky looked up, startled. "Get Julie back?"

"If that's her name. I got my dad, didn't I?"

"It's not the same. I mean, he didn't even know about you, so you can't blame him for not being there. But Julie knew...about me, I mean—" she said this last bit with difficulty, because it always made her feel funny somewhere in the middle of her stomach "—and she left, anyway."

Susannah kicked a rock. "She was a jerk."

Becky thought so, too, but she felt obligated to say what her father had always told her. "She just couldn't handle things. Daddy says she didn't know what she was getting into marrying him. The rodeos and the ranch and all. She was from New York City."

"That's no excuse."

"No." Becky agreed with that. "Well, you can see why I don't want her—if I've got to find a mother, I mean." She kicked the rock Susannah had kicked. They followed it up the road, taking turns.

"Then we'll find you another one."

"I'm not having Kitzy Miller!" Kitzy Miller worked in the Minimart. She chewed gum a pack at a time, had zits but called them freckles, and practically drooled on Taggart's boots whenever they stopped to buy gas or milk or bread.

There was no doubt in Becky's mind that Kitzy Miller had her eye on Taggart—and no way on earth was she going to have Kitzy for a mother!

"Definitely not Kitzy Miller," Susannah agreed fervently.

"Then who?"

They looked at each other hopefully, but neither could come up with another name. There were not a lot of unattached women in Elmer, Montana.

Becky kicked the rock. "Miss Setsma's nice."

"Miss Setsma's old as your grandma!" Susannah said about their piano teacher. She gave the rock an extrahard kick. "What about Brenna Jamison? She's young—and she's pretty."

Brenna lived up the valley on the biggest ranch around— when she was home, which wasn't often. Mostly she was somewhere else doing art. She was a very famous painter, and she only came home when her daddy, old Otis Jamison, required what Taggart called a command performance. There didn't seem to be very many of them.

"I don't think so," Becky said. "I mean, she's nice...but I don't think she wants to stay around here."

They'd reached the gate where the bus stopped, and they

slid between the posts without undoing the wire that held it fast. The bus was just coming over the rise.

"Tuck might know somebody," Susannah suggested.

"I know everybody Tuck knows," Becky said glumly. Tuck had been her best friend before Susannah came. Now he was nine and couldn't always be bothered with her. "There's no one."

"Then we'll pray."

Becky's eyes widened. "Pray?"

"Why not?" Susannah said as the bus stopped and they climbed on. "It worked for me."

Probably because Susannah was a lot better person than she was, Becky thought, slumping in her seat. The bus started up again and Becky stared out the window as it rumbled its way toward town. Susannah probably never climbed trees her daddy told her not to, and she always studied her spelling words, and it was even possible that she ate all her carrots. Becky hated carrots.

Would a mother make her eat carrots?

Maybe she could pray for one who would not. That might be worth a shot. As the bus trundled on, she screwed her eyes up tight and sent a prayer winging heavenward. The bus wound up the hill and down, then up another and down. It stopped. Becky kept praying, unsure how long she was supposed to keep it up. The bus began its journey once more.

"You got a pain or somethin'?"

Becky's eyes popped open. A red-haired, freckle-faced boy was standing in the aisle, staring at her. "Oh, hi, Tuck. I'm prayin'."

He looked dubious. "You? For what?"

Becky hesitated, unsure if she was supposed to tell or not. Was it like a wish that didn't come true unless you kept it a secret? She turned to ask Susannah, but she was leaning over the seat in front, talking to that snotty Lizbeth Caldwell. Becky certainly wasn't going to betray her ignorance in front of Lizbeth!

"I'll tell you later," she promised, partly for fear of jinxing a prayer she had no very great hopes for anyway, and partly because she knew Tuck would think she was out of her mind if she told him.

"A stepmother? You're prayin' for a stepmother?" he'd say. "Like Cinderella's?"

No way. She didn't want that! She wasn't sure what she wanted—besides no carrots. She tried to think about it. It would have to be someone who'd appeal to her dad, she guessed. Someone pretty who looked good in jeans would be a start. But then, she'd also have to be fun to have around. And she'd have to know about barrettes and Band-Aids, and it would be good if she could bake cookies and didn't care if kids got dirty sometimes or fell out of trees they weren't supposed to climb in the first place. They needed someone who'd love her and Taggart both.

A pretty tall order since her own mother obviously hadn't.

Becky thought it was asking an awful lot—even of God.

And then the bus stopped and she got off and walked into her class—and saw Ms. Albright standing there.

They were following her again.

When she stopped to stare at the display of nails, screwdrivers and wire cutters in Gilliam's Hardware, Felicity could see them reflected in the glass as they ducked behind the dusty Dodge pickup truck parked beside the curb. It was the third time this week she'd been tailed—by two little girls.

Becky Jones and Susannah Tanner.

Her students.

If she were still teaching in Southern California, Felicity might have understood. There, in the midst of the anonymous urban sprawl, stalking had sometimes seemed a way of life.

But *here?* In *Elmer, Montana?*

By a pair of third- and fourth-grade girls?

Felicity wondered if she was losing her mind. She didn't think so. In fact, for the first time in two years, she'd begun to think she'd finally recovered it.

Moving to Elmer had been the start. She had come last month when she inherited Uncle Fred's house. It was a completely unexpected windfall. She hadn't seen Uncle Fred since she was ten years old, when she and her mother had visited him for two weeks in the summer.

He'd been the eldest of her grandfather's brothers, the one with the wanderlust. He had traveled everywhere on the globe before finally settling in Elmer and taking over its small newspaper. When she came that summer, he'd let Felicity help him print it. She remembered being ink-smudged and totally happy. Those two weeks had been among Felicity's fondest memories.

They had apparently been among Uncle Fred's happiest, too, for in his will he left her his house and everything in it—lock, stock and printing press.

Felicity had been flabbergasted. And yet it had seemed like fate—a godsend—coming as it had, exactly two years to the day after her husband Dirk had been killed.

Dirk. Dear, wonderful Dirk. They'd only been married two-and-a-half years. Their lives, their hopes, their futures, were ahead of them as they waited for Dirk to finish school.

A graduate student in music, Dirk Albright had been a talented cellist—a gifted musician, but an even more gifted teacher. Everyone knew it—especially Felicity. She and Dirk had grown up together, they'd gone to high school and university back in Iowa together. When Dirk won a graduate fellowship at UCLA, they'd married and moved to California together.

"I don't want to go without you," he'd said to her. "Please come."

And over her family's objections, she had. She'd never considered doing anything else because she'd loved Dirk as desperately as he loved her.

They'd lived on a shoestring budget in a tiny apartment above a garage in Westwood. They ate macaroni and cheese, Ramen noodles and peanut butter sandwiches seven nights a week, and thought they were the luckiest people on earth. Felicity drove an hour and fifteen minutes each way to the school where she taught. But Dirk could ride his bike to the university. What little they could save, they put toward the house they'd buy someday wherever Dirk got a college teaching job. They had plans, hundreds of them. They talked about them every night.

And then one afternoon after school Felicity had looked up to see a policeman standing in the door to her classroom. Gently, quietly, he told her that Dirk was dead.

Riding his bike home from class as he did every day, he'd been hit by a car.

"He never knew," the policeman assured her. "He didn't suffer."

Felicity did. For the past two years she had mourned her lost husband, her lost hopes, her lost dreams. Everything she'd hoped to be had depended on her life with Dirk. In the space of a single moment, she'd lost it all.

"Come home," her parents urged her. "Come back to Iowa."

But she couldn't. There were too many memories there. Everywhere she turned she would come face-to-face with the past she and Dirk had shared. "No," she told them. "I'll stay here. I have my job. I love the kids. I'll survive."

She did. She got through the next school year by submerging herself in her work, letting it consume her. If she didn't stop, she didn't have to think, to plan, to face life more than a day at a time. That was enough.

Then, a little more than a year after Dirk's death, her friend, Lori, said, "Listen, Felicity...I have a friend I'd like you to meet."

A man, she meant.

Felicity knew Lori meant well, but she wasn't interested. She didn't want to know that his name was Craig, that he was an aeronautical engineer who lived in the same apartment complex as Lori, that he liked music and surfing and playing basketball. "I can't," she said.

"So, maybe he's not the right one," Lori said philosophically. "I know another guy, a friend of my brother's."

But Felicity wasn't interested in him, either. There were other men over the next few months—men Lori found for her, men her brother Tom and her sister Cassandra told to drop by and see her while they were in L.A. There were even some men who found her without any help at all. Nice men, all of them.

But not Dirk.

"You can't mourn him forever," Lori told her. "He wouldn't want you to stop living, you know."

Yes, Felicity knew. Intellectually she nodded her head and agreed, but she couldn't make herself show any interest in men. The very thought of dating again left her numb, as if her feelings were encased in ice.

"There are a million eligible men in Southern California," Lori had told her impatiently one night. "There must be one who's right for you."

But if there was, Felicity didn't care. She had no desire

to look for him. And she wished everyone else would stop looking, too.

But they didn't. So, when news of Uncle Fred's legacy dropped into her mailbox like the proverbial roast duck and Felicity remembered those few carefree days of childhood joy, the memory translated itself into a desire to go back once again.

Why not, after all? She had nothing to keep her here.

"You're going *where?*" Lori demanded.

"Elmer, Montana."

"You'll be back," Lori predicted.

But once she'd arrived, Felicity's chest expanded, her breathing deepened. She felt, as she looked around at the tiny higgledy-piggledy town, the high mountains and the big, big sky, as if that first deep breath had finally cracked the ice. The pain and numbness she'd lived with since Dirk's death began almost imperceptibly to melt away.

Felicity had looked around the town and smiled at its prosaic name. Nestled against the foothills of the Bridgers, looking across the fertile Shields Valley toward the mysterious Crazy Mountains, Elmer had, to Felicity's way of thinking, been misnamed. It should have been called Eden—or Paradise.

She decided to stay.

"You haven't seen it in the winter," Polly McMaster, who ran the post office, said.

But Felicity was looking forward to winter. The sameness of Southern California's seasons was one of the things she had never got used to. "I grew up in Des Moines. I can hardly wait."

Polly had looked skeptical, but Felicity knew it was true. And she felt alive here for the first time in two years. She went back to California just long enough to resign from her job and pack her things.

"You're kidding," Lori said.

Felicity shook her head and kept packing.

Lori watched, then sighed philosophically. "Well, fine. Maybe you'll meet a cowboy."

Felicity looked at her askance. "A cowboy?"

"This is Montana, isn't it?"

But Felicity hadn't met a cowboy yet. She had met most of Elmer's 217 inhabitants, though. Their sympathies had been immediately engaged by the pretty young widow Fred Morrison had left his house to, and they thought she was a right smart lady when she preferred Elmer to Southern California. It wasn't long before Maudie Gilliam, whose husband ran the hardware store, was bringing her gooseberry pies and Howie Ward was fixing her window screen and two old schoolteachers called Cloris and Alice were inviting her out for meat loaf at the Busy Bee, and old Mr. Eberhardt stumped over every afternoon with yesterday's Bozeman *Chronicle* so she'd have a big-city newspaper to read.

"Fred always liked to keep up," he told her.

"So will I," Felicity had assured him. She could read the want ads, she thought, and look for a job.

Serendipitously, a job found her.

Polly's sister, who had been the third- and fourth-grade teacher in Elmer's seventy-six-student school, discovered in mid-August that the long-hoped-for baby she was expecting was actually going to be triplets.

"She has to take it easy," Polly had told Felicity. "Stay flat on her back. And the babies aren't due until January."

So Felicity had a job.

And—for some unknown reason—two little girls tailing her.

She stopped as usual in the post office to pick up her mail. When she came out they were still there, one dark head and one light brown, peeping over the hood of a pickup. Felicity smothered a smile and turned up Apple Street, heading home.

Two small girls ducked and bobbed along behind.

They only came halfway down the block, just far enough to be sure that she was going into her house. When Felicity peeked out again moments later, they were gone. "What are you two up to?" she murmured as she let the curtain fall.

At first she had thought they had questions they were too shy to ask in class. Now she knew better. Susannah, a fourth grader, never seemed to have questions about anything, and every piece of work she turned in was excellent. Becky was a different story.

Not shy at all, Becky had all sorts of questions. Work was another matter. A third grader with bright green eyes and a quicksilver smile, Becky Jones had done absolutely nothing in three weeks.

Nothing—except wear spurs every day to school.

"They missed the bus *again?*" Taggart scowled when Noah put the cellular phone in the truck and ambled back to the corral to report the conversation he'd just had with his daughter. "How many times this week is that?"

Noah shook his head and began once more to slap paint on the fence. "Three. And three last week. You reckon Orville is takin' off the minute the bell rings?"

"Naw. He's been driving that bus since I was on it. It's gotta be that new teacher of theirs. She must be keeping 'em after."

"Susannah never does anything to get kept after school!"

"Takes after her mother, does she?" Taggart grinned.

"Well, she will if she hangs around with Becky long enough."

It wasn't that his daughter was a bad kid; she was just a challenging one. He figured it must run in the family. His dad had always said Taggart made life "interesting" for his parents. He supposed it was only fair that Becky made life interesting for him.

"So, who goes and gets 'em today?" Noah asked.

"Oughta make 'em walk," Taggart grumbled, but he set down his brush and started toward the truck. "I'll go."

Noah grinned. "Want to get a look at the teacher, do you?"

Taggart stopped. "No, why?"

Noah shoved his hat back. "Susannah says she's a looker. Long blond hair, deep blue eyes. Didn't Becky tell you?"

"Becky wouldn't notice."

If it didn't have four legs—or eight—his daughter didn't know it was there. Becky noticed frogs and spiders and mice. She played with cats and puppies and colts. She didn't pay the least bit of attention to people—unless they were riding on horses. Or bulls.

He doubted if she even knew her new teacher's name. And it would certainly never occur to her to tell him the woman was pretty.

Not that he'd be interested if she did.

Taggart Jones might have a wistful hormonal twinge every now and then—hell, what thirty-two-year-old man in possession of all the right hormones didn't?—but he could handle them.

Far better than he could handle another marriage.

So what if Noah and Tess were disgustingly happy in theirs? So what if both Noah's brothers, Tanner and Luke, and Taggart's friend, Mace—all well married—were as pleased as pigs in mud? That didn't mean he would be, even if he found someone he was ga-ga over.

Which he hadn't. Wouldn't. Because, damn it, he wasn't looking.

Oh, maybe he allowed his eyes to follow a pair of long legs and a curvy bottom in a pair of tight jeans from time to time. And maybe he wondered sometimes what it would be like these days to kiss a girl over the age of eight. But those were his hormones talking, not his common sense.

Taggart's common sense told him that he'd had his shot with a woman and he'd blown it—big-time. It had taken him less than a year to drive Julie away. He didn't imagine another woman would want to hang around any longer than she had, even though he wasn't going down the road all year long anymore.

He had other drawbacks now—like an almost eight-year-old girl.

Not that he personally considered Becky a drawback. As far as he was concerned, his daughter was the best thing that had ever happened to him.

He might not think too highly of Julie in other respects, but he thanked God every day for the daughter she'd given him. And since she'd hated him and their life so much, he even thanked God that she'd left. He did it again now as he started up the truck and headed toward town.

He and Becky were doing fine just the way they were.

Two

"**M**ay I please speak to Mr. or Mrs. Jones?"

Accustomed to calls from cowboys wanting to sign up for bull- and bronc-riding school or livestock dealers intent on selling him or his dad some cattle, Taggart was startled when the voice he heard was female, soft in his ear, yet clear and warm like honey. His folks must be making new friends.

He leaned against the barn door and tucked the cellular phone against his shoulder. "Sorry. They've moved to Bozeman."

"Bozeman?" The woman sounded flustered. "But I thought... This is Felicity Albright. I teach their daughter, Becky...."

Taggart fumbled the phone. Hell, how was he supposed to know she wanted him? Nobody ever called him Mr. Jones! And everybody knew there wasn't a Mrs. Jones, didn't they? He'd forgotten that Becky's teacher was new in town.

He rescued the phone and cleared his throat. "Sorry. I thought you meant…never mind. I'm Becky's dad."

"Ah." He could hear relief in her voice. "I'm so glad to reach you, Mr. Jones. I'd like to talk with you. I wondered if you could drop by some afternoon?"

"Talk with me? Like a conference, you mean? I thought conferences were in October."

"Well, yes. I realize it's a little early, but—" she hesitated "—there are some things I'd like to discuss with you."

Like why she was making Becky miss the bus every night? That'd be nice, Taggart thought. He straightened, shrugging his shoulders against the wooden door. "I wouldn't mind discussin' a few things with you, either, Ms., um—" What the hell had she said her name was?

"Albright," she supplied in his groping silence. "I gather Becky hasn't been talking much about school?"

"I reckon she's got other things on her mind."

"I reckon." Her echo of his words seemed somewhat dry. "That's one of the things I'd like to discuss with you, Mr. Jones. When can you come?"

"Tomorrow?" Might as well get it over with. Maybe she'd stop keeping Becky after school that way, too.

"Wonderful. About three-fifteen or so?"

"Why not? I been coming in three times a week anyhow. You know they been missing the bus, don't you?" He knew he sounded accusing, but he had a right to. She'd been inconveniencing everybody. He'd intended to tell her yesterday when he picked the girls up, but she hadn't been anywhere around.

"I thought they must be."

"And you kept 'em, anyhow?"

"I haven't been keeping them, Mr. Jones. Becky and Susannah are choosing to stay late."

His brows hiked up. He'd always known his daughter was bright and clever and capable, but he'd never known her to expend much of that brilliance or cleverness on school before. "How come?"

"I was hoping you could tell me."

"What do you mean?"

"Perhaps it would be better if we discussed it tomorrow. I do want you to know, though, how much I've been enjoying Becky in class. She's very...interesting. A challenge."

That sounded ominous. But then, maybe this Ms. Albright was one of those rigid, toe-the-line types who didn't appreciate a little girl who marched to a different drummer. Taggart rubbed his back against the barn door again and vowed to stick up for Becky. "She's a good kid," he said defensively.

"Yes, she is. I'm looking forward to meeting you, Mr. Jones."

"I'll be there."

Felicity felt a little foolish asking for a conference with Becky's parents. It wasn't as if the little girl was doing anything dreadful. She wasn't.

She wasn't doing anything at all. No work. No papers. Nothing.

Except wearing spurs. And tailing her teacher after school. And on Saturday, too, now—if last Saturday was anything to go by.

Felicity had been standing in the checkout line at the grocery store when she glanced up and saw Becky and Susannah peeping in the window. The moment they realized she'd seen them, they ran off.

Felicity had been tempted to ask Carol Ferguson, the checker, if she'd ever been tailed around town. Was it perhaps something all newcomers to Elmer experienced? But somehow the topic never came up—and it wasn't easily worked into a conversation. But eventually Felicity expected she'd get to the bottom of it. Maybe when she met the Joneses.

She had to admit to a certain curiosity about Becky's parents. Her father, according to Becky, was a bull rider. A world champion bull rider.

"He rode nine out of ten bulls at the National Finals two years ago. And I'm gonna be just like him when I grow up." She never mentioned her mother. Obviously the father had all the charisma in the family.

Felicity supposed his wife was one of those long-suffering women who stood by their men or, in this case, stood waiting for them to come home, which might not seem very romantic to a child, but certainly, to Felicity's way of thinking, wasn't to be scoffed at.

She knew very little about rodeo herself. She'd never met a bull rider. A third-grade teacher who'd been married to a concert cellist didn't travel in the same circles with professional bull riders. It seemed a pretty exotic thing to be. She was amazed that you could make a living at it. She doubted very many people could. But apparently until two years ago, Becky's father had. Now, according to Becky, he was staying home.

"Teaching," Becky had announced just last week. "Like you."

"I thought you said he was a bull rider."

"He was. Is. Now he teaches. How to ride bulls."

Felicity couldn't imagine. Did he give tests? Homework? Draw up lesson plans?

She'd have to ask him, she thought with a smile as she

sat at her desk and graded a math quiz. The Joneses would be here any moment. Without their daughter. Becky and Susannah had made it onto the bus this afternoon. Felicity had stood right next to it until it pulled away just to make sure. Not that they seemed to have any desire to linger.

Becky had, in fact, been bouncing with suppressed excitement all afternoon. Felicity wondered at it, but could hardly ask. Did she know her parents were coming to meet her teacher? Was she pleased?

It didn't seem likely—not since all Becky had to show for the first three weeks of school was a string of zeroes in the grade book after her name.

The sound of footsteps at the doorway made her look up, smiling in the expectation of seeing Becky's parents.

She saw the handsomest cowboy she'd ever seen.

Lean and tanned, broad-shouldered and narrow-hipped, he was the epitome of every woman's western fantasy. Lori, she thought irrelevantly, would have approved.

His hat was a Stetson, his jeans were Wranglers, and his dusty boots looked like they had been places that would turn an urban cowboy pale. He was not, she noted, wearing spurs. Obviously, then, he was not Mr. Jones.

Her perusal took far longer than it should have. When she recollected herself, she realized he'd been making an equally astonished study of her. She reddened. ''May I help you?'' she said coolly, trying to regain her equilibrium.

He reached up and jerked off his Stetson, baring a short thatch of thick dark hair. ''I'm…looking for Ms. Albright?'' He clearly thought he hadn't found her.

Felicity wiped suddenly damp palms on her jungle-print skirt and stood up, holding out her hand as she came around the desk. ''I'm Felicity Albright.''

''Taggart Jones.'' He took her hand.

"I...I'm so glad you could come, Mr. Jones," Felicity said, her mouth oddly dry.

"Taggart," he corrected her. "If you call me Mr. Jones, I'll be lookin' over my shoulder for my dad." The grin he flashed her must have sent women all over the rodeo circuit into a tailspin.

Felicity, who had been immune to that sort of thing from anyone other than Dirk, felt a faint stirring deep within. It surprised her so much that she jerked her hand out of his grasp.

He didn't seem sorry to break the contact. He quickly stuffed his hand into the pocket of his jeans. The other tightened on the brim of his hat. "Pleased to meet you, ma'am." He dipped his head, and for an instant, his gaze trapped hers. He had the most intensely green eyes she had ever seen. Deep-set and sparkling, they reminded her of a pool in a forest glen, a pattern of sunlight and shadow on a jade both still and deep.

How fanciful is that, she chided herself, disgusted. She didn't ordinarily wax poetic about the parents of the children she taught. "I'm delighted to meet you, too, Mr., er...Taggart. Won't you sit down?" She gestured toward one of the children's chairs. "Becky has talked a lot about you."

"She has?" He sounded doubtful. He tried to sit in one of the children's chairs, then another. Both were far too small, and after trying for several seconds to find a comfortable spot, he gave up and swung himself up to sit on the waist-high counter above her storage cupboard, his boots dangling.

"Sorry," he apologized, but his grin was as unrepentant as Becky's. "I used to get into trouble for sittin' up here when I was in school. You gonna make me get down, too?"

Felicity tried to resist his grin. "I'd have to," she told

him in her best severe-schoolmarm voice, "if the children were here. Since they aren't—" she shrugged and smiled, her tone softening "—no, I won't."

Their gazes caught again. Something electric seemed to hover in the air. Abruptly, Felicity looked away and slipped behind her desk, grateful for the solid expanse of wood that separated her from Taggart Jones.

What was the matter with her? He was Becky's father! He was *married!*

It was just that dratted Lori and her subliminal suggestion about a cowboy, Felicity told herself—and the sudden reactivation of her two-years-asleep hormones. She drew a steadying breath and pulled out her grade book. "I'm sorry Mrs. Jones couldn't make it."

"There isn't one."

The baldness of his statement rocked her. His tone was matter-of-fact, but embarrassment burned her cheeks, anyway. Why hadn't she checked? When half her California students had been from single-parent families, why had she assumed that none of her Montana kids would be?

"I'm sorry," she said.

He shrugged. "Not your fault. She left us when Becky was two months old. It's common knowledge hereabouts. I should've said when you asked for her, but that was when I thought you were asking for my mom. And then when you weren't, I guess I was more concerned about Becky."

Felicity felt like a fool. She twisted her pencil and finally mustered a smile. But when Taggart smiled back, and all those dormant hormones suddenly took it upon themselves to dance around again, she looked down at her grade book. "Er, yes, well, um...Becky. She's quite a...an interesting child. She told me she wants to be a bull rider like her father."

Taggart rubbed a hand against the back of his neck. "It's

what she knows. She'll figure out sooner or later that there's plenty better ways to make a living."

"She's very proud of you."

"I'm proud of her, too." Their gazes met again. This time Felicity kept her hormones under strict control.

"Of course you are," she said, and wondered how she could gracefully ease into the part of the conference that he might not be so proud of.

"So, what's wrong with her?" he said, neatly solving her dilemma.

"Wrong?"

He grinned. "Nobody ever called my folks to talk about me when I was doin' everything I was supposed to. You got a problem with Becky, I want to hear it."

Felicity sucked in her breath. "You're absolutely right. There are one or two things I hope you can help me with." She opened her grade book. "As you can see—" she turned the book so he could follow the line of zeroes her finger traced "—Becky hasn't turned any work in all year. Now, there may have been some things she wasn't quite sure about, but I'm certain she can—"

"Hasn't turned anything in? *Nothing?* All year?" Taggart's grin vanished. He bounded down off the counter and came to loom over her.

"There have been several reading work sheets due already, as you can see. Not large assignments, of course. But she hasn't done any of them. And here—" she turned the page "—is a record of the arithmetic assignments I've given them." More zeroes. "We've finished our first unit in social studies." Still another line of zeroes. She showed him the incomplete for the science project, the penmanship grade— "Not really important," she allowed. "But another indication…"

Taggart's jaw tightened. The deep tan on his face was

underlined by an even deeper red beneath. He scowled fiercely. "Becky always does her work! She never misses." Felicity didn't know whether he was talking to her or to himself.

"In the past, you mean? Then...there isn't any reason, um, at home...why she might not be..."

"A reason at home for her not doing her work? Hell, no. But I'll give her a damn good one for doing it!"

"I'm sure you will." Felicity felt a flicker of sympathy for Becky Jones. "But I'd really like to know *why* she isn't doing any now—especially if you say she's always done her work before."

Taggart shook his head. He walked across the room and stared at the children's stories she'd hung on the wall, scowling at them. "Susannah doin' hers?"

"Yes, all of it. And very well, too."

He raked a hand through his hair, ruffling it where his hat had jammed it down. "I don't know, then. I figured maybe if Susannah wasn't doin' hers, either... They're friends, you see."

"I know. They...do a lot together. That's another thing I wanted to talk to you about." She hesitated, unsure how to phrase it.

Taggart leaned against the counter, arms folded across his chest. Felicity had to look up to meet his gaze. If she didn't, her eyes were on a level with his big gold world championship belt buckle. She studied it. Her eyes lowered a bit farther. Bad idea.

"What else?" he demanded.

There was only the bald truth. "Becky and Susannah seem to be...following me."

"Following you?" He gaped at her.

"You said they were missing the bus," she reminded him quickly. "Some days after school when I'm walking home or to the grocery store or wherever I'm going, I look back and they're...following me.''

Taggart frowned again, but it wasn't so much a frown of anger now as one of total bafflement. "This is a small town. You could just happen to look around and see them.''

"I know it's a small town. That's how I know they're following me. You notice things like that. *I* notice things like that. And whenever I glance over my shoulder—at the library, at the Laundromat, at the grocery store—there they are.''

"An' you think they're doing it deliberately?''

"I would say so, yes. It's happened several times a week since the beginning of school. I thought you might have some idea...''

"Not a clue. She's never done anything like it before. Of course, she's never not done her work before, either. Damn.'' Taggart scratched the back of his head. He slapped his hat against his thigh and shoved away from the counter. "I'll sort her out. I'll get to the bottom of it, Ms. Albright. Believe me.'' He started toward the door.

Felicity went after him. "Uh, Mr. Jones? Taggart?''

He turned. "There's more?''

"One...other thing.''

He waited, not speaking.

"Spurs.''

"What?"

Felicity shrugged helplessly. "She's wearing...spurs.''

He stared. *"To school?"*

Felicity nodded. "Every day. Except the first day. I don't remember her wearing them then. But it was pretty chaotic. Still,'' she mused, "I think I would have noticed.''

"I'd bet on it,'' Taggart said darkly. He smacked one fist into his other palm. "When I get my hands on that kid—''

"There isn't really a rule about it," Felicity said quickly. "I checked."

"Don't reckon anybody ever figured you'd need one." Taggart strangled his hat brim. "Spurs! Damn that kid. What's she up to?"

"Perhaps she wants attention."

"She'll get it, believe me."

"I didn't ask you to come in so I'd get her in trouble," she said quickly. "I simply wanted to understand what was going on."

"You and me both." He fixed his gaze on her. "Did you ask her?" he said. "About the spurs?"

"She said she needed to wear them."

"Needed to?" Taggart's eyes narrowed. He frowned, and the line between his dark brows deepened. "And what about the following business? Did you ask her about that?"

"I didn't want to accuse them of something." Felicity gave a little shrug. "I mean, I'm not from Elmer and I didn't want to...get off on the wrong foot. I thought it was maybe some local custom...."

"Not one I ever heard of." Taggart started toward the door again, then turned back once more. "Is that all?"

"That's all." She ventured a smile.

He didn't return it. "It's enough." He drew himself up straighter and squared his shoulders. "I appreciate your calling me, ma'am. I'll take care of it. And there'll be lots of work and no more following you around, I promise."

"Thank you." Felicity gave him a grateful smile. "And the spurs?"

"No more spurs." Taggart set his hat on his head and tugged it down tight. "Count on it."

He didn't know whether he was madder at Becky or at himself. He was plenty annoyed at his daughter, that was for sure. And puzzled, too. But he'd sort her out pronto, no two ways about it. He only wished he could sort himself out as quick.

That was Becky's teacher? That young knockout of a blonde? They sure as hell hadn't made teachers like her when he was a kid!

"A looker," Noah had called her. The word didn't begin to describe Felicity Albright. When he'd first glanced at her sitting there behind the teacher's desk, Taggart had thought she was some high school girl who came to help out. But then he'd taken a closer look and realized she was old enough to teach. She was just too damn pretty!

And all his wistful hormones sure as hell noticed. He couldn't remember being knocked for a loop like that since Julie. And the simple memory of that had nearly sent him running.

She wasn't Julie, he reminded himself. She was a teacher. His kid's teacher. And he'd been there to talk to her—like the concerned, intelligent, mature parent he was.

Still, he was lucky he'd managed to cross the room without stumbling over his boots. Remembering the way he'd stared and his initial stammering awkwardness, Taggart cursed under his breath now as he drove up the highway toward the ranch. The beautiful Ms. Albright must think he was an idiot.

And that he had an idiot for a kid.

Damn Becky, anyway! What on earth was she doing? How could she not turn in any work for three full weeks? How could she tail her teacher after school? And for God's sake, what was with the spurs? *Spurs!*

Taggart's fingers tightened on the steering wheel. Was she upset because his folks had moved away? Was she trying to say she'd be happier if he let her go live with them in Bozeman?

His mother had offered to let her come with them, though she knew Taggart would never agree. When he left rodeoing after the accident, he'd done it because he wanted to be with Becky. He still wanted it.

Didn't she?

Maybe not. Maybe…oh, hell, there were a million maybes. Most of the time his daughter was an open book. Not for her the feminine wiles that so entranced and then entangled him with Julie! She wasn't ever going to be like her mother, he assured himself time and again.

Now he wondered if he knew her at all.

As he pulled into the yard at Noah's new house, he saw Becky's sun-streaked hair and Susannah's dark head in the window of the tree house he and Noah had built for them. They peered down at him as he shut the engine off, but the moment he opened the door, both heads abruptly disappeared.

He stalked over to the tree. "Rebecca Kathleen! Get your rear end down here!"

There was a mouselike scuffling overhead, then Becky's green eyes appeared in the window. "Oh, hi, Daddy."

Hands on hips, he glowered up at her. "Down. Now."

"But we were just—"

"Down, Rebecca."

Her head disappeared again.

"That's twice he's called you Rebecca," he heard Susannah whisper. "You'd better go."

"I'm goin'." Becky didn't sound nearly as nervous as she ought to. Taggart tapped the toe of his boot on the dirt.

"Taggart!" He turned to see Tess, with Clay balanced on one hip, waving at him from the kitchen door. "Have time for a glass of lemonade?"

"Not today. Thanks, anyway. Just collectin' my kid."

When he turned back, Becky was climbing down the

ladder. She was wearing dusty blue jeans, a T-shirt. And spurs. Taggart's teeth came together with a snap.

"I gotta get my backpack," Becky said the instant her feet hit the ground. She skirted around him quickly, heading toward the house.

"Got a lot of homework, have you?"

Becky looked back at him guiltily, gave a tiny nod, then scurried toward the house. She seemed, for the first time, just a little nervous.

She damned well ought to be. Taggart went back to the truck and leaned against the door, arms folded across his chest. Out of the corner of his eye he could see Susannah peeking down at him from the window of the tree house. Usually she came skipping right up to him, ready to share some bit of news. Not today.

Becky retrieved her backpack, answered something Tess had said, then trudged toward him across the yard. There was a definite reluctance in her walk now. She didn't look at him, just climbed into the passenger side of the truck and fastened her seat belt without him even having to remind her.

Taggart got in, flicked on the engine, threw the truck into reverse and backed around. Becky sat silently beside him. Every now and then she slanted him a quick glance, like someone checking the fuse on a stick of dynamite she'd set.

The entire ride was accomplished in silence. She didn't even ask to steer the truck through the gate while he opened and closed it. Taggart didn't remark on it. They reached the kitchen before either of them said a word.

Becky headed for the stairs. "I gotta go do my homework."

"Why start now?"

She flinched as if she'd been shot. Then she ventured a

wary look at him over her shoulder. He beckoned to her. Sighing, she turned and came to stand in front of him, looking up at him solemnly, like a condemned prisoner about to face the firing squad. Taggart felt a momentary remorse, then promptly squelched it. She was in the wrong, not him.

"So," he said evenly, "why don't you tell me what's going on?"

Becky blinked. Her eyes widened fractionally. "Going on?"

"You know I went to see your teacher today."

She nodded.

"And you must have a pretty good idea what she told me."

Another nod, this one a little more hesitant.

"Want to guess what she told me?"

"Um...:" She paused and ran her tongue over her lips. "That I didn't do my homework?"

"Homework, hell! You haven't done *any* work! Not a lick. Not since school started!" His eyes narrowed when she nodded again. "You're *agreeing* with me?"

She swallowed audibly, then straightened her shoulders and looked at him steadily. "Yes."

"She also told me you're wearing spurs to school."

Becky pressed her lips together. Something flickered in her gaze and was quickly suppressed. She shifted her feet. The spurs jingled. "Uh-huh."

Taggart felt a muscle in his jaw tick. "And she said you're following her all over town!"

Becky looked at him, horrified. *"She saw us?"* Then she sighed and stuffed her hands into the pockets of her jeans. Once more impassiveness covered her features. Her green gaze met his unflinchingly.

"So maybe you'd like to tell me why?"

Becky dug the toe of her cowboy boot into the linoleum

floor, contemplating it for a moment before she lifted her gaze. "So she'd notice me."

"Oh, she did that," Taggart said dryly. "At the Laundromat. At the grocery store—"

"Not the followin'," Becky amended. "We didn't want her to notice *that*. Just the other stuff."

He shook his head, uncomprehending. "Why?"

"So she'd call you."

Which left him no more enlightened than before. He scratched his head. "You wanted her to call me?"

"Uh-huh."

He stared at her as if he might find the answer to his unspoken question emblazoned on her forehead, but he didn't. So eventually he had to ask again. "Why?"

"So you could meet her before some other guy did."

"What?"

Becky shrugged guilelessly. "She's better'n that lady at the rodeo in Missoula. Heaps better. Better'n Kitzy Miller, too."

Taggart took a step back and gripped the doorjamb for support. "Better than *what* lady in Missoula? What's this about Kitzy Miller?"

He knew he was perilously close to shouting at her. All right, he *was* shouting at her, but she wasn't making any sense! He swallowed hard and looked at her closely. "Explain."

Becky hunched her shoulders. "Well, I know she's not Tess, but she's the next best thing and—"

"Whoa. Hang on here a minute, sweetheart. What's this about Tess?" He hesitated, a notion suddenly occurring to him. He crossed the room and hunkered down to get on eye level with his daughter. He settled his big hands on her narrow shoulders. "Is this about mothers, Pard?"

She shifted under his hands. "Sorta." She wouldn't meet his eyes.

The vague worry that sometimes bothered him in the dark of night began to creep up on him in the bright light of day—the worry that said he wasn't a good enough parent, that he'd failed Becky as well as having failed her mother.

He made himself ask, "Do you want a mother?"

Her toe scraped. A spur jingled. "Not exac'ly," she said at last. "But if I'm gonna get one," she added firmly, "I'd rather have Miz Albright than Kitzy Miller or that lady at the rodeo."

Taggart stared at her, astonished. "What makes you think you're going to get any of them?"

"The way you look at 'em."

Taggart felt a flush crawl up his neck. He stood abruptly and tugged at the collar of his shirt. "How do I look at them?" he asked, then wasn't sure he wanted to know.

"Like you want 'em," Becky said bluntly. "The way I looked at dogs before I got Digger."

Taggart rubbed a hand down his face. "God," he muttered. He wasn't sure if it was supplication or blasphemy—probably the former. Heaven knew he needed all the help he could get. He looked like he wanted a woman? *That* was why his daughter hadn't been doing her schoolwork? *That* was why she and Susannah had been following Felicity Albright around town? *That* was why she was wearing spurs to school? So he could meet her teacher and—

And what?

Bed Felicity Albright? He didn't think that would have occurred to Becky.

Then what?

Marry her?

Taggart groaned and closed his eyes.

Three

—

He tried gentleness; he tried firmness; he tried logic; he tried emotion. Basically, he ranted and raved about how finding a woman was his responsibility, not hers, *if* he wanted a woman, which he didn't. Did she understand? He glowered. He glared. He stomped from one end of the room to the other and back.

Through it all Becky sat against the back of the couch, hands folded in her lap, moving only to point the toes of her boots in and out, in and out, as she watched him pace.

"It's not that I don't appreciate your…efforts," Taggart finished finally. "I know you…mean well. But—" here he stopped and fixed her with a steely look "—it's wrong to meddle in other people's lives. And you have to admit that not doing any work was pretty ill-advised."

For the first time Becky's lower lip jutted and began to quiver just a little. He took heart, glad he was beginning to get through to her.

Determined, he pressed on. "And so was wearing those da—dratted spurs." He gave her a hard look. "There will be no more spurs in school. Got that?"

Becky nodded once. She looked suitably chastened now. He almost hated to bring up the following Ms. Albright business, fearing it might be overkill, but he needed to make sure she got the point about that, too.

"And you will not follow your teacher anymore, either. Understand?"

A quick, flicking glance in his direction. "Yes, Daddy." Then she lowered her eyes again.

"Good." He gave a satisfied sigh, glad they had that straightened out, glad she realized she had no business meddling in his love life, glad there would be no more matchmaking.

Her head was bent. She was still studying her hands. Taggart, looking at her, was sure he felt worse than she did about her chastisement. Then she gave a tiny sniffle.

"Ah, hell, Pard," he muttered, undone, and strode over to grab her off the couch. She practically leapt into his arms, hugging him fiercely around the neck and wrapping her legs around his waist, kicking him in the butt with her spurs as she did so. He didn't care. He relished the strength of those small arms hugging him. He hugged her back and nuzzled her neck, making her squirm and giggle.

"I love you, Pard," he said at last, his throat tight.

She grinned and gave him a smacking kiss. "Love you, too, Daddy." She squirmed some more until he let her slide to the floor. Then she looked up at him, and they smiled at each other.

"I'll start dinner," he said. "You go get your school-work done." He picked up her backpack and handed it to her. She took it and started toward the stairs, then stopped and looked back at him.

"Miz Albright's awful pretty, isn't she, Daddy?"

"Becky!"

But he knew that his strangled exclamation and flushed face had given her the answer she was looking for.

"He likes her," Susannah said, looking up from the report she was writing on the history of the Shields Valley. It was part of the local history project that Ms. Albright had assigned, lots better than the boring stuff most teachers made them do. But today they had more important things on their minds.

"He thinks she's pretty," Becky corrected as she bent over her map. She was supposed to be making a flour-and-water version of the Crazies, but the flour wasn't cooperating. Neither was the water. There was a lot more of both on her hands than there was on the fiber board.

"Men are like that," Susannah replied knowledgeably. "It's a start."

"Huh." Tuck snorted. He was sitting at the desk next to Becky, drawing an Indian on horseback, one of a series of illustrations he was making to show the people who'd lived in the valley throughout history, and it took all his concentration. When Tuck drew, he never paid attention to anything else. Becky was surprised he'd even heard them talking.

"'S true," Susannah said. "It's how come my dad fell in love with my mom—at first."

Tuck stuck his tongue in the corner of his mouth and bent over his drawing. Becky tried to scrape some of the flour-and-water paste off her hands onto the map and make it look like a snow-capped peak. Her nose itched and she wanted to scratch it. She wiggled it. That didn't help.

"Scratch my nose," she said to Sam Bacon, the other member of their group. On Monday Ms. Albright had divided the class into groups of four and put them to work on projects.

"Multimedia events," she called them. Susannah, who had the neatest handwriting, was doing the report; Tuck, because he was by far the best artist, was drawing the people; Becky—because she was the messiest probably—was making the map; And Sam, who wasn't much good at reading and writing, but could do anything with his hands, was sanding the butt of the wooden rifle replica he was making. Now he scratched her nose for her, then went back to sanding.

"How's the Shields Valley crew?"

Becky looked up to see Jenny Nichols, the school's one teacher's aide, smiling at them. Becky had to remember to call her Mrs. Nichols during school days. Outside of school she was always just Jenny. Becky had known her as long as she could remember.

Jenny and her husband, Mace, lived on the old Galveston spread up past Flathead Creek. They'd finally saved enough to buy it just a year ago. Before that Mace had cowboyed for Becky's grandpa and had run his small herd with Will Jones's bigger one. As soon as Becky was big enough to walk, she'd followed Mace.

"Shadow," he called her, and then he'd grin the most gorgeous grin Becky had ever seen and her heart would do a flip-flop. With his black hair and deep blue eyes and that wide white grin, Mace Nichols was the handsomest cowboy Becky had ever known.

And the nicest—next to her dad.

Sometimes she wished Mace wasn't already married to Jenny, because then he could wait and marry her. But she'd always liked Jenny, too. Once or twice she'd even thought it would be nice to have Jenny for a mom. If Jenny divorced Mace and married Becky's dad that would leave Mace free to someday marry her. She wondered if he'd like having his ex-wife for a mother-in-law.

Maybe it wasn't such a good idea, after all.

"Mace wants to know when you're coming out to visit us," Jenny said. Sometimes her dad let her go spend the weekend or a few days in the summer with Mace and Jenny, but she hadn't gone now since school had started. She'd been too busy trying to get her father together with Ms. Albright.

Now Becky shrugged. "I dunno. I've got a lot of work to do here."

Jenny grinned. "So I heard."

Becky flushed, realizing that Jenny knew about her three weeks of missing schoolwork. She hoped Mace didn't find out. He'd be disappointed in her.

He might approve if he understood why she was doing it, though, because he and Jenny were happy enough. But then again, maybe he wouldn't because he was a good friend of her dad's, and sometimes grown-ups stuck together.

"How about coming out this weekend for a while," Jenny suggested.

"Maybe." But Becky knew she couldn't. She and Susannah had to carry out the second phase of their plan.

"There's more?" Becky had said doubtfully when Susannah proposed it.

"He didn't propose to her the first time he saw her, did he?"

"Well, no," Becky had admitted. So they were moving on to phase two—as soon as Taggart had a week or so to calm down.

Becky slanted a quick glance at Ms. Albright. Did she think Taggart was handsome the way Becky thought Mace was handsome? Did he make her feel all hot and cold and kind of quivery inside?

Was that the way her dad made Kitzy Miller feel?

Becky didn't like to think about that. Her cheeks warmed suddenly when she realized that Ms. Albright had lifted her eyes from the paper she'd been reading and was looking straight at her. Becky ducked her head and shoved her hands in her pockets.

Only then did she realize they were still covered with paste.

She missed them.

Perverse as it might be, Felicity felt just a little bereft every afternoon when she left school and glanced over her shoulder to discover that "the shadow twins," as she'd come to think of them, weren't lurking there.

They weren't at the grocery store on Saturday morning. They weren't at the museum-cum-library Wednesday afternoon. They weren't outside the Laundromat on Tuesday when she carried her basket of folded laundry home. Every day after school they got on the bus like good little girls. Becky wasn't even wearing spurs.

It was just the way it should be.

And yet Felicity kept wondering what had caused Becky's behavior in the first place.

She'd hoped that Taggart—she really did think of him as Taggart even though she told herself she ought to be calling him Mr. Jones—might call and tell her. But three days went by, and then a week, and he never rang.

Even more perplexing was the new mystery she had to contemplate: why she spent so much time thinking about Taggart Jones?

If he'd been at all like Dirk, she might have understood it. But he wasn't. Dirk had been tall, three inches over six feet, with straight fair hair that, in the sun, turned to strands of spun gold. He'd had deep brown eyes all the more striking because they were at such odds with his pale coloring. He was quiet, introspective, a man in tune with music very few people heard.

Taggart Jones was average in height, his skin weathered and suntanned, his green eyes framed by lines drawn by laughter and the sun. His hair was short and dark, what she could see of it. Mostly it was hidden by his hat. His *cowboy* hat, she reminded herself.

Never in a million years had she anticipated being interested in a cowboy.

She wasn't really interested, she'd tried assuring herself. Her hormones had suddenly come back to life, and he'd happened to be around at the time.

It could have been any man.

If Elmer had more of a social life, she could have tested out her theory. But single men were not thick on the ground in Elmer, and so she spent more time than she wanted to recall fantasizing about Taggart Jones.

Not at school, of course. She never had time at school. But at night when she was sitting at home grading papers or cooking dinner or fooling around with Uncle Fred's old printing press, she'd find herself daydreaming about a dark-haired cowboy who wore a Stetson and boots and a big gold buckle and had eyes the color of a mountain glade.

It was just that there was nothing else to think about—besides school—she told herself. And school meant thinking about Becky, and thinking about Becky meant thinking about Taggart—and there she'd be, thinking about him again.

He had certainly been as good as his word.

Becky had appeared sans spurs the next morning, and she hadn't missed an assignment since. In fact, she had turned in every single assignment for the entire first three weeks!

"It's too late to get credit," Felicity had said.

"Don't matter." Becky thrust the papers at her. "My dad said to do 'em."

And she had. Very well. She'd understood everything, which told Felicity that lack of comprehension hadn't been the problem.

Then what was?

"My dad says to apologize to you, too. For the spurs. An' the work I didn't do." Becky flushed. "An' the following." She ducked her head briefly, then raised it again. Her eyes were mountain-glade green and as steady and direct as her father's.

"Apology accepted." Felicity smiled at her.

Becky smiled back. A hopeful smile? That's what it looked like to Felicity, but she didn't know and Becky didn't explain. She just took off running toward the playground.

Bemused, Felicity watched her go, still wishing she knew what had been going on. But short of calling Taggart and asking him, she didn't suppose she ever would. Still, she thought now, with an odd little hope of her own, Elmer was the small town he'd claimed it was. Maybe if she waited long enough, she'd run into him sometime.

He ran into her everywhere.

Of course, it was his fault. Every time he turned around now he seemed to have to go into town. Wednesday just before dinner, for example, Becky remembered the book she'd forgotten to get to do her report. So they'd had to drive into Elmer to the tiny museum-cum-library to pick it up. And coincidentally the woman standing talking to the museum volunteer was none other than Felicity Albright.

"Oh, hi," Becky said cheerfully. "You remember my dad?"

"Of course," Felicity said, smiling.

Taggart, remembering what Becky wanted him to do with this very same Ms. Albright, muttered hello and felt himself blush to the roots of his hair.

"She really is nice," Becky had said on their way out. "Don't you think so, Daddy?"

"Um," Taggart said. He didn't want to think about Felicity Albright. It wasn't good for his hormonal health.

But on the following Saturday morning, they'd had to go into town to buy a gallon of milk and damned if they hadn't run into her again. Taggart didn't understand how they could have run out of it since he'd just bought a gallon two days before.

"Did you finish all the milk?" he'd asked Becky, scowling.

"Me an' Susannah an' Tuck," she'd said. "Isn't that all right?"

What was he supposed to do, ration the kid's calcium intake? They drove to town to the grocery store. Felicity Albright was there buying apples.

"Hi, Ms. Albright!" Becky sang out.

Taggart wished he could sink through the floor.

Felicity smiling at him like that made him want to dig the hole even deeper. And when she said, "My, but Becky has certainly been working hard lately. I can't imagine what must have been the problem earlier," Taggart thought that if he dug clear to China, he still wouldn't be far enough away.

And then there was the Laundromat.

Ordinarily Taggart never set foot inside the Laundromat. He had his folks' old washer and dryer, and they did the job just fine. But Tuesday afternoon when he went to put in a load, the washing machine had gone clunk, clank, sputter.

"What the hell's wrong with you?" he asked it. Not surprisingly, he got no answer, except Becky saying plaintively, "What'm I gonna wear?"

Her clothes—*all of them*—were muddier than he'd ever seen them.

"You said you used to get your clothes muddy when you were a kid," Becky reminded him when she heard his teeth come together with a snap.

"Not all at once," Taggart muttered under his breath. "Come on. I can get the gate welded while we do the laundry."

He supposed he was lucky Felicity wasn't having her gate welded, too. It was bad enough that she was right there, putting her clothes in the dryer, when they walked in the Laundromat door. Taggart stopped and stared.

"Gosh, Dad, look who's here!" Becky said.

Taggart didn't move. Or at least not all of him did. He cleared his throat. "Almost forgot. I gotta see a man about a...a cow." He gave Felicity a quick nod, thrust a handful of quarters at Becky and took off for the barber shop hoping to find some male reinforcements.

But Nick the barber only wanted to talk about that good-looking new schoolteacher. Didn't Taggart think she was somethin'? Taggart's mumbled response caused Nick to lean into him with the clippers. He felt lucky to escape with any hair on his head.

At least when he reappeared in the Laundromat, Felicity was no longer there. He breathed a sigh of relief.

Still, seeing her so many places was eerie. It was uncanny.

It was planned.

A guy only had to look at the sphinxlike smile on his

daughter's face every time they'd run into the gorgeous Ms. Albright to know he'd been had.

The last straw came on Sunday morning.

"You want to go to church?" Taggart looked at his daughter, astonished. Becky was no more a fan of long-winded sermons than he was. He figured he and God were on a pretty friendly footing—any guy who faced meeting his Maker as often as a bull rider did, kept his priorities straight—but never once had he gone at the urging of his daughter.

Still, maybe this was part of growing up—taking on a new interest in religion. At least that's what he told himself until he came in from parking the truck to find Becky planted in the pew right behind Felicity Albright!

He stopped right where he was. Then Becky turned around and saw him. She waved enthusiastically. "Dad!" she said in a loud whisper.

He glared. But once she'd got his attention, Becky turned around and sat, head bowed, eyes closed in presumably pious contemplation. Her devoted pose was only ruined by the fact that he could see her biting her lip to keep from grinning.

Taggart wanted to bite her head off. He wanted to take off and never look back. But there were people coming up behind him, waiting for him to move, and so finally he walked down the aisle and slid into the pew next to her. His fists clenched on top of his thighs as he stared straight ahead. He ended up staring directly at the back of Felicity's beautiful blond head.

He could, of course, have closed his eyes. He tried. That was worse.

It gave his imagination full rein. It hauled up every fantasy he'd spent the last couple of weeks trying to keep at bay. It spread all the lovely golden hair out on a pillow—

his pillow—and encouraged him to run his hands through the curly, silken tresses.

He had told himself he didn't like blondes—not after Julie. But Felicity's hair wasn't the cool silvery platinum that Julie's had been. It was a deeper, warmer, burnished golden color. Julie's hair had always made him want to reach out and stroke its almost shiny smoothness. Felicity's, on the other hand, made him want to tangle his hands in it, to tug its gentle waves, to thread his fingers through it, to explore its softness. He wanted to explore the softness of her—all of her. In his dreams he had.

And in his mind he was going to right now—in the middle of church—unless...

He jerked open his eyes and sucked in a desperate breath.

Big mistake. Unless that soft lilac scent was some new-fangled incense the minister was using, it was Felicity's scent he was breathing in.

He tried holding his breath. Also unwise. He couldn't hold it for an hour. And when he finally did have to breathe he took such a desperate gulp of air that Becky whispered loudly, "'S matter? You sick?"

Taggart jerked back and shot his daughter a hard glare. She knew damned well what the matter was! And if she didn't understand the specifics at her age, she could guess.

Felicity turned her head. He could see her face in profile now, the soft curve of her cheek, the slight tilt of her nose. If she turned much farther, she'd see him sitting right behind her. He could well imagine the look she'd give him then.

He'd seen it often enough in the past week—that startled, slightly bemused glance, that softly knowing smile. She didn't really know, did she? The very thought made his blood heat.

Did she think he was trying to follow her the same way Becky had been? God help him.

"Let us pray," the minister intoned.

Taggart did. Fervently. But if God heard anything he said about wanting to be cool, calm and disinterested, He certainly didn't give any indication. Maybe God didn't listen to liars, Taggart thought grimly, for as devoutly as he seemed to be asking for deliverance from the temptation of Felicity Albright, so equally determinedly did his eyes seek her out and his mind come up with scenarios better played out anywhere other than in church.

He squirmed, wondering if there was any way to get out of here without Felicity Albright seeing him. There wasn't.

Worse, at that very moment, the Reverend Mr. Wilson decided that loving one's neighbors began with getting to know them.

"Look around you! Greet your Sunday morning neighbors," he exhorted them, waving his arm to encompass them all.

And the next thing Taggart knew he was staring into Felicity Albright's startled eyes. Would she look at him like that gazing up from a pillow?

Oh, jeez. He grabbed her outstretched hand and shook it.

It was even softer than he remembered. Or maybe he was simply more aware of the callused roughness of his. Jerking his hand back, he stuffed it into the pocket of his jeans.

"Morning," he muttered.

Felicity smiled. "Good morning, Mr. Jones. Taggart," she corrected herself. Hearing his name on her lips sent a shiver down his spine. God, it was worse than being fifteen again. What had Becky done to him?

"Lovely day, isn't it?" Felicity went on.

"Lovely," he managed, strangled. He didn't usually

have trouble talking to women. Usually he could charm the socks right off them—and other things, too, if he so desired. And there he was again, with his thoughts winging off in a definitely nonspiritual direction.

Felicity held out a hand to Becky. "And good morning to you, Miss Jones," she said with a smile. "Have you had a good weekend?"

Becky nodded eagerly. "We got a new bull! Sunfish! He's really mean. Fer-ocious! You wanta come see him?"

Felicity blinked. "Well, thank you. I—"

Taggart considered stuffing a hymnal in his daughter's mouth and was grateful that, before Felicity could answer, Reverend Wilson had moved on to the sermon.

Becky tugged on his hand. "Sit down, Daddy! Everybody else is sittin' down."

So they were. Mortified, Taggart sat.

Reverend Wilson embarked on a rambling discourse about loving your enemies and being kind to the people who tried to do you ill. "It isn't easy," he told them. "Not easy at all."

Taggart figured that it was a damn sight easier than loving your daughter when she was trying to manage your love life. He glowered. Becky sat in pious justification, ignoring him.

The minute the service was over, he didn't give her a chance to renew her invitation. He grabbed her hand and bolted for the door—only to be trapped by Reverend Wilson, who wanted to inquire about his parents.

"Haven't seen you in a while, Taggart," he said easily, grabbing Taggart by the hand and shaking it heartily. "We've missed you. Missed your parents, too. How are Will and Gaye?"

"They're fine." Taggart tried to free his hand. The Reverend hung on.

"Good, good. How do they like it down in Bozeman?"

"A lot," Taggart assured him, trying still to ease out of the minister's surprisingly strong grip. "They'll be back for a visit one of these weekends. I'm sure they'll come by to see you."

"I'll look forward to it. You tell them we miss them," Reverend Wilson commanded him. "We don't get such a lot of new people moving in that we can spare them. Except of course, Fred's lovely niece—" He reached around Taggart to snag someone else's hand and draw her over. "Have you met our new parishioner, Miss Albright?"

Only thirty or forty thousand times, Taggart thought desperately. In person and in his dreams. His gaze met Felicity's, and he saw that she was laughing.

"I teach his daughter," she explained to the minister, still smiling. "And we've run into each other quite often in town, haven't we, Mr. Jones." Her eyes sparkled with amusement, inviting him to share the humor.

But Taggart was beyond thinking anything was funny. Between her reality and his fantasies he had reached the end of his rope.

"I don't know what you think, but I wasn't following you," he said abruptly. "In fact, I don't want anything to do with you!"

And leaving an openmouthed minister and an astonished Felicity Albright staring after him, he grabbed Becky's hand and took off for the truck.

"You were rude," Becky said.

Taggart didn't reply. He turned onto the gravel road that led to the ranch house, his knuckles white on the steering wheel. The truck kicked up gravel as he drove.

"I bet you hurt her feelings," Becky persisted.

Taggart stomped on the accelerator. The truck hit a pothole, bouncing him so high he smacked his head. He cursed under his breath and saw Becky grip the edge of the seat in silent desperation. Sighing, he slowed down.

"You could say you're sorry."

"So could you," he bit out. Who had goaded him into it, after all?

His daughter chewed her lower lip. "I only wanted to go to church."

"You only wanted to throw me at Ms. Albright!"

"I wasn't sure she was gonna be there."

"Just like you weren't sure she was going to be at the Laundromat or the grocery store or the library."

"I wasn't," she said stubbornly.

"A trial lawyer might get you off on a technicality like that. Your father isn't buying."

Becky scrunched lower in her seat and gave him a put-upon look which he met with a hard glare. She sighed and looked out the window. The truck bumped along the road. Neither of them spoke again until he pulled up in front of the house and shut off the engine. The utter stillness between them seemed to magnify the mere sound of their breathing.

Finally Becky slanted a quick glance his way. "Sorry." Then she unhooked her seat belt, opened the door of the truck, slid down to the ground and started toward the house. Her small shoulders were hunched, as if she were carrying the world—or her father—on her back.

Taggart sat staring after her until she reached the house. Only then did he get out. He didn't head for the house, but for the stock pens and the "fer-ocious" Sunfish he'd bought the day before.

Pitting his desperation against a ton of bovine irritability seemed a good idea right about now.

* * *

"He said what?" Susannah was clearly horrified when Becky called her on the phone and reported what had happened at church.

Becky repeated it word for word. She tried to tell herself it wasn't as rude as it had sounded, but even she knew better than that. But he was right, it wasn't only his fault. She had pushed him too far.

"Maybe if I hadn't put the wrench in the washing machine and got my stuff all muddy," she murmured.

"Too late. Besides, it might be the best thing that ever happened." Susannah was ever the optimist.

"I don't see how," Becky said.

"Easy," Susannah said cheerfully. "Now he'll have to apologize to her."

Every Sunday night after supper since Felicity had arrived in Elmer, two retired schoolteachers, Cloris Stedman and Alice Benn, had spirited her off to the Busy Bee for pie and coffee.

"Think of it as 'girls' night out,'" Cloris told her cheerfully. "Besides, what else do you have to do?"

Other than grade papers, miss Dirk and, for the past two weeks, daydream about Taggart Jones, nothing at all. So every Sunday night, Felicity had gone.

Until tonight.

Tonight when Cloris and Alice appeared on her doorstep promptly at seven-fifteen, she declined.

"Hot date?" Alice asked, bobbing her spectacles up and down on her nose and looking about expectantly.

"No date," Felicity assured her.

"No man." Alice made a tsking sound. "You need a man in your life, my dear." Both she and Cloris were widows, too, but they'd had long and apparently happy marriages. They thought Felicity should start looking around again.

Maybe Felicity would have—if Taggart Jones hadn't said what he'd said this morning in church. She knew she was foolish to have spent the day dwelling on it. But she couldn't believe how much those few harsh words had hurt.

Used to feeling virtually no interest around any man who wasn't Dirk, she had spent the past two weeks speculating about her hormones' revival where Taggart was concerned. When she'd happened to see him all over town, it had somehow seemed to confirm the rightness of those feelings, as well as being uncanny, but really sort of funny—like their own private joke.

Obviously it wasn't funny to Taggart Jones. *I wasn't following you. I don't want anything to do with you!*

His words had echoed in her head all afternoon. At the time, they'd made her feel like crawling under a rock. Fortunately, she didn't think anyone else had heard except Reverend Wilson and, of course, Becky. She'd managed to laugh it off with Reverend Wilson after Taggart had stormed off, dragging Becky behind him.

It wasn't so easy to laugh when she was alone.

I don't want anything to do with you!

Well, fine. She wasn't exactly keen on having anything to do with him, either—not now.

In fact, she wasn't going to the Busy Bee tonight because, wholly irrationally, she was afraid she might run into him if she did. And if he was there, what would he say this time? She didn't want to know. "It's just that I have lots and lots of papers to do," she said vaguely.

Cloris and Alice muttered a little, but then took themselves off. Felicity watched them until they reached the end of the walk. Their heads were together, discussing her, no doubt. Too bad. She needed a little time alone tonight—a chance to lick her wounds.

She went back and sat down at the kitchen table to face a stack of papers. What she'd told them about having papers to grade had been nothing but the truth. She sat down and forced herself to get on with them, but her mind kept wandering, kept remembering, kept hearing Taggart's hurtful words. She was almost relieved to hear a knock on the door an hour later.

Cloris and Alice must be back, bringing her a piece of pie, unwilling to let her miss the fattening part of the evening, even if she declined to accompany them.

"You didn't have to—" she began as she opened the door.

It wasn't Cloris. Or Alice.

It was—heaven help her—Taggart Jones.

Four

And he looked, for all the world, like he'd just come from a bar fight.

"What on earth happened to your face?"

He actually looked startled at her question. He lifted a hand and touched his raw cheek and partially closed right eye almost absently. "This? Nothin'. Just a little run-in with a bull."

"A bull?"

A tide of color crept above the collar of his blue chambray shirt. His mouth twisted wryly. "That mean ol' one Becky told you about, remember? He did what you should've done to me."

"What's that?"

"Kicked me in the ass. Knocked me on my head. I was rude to you this morning. I've come to say I'm sorry."

Felicity stared at him, astonished. If seeing Taggart on her doorstep was unexpected, his apology was even more so. She became aware of her heart hammering just a bit too quickly and deliberately sucked in a slow, careful breath. All she could think was that a woman could get lost in the green depths of Taggart Jones's one good eye. He was looking at her steadily, waiting for a response, she guessed.

She felt a little giddy. "Thank you. I…appreciate that."

They stared at each other. He swallowed. So did she. His swollen eye blinked shut.

"Are you sure you're okay?"

"Fine. It's an occupational hazard. Don't worry about it."

But Felicity couldn't help but worry. She wasn't used to occupational hazards like his. Sitting on tacks and finding the odd frog in one's desk drawer didn't compare. "You ought to put ice on it. Come in here and I'll give you some." She opened the door wider, and, after a bare second's hesitation, he came in.

"Sit down." She didn't stop to think that the room seemed suddenly smaller, closer, warmer. She nodded toward the chairs at the table. He dragged out a chair and sat. She went to the refrigerator and took out a tray of ice cubes, thumping it on the counter to crack them into smaller pieces. Then she put the cracked ice in a plastic bag, wrapped it in a thin dish towel, and handed it to him.

He took off his hat and she noted his recent haircut. It made him look younger, more vulnerable. Or maybe that was the black eye and scraped face.

"You seem to have a little experience with this sort of thing." He set his hat on the table and pressed the makeshift ice bag against his eye.

Felicity wiped her palms on her jeans. "I had brothers. And once my husband broke his foot—"

"Husband?" Taggart's gaze jerked up. He looked around as if he expected to see Dirk in the doorway.

"He died two years ago," Felicity said quietly.

"Oh." Taggart let out a slow breath. "I'm sorry. I didn't know."

"I don't advertise it. It's just...there. Like you...and your...wife." The shuttered look that came over Taggart's face the instant she said the words made her regret them.

"Ex-wife," he corrected.

"Ex-wife," Felicity repeated. "Sorry."

"Not as sorry as I am." He said the words so softly she barely heard them. He didn't look at her, but kept his head down, the ice pack pressed to his eye.

He must have loved her a lot, Felicity decided, and thought for the first time that there might be a harder way to lose a spouse than to a sudden, unexpected death. Wouldn't it be worse to feel rejected? Unloved?

She wanted to go to him, to put a hand on his shoulder, to touch his hair, his cheek. To offer comfort. She wrapped her arms tightly across her breasts, squelching the notion.

"It was...kind of you to come and apologize. You didn't really need to. I don't blame you for being a little...testy. It must have been a shock to see me right in front of you in church after seeing me all those other times." She gave an awkward little laugh.

Taggart raised his one good eye and met hers. "A bigger shock than it ought to have been."

"What do you mean?"

"I mean I should've realized about all that following Becky and Susannah were doing."

"What about it?" Felicity looked at him, confused.

"We were being set up."

"Set up?"

"By a pair of scheming girls." Taggart dragged the ice bag down his face, then looked at her over the top of it and said flatly, "Becky reckons you'd make a fine mother for her—and a wife for me."

Felicity was grateful she was clutching the back of one of the chairs. Otherwise, she might have sat right down on the floor. She stared at him, astonished.

"A wife! *That's* what they were doing?" She felt her cheeks warm. His face was red, too, and not just from the ice. Felicity thought about all the times in the past two weeks when Becky had turned up in those very same places with her father in tow. She thought how odd it was, what a small town they lived in. She hadn't connected it, but Taggart had known! No wonder he'd dragged Becky off after church today. No wonder he'd said what he had!

"Oh, my," she said now.

Taggart lifted his head. "Oh, my, indeed."

Flustered, she sat down, then bounced up again, feeling somehow that she was contributing to an excess of familiarity by simply seating herself in her own kitchen. She did a lap around the tiny room, picked up the dish cloth, put it down again. "Oh, my."

"Don't worry. I set them straight. At least I thought I had." He shrugged. "Judging from church this morning, I didn't do a very good job."

"Whatever would make them think that we..." Now her cheeks were burning!

"Susannah, I'd bet," Taggart said grimly. "She got her folks together a couple of years back."

"They were separated?"

Taggart shook his head. "They weren't married. Noah didn't even know Susannah existed."

Felicity goggled. "Didn't know?"

"Not till we got in an accident two Christmases ago comin' back from the National Finals. We got smacked by a semi on the Interstate near Laramie in a snowstorm."

Felicity shuddered. "Were you badly hurt?"

"Concussion. Broke my leg. Once I came around and they got things sorted out, I got to come home pretty quick. But Noah punctured a lung and hurt his knee and wrist and shoulder. So he ended up in Laramie doing physical therapy over Christmas. He knew Tess—she's a nurse—'cause he'd recuperated there once before. He reckoned maybe she'd take him in again, so he showed up on her doorstep—" he paused "—and met Susannah."

"Tess hadn't ever told him?"

"She didn't figure he'd want to know." Taggart gave an awkward shrug. "They hadn't parted on the best of terms. There isn't much future if one of you is goin' down the road all the time." His mouth twisted wryly. "Guess I should've figured that out for myself. Anyhow, Susannah talked her mother into letting Noah stay. Just for Christmas, you understand. But, well...Noah wasn't about to let her go again, and eventually they got together, happy as pigs in—" He flushed and broke off. "So, I figure it went to her head and now she and Becky are convinced they can do equally well for me. And you."

"Not your...ex-wife?" She was careful to get it right this time.

"No, thank God." His tone was fervent. Maybe he didn't love her anymore. Maybe he was getting over it. Like she was getting over losing Dirk.

Was she getting over losing Dirk?

Certainly Felicity had never felt as intensely aware of any man since Dirk's death as she did of Taggart Jones. But *marry* him? That was a little drastic.

"Have they done this before?" she asked cautiously.

"Never. And they won't do it again, I promise you."

She smiled. "I'm sure they were only...trying to help.

They're young. They'll realize before long that you want to pick your own wife.''

''I'm not in the market for a wife.'' His tone was flat and hard, brooking no argument.

''Oh.'' Felicity felt oddly deflated. ''I see.''

Something in her tone must have made him take notice. ''Not that you wouldn't be a great candidate if I were,'' he said quickly.

She gave him a faint smile. ''Thank you. I think.''

''Hey.'' His own smile was rueful. ''Can't seem to stop sticking my foot in my mouth, can I?''

''Don't worry. I won't be coming after you with a wedding ring. Actually,'' she admitted, ''I came up here to get away from matchmaking friends in L.A.''

''All the way to Elmer? Wasn't that a little drastic?''

''Well, I didn't see myself staying in Los Angeles, and I didn't want to go back to Des Moines—that's where I grew up. So when Uncle Fred died and left me the house, well, it seemed like fate, I guess.'' Her cheeks warmed slightly as she thought he might consider her foolish, but a glance told her that he was simply listening, not judging at all.

Encouraged, she went on. ''I remembered how much I loved it here. I spent a summer here with my mom when I was ten—helping Uncle Fred put out his paper, going hiking in the mountains, riding horseback, picking berries—they're all part of my fondest memories. And so—'' she shrugged ''—I came.''

''And?''

''I love it.''

''Love it?''

''I do.'' And as she said the words, she knew firmly and fully that they were true. She'd been living in what had amounted to a holding pattern all the while she'd stayed in

Los Angeles after Dirk had died. Perhaps at the time she'd needed to.

But she needed to no longer; in fact, she needed to be somewhere else, to *grow* somewhere else. Elmer.

"Good for you," Taggart said after a moment. His voice was a little gruff, and he looked at her only for a moment, then stared away into space.

"Can I get you a cup of coffee or something?" Felicity asked. She felt hesitant, not wanting to break the tentative rapport that seemed to be developing.

Taggart's eyes focused on her once more. He blinked as if he was suddenly aware of the intimacy of their surroundings and of the possibility that his daughter might be already busy picking out Felicity's engagement ring. He set down the ice pack and stood abruptly. "Nope. Thanks, but I've gotta get going."

"I won't try to marry you tonight," Felicity said lightly, forcing a smile. "If that's what you're worried about."

Taggart flushed. "Sorry. I just...don't want you to get the wrong idea...thinking I'm trying to...you know." He shrugged awkwardly.

"I know," Felicity said gently.

"I really do have work to get done."

"Teaching bull riding?"

"Not tonight. Paperwork. An ad to put together. Some correspondence."

"For your bull riding school?"

"Yep."

"What's it like, teaching bull riding? I can't imagine."

"Fun. Challenging. I've got some two-day schools. Some three. Some five."

"And what do you teach? How, I mean?"

"We go over fundamentals—the way the bull moves, the way the rider is supposed to move. How to get your head screwed on straight. Bull riding is a mind game as much as a strength game. You're never really stronger than the bull, so you have to succeed some other way. You have to understand that and go with him.''

Felicity was fascinated. "How did you get started?"

"It was just something I did. I won a ribbon ridin' a sheep when I was five. Mutton bustin' they call it. Then I started on steers, and when I was in high school, broncs and bulls. Kids hereabouts do that. It's not all that rare. I was good at it. I liked the bulls the most. I was never much for sittin' still.''

No, she could see that. She could see it in his daughter, come to that. "But teaching?"

"I like that better than riding most of the time." A smile turned up the corners of his mouth. "I like figuring things out. Helping guys make the best of themselves. They won't all go on and be world champs. In fact, damn few of 'em will even go pro. But what they learn, they can use in whatever they do.''

"What do you mean?"

"Confidence. The ability to focus. The determination to do something hard and follow through.''

"Yes, I see." At least she was beginning to. "And there really are enough hopeful bull riders around for you to do that full-time?" She flushed at her nosiness. "I'm sorry. That's none of my business.''

But Taggart didn't seem to mind. "I teach maybe fifteen schools at home a year. I do about the same number on the road. Noah does the same with bronc riding. It works out.''

"I'm impressed."

He shifted from one foot to the other, looking embarrassed. He tugged on his hat. "You oughta come out sometime.''

"Maybe I will." She smiled at him.

He swallowed quickly and took a step backward, then gave a quick, jerky nod. "Well, good. Now, I really gotta get goin'." He started for the door.

Felicity rose and followed him. "It was...kind of you to come."

"Had to, after what I said this morning. I was an ass."

"You were embarrassed."

He grimaced. "Ain't that the truth?" Then he grinned and shook his head. "Reckon I'll have to keep a firm hand on that girl."

Their gazes met, clung, electricity arcing once more. Felicity nodded. "Reckon you will."

"Didja see her?" Becky asked. They were in the truck driving home from Susannah's, where Taggart had dropped her while he'd gone to apologize—not that he'd told her so. "Have to see a man about a bull" was all he'd said.

"See who?" he asked his daughter now.

"You know who." Becky looked up at him unflinchingly, waiting for a reply.

"I saw her," Taggart admitted, his tone gruff.

Becky got a small smile on her face. Then she gave a little bounce. "I like her. Lots."

Trouble was, so did he.

Her daydreaming about Taggart Jones should have abated. Realistically, she told herself, there was no point. The man had out and out said he didn't want another wife. But then, she wasn't really in the market for a husband, was she?

Of course not. And besides, these were just dreams. They didn't require confirmation in reality. They were, by their very nature, fantasies—unrelated to real life.

Whatever they were, Felicity had a ton of them. Every sleeping moment. Almost every waking one.

It was because she'd been emotionally dead for so long, she reassured herself. It was healthy. Promising. It meant she was waking up to live again, thinking about the future, about moving on.

Mostly, though, she was thinking about Taggart Jones.

Perversely, she no longer saw him everywhere she looked. In fact, he might as well have dropped off the face of the earth.

She should have taken it for the message it undoubtedly was: that he wasn't interested in her. He was annoyed and embarrassed by his daughter's actions. He'd been embarrassed and ashamed of his own, and he'd done what needed to be done to put things right. End of story.

Still, Felicity looked for him. And when she didn't see him, she asked about him.

"Taggart Jones?" Cloris said.

"Oh, my, yes. Of course we know Taggart." Alice's face was wreathed with a smile, and she gave a little giggle. "Isn't he just the sweetest boy? Always was."

Cloris sniffed. "Bit of a devil, if you ask me."

Alice made a tsking sound. "You're just saying that because of the cow pie, and you know it."

"Cow pie?" Felicity was agog.

Cloris pressed disapproving lips into a thin line. "Don't ask," she said, folding her hands in her lap and giving Alice a quelling look.

But very little, Felicity had begun to realize, quelled Alice Benn. She just giggled and said, "Well, it was rather funny."

"You," Cloris pointed out, "didn't sit in it."

"Oh, dear." Felicity stifled her own giggles as she imagined the very proper Cloris as an unsuspecting victim of a well-placed cow pie.

Cloris gave them both a steely glare, but even as she did so, Felicity detected a glimmer of amusement in the older woman's eyes.

"As I recall," Cloris said tartly, "his daddy made it a little difficult for him to sit down a day or two after. I suppose he didn't turn out too badly," she allowed after a moment. "He seems to have done rather well with that little girl. She's in your class, you say?"

"Yes." Felicity told them about Becky coming to school in spurs.

Alice laughed heartily. Even Cloris cracked a smile.

"Chip off the old block, isn't she?" Alice said. "Why ever did she wear them, do you suppose?"

"She's her father's daughter," Cloris said dryly. "What other reason does she need?"

Which was a fortunate comment because it saved Felicity from having to give the real explanation. She had no intention of telling them it was a matchmaking ploy. Even though neither of them had commented today on her need for a man in her life, last Thursday evening, when she'd had dinner with Alice at her house, the entire conversation had focused on the vital statistics of both of Alice's unmarried grandsons.

"You could do worse, dear," Alice had told her.

"I'm not really interested," she'd said, so she certainly didn't want them getting ideas about her and Taggart now!

She wondered if his eye was still black and swollen, if his cheek was still raw. She remembered the briefest touch of his callused fingers on hers when he'd taken the ice pack. In her fantasies his touch lingered.

"...distracted this evening, dear," Alice said.

Jolted, Felicity tried to follow the conversation. Both

older women looked at her indulgently. She flushed. "I'm just about to start a new project with the children," she lied. "And I've been thinking about that."

"*More* projects?" Cloris's brows arched. She wasn't quite sure about this "project" nonsense. A little old-fashioned reading, writing and arithmetic never hurt anyone, she told Felicity. Felicity had assured her the children got that within the projects, but she could tell Cloris wasn't convinced.

"This one's about families," she said. "Occupations. I want the children to begin thinking about the way their parents earn a living—what skills it takes, how they began to learn those skills as children, how they might already be learning skills themselves."

Not bad since she was making it up as she went along. A curriculum committee with its nose in every teacher's classroom would have a fit about her improvisation. But the more she thought about it, the better it sounded. She'd often told Lori that her California students had no idea what their parents did all day while they were at school. And they lived, in many cases, so far away from the places their parents worked, that they had no sense of how their parents contributed to the life of the community. It would be easier to make the connection in Elmer. It would be good for the students—and good for the parents.

And, incidentally, it would allow Felicity to watch Taggart Jones teach his students how to ride a bull.

"You don't mind, do you?" Becky asked. She had on her innocent waif look, the one he knew was designed to make him give in. She stood looking up at him while he flipped pancakes for their breakfast.

He sighed. "No, I don't mind."

He did. But how could he possibly tell her that Ms. Albright wasn't welcome to observe a session of bull riding school tomorrow afternoon? Especially when he'd all but invited her himself.

"It's for school," Becky informed him. When he raised his eyebrows in doubt, she added, "We're doin' occupations. 'What keeps our valley alive,' Ms. Albright calls it. We're makin' a documentary."

Taggart's brows lifted even higher. He didn't even know Becky knew the word *documentary,* much less what it meant.

"We're writing the script, and she's doin' the videotaping. Showing what our parents do. Then we're gonna do voice-overs, an' when we get done, we'll have a real movie."

It didn't sound like school the way he remembered it. He was reluctantly impressed. But he still wasn't sure he wanted Felicity Albright hanging around his bull riding school. He'd had a hard enough time putting her out of his mind this past week. Now that he could imagine her in her house, at a table, leaning her cheek against her palm as she listened to him, smiled at him, it was all that much easier to imagine her other places—like in his bed. He'd made sure he didn't run into her again. But even the "out of sight" business wasn't as successful as he'd hoped.

He slid the turner under the pancakes on the griddle and scooped them onto Becky's plate. "Eat," he told her. "I'll run you up to the bus. We're late."

They wouldn't have been if he hadn't burned the first two batches. It was because she'd kept prattling at him, telling him all about what Ms. Albright had done this week—the stories she'd told them about growing up in Iowa, about living in Southern California, about traveling around Europe with her husband. Her husband, according to Becky, had been a concert cellist.

"That's a very accomplished musician," Becky informed him.

He sure as hell didn't think it was a calf roper.

When he dropped Becky off at the bus stop, he didn't go right home. He stopped the truck on a rise overlooking the pasture. He sat there, letting the engine idle as he stared at the bulls. His pride and joy, bread and butter.

He tried seeing them through the eyes of a woman who'd been married to a cellist, a woman who'd traveled around Europe on her holidays, a woman with golden wavy hair and a smile that made the ice around his heart begin to melt. He tried to imagine what she'd think of a man who rode them for a living—who even went so far as to teach others to ride them.

He didn't have that good an imagination. Until he remembered how Julie had come to see him.

Then he gunned the engine and headed home.

Even though she had a rough idea of what Taggart must do, Felicity didn't quite know what to expect the morning she showed up for bull riding school. Surely they didn't sit in rows and listen to lectures and raise their hands to ask questions, did they?

What she saw when she opened the door to the "classroom," which was a steel-sided building beside the barn, was a sea of cowboy hats. Black and white and ivory, wool felt and straw, they topped the heads of more cowboys than Felicity had ever seen in one place in her life. Where, she wondered, had they all come from? There must have been twenty at least.

"Twenty-three," Taggart told her later.

But right then she couldn't see him behind the hats. She could hear his voice, though, easy and confident over the sounds of boots on wooden flooring and the clink and rattle of the rowels of twenty-odd pairs of spurs. It was a sound Felicity recognized all too well.

She'd have looked around for Becky, but she knew where the little girl was—right beside her. She had been since Felicity arrived ten minutes before.

"What are they doing?" she asked as she watched them show Taggart their spurs.

"He's seeing if they're too sharp," Becky said. "You don't want to hurt the bull. You just want 'em to grip with. And he's gotta make sure they got the right kind of spurs, too."

"Right kind?" A spur wasn't simply a spur?

"They got big dull rowels on 'em, see?" Becky pointed to a pair that one young cowboy had in his hand. "Not little ones like bareback riders use. Bronc riders use little ones, too. An' the rowels spin free on theirs, too, 'cause they gotta mark their horses out."

There was obviously a whole specialized vocabulary here that Felicity didn't have a clue about.

"I see," she said, and was determined she was going to before the day was out.

She shouldn't really be spending a whole day on one parent. She'd spent an hour with Lonnie Gilliam's dad in the hardware store. She'd spent another with Sylvie Sorensen's mom, who cut hair. She'd spent at most four hours with Damon Kerrigan's parents, who were wilderness outfitters, watching them prepare for a week-long expedition, taping them packing gear, buying food, going over safety regulations, tying flies and discussing topographical maps.

Surely she'd get enough of Taggart Jones on tape in an hour or two to satisfy the needs of the classroom documentary. Of course she would. But she wouldn't satisfy herself.

Besides, it was Saturday. Her day off. She could do what

she liked—even if it happened to be watching one of her student's fathers teach cowboys how to ride a bull.

There were plenty of chairs, but no desks in the classroom. There was also a large-screen television and a barrel sort of contraption braced by two long poles and upholstered with foam padding and a carpet remnant. The poles rested on the ends of a pair of tables. Felicity looked at it warily. It was clearly a nonmechanical surrogate bull.

This was how he taught bull riding? She took a seat at the back of the room and waited until the cowboys had finished milling, the spurs had all been checked, and things were starting to settle down. When the men sat down, she glimpsed Taggart in the corner of the room.

He was examining a braided rope one of the cowboys had handed him. He said something, and in reply the man lifted his left hand. Taggart shook his head. The cowboy grimaced, then shrugged.

"What's the matter?" Felicity asked Becky, needing an interpreter already.

"He musta had a right-handed bull rope," Becky said matter-of-factly. "An' he rides left-handed."

Felicity stared at her, nonplussed. She'd heard of cowboys telling tall tales. But, "a right-handed bull rope"?

She heard a laugh behind her and turned to see Noah. "When you grip the rope, you want the braid working away from the way your hand will turn so it will flex, but not give, see?" He borrowed a rope from one of the cowboys standing nearby and demonstrated. "It's easier not to get hung up, and it gives you better traction and grip."

Felicity looked skeptical, but she took the rope when he handed it to her, then let him wrap it around her fingers the way she would hold it if she were on the back of a bull.

"Turn your hand," Noah said. She did. It slipped. "Now the other." He wrapped it the same way. "Turn," he commanded. She did, and saw at once what he meant. She looked at him with wide eyes.

"Lots of guys ride a bull for the first time at one of the schools. They learn, just like you have, from the ground up."

Felicity figured that most of them would be learning from the bull down before long. She knew she would be! It would have been a treat to simply sit back and watch, but she knew she had to justify her presence, so she got out her video camera.

"Are you teaching today, too?" she asked Noah. He dropped into the chair beside her and stretched his long legs out, crossing his boots at the ankles.

"No. We alternate weeks usually. I shoot the video for Taggart while he works with his guys, and he shoots for me while I work with the bronc riders. When we give schools on the road, though, we usually try to go together at least some of the time. Although lately, with Tess being so far along, Taggart's been going alone and so have I. That way one of us is always home."

"You're good friends." That was abundantly clear.

Noah nodded. "We went down the road together for a lot of years. You know whether you can depend on a guy when you spend that much time with him. Taggart's as good as they come."

There was a quiet certainty in his tone that told Felicity as much as his words about his opinion of the man who was now moving to the front of the room. She picked up the video camera, and, as he began to talk, she began to shoot.

More went into riding a bull than Felicity had ever thought. Taggart didn't simply talk about the care of the equipment—glove, rope, resin, bell, spurs, boots—he showed by his very meticulous preparation that this was serious business. Twenty-three hats nodded at every point he made, everything he said.

Felicity listened intently, which she was sure he was aware of, though he gave no sign. Everyone was aware of her. Taggart had even fielded a few teasing remarks about her presence.

"Gonna get the pretty lady on one of them critters, Taggart?" one brash young cowboy asked.

"Ain't one of those bulls gonna buck her off," laughed another, even more brash.

Taggart's gaze leveled on him with the precision of a battery of guns taking aim. The cowboy flushed and looked quickly away. "Sorry, ma'am," he said to Felicity. "No disrespect intended."

Felicity, who had heard plenty of far more disrespectful things on California beaches, gave him a small nod.

Taggart, point made, nodded, too, then turned his attention to the videos. "Watch these guys. These are guys who do things the way they ought to be done."

Then, with each ride, he stopped the tape and pointed out the correct position. "See here how he's movin' up and forward when the bull does? See the way he's bent into the thrust? And now—" he moved the video forward a few frames "—look at the way he's movin' back to meet the kick."

The hats nodded.

"The mechanics are the same for everybody," he went on. "That's the physics of riding. Gravity and balance and the weight of the body in motion. But style, well, that's different. That depends on each guy personally, his build, height, flexibility, aggressiveness." He grinned. "That's what makes me, me. It's what makes Tuff, Tuff—and Ty, Ty. But the mechanics don't change—and that's what we're gonna be working on here."

He got on the makeshift bull and showed them each move in slow motion. "Build muscle memory," he told them. "Practice. Over and over. Break it down into single tiny movements and work on each one."

Felicity watched, entranced, as he showed them how. She understood exactly what he was telling them about muscle memory. It was what Dirk had trained his fingers to do. He'd played passages over and over, broken pieces down into manageable bits and committed them to the memory of his fingers—exactly the same way Taggart did with bull riding.

"Right, then. Ready to get on and put some of this theory to work?" Taggart asked them at last.

There was a general eager murmur of assent, a scraping and shoving back of chairs, and a jostling toward the door as the hats stampeded toward the bucking chutes. Felicity stood up, too.

Taggart crossed the room and came toward her. "Seen enough?"

She smiled. "Not nearly. I'm fascinated."

He rolled his eyes. But he didn't object when Felicity followed him and Noah and Becky out to the arena. The cowboys had gathered by the chutes. Felicity hadn't taken the time to go up close when she arrived. Now, for the first time, she came within arm's length of a snorting, glaring bull.

It didn't matter that he was on the other side of a metal fence gate. It didn't matter that he was in the chute and she wasn't. She could sense his power, his irritation, his desire to make roadkill out of the cowboy who would settle onto his back.

She stopped where she was.

Noah laughed. "Want to ride?"

"Not on your life." She looked doubtfully at the young

men who were clustered around the chutes, wondering at their sanity.

"He's a nice one," Becky told her.

"Nice?"

"We rank them," Noah explained. "He's an easy ride."

He didn't look easy to Felicity. "If you say so."

Becky hopped up and down. "Are you gonna ride, Daddy?"

Felicity looked at Taggart, horrified. She hadn't even thought of that. Now she remembered his black eye and scraped cheek. He'd broken ribs before, Becky had told her. And dislocated his thumb. And got kicked in the knee. And had a groin pull. Some men had died. She knew that, too. She looked at him.

He was looking at her.

"Ah, go on. Ride," Noah said, grinning. "You know you want to."

Still Taggart hesitated.

"We'll pick up the pieces." Noah winked at Becky and Felicity. "Just kidding."

Becky giggled.

Felicity looked at Taggart, her eyes wide and worried.

Taggart looked back. Something passed between them—something Felicity couldn't quite define. Challenge? Determination? Daring? Pride?

Taggart nodded his head. "All right," he said. "I will."

Five

Taggart never rode bulls in his schools.

It distracted his students from what they were there for even though they thought it was cool. It distracted him. He was there to teach them what to do, not show off. He'd already proved what he needed to prove.

Hadn't he?

Apparently—if the gnawing in his gut and the nibbling at the edges of his concentration were anything to go by—he hadn't. Not quite.

Besides, distraction seemed to be the name of the game where Felicity Albright was concerned. Taggart hadn't been single-mindedly focused on the job at hand since he'd known she was coming to watch.

He'd be moving bulls or putting together his videos or going over his notes, and the next thing he knew he'd be thinking about Felicity's gentle smile or the way she ran her fingers through her hair. His fingers itched to do it, too.

Don't think about it, he told himself. *Don't think about her.*

It shouldn't have been hard. He was a whiz at mind control, at focus, at seeing only what needed to be seen and doing exactly what he needed to do. If he'd controlled his attention two years ago in Vegas the way he was controlling it around Felicity Albright, he'd have been a cow pie on the Thomas and Mack Arena floor instead of the world champion bull rider of the year.

He had focus, all right. And right now, every bit of it was on her! He'd been aware of her every movement since she opened the door to the classroom that morning. He'd done his damnedest to ignore her, barely letting his gaze light on her when she came in with Becky on her heels like a faithful herd dog.

She didn't matter to him, he assured himself; she didn't have spurs for him to check or a bull rope to look over. She wasn't the issue he needed to concentrate on. Still, he was aware of her; it felt almost as if the very air pressure in the room had altered the moment she'd come in.

He was a professional, for heaven's sake. He was being paid good money to teach twenty-three guys everything he could about bull riding in two short days. If he spent twelve or thirteen hours with them each day he would barely scratch the surface even if he—and they—focused every minute.

Why the hell had he said he'd ride a bull?

Because he was thinking not with his head, but with that gender-specific equipment tucked away in his Wranglers. Damn it.

"C'mon," he said, raising his voice now. "Let's get moving!"

He got a cup of coffee from the urn on the small card table outside the arena. Then, cup in hand, he climbed over the fence and headed toward the chutes where Mace Nichols and Jed McCall, Tuck's uncle, were running in the bulls.

Out of the corner of his eye he could see Felicity sitting at the top of the small set of bleachers he and Noah had built last summer. Becky sat with her. Noah, who was supposed to be on the platform next to the bleachers manning the video camera, was in fact sitting on Felicity's other side, chatting. Taggart watched as she leaned toward Noah and nodded at some comment he made. He said something else and they both laughed, then looked in his direction. Irritated, Taggart jerked his gaze away.

He climbed up on the chute gate and began talking to his students. Most had ridden bulls before; some were just there for a refresher course—a "tune-up," Noah called it. But there were three complete rookies, guys who hadn't so much as touched a bull.

"Gotta start somewhere," Taggart said, giving them a grin of encouragement. They all looked white-faced with apprehension.

He went over the fundamentals slowly and carefully. How to resin the rope and glove, how to put the rope on the bull, how to hook it under, then pull it up tight, how to make the wrap tight and secure around your hand. He fitted them with protective vests, which wouldn't save them from all injuries—in bull riding, he reminded them, it wasn't a matter of *if* you get hurt, it was *when*—but they could save a life. He knew cases where they had, and other sadder cases where they could have, if only the cowboy had been wearing one.

While he talked, the bulls clanked against the metal railings, kicking and blowing. One of the new guys muttered under his breath. Taggart stopped to sip his coffee. A bull reared up, hooking his horns at a cowboy on the top rail. He scrambled out of the way.

"Some of 'em come right straight up," Taggart cautioned. "Don't be gettin' in there till you're ready to ride."

"Yes, sir." This particular cowboy looked as if he was ready to hit the trail.

Taggart smiled at him. "You ready?"

It was one of the novices. He shook his head.

"These bulls are a little too snuffy for a first-timer, anyway." Taggart ranked them according to how tough they were to ride. Mace and Jed had filled the chutes with number-two bulls, animals to challenge the better riders. "How 'bout another volunteer. Jason?"

A lean, tough kid from a ranch near Dillon, Jason Dix had been to one of his schools last year. He'd also competed in the Montana State High School Finals Rodeo in both bronc and bull riding last summer. Jason scrambled over the railing to put his rope on the first bull. One of the other experienced cowboys dropped down into the arena to fish it out and pass it up to him. The new guys got out of the way.

One by one, they rode. Jason and three or four others lasted more than a few seconds. Some barely got out of the chute. Taggart cheered all of them on, regardless, watching intently, never once letting his gaze drift over to where Felicity sat.

"That it?" Mace asked when the last of the new guys had been dumped in the dust.

Taggart hesitated. "Run in Sunfish."

Mace raised his eyebrows. "Who's that good?"

"Me."

Felicity had watched all the other cowboys ride with a combination of nervousness and exhilaration. She felt no exhilaration now—only terror. She knew, of course, that Taggart Jones rode bulls. She knew he'd been champion of the world. He was, without question, a man who would be good at what he did.

But even though he was wearing a vest, even though he knew the risks he was taking, she still didn't want to look. He could get killed.

Of course, she didn't say that. Who would she say it to? Becky? His daughter sat next to her, bouncing up and down with excitement.

"He never rides bulls in his schools," she'd informed Felicity only moments before. "He must be doin' it for you!"

He didn't have to do it for her, Felicity wanted to tell him. Please God, that was the last thing she wanted him to do! She should have left. She had enough tape of Taggart Jones to more than suffice for the part he would have in the class's video. She could leave now.

If she could make her feet work. If her legs would hold her. They felt like jelly. Felicity stayed where she was. She tried to look away, but a heretofore untapped morbid fascination gripped her as Taggart braced himself above the bull's back, his booted feet on the rails on either side of the chute, and prepared to lower himself down.

Felicity swallowed, her mouth as parched as Death Valley. Her fingers clutched the video camera in a death grip.

"Aren'tcha gonna tape him?" Becky asked. "You oughta tape him."

Felicity's hands shook. She'd taped other cowboys—most of whom had barely got out of the chute, one or two who'd made it through a kick and a thrust and spin. "I've got quite a lot on tape," she told Becky.

"Not like my dad."

No, not Taggart. Felicity sucked in a breath. Maybe Becky was right. It might help. Maybe if she watched him through the viewfinder it would seem like nothing more frightening than a car chase on television. She picked up the camera and pressed her eye against the viewfinder. Her finger found the zoom, and she closed in on him. She saw him, feet still braced, pull up on the rope once, test it, then haul it tighter yet. Then he pulled his glove out of his belt and tugged it on. Then he rubbed his gloved hand up and down the rope before beginning to wrap his hand.

The rails were in the way, so Felicity couldn't see his hands. She didn't care. She watched his face, the tight look of concentration that came over him as he settled down and shoved himself forward into his hand, the flat press of his lips and the bunch of his jaw. The mike picked up the mutters of half a dozen chattering cowboys. Taggart didn't make a sound. He shifted, centered, stilled, then nodded his head.

The gate swung open and the bull exploded into the arena.

Felicity jerked the camera aside, unable to zoom back fast enough to catch more than the whirl of color and movement that was Taggart and the bull. She clutched it against her breasts, forgotten. Her heart pounded as she watched the intricate dance of man and animal—the arch and thrust, the kick and leap of the bull, complemented by the movements of the man who sat on his back.

Having just seen twenty-three young men flung around like sacks of potatoes, then stomped and kicked in the dirt, Felicity had asked herself why anyone would do such a thing.

She got a glimpse of the answer now. It wasn't a simple answer, either; she saw that, too. Riding a bull the way Taggart was riding this one was both a test of courage and

a celebration of life. It was a walk on the edge of disaster—
a balancing act of beauty and terror, of power and grace.
Well done, it was a compliment to both the man and the
animal. It showcased the animal's force, his cunning, his
strength, his determination. And it pitted them against a far
weaker, but equally graceful, wily and determined human
being. It was a ballet of stimulus and response, a waltz of
twist and spin.

It lasted an eternity. It lasted eight seconds. Maybe ten.
There was no whistle, no buzzer. Only at last, a ducking
movement on the part of the bull, a hard backward thrust
of his hind feet, a jerk of his head, a sideways twist, and
Taggart's compensating moves weren't quick enough or far
enough. He slipped, his free hand dipped. He tilted, loosed
his hand, and as the bull bunched and thrust forward again,
Taggart leapt away.

He landed flat on his back in the dust. As the clownishly
dressed bullfighter distracted the animal, Taggart scrambled
to his feet and sprinted for the fence, hauling himself up
and over. Then, without so much as a pause, he took his
cup of coffee back from the cowboy who'd been holding
it, took a long swig and, finally, glanced over at her.

Felicity was conscious suddenly of clutching the camera
so tightly against her that it was making grooves in her
arms and pressing her breasts flat. She eased her grip,
opened her mouth and sucked in a deep draught of dusty,
bovine-scented air.

"Good goin', Daddy!" Becky yelled. She looked up at
Felicity, a grin on her face. "Didja see him? Didja see that?
Wasn't he great?"

"Great," Felicity echoed hollowly. She felt the strength
beginning to return to her legs. "I—think I ought to go."

"Go?" Becky's face fell. "You can't! You gotta watch

the rest of it. You don't really wanta go, do you?" She looked beseechingly at Felicity.

No, Felicity thought, *she didn't.* "All right," she said. "I suppose I can stay awhile longer."

Becky beamed. "C'mon." She bounded down off the bleachers, leaving Felicity to stumble after her. Felicity's knees wobbled as she climbed down, just as if she were the one who'd spent all that adrenaline, not Taggart.

"What next?" she asked Becky.

"Critiques."

Critiques, Felicity found, meant that the entire brigade trooped back to the classroom, where Noah handed the camera over to Taggart and flashed Felicity a grin before he disappeared.

"Gotta go check on my missus," he said as he headed for the door. "You wanta come and play with Susannah, Beck?"

Becky edged closer to Felicity. "No. I wanta watch."

Noah's eyes met Felicity's over Becky's head. He grinned and gave her a wink. "I'll be back."

Felicity sat in the back of the classroom with Becky at her side and listened to Taggart painstakingly critique each bull ride, playing the video in slow motion, freeze framing it to point out the good moves, then to point out where things began to go wrong.

"You don't hurt yourself with one big mistake usually," he told them. "It's a buildup of little ones. They're cumulative. A little slip here where you don't quite get set right—" he pointed at the frozen cowboy on the television screen "—and that throws you off for the next jump. Next thing you know you're flat on your butt in the dust."

The hats nodded. Taggart moved on.

"Here now," he said to one cowboy. "You got good form here when you come out of the chute, but watch—"

the video moved forward a couple of seconds "—now you're sittin' back on your pockets. You're givin' him all the advantage 'cause you're off-balance and you can't grip him with your calves. This isn't bronc ridin', Danny. You don't have to mark 'im out."

There was a general chuckle at Taggart's reference to the bronc and bareback riders being required to have their spurs high on the horse's neck when they came out of the chute. The cowboy called Danny grinned, then nodded. "I'll get 'im next time."

Felicity watched Danny's ride end with him being flung hard against the arena fence. She winced at the sound of the clang and rattle when he hit. And he was going to do it again?

Apparently they all were.

Felicity was sure they'd take a break, instead they headed back to the arena for another ride. Only after they'd all taken another turn did Taggart call a break. Tess Tanner and Jenny Nichols had set up a table under the trees and were cooking hot dogs and ladling up bowls of chili. She was so hungry the enticing smells rendered her weak in the knees.

That was what did it, she assured herself, not a lean and still slightly dusty Taggart Jones, climbing over the fence, coffee cup in hand, to smile crookedly and say, "How about some lunch?"

After a quick meal, during which half a dozen guys came up to ask him specific questions, Taggart herded them back to the classroom and went over each cowboy's ride with the same thoroughness that he'd used on the first ones. Becky lost interest and went out to follow Jed and Mace around.

Felicity stayed in the classroom, watching the videos. She began to understand what Taggart was talking about when he pointed out somebody being too far back or being told he looked like he was waving to the crowd. She saw the little mistakes that led to bigger ones. She saw how the mechanics that Taggart was talking about came into play time after time after time.

It was past five when he finished the critiques and said, "Not bad. You're gettin' the hang of it." He gave them a thumbs up, and Felicity, glancing at the clock, started to pack up her things.

"Okay—" Taggart clapped his hands together "—back to the chutes. Get on, get set, get out. We got plenty more stuff to cover 'fore we go home tonight."

Felicity stared, dumbfounded. But the cowboys, some of them stiff, a few of them bloody, all of them far dirtier and dustier than they had been in the morning, hauled themselves to their feet and headed out the door.

Taggart followed. "You don't have to stay," he said to her.

"You're going to go through another entire round?"

"Yep. I'd rather do this in three days. But we've only got two, so we're makin' the most of it. Shut off the light when you leave."

Felicity got to her feet. "I'm not leaving."

They didn't finish until almost ten—after another full round of rides and critiques. Then Taggart showed a video of little kids riding sheep. The oldest couldn't have been more than five or six. One of them, the last one, was barely three or four.

"See that?" he said as the little girl clung and rode…and rode, then waved her hands in triumph when she landed on her bottom and bounced up again. "That's my daughter."

There was a giggle from the doorway. Felicity and those cowboys who still had enough cooperative muscles to turn around looked back to see Becky grinning.

"What's the word?" Taggart asked her.

Becky grinned even more broadly. "If I can do it, you can do it," she told the assembled cowboys. "See you tomorrow."

He wouldn't see Felicity tomorrow. She wouldn't be there. He was surprised she'd stayed so long today.

Taggart felt uncomfortably flattered. Julie's attention span where his bull riding was concerned was barely longer than the eight seconds it took for a qualified ride. He didn't try to kid himself that she would have been happier if he'd stayed home and taught bull riding instead of going down the road.

Marrying him had been a whim. Most girls felt the same way about even dating him. He didn't inspire commitment. Most women weren't as crazy as Julie, though, so they never even pretended otherwise. And frankly, he'd never cared. Which was why Felicity Albright made him uncomfortable.

She made him want to care.

He wished she'd left. He'd thought maybe seeing him ride the bull would send her on her way. Some women got passionate about men who did stupid, dangerous things for a living. He seriously doubted that Felicity was one of them.

But she hadn't left. In fact, her mind didn't even seem to be wandering. She didn't paint her nails or read a magazine the way Julie had. She taped him talking in the classroom, making him feel awkward and like he ought to be dropping pearls of wisdom instead of just talking about where to put your free hand so you had the best balance and why you shouldn't try to second-guess bulls. That was bad enough. But at other times, she'd simply sat watching him. And that was worse. He felt like he ought to wipe his face or check to see if his fly was open.

He'd tried not to look at her. She wasn't important.

Yeah, sure.

He knew that for the lie it was Sunday morning in the middle of reviewing mechanics and talking about role models, when the door opened and Felicity slipped in.

She gave him a quick, almost guilty, smile and slid into a seat at the back of the room. He kept right on talking, but his voice felt suddenly stronger, as if his earlier words had been mere rehearsal, as if it was Felicity he'd been waiting for.

Get your head on straight, he commanded himself. *Focus, damn it.*

He tried. "Take your time," he told his students. "Practice. Every day. Every movement. Even if it takes you ten minutes to get something right once, get it right. Give your muscles something to remember. I can teach you the movements. But I can't teach you to try. That you get on your own, from inside. You put the two together and you'll be just fine." He looked at them steadily. "Now, let's go ride some bulls."

They were out the door almost before he finished speaking. Felicity, however, moved more leisurely, as if she was waiting for him, and he fell into step beside her, trying to mask the eagerness he felt.

"You're back?" He made it a question.

She favored him with a smile. "I couldn't stay away."

He tripped over his boot. "What?" He shot her a quick sideways look.

Her smile widened. "I love watching you teach. You're so good at it. You inspire them. You make them understand. They're getting kicked and stomped and run over in the dust and they love every minute of it."

He laughed. "Yeah, well, nobody said bull riders were real bright."

"Some of them are very bright, and all of these guys are very dedicated. The dedication they're showing is something that will carry over no matter what they go on to do."

He nodded. "That's the point, really. If they learn how to apply themselves to bull riding, there's no reason they can't do it wherever they want."

"Dirk used to say the same thing to his students," she said softly. "My husband," she added, when Taggart's head jerked around.

"I remember." The comparison surprised him. He didn't think he could possibly have anything in common with her cello-playing husband.

"He loved teaching, too. He was good at it, just like you are. He reached different people, but he taught them the same basics. You're really very much alike."

They'd reached the arena by that time and she left him to climb up and perch at the top where she'd sat yesterday. He started to climb the fence. His foot slipped and he whacked his chin on the top rail.

"Been walkin' long?" Noah grinned from his spot on the platform.

Taggart swallowed blood from biting his tongue. He tugged his hat down and tried the fence again. "Come on," he shouted to the first cowboys in the chutes. "Let's go."

There were four steps up to the entrance to the classroom. By six o'clock Sunday evening very few cowboys were taking them two at a time. Two or three even had to use the handrail to pull themselves up. The grimaces Felicity saw on their faces betrayed feelings their words would belie—if anyone asked how they were, which no one did.

They were fine. They were cowboys.

Would that Dirk had seen the same dedication from his cellists, Felicity thought. One or two had actually shown a similar determination, but she doubted if even they would have turned as a group to shush the EMT talking loudly while he sewed up one guy's leg in the back of the classroom after the final bull ride Sunday night, just so they could hear what Taggart was saying.

Felicity knew she had never seen that kind of dedication among any of her students! She'd never, ever, heard one of them say, "Be quiet so I can hear Ms. Albright explain how to divide whole numbers." Not once had any of them said, "Shut up! I want to hear Ms. Albright tell us the difference between proper and common nouns."

Ah, well…maybe if she taught them how to ride bulls.

And they had hushed and paid attention when she got them interested in studying the history of the valley they lived in, when she told stories of the Indians who'd hunted there and the white settlers who had come to ranch and to farm. That meant something—just like Taggart's instructions meant something to these guys—and when she was lucky, she got in the division and the nouns through the history they read and the stories she told.

He ended with a pep talk that she taped so she could listen to it over and over. "Dedication is what it's all about," he told them. "You got to want it. If you want it, you can make it happen. And that's what you have to think about—making it happen, believing it can happen." His gaze moved slowly from one cowboy to another, connecting with each and every one of them. Then he nodded slowly. "Believe in yourself. If you don't, you not only won't finish, you won't even start."

Felicity sat in the back and watched the cowboys straighten up slowly. They were aching, all of them. Sore muscles, scrapes, abrasions abounded. They'd ridden five or six bulls in the past thirty-six hours. Every fiber of their bodies hurt. But they straightened anyway, they sucked in their breath, nodded their heads.

Taggart watched them; his eyes traveled over them once more and a slow smile spread across his face. "You all got what it takes," he told them. "Good luck."

She stayed till the bitter end. The last cowboy had climbed into his truck and rumbled down the road, and Felicity was still sitting in the classroom watching the video he'd left running. Taggart stood in the doorway, watching her, just enjoying the view. She was writing something in a notebook, her head bent, her wavy golden hair obscuring his view of her profile, but he didn't need to see it to know exactly what she looked like.

Suddenly she seemed to realize he was there because she turned guiltily, then jumped to her feet.

"I was just...digesting."

"Enough to give you indigestion, was it?"

She smiled, shaking her head. "No. It was wonderful. You were wonderful."

He dipped his head. "Thanks, but I don't do it alone. Noah, Mace, Jed, Jenny, Tess. There's a whole lot of people involved. I'm only as good as my cast and crew."

"And bulls."

He grinned. "Them, too."

He waited while she packed up her camera and put away her notebook, then started to slip on her jacket. Automatically he reached around to help her. Easing it up her shoulders, he touched her hair. It was as soft as he'd imagined it. He let it curl through his fingers, rubbed his thumb against a strand. Then, reluctantly, he stepped away and followed her out into the cold October night.

A canopy of stars and a sliver of moonlight showed in the ink black sky overhead. It was the sky he saw every night, and yet tonight it felt different, new.

Felicity's shoes made a scrunching sound on the gravel as they walked down the path toward her car, and Taggart was suddenly aware that they were alone. Becky had long since gone in to bed, and Noah had just left for home. In fact Taggart could see his taillights disappearing over the rise right then.

It was just him...and Felicity Albright.

A shiver slid up his spine that had nothing to do with the cold. All sorts of ideas began swirling in his head—ideas as inappropriate as they were unlikely. It was Becky's fault, he told himself. If she hadn't said...

But it wouldn't have mattered what Becky had said. He was perfectly capable of appreciating a beautiful woman without the help of his daughter. The question was, What was he supposed to do about it?

The answers that occurred to him made his tongue stick to the roof of his mouth. He couldn't seem to say a word.

They stopped beside her car.

She turned to him, so close he could smell the soft flowery scent of her shampoo. He sucked in his breath. She smiled up at him. "Thank you for letting me come."

He swallowed, shifted from one booted foot to the other. "My pleasure. I hope Becky didn't do too much arm-twisting."

"Becky had nothing to do with it."

"What did?" The question was out of his mouth before he had a chance to stop himself. *Your job is to react, not to think,* he told his bull riders. Yeah, sure, he thought desperately now. And look where that gets you.

"Because I wanted to come," Felicity said quietly. "I

was enthralled. I wanted to watch them learn." She hesitated. "And I wanted to watch you."

Before he could think *or* react to that, she went up on her toes just enough to brush a quick kiss across his lips. Then she opened the car door, got in, started the engine and drove away.

Taggart was still standing there five minutes later when her taillights vanished over the rise. His knuckles rubbed against his lips.

For the first time in memory he was scared.

Six

She should *never* have kissed him.

Heavens above, what *had* she been thinking?

Well, she hadn't. That was precisely the problem. She'd simply reacted—to the man, to the moment. And now she felt like a robber stealing off in the getaway car, half expecting the propriety police to be blaring their sirens and racing down the road after her to haul her in.

She had *kissed* the father of one of her students!

Where were her ethical standards? Where was her professional demeanor? Where were her brains, for goodness' sake? Men were the ones who were supposed to be governed by their hormones, not women.

How sexist is that, Felicity Jane? she asked herself.

Very. And it obviously wasn't true, either. God, what must Taggart be thinking?

She could feel her cheeks burning even now, twenty minutes later. She rolled down the window of the car and let the cold night air nip at them as she drove. But she'd need a blizzard to take the heat out of them after what she'd done.

"A cold shower for you, kiddo," she prescribed as she skidded around the turn that took her off the gravel road and onto the paved county highway.

But even the icy shower she forced herself to endure when she got home didn't totally relieve the burn of awareness or the memory of Taggart's lips against hers. It had been so fleeting she couldn't imagine why she could still feel their touch.

She told herself he wouldn't think anything of it. Taggart Jones had surely been kissed by plenty of women in his life. She doubted there was a man alive who'd been a world champion bull rider and never been kissed. One more wouldn't faze him a bit. He probably wouldn't even remember she'd done it.

And she might have made herself believe it if she hadn't glanced in the rearview mirror—and spied Taggart, standing stock still right where she had left him, staring after her, his fist pressed against his mouth.

"Fool," she called herself. "Idiot."

She went to bed and tossed and turned, hugged her pillow, then thumped it and tried to get comfortable. There was no comfort. She got up again and turned on the light. She would read. Reading would take her mind off things— off Taggart.

She reached for the book she'd left on the bedside table. And saw Dirk.

Of course every night she saw Dirk. She had his picture right where she would see him the last thing before she turned out the light and settled in. It was habit. It was ritual. She smiled at him, told him about her day, touched his smile, said good-night. Every night.

Except tonight.

Tonight she hadn't even remembered. She'd shut off the light and flung herself onto the bed, her mind whirling so fast she couldn't think, only feel.

"Oh, Dirk." She reached for his picture, then sank down on the bed, holding it, cradling it in her hands, looking down at him. "Dirk, what am I doing?"

He smiled at her the way he always had, supporting, encouraging. Dirk had always been the more even tempered of the two of them. He'd always rolled with the punches far better than she had. He'd been able to look at the bright side when Felicity had only seen the gloom.

She wondered what he'd see if he looked at Taggart Jones.

"I think you'd like him," she told Dirk's portrait. She ran her thumb lovingly over the glass that protected his smile. "I do."

But she shouldn't have kissed him.

She lay back on her bed and drew her pillow tight against her breasts. "Should I apologize to you?" she asked. It wasn't Dirk she was talking to.

She didn't have a chance.

"He's out of town," Becky told her when he didn't come to the screening of the tape about the parents' occupations. The students had all made invitations and taken them home. Most of the parents came. Only Sam Bacon's and Teresa Faraday's weren't there. And Becky Jones's father.

"He's got a school in Oklahoma this weekend. He left last night," Becky told her glumly.

Felicity had chosen a Friday to show the tape. Now she wished she'd picked a Monday or a Tuesday. Any day when Taggart would have been able to come. Two weeks had passed since her foolish kiss—long enough for her to be convinced that he'd forgotten—even if she couldn't possibly. She remembered it—*him*—more intensely than she wanted to. It was an odd feeling. Unrequited. Not at all the way she'd felt about Dirk. Except the interest. The interest was definitely there.

"He can stop by and see it after school someday," she told Becky. "You tell him."

But when Becky came back to school on Monday, she said, "He wants to know if you'll send it home with me so he can run it in our camcorder." She didn't look particularly happy about the request. Felicity wasn't, either, but she could think of no reason to refuse.

She hoped he might bring it back himself. He didn't. She thought he might ring her up and say he'd enjoyed it, that she'd done a good job with his bull riding part. She had, damn it.

But another week went by and she never heard a word.

She shouldn't have been surprised. He'd made it quite plain that he didn't want to get involved. Not that she was desperate to get involved, either, she tried to tell herself.

But the more time passed, the more she knew that wasn't entirely true. She had mourned Dirk for two years. Somewhere deep inside, she loved him still; always would. But she was alive, too. She wasn't even thirty years old. She wanted to love again.

And even though she told herself it was pointless, she wanted to love Taggart Jones.

At least she wanted to *try* to love him. Or even get to know him! Was that asking so much?

Apparently Taggart thought so. He clearly had no burning desire to get to know her. Her only consolation was that he would have to show up for the class production about the history of the valley. Wouldn't he? No, he wouldn't. Not if he could manufacture a commitment elsewhere.

Unless she got him to make a commitment to her.

He wasn't cooperating, Becky told Susannah. "Whenever I try to talk about her, he changes the subject. He won't even listen to what I do in school anymore. And he hasn't seen her in weeks! He won't go into town, either."

"Really?" Susannah said, a tiny smile playing at the corners of her mouth. "Good."

"Good?" Becky muttered. "I needed pencils and we could've got 'em at the grocery store, but he says we have to wait till we go to Bozeman. And he's grouchy all the time, too."

"Even better."

"Easy for you to say."

Susannah just laughed. "He wants to see her, but he's afraid to."

"You think so?" Becky said doubtfully.

"Of course." Susannah's tone was airy. "That's the way men are."

"You did *what?*" Taggart, who had been stacking bales of hay when Becky appeared bearing news, turned and glared at his daughter.

She stood her ground. "I told Ms. Albright you'd videotape our local history projects on Wednesday. She asked," Becky added when his glower deepened.

"She just came up to you and said, 'By the way, Becky Jones, I wonder if your dad would mind videotaping for us on Wednesday?'" Taggart wasn't usually sarcastic to his daughter. This time he couldn't help it.

She bobbed her head. "Yes. She did! You don't think I'd tell her you would, do you? Without askin' you?"

"Yes," Taggart replied dryly.

Becky flushed, then gave him a long-suffering look. "Well, I didn't. You're too crabby lately. I'd never do that. You'd yell."

"I would not."

"You just did."

He flushed and rubbed the back of his neck. "I'm just…surprised."

And dismayed. He didn't want to go to Becky's class. He didn't want to see her teacher. He saw Felicity Albright often enough—in his thoughts, in his fantasies, in his dreams. He relived the kiss Felicity had given him so often you'd have thought it was the last one he was ever going to have.

It was sure as hell the last thing he'd ever expected.

He chewed at his lip now, aware that just thinking about it made him remember the feel of Felicity's soft mouth brushing his. It had made his nights long and his body hungry. He'd wanted to see her again—and knew he didn't dare.

He'd stayed on the ranch since, not risking even one trip to town. He'd got Tess to pick up groceries for him or he'd driven down to Bozeman. He'd had Noah take in the horse trailer to get the broken brace welded. He'd only left to drive straight to the airport, and even then he'd been looking over his shoulder.

He knew, of course, that he couldn't avoid her forever. But he figured he'd have his libido under control by the time he had to go to Becky's parent-teacher conferences. He wasn't there yet.

"Why me?" he demanded.

Becky shrugged. "Most parents don't know how."

"Noah does."

"Yeah, but—" Becky scuffed her toe in the dirt, then studied the mark it made.

"But what?"

She slanted him a look. "You want me to hafta tell Susannah you're chicken?"

"What?"

"Afraid of Ms. Albright." She spelled it out for him.

Taggart's jaw worked. He scowled at her, furious. *"I'm not afraid of Ms. Albright!"*

"Well, what would you call it?" Becky's stubborn little chin jutted out, dared him to come up with a better description.

He cussed under his breath. He fumed and muttered. He took off his hat, slapped it against his thigh, then jammed it back down on his head. "Oh, hell, all right."

Felicity wanted everything to go perfectly. She wanted the kids to say their pieces with the same enthusiasm she saw every day in the classroom. She wanted the parents to be proud of their accomplishments. She wanted them to think she was doing well by their kids. She wanted Taggart Jones to smile at her.

He was coming; Becky had said he was. She'd tried to search the little girl's expression for some idea of how Taggart felt about being asked—as if she didn't know—but Becky gave nothing away.

Now Felicity wiped her palms on the sides of her navy pleated trousers and tried to get the kids to focus on their math assignment. But most of them were far too keyed up at the notion of the program they were putting on for their parents in half an hour.

Felicity was keyed up, too. Because Taggart was coming.

"I hafta go to the bathroom," Geri Tibbets interrupted for the fourth time that morning.

So do I, Felicity thought, but she could hardly keep running to the lavatory. "Go on," she said.

"Can I get a drink? My mouth is dry," said Randy Decker.

So is mine, Felicity thought, but trips to the drinking fountain were equally unacceptable. She wet her lips with her tongue. She was always slightly nervous before such events because she wanted everyone to do well, and it was, of course, out of her control. But she couldn't ever remember being quite this strung out before.

"He's here," Becky said suddenly in the hush that fell over the classroom, and Felicity looked up to see Taggart in the doorway. It was the first time she'd laid eyes on him since she'd kissed him. If she'd entertained any notion that she might have got over her awareness of him in the ensuing weeks, she was glad she hadn't counted on it. She was as aware as ever. More so. Her eyes went right to his lips. Heat burned her cheeks.

She managed a smile. "Ah, Mr. Jones. I'm so glad you could come and help us out."

"Ms. Albright," he drawled. "I wouldn't have missed it for the world."

Becky and Susannah exchanged significant looks, which caused Felicity's cheeks to heat even more. Her mouth felt like it was filled with cotton. "We appreciate your willingness to help out."

"My pleasure." He didn't look as if he'd been dragged here kicking and screaming. But he didn't look all that happy to see her, either. Probably he hadn't given her a thought. Probably he'd just been busy, not avoiding her.

Oh, Felicity, you ninny, she chastised herself. *You silly dreamer.* Her feet landed back on the ground.

Taggart slipped off his backpack. "Brought my own camera."

"I have one."

"Easier to work with the one I know." He was opening the pack even as he spoke, not really looking at her, just taking out the camera and battery with the same quick competence with which she'd seen him tighten a bull rope or climb a fence with a cup of coffee in his hand.

The children, who had quieted when he came in, began to murmur again when they saw him begin to get the camera ready, as if they suddenly realized why he was there. The nervous chatter rose to a crescendo. Felicity cleared her throat.

"Girls and boys," she said in her best soothing tones. "Having someone come into the classroom is no reason to forget what we're supposed to be doing. We just have a few more minutes to get things in order before our presentation, so let's use them wisely. Moaning doesn't help, Lizbeth, Randy." She singled out the two most vocal grumblers. "I think most of you know Becky's father, but if you don't, this is Mr. Jones. He's going to help us today by making a videotape of our local history presentation."

Talking steadied her, made her focus on the children, on her job—not on Taggart. As she talked, the experienced teacher in her took over.

Taggart settled into the back of the room, fiddled with the equipment, gazed into the viewfinder, followed her with it. That was a little unnerving, but Felicity soldiered on, doing her best to ignore him. But out of the corner of her eye she watched him.

She saw Tuck McCall sidle up to where Taggart was perched on the back counter—still flouting the rules, Felicity thought, smothering a smile.

"Hey, Taggart."

"Hey, Tuck. How's it goin'?"

"Okay." Tuck stood watching while Taggart panned the classroom, catching Felicity looking at them. Quickly she looked away. "Can I come watch your school sometime?"

"Sure. Got one in two weeks. You gonna learn to ride?"

"Naw. I wanta draw them bulls."

Taggart lowered the camera. "Draw 'em?"

Tuck nodded gravely.

Taggart gave Tuck a slow smile. "Well, sure, why not?"

Tuck grinned. "Thanks. Me an' Jed saw a coyote last night. Up near Flathead." He launched into a tale that amazed Felicity. It was the most voluntary conversation she'd heard from Tuck McCall. Having tried to converse with his uncle and guardian Jed McCall about participating in the "parents' occupations" video to no avail—"Can't," Jed had said—she had suspected Tuck's reticence was genetic.

Perhaps she'd been wrong.

She had no more time to consider the notion, though, for more parents were beginning to straggle in.

Most of them she'd met while doing the earlier video. Both Tess and Noah Tanner arrived, Noah carrying a little boy and Tess waddling alongside, so pregnant that Felicity found herself hoping she didn't deliver during the presentation. Randy Decker's mom was there. His father, a truck driver, couldn't make it. Neither, not surprisingly, could Jed McCall. Geri Tibbets had a full complement of parents and grandparents in attendance. Sam Bacon's father didn't come, but his mother was there. That pleased Felicity, because she knew Sam needed all the encouragement he could get. He was clever and quick with his hands, but his strengths didn't lie in the area of traditional learning. She'd heard from his teacher last year how little success Sam had had in school. He'd had quite a lot in the local history project. He'd started it rather apprehensively, but by the time they were finished, he was contributing as much as anyone. She was happy his mother would see how well he'd done.

She smiled in Mrs. Bacon's direction. The woman gave her a tight smile in return. A few more parents came in.

Felicity greeted them all, then quieted the kids, nodded at Taggart to start taping and began to introduce the program. "It's important for our children to know something about the world in which they live. The immediate world," she added. "And that means the valley they're growing up in. They need to see themselves as part of a larger context—a process, if you like, of which they are a small but significant part. It's been going on for a long, long time. Eons," she told them, scanning the crowd of proud and interested faces. "And so we'll begin with the geology of the region. Becky?"

Becky, face flushed, got up and walked over to the map she'd labored over so long. Together she and Sam propped it against the blackboard. Felicity held her breath, but the mountains stayed put, and so did the trees and the tiny ski resort stuck in the Bridgers.

"This is where we live," Becky said in a serious, grown-up tone. And then she began to explain how the valley had come to be. She talked about the formation of the valley, the shift in the earth's plates. On cue, Tuck and Sam got up and showed, with pieces of corrugated cardboard, exactly what had happened, how the earth's crust had slipped and buckled. While Becky talked about the inland sea that had covered much of the earth's surface, Tuck showed drawings he'd made of the plant life that had left fossils in the region. Then, when Becky had covered the geological history of the area, she started pointing out things as they were in the valley and surrounding mountains today.

Felicity glanced back at Taggart. He was watching his

daughter through the viewfinder. He was also grinning all over his face.

Felicity sent a prayer of thanksgiving heavenward, then turned her attention back to the class.

After Becky, Susannah gave her report on the people who came to the valley, and Tuck showed drawings he had made to illustrate them. Then Sam showed his display of the replicas of artifacts he'd made: the rifle, the bow and arrows, the powder horn, the buffalo horn spoon. He talked, at first haltingly, and then with more enthusiasm, about what he'd learned.

When he sat down, with obvious relief, he was smiling, too. He looked at his mother and grinned. He got another of the tight smiles she'd given Felicity earlier.

Poor little kid, Felicity thought. But she couldn't spare him much more consideration just then, because Randy and Teresa were getting up to talk.

Each group in turn shared the results of their explorations. One group wore costumes that depicted the clothing of the various people who'd lived in the valley at certain times. They explained why the clothing was appropriate to the lifestyle of the time. Another group talked about the animals and birds of the valley, using photos and a record of bird songs and a deer skin.

At the end, Felicity led them in singing a song they'd made up about the valley and the people and the animals who had lived there. Becky, she noted, sang louder than anyone.

Only when the parents had finished their enthusiastic clapping did Taggart stop taping. But when he put down the camera, he was still grinning. For an instant his eyes met hers.

Felicity felt the combined weight of the entire third and

fourth grades of Elmer Elementary School slide from her shoulders. She breathed again.

Afterward, parents and children crowded around, looking at each exhibit more closely, talking among themselves and to her. There was excitement in the air. Enthusiasm. Noah and Tess shook hands with her, telling her how much they liked the program, how much they thought Susannah was learning. So did Geri Tibbets's mother and Lizbeth's and Randy Decker's.

Sam's didn't. She was gone almost as soon as the program ended.

So was Taggart Jones.

Felicity hadn't been in any hurry to get through the throng of parents. She didn't imagine she would need to be. Of course, he'd stopped taping, but that didn't mean he was going to leave immediately, did it?

Apparently it did, for when she looked around after most of the parents had disappeared, Taggart was no longer there. The videotape lay on her desk. She picked it up. It was still warm.

Swallowing the lump of disappointment in her throat, she dredged her peppiest smile up from her toes. "You were wonderful," she told the class. "I couldn't be prouder of you. How about an extralong recess?"

The whoops and hollers were deafening.

"If," she said severely, "you can be quiet until I get you outdoors. There are other classes in the building hard at work, and you can't disturb them." They quieted down, and once they had she led them outside for recess. Jenny Nichols stayed outside to watch them while Felicity went back to the classroom.

She needed a little space, a little time to think. Time to recover. Not from the program. But from seeing Taggart come—and go—without a word to her.

She still held the tape in her hand. The product she had asked for. Not at all what she wanted. She lifted the tape to her cheek and pressed it there.

"Felicity?"

She spun around.

Taggart stood in the doorway.

"I was wondering...would you like to go out to dinner?"

Seven

He should be minding his own business! He should be getting into his truck and heading home.

He'd done what he'd come for—to see Becky do her presentation, to make the videotape as Felicity had requested. He didn't have any further reason to stick around.

Except to tell Felicity what he'd heard.

It wasn't his problem. It certainly wasn't his business. He'd told himself that all the way out to his truck. He'd even got in and started the engine.

But then, just as he'd started to leave, he looked over and saw Felicity letting the kids out to play. They'd spilled down the steps, hooting and hollering, and she stood there watching them, smiling at them. She'd looked young and innocent and happy.

Then, as he'd watched, her smile faded. She looked lonely, lost, almost, as she ran a hand through her windswept hair. She turned and said something to Jenny Nichols. Then, hugging her arms across her breasts, Felicity went up the steps and disappeared into the building once more.

And Taggart had gone after her.

Where the invitation to dinner came from, he wasn't sure.

He certainly hadn't had to ask her. He'd wanted to. There was that kiss, after all.

Not that he'd asked her because of the kiss! God, he'd been running from that kiss for weeks. But it wasn't working—the running. He was thinking about her all the time. Maybe it was better to see her—eat with her—get to know her. *Get over feeling the way he felt around her.* Yeah, that must've been why he'd done it. Self-preservation.

"It has nothing to do with—with what Becky wanted," he said to her now, not wanting her to get the wrong idea. "It's not a date."

"Oh." And damned if it didn't look like the light went right out of her eyes. Then Felicity straightened and met his gaze squarely. "Of course not." Her tone was brisk, but he felt as if he'd just kicked a pup.

"I didn't mean...I wasn't..."

"No, I understand," she said quickly. "You're telling me what the rules are because last time I...broke them."

He swallowed. "You mean the...kiss?" He damn near strangled on the word. "Don't be silly," he said, lying through his teeth. "It doesn't matter. I don't get kissed and tell, if that's what you're worried about. It didn't mean anything," he added, and dared a direct glance at her for confirmation.

She didn't nod. Hell.

He scuffed his toe on the linoleum floor. "You don't have to come," he said gruffly.

"I want to come." Her soft voice pierced the armor he was trying hard to keep up.

Their gazes collided again. Taggart quickly looked away. "Fine." If it wasn't a date, why the hell did it feel so much like one? "I'll pick you up at six."

She folded her hands on the desk and looked at him. "Thank you for making the tape. I really ought to be taking you to dinner."

"This one's on me."

Outside, children shrieked and yelled. Down the hall he could hear chairs scraping and some teacher droning on. That was what he remembered about school, the droning. He couldn't imagine Felicity droning. And what he could imagine he wasn't supposed to be thinking about at all.

He ran his tongue over his lips. "Right. See you then."

"Where are you going, Daddy?" Becky asked. She was perched on the toilet seat lid, watching him shave. It had become something of a ritual over the years, a time to talk, a time to laugh. Sometimes he put a shaving soap mustache on her face and made her giggle. She had one now and was watching him with bright, eager eyes as she swung her legs back and forth, kicking her boots against the porcelain bowl.

He kept his eyes firmly on his own mirror image as he scraped the razor up his cheek. "Out to dinner."

"Can I come?"

"Tess invited you over."

She sighed. "I always go to Tess's."

"And you're going again tonight."

"Where you going?"

Why, he wondered, did they have to play twenty questions? "Down to Livingston. No big deal."

"To the pizza place?" Becky got that desperate, hungry look on her face.

"Not the pizza place."

"How come?"

"Because I'm not in the mood for pizza."

"Are you in the mood for love?"

Taggart's razor damn near slit his throat. *"What?"*

Becky stifled a giggle, but her expression was guileless. "It's a song Tess sings sometimes."

"Oh." He breathed a little easier. Not much. Tess needed to censor her singing material. He grabbed a tissue and stanched the flow of blood from the cut on his neck.

"Who you going with?"

"A friend."

"A *girl*friend?"

"Just a friend." He'd envisioned having this conversation with her one day. But in his version, *he'd* been the one asking the questions.

"A girlfriend," she translated hopefully. Then, stricken by a sudden thought, she blurted, "Not Kitzy Miller?"

Taggart's eyes met hers in the mirror. "What's wrong with Kitzy Miller?"

"Her hair is stiff and her eyelids are purple."

Taggart smothered a grin and lied, "I never noticed."

Becky rolled her eyes. Then she gave a little hop and her eyes grew wide. "Is it Ms. Albright?"

Taggart cut himself again. "Damn!"

Becky, beaming, handed him another tissue. "I'm glad," she said and gave a deep sigh of contentment.

"I didn't say I was going with Ms. Albright!"

Apparently he didn't have to. Everything he did must be transparent to the eight-year-old female mind. He felt hopelessly outclassed and outmaneuvered.

"You're not to make anything out of this," he told her

sternly. "I just need to talk to her about a few things—related to school."

"Sure." She looked at him owlishly. "Wait till I tell Susannah!"

Taggart nailed her with his fierce father expression. "If you say one word to Susannah about this, I'll ground you till you're married."

Becky just giggled. Then she threw her arms around his waist and hugged him hard. "Don't worry, Daddy. I won't tell."

Felicity heard his truck come up the street a few moments past six. Running the brush through her hair one last time and praying for the good sense not to do anything rash—like kiss him again—she drew a deep breath and went to the door. She wasn't prepared to have him practically bolt inside the moment she opened it.

"What's wrong?" A wind had come up this afternoon, blowing down from the Bridgers, but Taggart didn't look like the wind had blown him in. He was glancing over his shoulder like he had a posse after him. He jerked off his hat and ran a hand through his hair, then leaned his back against the door. "You didn't happen to mention that you were going out to dinner tonight, did you?"

"Just to Maudie Gilliam."

"And with who?"

"She asked," Felicity said, feeling just a bit defensive. Taggart groaned.

"I didn't know it wasn't allowed. She brought me some leftover meat loaf when I got home from school. She was going to stay and eat with me, but I said I was going out."

"Figures. And now the whole damn town has ideas." He looked hunted.

"Ideas?"

"About us. You and me."

"I told her it wasn't a date. Well, that's what you said," she reminded him when he groaned again.

"Great. You didn't think that was maybe protesting a bit too much. Jeez. Those old biddies will put Becky to shame."

Felicity sniffed. "Don't be ridiculous. They aren't interested in what I do."

"You see Maudie out there weeding just now? There hasn't been a weed in her yard since World War II. And Mrs. Benn was sitting on her porch with old Horrible Cloribel starin' at me when I drove up the street. Even Sam Eberhardt was giving me the eye. And when have you ever known Sam to rake leaves?"

"Well, I haven't. But I haven't been here long. Who's Mrs. Benn? Oh, you mean Alice. And horrible Cloribel?" Felicity's brow creased. "Not *Cloris Stedman?*"

"It's what we called her in school." Taggart strode over to the sink and pulled back the curtain to peer out the window. It took only a quick look apparently. He let the curtain fall. "I had both of 'em. Cloribel for two years."

"Did you flunk?"

He grimaced. "No thanks to her. She taught fourth *and* fifth grade. I reckoned she didn't think it was enough to make my life miserable for one year."

Felicity grinned. "From what I heard, you made her life pretty miserable, too."

Taggart almost smiled. "She told you about the cow pie?"

"Mentioned it."

"Served her right." He tugged his hat down on his head as if to emphasize his words.

"Alice is very fond of you."

Taggart grunted. "She had a sense of humor. Ol' Cloribel didn't."

"You might be surprised," Felicity said dryly. She lifted the curtain. A convention of neighbors had gathered in the middle of the block, talking among themselves and looking at her house and Taggart's truck. Alice was beaming.

"I'm sorry…about telling Maudie, I mean. I didn't realize they'd all be outside watching. Are you sure it isn't just coincidence?"

Taggart gave her a dark look. "What do you think?"

Felicity thought he was probably right. "We don't have to go."

"We're going. Are you ready?" He looked her over briefly, and a hint of color rose in his cheeks as he took in her eager face. "I guess you are. Come on. Let's go."

The sharp wind had brought cooler weather, so Felicity grabbed her jacket along with her purse, then followed him down the steps and across the yard. She thought he'd head for the Busy Bee, but he headed for his truck.

"We're going to Livingston."

"Oh." Felicity supposed if they went to the Busy Bee, all the neighbors would come, too. It might be good for the local economy, but it wouldn't do much for Taggart's peace of mind. Or for her own. She nodded and got in.

Taggart got in, too, flicked on the ignition and backed around. Then he shot down the street, spraying gravel everywhere.

"Taggart!"

He grinned unrepentantly. "They want to stand in the street, they gotta take what they get."

But he slowed down before he got to where they stood. Still, he stared straight ahead while Felicity waved at them all as he drove past. By the time they got to the end of the street, she was laughing.

"It's insane," Taggart grumbled. "I'm glad I never courted a local girl. I don't see how Jenny and Mace Nichols survived."

"Jenny grew up here?"

Taggart nodded. "She's the same age as my sister, Erin. Jenny and Mace were high school sweethearts." He made a face that told Felicity he didn't think much of the idea. "Mace was always nuts about her. And she was about him, too."

"They seem very happy."

"Happy? I guess so," he said gruffly. "They been married over ten years. More power to 'em, I say."

Felicity heard the strain in his voice. She glanced over at his hard profile. Was he thinking about his own marriage? She didn't dare ask. Instead, after a moment, she turned and stared out the window, watching as cirrus clouds blew east above the Bridgers. The peaks were already capped with snow left earlier in the week.

"Winter's coming," she said softly.

At her words, Taggart seemed to breathe again, and she realized that since he'd made his comment about Jenny and Mace, he must have been holding his breath. His fingers flexed, then loosened, on the steering wheel. "Let's hope it doesn't come too soon. Those clouds aren't a good sign."

Felicity studied them for a moment. In California, except for occasional torrential rains that the drainage system wasn't equipped to handle, or bouts of drought that brought about water-use strictures, she hadn't had to pay much attention to weather. In Iowa it had been more of an issue, but it seemed slightly more predictable than Montana. The year she and her mother had come to stay with Uncle Fred there had been snow on the Fourth of July. And once Uncle Fred had sent her a picture of a picnic in February.

"I should have had one of the children do a section on weather. I could definitely use some instruction," she said.

"Just ask. We'll bore you for hours. Cloribel was big on weather. Actually," he reflected, resting his arm on the window ledge, "I learned quite a bit from her."

"She'd be pleased to hear it."

"She never will from me."

"You aren't fond of teachers."

He slanted a glance her way. "You're pretty damn good. That program today was impressive. I was surprised how much the kids knew."

Felicity was startled, then inordinately pleased at his praise. "They worked so hard. Every chance they could get. People often say kids aren't motivated, but they are if they're interested."

"They were obviously interested. And wired, too. Becky was practically going nuts last night—worrying about getting everything right."

"I hope she slept. I never thought about that."

Taggart grinned. "After thirty or forty drinks of water and bounces up to make sure she had everything written down, she went out like a light."

"I'd hate to have parents coming after me with shotguns!"

"They wouldn't do that." There was a second's pause. Then, "I hope," he muttered.

"What?"

"Nothing." He cleared his throat and flexed his hands on the steering wheel. "The only other time I remember Becky gettin' like that was before the Christmas program last year," he went on firmly. "And then she was just standing in a row singing. The year she actually had a part—as a snowman—I missed it."

"Because of the accident?"

"You know about that?"

"Becky told me a little. It…reminded me of Dirk's. One minute everything was fine, the next the world had changed."

His hand left the steering wheel, stealing over to enfold her fingers in a warm, gentle grip. Felicity felt the comfort offered, the kindred feeling. Neither spoke. Taggart continued to watch the road, and Felicity stared out at the clouds beginning to build over the hills to the west. But all her attention was concentrated on the fingers Taggart held in his hand. It felt so good, so right.

"Tell me about when Becky was little," she said after a moment. "What was she like?"

Taggart started to smile. "A trooper," he said. "Becky's always been a trooper. I took her down the road with me, did you know that?"

"To all the rodeos?" She couldn't hide the surprise in her voice. But she was smiling, too, at the thought of this tough, hard man caring enough about his daughter to want her with him all the time.

"Almost all of 'em. Now and then I'd leave her with my folks, but mostly it was her and me and Noah. We went all over." He grinned. "Even went to Disneyland once. Got some of those ears. Guys were callin' us The Three Mouseketeers."

Felicity laughed and settled back to listen. It was the right question to have asked. Talking about Becky was something Taggart did easily and with enthusiasm. Every little girl should have such a father, Felicity thought. The miles passed all too fast.

The wind was equally strong in Livingston. Not surprising. The town had a reputation for being one of the windiest in the West. Now she shivered and wished she'd brought a warmer jacket. But Taggart found a parking place only a few doors down from the old brick building that housed the restaurant, so it didn't really matter.

The dining room was paneled in dark wood, and overhead fans hung from what Felicity assumed was the original pressed-tin ceiling. A long, ornately carved bar with a brass rail and a beveled mirror sat along one wall. Along the other was a row of booths. In the middle and at the back diners sat at heavy oak tables.

"Right this way," the hostess said, and led them to a discreet corner table. The sort of place one put couples who wanted to be alone together. Felicity sneaked a glance in Taggart's direction. His face was impassive. He held her chair for her, then sat down opposite. Felicity picked up her menu, but over it she watched Taggart. All right, she thought, it isn't a date. But then, what is it?

Taggart waited until they ordered before he told her. "I heard something today I thought you should know." His fingers drummed briefly on the tabletop. Then he dropped his hand into his lap.

"Something you heard?" Felicity wondered what could possibly make him take her clear to Livingston to talk about it. "This afternoon? At the program, you mean?"

He nodded. "A couple of the parents were... complaining."

Her brows knitted. "About the program?"

"About you."

"*Me?*" She stared at him.

He shrugged as if he wished he hadn't brought it up. "They're a couple of whiners. Nothin' makes 'em happy, but—" his mouth twisted "—sometimes they can get out of hand."

Felicity looked at him warily. "What do you mean, out of hand?"

"They get a bee in their bonnet about somethin' they don't like, and they want to get rid of it, you know?"

"Get rid of me, you mean?"

His fingers started drumming again. "Not necessarily. I mean, I don't think they're aimin' to get rid of you, exactly. Not yet, but…" His voice trailed off. It was pretty clear to Felicity that if they weren't there yet, Taggart thought they were soon going to be.

"What did they say?" she demanded. "Exactly."

"Well, I can't say word for word, but—"

"You must have a pretty good idea. You asked me out to dinner on the basis of it."

He shoved back in his chair and raised his hands as if to defend himself. "Hey, I just thought you had a right to know."

"So tell me!"

But he studied the tabletop for a long moment before he finally raised his eyes to meet hers. "They said you were playin' games. They said you weren't doing basics. They said the kids weren't learning the right things."

"Not learning the right things? They're learning history! They're learning to read and write and understand how their world works!"

"But not the way we used to."

Her gaze narrowed on him. "You mean if it's boring, it's better?"

"No! Hell, no. I didn't say that!"

"But that's what you're implying."

"*They're* implying. Not me. I think they're full of you know what." He paused. "But—" He lifted his shoulders in a gesture of helplessness.

"But what?"

"But Orrin Bacon is on the school board and—"

"Sam Bacon's dad? He wasn't even there!"

"Elizabeth was. His wife," Taggart explained. "Orrin's probably on the road. Couldn't make it, but—"

"Then exactly how is he qualified to judge my teaching?"

"I never said he was, just said he's doing it."

Felicity felt her mouth open, then close, then open again. A hundred responses crowded her brain. None of this made any sense! "Are you telling me my job is in jeopardy?" she asked him finally.

The waitress came bringing their steaks. Felicity had lost her appetite. She waited, but Taggart didn't reply until the waitress had left. "I don't know," he said, his gaze level, meeting hers. "Orrin's a pretty tough guy to buck. He's got plenty of opinions and he doesn't hesitate to make them known."

"But Sam's doing well!"

Taggart's mouth twisted. "By your standards, maybe."

"By anyone's standards, I should think. He wasn't doing any better with traditional methods! Damn it." Felicity attacked her steak with the desire to cut Orrin Bacon in two. "I can't believe this!" Felicity pointed her knife at Taggart. "Do you know how hard Sam has had it in school? No, of course you don't. And I shouldn't be telling you." Another breach of professional ethics. She went back to sawing her steak.

"I know," Taggart said quietly. He spread his hands when she looked up at him warily. "How could I not? This is a small town, remember? Everybody knows I took you to dinner. I know Sam has trouble in school."

"Well, then, do you know that I'm finally reaching him?"

He shook his head. "No, I didn't know that."

"Because the darling Bacons aren't talking about it, obviously."

"But if you are, why aren't they pleased?"

"I don't know! Because they're perverse. Because they're stubborn. Because they're determined stick-in-the-muds who only want success if they get it their way!" Felicity brought her silverware down with a clatter.

"Hey," Taggart said gently, "careful with the dishes. And don't kill the messenger."

Felicity sighed. "Sorry." She managed a smile, but it was a pained smile. How could the Bacons be the ones complaining? Of all the parents, they ought to be most pleased. "Does anyone else have problems?"

His gaze flickered away for a moment. "One or two. Nothing much."

"What?" She wanted all the cards on the table now.

He shrugged awkwardly. "A couple said the program was...frivolous."

"Frivolous." She repeated the word with deadly calm.

"The costumes and the...I don't know what you'd call it...multimedia approach, I guess. Hands-on, maybe that's the word. They thought it was...unnecessary. They thought the thing on parents' occupations was, too." He gave her a helpless look. "I don't mean I'm agreeing with 'em. I just thought you ought to know. They don't like frills."

She stared at him, stupefied. *"Frills?"*

"They want their kids memorizing things, doing papers, turning 'em in, getting a grade. Going on to the next subject."

"And it doesn't matter if their kids learn anything?"

"Kids *do* learn that way. I did," he added defensively.

"And loved every minute of it, obviously. I remember all those happy stories you told me...about you and Cloribel the Horrible."

He looked uncomfortable. "I did learn from her. I told you that."

"And you so clearly enjoyed every minute."

"I didn't need to."

"Wouldn't you rather have enjoyed it?"

"Of course, but—"

"Then what's wrong with making what they have to learn anyway interesting and enjoyable? Why make them hate it? I believe in what I'm doing. And I think I've made a difference for the better. For all the kids, Sam included. Especially Sam. What are the Bacons going to do?"

"What do you mean, going to do?"

"I mean, you're obviously concerned about this. You braved having dinner with me to tell me." He scowled at her wording, but she didn't care. "So what's going to happen? Is he going to shoot me? Run me out of town?"

"Of course not. He can't do either. But he might have the power to see that your contract isn't renewed."

She wanted to say, "So what?" She couldn't, because there was nothing "so what" about it. She cared—far more than she thought she would—about keeping this job. Elmer, in the few months she'd been here, had come to seem more like a home to her than California ever had. It was the place where she'd discovered how to live again after Dirk's death. And to have it threatened right out of the blue— especially when she knew she was doing a good job! Her stomach knotted. So did her fist around the knife.

Taggart watched her worriedly. "I didn't tell you in order to upset you," he apologized.

"I know. I'm sorry. It's just not fair. I thought people were pleased."

"People ought to be," he said firmly. "I am. Becky's a bright enough kid, and she's done well in school—when she's worked," he added wryly. "But she's never liked it the way she has this year. And it's not just because...

because she thinks you'd be…uh, because you'd be…'' He stumbled, then stopped. "Aw, hell."

"Because I'd be mother material?"

He shot her a glance from beneath lowered brows. "She knows better now. I straightened her out," he said firmly.

"I gathered you had."

She tried to look upbeat, but she must not have done a very good job, because Taggart said, "It isn't that I don't…like you. I just don't want to get married."

"You don't have to explain," she said, feeling her cheeks warm.

"Yes, I do. I don't want you to think I'm…findin' fault. Like the Bacons, you know?" He looked at her earnestly.

Felicity smiled faintly. "So I won't feel like I'm a complete all-around failure, you mean?"

"Cripes, no, I never meant *that*."

He was flustered now, she could tell, and she knew she had to take pity on him.

"I understand, Taggart. I was teasing."

"Oh," he mumbled. "Yeah." He bent his head over his dinner, sawing doggedly at his steak.

Felicity cut hers, too, and took another bite, but all the while she chewed, she couldn't take her eyes off Taggart Jones.

She knew it was a lost cause. She'd finally awakened to the possibility of having a new man in her life, and the new man she had awakened to had apparently vowed to become Rip Van Winkle where women were concerned.

Still, she watched him. She couldn't seem to get enough of watching him. She'd played her video of bull riding school over and over again, watching not just the bull rider, Taggart Jones, who was impressive, but the teacher, Taggart Jones, who impressed her even more.

"*You* teach the way I do," she said suddenly.

His head jerked up. "What? What are you talking about?"

"You don't teach your students out of books. You show them things—videos, even—and then you put them on the bulls."

"Because I'm teaching bull riding," he said patiently.

"But it has to do with life. You said so. And I'm teaching my students what they need to know in life, too. I'm teaching them subjects—like reading and history and arithmetic. But more important, I'm teaching them *how* to learn, *how* to find out things later on when they're out of school. They won't bother if they think it's all drudgery. But if I show them that there are alternative ways to learn things—" she was poking her knife at him again, she realized. Deliberately she set it down. But then she looked back up, fire in her eyes. "If I show them ways to learn that they can understand, they'll use those ways in the future. They'll have the tools they need to learn whatever they need to!"

She looked at him, impatient, waiting for a response. He wasn't agreeing enthusiastically, that was for sure.

But finally he nodded his head. "Yeah. You're right."

That was all he said. He wasn't fired up the way she was, but there was a quiet certainty to his tone that was just as good. Better, perhaps, because she suspected she could count on it. Felicity smiled at him, justified.

Slowly, almost reluctantly, Taggart returned her smile.

Eight

There. He'd done it. He'd taken her to dinner. He'd told her about the grumblings of Sam Bacon's mother, he'd hinted at the furor he knew damn well Orrin Bacon could stir up. He'd done his duty. He'd even managed a bit of small talk on the side.

After they'd disposed of the Bacons, he'd asked her about her time in California. And then, later, about Europe. "If you don't mind talking about it," he'd said hastily, realizing she might not want to relive memories of trips with her husband with him.

But she didn't seem to mind. In fact, she talked about him quite willingly and at length. Dirk Albright sounded like a damned paragon. But Taggart couldn't dislike a guy who'd built a car out of spare parts as a teenager, who'd spent an entire summer canoeing in northern Canada with his brother, who'd swept Felicity off her feet in junior high by writing her messages in Morse code.

"Love letters," Felicity had giggled.

For a cellist, he actually sounded almost like a regular guy. Maybe even a fun one. Taggart sort of wished he could have met him. Sort of.

It was obvious how much Felicity had loved her husband. It showed in her face, in her eyes, in her smile, even the wistful one. Part of him wished he'd never brought Europe up—or Dirk. Another part told him it was salutary that he had.

He knew Felicity had had a wonderful marriage, just like he knew he'd had a lousy one. They had nothing in common, see?

He saw. It didn't help.

Because he also saw a woman he wanted. When she told him about traveling to Europe—to Paris and Vienna and Salzburg the summer after she and Dirk had graduated from college, camping and staying in hostels—she made it seem not very different from the way he'd lived, going down the road from town to town. Only a little more exotic. He thought he'd like to see some of those places some day. He said so.

"You'd love it," she told him eagerly, eyes sparkling. They'd finished their dinner and were drinking coffee. It was getting late, and he should be taking her home, but he made no move other than to sit and sip. He even dared look at her now and then for longer than a split second.

"Yeah, I probably would," he said now, reflectively. He wished he could see it all. With her.

But that would never happen, he told himself firmly. Tonight was a one-off. A sort of test. Like riding a bull. He was pitting himself against an unknown force, setting himself up against the temptation of succumbing to Felicity Albright's charms.

He'd needed to. To prove that he could do it—and survive.

And he had. Even though he wanted her more now than he had this afternoon.

Taggart finished his coffee quickly and paid the bill. Then he ushered her ahead of him toward the door and held it open so she could precede him.

Out into the swirling snow.

Snow?

Small sharp flakes stung his eyes as the wind whipped them in his face. An icy north wind bit into him. Oh, yes, snow. Unseasonable, unpredictable, entirely possible Montana snow.

Felicity shivered and turned to him, incredulous. "I don't believe this."

"I do," Taggart said darkly, cursing his lack of forethought. The National Weather Service hadn't said anything about a coming storm, but he didn't need them to have seen the high, fast-moving cirrus clouds that had come over the mountains from the west earlier in the evening. He didn't need them to tell him about the sharp wind. He'd just been too strung out over Felicity to notice. And now he was going to pay.

"Is it…safe to drive back to Elmer in this?" Felicity asked.

Safer than spending the night in a motel room, Taggart thought. "It'll be fine," he promised. "There's only a couple of inches on the ground so far. We can make it." Taking her arm, he steered her toward the truck. He could touch her through her jacket with immunity, he was certain. Well, maybe not so certain. She was so close she radiated warmth as she stumbled along beside him, her head ducked down.

"It won't be bad, will it? It's only October," she said hopefully.

"The worst storm I ever saw was in October," he replied before he thought.

She winced. "Then you think this is going to be a big one."

"Naw. I doubt it," he said, not wanting to make things worse than they already were. "It'll probably let up soon."

"Says the guy who isn't wearing sandals."

He glanced down. Her bare toes were peeking out at him. "Damn!" He bent, reached around and swung her up into his arms.

"Taggart!"

"You'd rather get your feet frozen? Relax. It's only a few feet."

It really wasn't far distancewise. She wasn't even very heavy. Heck, he slung Becky around all the time—not to mention saddles and hay bales and other ranch gear. The trouble was, Felicity didn't feel like any ranch gear he'd ever lugged. She didn't feel very much like his daughter, either.

He cursed under his breath, all too aware of the firm warmth of her body in his arms. Her mouth was so close that her breath warmed his cheek. He turned his head. Even so, he could smell a flowery scent. Lilacs, he thought.

In the snow? Was he losing his mind? Yep. And his composure.

He almost dumped her next to the truck, then opened the door. She slipped in with a grateful sigh. Taggart caught her feet and brushed the snow off her bare toes. They were cold and trembled at his touch. She gave a tiny giggle that sent a shaft of need zinging through him.

He backed away hastily. "There's a blanket in the back of the cab. Can you reach it?"

She was tucking it around her when he climbed in the other side. "You come prepared." She turned a smile on him. Snowflakes glistened on her lashes and shone in her hair like tiny diamonds. He wanted to touch one.

No, you don't, he told himself firmly, sucking in his breath and flicking the key in the ignition. That way lay disaster. He was almost home free.

But he wasn't home yet.

"Got to be prepared in Montana," he said brusquely. "You never know what to expect."

Something else Julie had hated, he reminded himself. "I don't mind cold weather," she'd said, "but some days it's 50 degrees below zero. The next it's 50 above. It rains one minute, then snows the next. And the wind. God, I hate the wind."

Felicity hugged herself. "This is wonderful."

Taggart's head jerked around. He shot her a wary glance. "What's wonderful?"

She was still smiling. "This weather. It's amazing. I love it."

He gave her a sour look. "And when there's a job opening in the Antarctic, you'll take it?"

Felicity laughed. "No, but I'm serious about this. California—where I lived in California, at least—the weather was always the same. You almost never even noticed it."

"Must have been nice," Taggart said dryly.

"It was boring."

"Well, whatever this is—boring it ain't." He put the truck in gear and eased out into the street.

He got them out of town and up onto the Interstate without too much trouble. Felicity settled in quietly beside him, apparently trusting him to be as good as his word. Taggart gripped the steering wheel and stared straight ahead.

Soon they'd be taking the highway north, provided he could see it. The snow had already covered the roadway and was still coming down so thick and fast that the signs were all but invisible. The headlights of a semi appeared dimly in the rearview mirror.

Taggart sucked in his breath. It had been in weather like this, the first snow of a heavy storm, that he and Noah had had their accident. A semi had come up behind them fast then, too. His jaw clenched. He felt a cold sweat break out against the back of his neck.

They'd been damned lucky that time. He didn't expect to be that lucky twice.

"Shall I put on the radio and see if I can get the weather station?"

He took a jerky breath. "Yeah, why not?"

Felicity did. Snow, they said in cheerful tones.

"No kidding," Taggart said through his teeth, one eye on the semi. It was getting closer.

High winds, they said. Low visibility. Not a good night to travel. Stay home if you could. Use chains if you were attempting one of the passes.

"We aren't attempting any passes, are we?" Felicity asked.

"No. We shouldn't have any trouble. This is pretty much a straight shot until we get to the hills leading up toward Elmer."

The wind shook the truck, making it harder to steer. The sign for the exit to the highway north loomed suddenly in the swirling whiteness. In his rearview mirror the semi seemed almost on his tail. His whole body tensed.

Then the off ramp was in front of him, he guided the truck onto it, and scant seconds later the semi roared past.

His body sagged suddenly as if all the air had gone out of him.

"Are you all right?" Felicity leaned toward him, her expression worried. "Taggart?"

He straightened and ran his tongue over his lips. "Yeah,

of course. I'm…fine." He loosened his grip on the wheel and found that his hands were shaking.

Felicity wasn't convinced. "Is it the storm? Should we be driving in it? Is it too bad?"

"No," he said, relieved his voice didn't sound as shaky as it felt. "I was just…it was…sort of a déjà vu. The accident…"

"Do you want to stop? Go back?" She reached over and laid a hand on his arm. Her touch felt warm, intimate. The last thing he needed right now. He shifted his arm, and she pulled her hand away.

"No. We'll be fine. It was just…seeing those headlights in the mirror." He drew in a deep, careful breath and let it out slowly. "Really. No problem." He turned and gave her the sort of tough-guy-in-charge smile he gave crowds after he rode a bull.

It must not have worked, because Felicity said, "If you want to stop, we'll stop."

"No."

The miles passed slowly. Taggart kept his eyes on what he hoped was the road, though signs of it were fast disappearing beneath the accumulating snowfall. Felicity sat silently, staring out the windshield. Every once in a while he could feel her turn her gaze on him. He kept his straight ahead. He couldn't go faster because visibility was poor. Even if it hadn't been, they wouldn't have made good time on the snow-covered road.

At least they didn't meet many vehicles heading the other way. A couple of trucks, a few cars. It wasn't a night to be out, that was for sure. The road curved and Taggart took his foot off the gas, slowing without braking.

"Look!" Felicity pointed across the road into the field that sloped off from where the curve in the road began.

"There's a car over there!" Through the falling snow, Taggart could just barely make it out.

A car coming the other way had missed the turn. As they got closer, Taggart could see two men behind the vehicle, pushing it, while a third tried to steer it back up out of the ditch onto the road. They weren't getting very far. The car had out-of-state plates. Taggart wasn't surprised.

He let the truck slide slowly to a stop on the shoulder. "Wait here." He shut off the engine, climbed out and crossed the road. "Need a hand?"

It turned out they needed more than a hand. Hunters, out for a week's vacation, they hadn't come prepared for the eventualities of fall in Montana.

"It's October," one of them complained. "My God, you're not supposed to have snow in October!"

"Hardly ever seen anything like it," another said, "and I'm from Illinois. My brothers—" he jerked his head at the other two "—live in Florida."

Figures, Taggart thought. He didn't say anything, just went back for his chains.

"Are they all right?" Felicity asked.

"They will be." Provided he could get them out. He thought with the chains he could. Then, if they drove slow enough and didn't try anything fancy—like using the brakes—they could make it to town. He carried the chains back to the car.

"How do you stand it?" one of the Florida brothers asked, shivering in his boots, while Taggart bent to put on the chains.

"You get used to it." Taggart worked in silence after that, giving directions only when he had to. It was easier to do it himself. Finally, when he had the chains on, he straightened up. The snow stung his cheeks. The wind tugged at his hat and he pulled it back down tight.

"That should do it. You steer," he commanded one. "We'll push." He leaned into the back of the car. In a matter of minutes they had the car back on the road.

They fell all over him saying thank you. Taggart shrugged it off. "Where're you headed?"

"Back to Bozeman when the snow lets up. *If* the snow lets up," one of the Florida brothers added with a sunbelter's scepticism.

"I'd wait till it quits snowing to go over the pass." He might have risked it himself. He knew better than to encourage them to. "You can take the chains."

"But—" The one from Illinois started to argue.

"My folks live in Bozeman. You can drop the chains off with them." Taggart reached inside his jacket and pulled out a pen and one of his business cards. He scrawled his folks' address and phone number on it and handed it over.

"Can't tell you how grateful we are," babbled the Illinois brother.

"Much obliged," agreed both Floridians.

"No problem." To be honest, Taggart had been grateful for the distraction. It was easier putting on chains in a blizzard than sitting next to Felicity in the warm cab of his truck. He stopped now and took a deep breath, gearing himself up for the last few miles. Finally, when the hunters were out of sight, he let out a frosty breath and opened the door to the truck.

It was toasty warm and welcoming, and Felicity was smiling at him. So much for distractions. He sucked in his breath.

"Local hero." She grinned at him.

Taggart knocked the snow off his hat and kicked his boots against the running board. "You got to help each other out when the weather's like this."

"They're lucky you came along."

"I'm a damn fool to be coming along," Taggart said grimly. "I should've paid closer attention this afternoon. I'd never have brought you down for dinner if I'd known."

"I don't mind," she said. "Truly."

I do, Taggart thought.

They moved even more slowly now. Miles he could cover in minutes on clear pavement took more than an hour in weather like this. He was glad Becky was asleep at Noah's. If she weren't, she'd be worrying. The road had completely disappeared by the time they turned onto the county road that led from the highway up into the foothills. Five miles more and they'd reach Elmer. It would feel like fifty before they got there.

Taggart was driving by instinct and feel now. There was no visibility. That was the down side. The up side, he told himself, was that his preoccupation with the storm kept him from thinking so much about Felicity. At least he knew the route like the back of his hand, and he figured that would make the difference.

But just as they came around the bend by the creek, a buck leapt out of the trees in front of him. Instinctively he hit the brakes—and saved the buck. It loped off into the snowstorm and disappeared.

They weren't so lucky.

The truck slewed sideways, then slid down the incline toward the creek.

"Are you all right?" Taggart's voice was in her ear.

Felicity, who'd banged her head against the door's window as the truck came to a halt, struggled to sit up as straight as she could. "Yes." She was shaken, nothing more. But the truck, she could tell, now sat a steep angle quite a ways down an embankment from the road.

"You're sure?" Taggart was peering at her worriedly,

bracing himself against the steering wheel so he wouldn't come sliding into her.

She nodded. "Truly. I'm fine. Are you?" He looked almost white in the light reflected off the snow.

"Okay." He tried to turn and open his door. It wasn't easy due to the angle at which the truck had come to rest.

"I can get mine open," Felicity offered.

"No. You stay here. No sense in you getting any colder." He managed to shove his door open and climb out. Felicity watched him walk around the truck, surveying the damage. She rolled down her window. "Is it bad?"

His mouth twisted. "Depends on what you call bad. The truck's all right."

"But?" she prompted.

He sighed. "But I don't see us getting out of here without the chains I gave our friend from Illinois." He stood, hands on hips, staring at the truck, a grim look on his face. The wind whipped snow into his face, and he turned, hunching his shoulders against its force.

"We can't push it back up?" Felicity knew even as she said the words what the answer would be.

"Nope." He scowled and kicked at the snow with one booted foot. The wind howled. Felicity wanted to roll up the window, but she didn't want him to feel she was deserting him.

"Come back in," she suggested.

"I'll call Noah on the cellular," he said, then cursed under his breath.

"What's wrong?"

"I forgot. I don't have the cellular with me. Damn it." He slapped his hand against the side of the truck, clearly furious with himself.

Not having a cellular herself, nor ever having had occasion to use one, Felicity wasn't as upset as he was. "Don't worry about it," she said.

"I'll walk."

"In this?" The snow had obliterated every landmark. Felicity had no idea where they were. She supposed Taggart did, but the wind was still howling down out of the northwest, making the already-falling temperatures seem even colder. "How far is it?"

"Three, four miles."

"You can't walk that far in this."

"I can," he said stubbornly. And he was a man who'd ridden bulls for a living. Probably he could.

"Maybe," she agreed. "But don't. Please, don't," Felicity repeated. "It's too dangerous."

"I know the road."

"You can't *see* the road."

"I could follow it without seeing it."

"But you might get lost. You might get hurt. You might freeze. I wouldn't have any idea if you were all right or not. And you have to think about Becky."

His eyes met hers. "What about Becky?"

"You said you stopped going down the road because of her. You didn't want to be away from her."

"So?"

"It wasn't just being away, was it? It was because you were afraid something might happen? That maybe you wouldn't be so lucky next time? That maybe Becky wouldn't have a dad if you kept on going?"

She could see by the look in his eyes that she'd hit him right where he lived. He sucked in his breath sharply. His teeth came together. His knuckles went white against the red frame of the truck.

"Don't go," she said.

* * *

She didn't know what she was asking of him. To climb back in the cab and sit there—for *hours*—beside her. Keeping his hands to himself. Sharing body heat but not the joy of physical intimacy. He'd die of frustration.

He'd rather die in a blizzard! A younger, more cocksure man would have scoffed at her and gone on his way. A single man with no responsibilities would have gone and to hell with the risk.

But Taggart had been minding his own business, hurrying home for Christmas, and been nailed by a semi. Taggart had seen laughing, joking colleagues—more than one—get on a bull and a minute later or a day later be stone-cold dead. Taggart had a daughter who had only one parent.

He wasn't taking unnecessary risks—not with his life, anyway.

Grimly, he hauled open the door and climbed in. Felicity smiled.

"Roll up your window, for God's sake," he snapped, shoving himself as hard as he could against the driver's-side door, but even gravity was against him, dragging him toward her.

She shot him a quick, nervous look and hastily rolled it up. "Sorry."

"No, I'm sorry." Taggart hunched his shoulders. "I shouldn't have jumped on you. I'm just mad. I should have brought the damn phone. I always bring the damn phone!" But he hadn't this time because he hadn't wanted anyone disturbing his evening with Felicity. He didn't want Becky calling him and checking up on him. He didn't want his folks ringing to see what he was doing for the weekend since they knew he had it free.

Wouldn't they like to know what he was doing? He swallowed a groan.

Felicity huddled in the far corner of the cab. At least she

didn't have gravity to fight with. Her legs were tucked up under her and she was sitting with her arms wrapped tightly around her torso, which Taggart could see shivering inside her thin jacket.

Since the engine was off, the heater was off, and because Felicity had opened the window to talk to him, the temperature in the cab had dropped dramatically. He shivered, too.

Felicity opened the blanket she had around her. "I'll share," she offered.

He scrunched back even further against the door. "No," he said. "I'm fine."

And so they sat. Or rather, Felicity huddled and Taggart braced himself, his arm against the steering wheel, his feet pressed into the floor. The wind flung snow against the truck, whipping it furiously, and on the windshield now some of it was beginning to stick, cutting visibility even more. Soon they were in their own little cocoon, just the two of them. Not something Taggart particularly wanted to dwell on.

He shifted, slipped and caught himself. He shoved himself back hard against the door.

Felicity looked at him. He looked at her, then away again.

"How long are you going to keep that up?" she asked him quietly after a moment.

"Keep what up?"

"Fighting the laws of nature." He glanced her way and saw a faint smile light her face. "Gravity, for instance."

He flushed. "You want me to fall on top of you?"

Her cheek dimpled as her smile widened. "It would be warmer."

He stared. Was she suggesting...?

He gave her a hard, searching look. She met it evenly,

steadily. God, she was lovely. Even half frozen, teeth chattering, she made his heart kick over.

Which was exactly the problem, wasn't it?

He didn't want his heart kicking over. He wanted to be immune. He didn't want to want what he knew he couldn't have.

If Felicity were just some buckle bunny, like the girls who hung around after the rodeo looking for a cowboy to spend the night with, well, he supposed he could handle that. A roll in a truck cab wasn't exactly his idea of great sex, but he could manage it. But that wasn't what Felicity would want.

Was it?

Oh, God.

He ran his tongue over his lips. "If I stop fighting...gravity—" he gave the word a harsh twist "—chances are that won't be the only law of nature I give in to."

There, he couldn't have spelled it out any more clearly than that. He looked at her, brows arched, waiting for some reply.

Felicity took her time. Finally, she nodded. "There is that possibility," she said slowly. Her voice was soft, soothing, almost. But was it a yes or a no?

At least with Julie he'd known that much! When she'd wanted him she was all over him like a case of measles. When she hadn't, she was yelling and chucking things at him, then packing her bags and slamming out the door.

With Julie there had been no *possibilities*.

"We're going to be here all night, aren't we?" Felicity asked him now in that same soft voice.

"Probably." There was a thread of strain in his. He wondered if she could hear it.

She shifted, untucked her hands from between her arms and sides, and held them out to him. "Then come here, Taggart. We'll keep each other warm."

Nine

The moment she said the words, she was afraid she had shocked him. She'd shocked herself.

Or maybe, to be honest, she hadn't. Not really. Maybe she just thought she ought to be shocked. It wasn't exactly typical Felicity Albright behavior, practically inviting a man into her arms.

But shocked or not, Felicity wasn't sorry she'd done it.

She had loved Dirk and she had mourned him. She had been two years without ever once feeling desire or even interest in another man. But now she did. She supposed it was perverse that it happened to be Taggart Jones—a man who clearly wanted nothing to do with her—on an emotional level, anyway.

But she knew from loving Dirk that the heart chose to love where the mind often did not. Common sense and so-called "good judgment" had little to do with it. If it had, she'd never have loved Dirk.

Certainly her parents had despaired of her interest in the weedy, gifted boy Dirk had been. Though he could do most anything he set his mind to, his consuming interest in music to the exclusion of almost everything else made him questionable boyfriend material, much less a good prospective husband.

But somehow she and Dirk had been the making of each other. He had taught her to look beyond the confines of their upbringing, to reach for the stars, to strive and work and hope. And she had taught him how to love, how to share a passion, how to engage others' interest even if they weren't as gifted as he. She had given him an anchor in the stormy sea of professional music. She had shown him that he had value as a person beyond how he played the night before. They were good for each other. Perhaps Dirk had suspected it. Felicity certainly had.

She felt the same way about Taggart now.

He was different from Dirk. He wasn't weedy, for one thing. He was hard and lean and muscled. He was dark where Dirk had been blond. He was a talker. Dirk had always let his music speak for him. But deep down he reminded her of Dirk.

He was intense, committed, determined, good at what he did and a gifted teacher, as well. She'd seen the way he could communicate with his students. She'd seen the hero worship in their eyes. She'd seen him earn it—not just with his bull riding, but with the concern and the vision he shared with each of the students who came to one of his schools. She knew he wasn't only preparing them to ride bulls. He was giving them the keys to a successful life. He was a man who inspired trust.

Felicity trusted him.

Probably, she acknowledged, more than he trusted himself. And she needed him—and not just to keep her warm tonight.

She needed him to warm her soul. And she dared to think he needed her, as well. Whatever had happened to Taggart because of his marriage, she had heard enough now to know that it hadn't been good. But that didn't mean marriage couldn't be good. She prayed he would give her a chance to teach him that.

He didn't move quickly. There was no eagerness. She could see the wariness, the strain in his face. The skin over his cheekbones was taut, the green eyes probing, looking for—what?

Love? She didn't think so. Not yet. Not more than the physical kind, at least. She knew well enough that he wanted that, but in the cab of a truck...?

"Trade me places," Taggart's voice had a slightly ragged edge to it.

Felicity slid forward, and he moved along the seat behind her until he was pressed against the passenger side door. Then he wrapped his arms around her, drawing her against him so that she was practically sitting in his lap. She snuggled back, pressing into his warmth. It felt so good. Not only the warmth, but the holding. It had been so long since she'd been in a man's arms.

But it wasn't just that, either. It was the man. Taggart. Taggart holding her. Taggart's breath against the back of her neck. Taggart's hands tucking themselves around, cupping her breasts. She could feel his fingers through the jacket she wore. His thighs were warm and hard beneath her bottom. She shifted, settling in more completely, her body molding itself to his. Shifting again, wriggling. Accommodating.

Taggart's arms tightened. She heard a swift intake of breath.

"What's the matter?"

"Nothing." There was a faintly strangled sound to his tone.

She twisted clear around on his lap to look at him. "You can't tell me you're all right," she said. "When we slid into the ditch...were you hurt?"

A muscle ticked in his jaw. His mouth was only bare inches from hers. So close she could feel the warmth of his breath when he spoke. "No."

"Then—"

He shifted then, too, shrugging against the seat as if to ease some discomfort, and suddenly she understood—and felt her cheeks burn. "Oh."

Taggart grimaced. "Yes. Oh," he echoed, his tone now ruefully self-mocking. "Sorry. I told you—those laws of nature."

"Do you want me to move off?"

But when she tried, he held her fast. "Do you want to stay warm or not?"

"Yes, but—"

He shifted her sideways slightly, so that her feet rested on the other end of the bench seat and her bottom pressed firmly into him. Then his arms tightened again. "Tell me some more about your trip to Europe."

She knew he was making small talk, but she obliged him. She talked—haltingly at first, but then with more ease, describing the hostel she and Dirk had stayed in near Lake Como. She told him about their visit to Venice.

"Did you ride in a gondola?" He sounded almost jealous.

She shook her head. "Too expensive. We took the vaporetto. Water bus," she explained. "We saw the same things—and just as romantically, really. The romance is within, I think."

"Yeah." His breath caressed her ear, making her shiver, and all her small talk went for naught. She was intensely aware of him again.

"Your turn," she said. "Tell me about...about..."

"Cheyenne? Reno? The Cow Palace? All those romantic spots?"

"Why not? I haven't been any of those places."

So he told her. About the places, about the people—and the bulls—he'd seen. It sounded fun and grueling and exciting and tiring. "Do you miss it?" she asked, turning her head to get a glimpse of his face. "The traveling?"

He looked thoughtful. "Some. Now and then. It gets in your blood, I guess. But I knew I couldn't do it forever. And with Becky I just had to quit a little sooner than I might have otherwise. I don't regret it, if that's what you mean."

He didn't sound like a man who had many regrets—besides his marriage. She wanted to ask about it and wondered if she dared. The wind rocked the truck again, and Felicity felt Taggart's arms tighten around her.

"Did your...wife travel with you?" she ventured finally.

"Once." His voice was flat. "She didn't like it."

"I'm sorry," Felicity apologized for asking. "It's none of my business."

"It's history," Taggart said. "Not very pretty history, so I don't talk about it much. We were two people in the throes of lust. We should have seen it for what it was. I do now. I won't make the same mistake again."

There was nothing to say after that. The snow buried them deeper. Felicity tried to imagine a woman who could only feel lust for Taggart Jones. It was so much less than she felt herself. She settled back more deeply into the warmth of his embrace. He shifted beneath her.

"Sorry," she muttered again.

"A little torture never hurt a guy."

She smiled. "I didn't know you were a masochist."

"I ride bulls, don't I?" He was smiling, too, but Felicity had seen the danger.

"Don't you…get scared sometimes?"

"If you concentrate on the fear, you might as well not do it. The fear is more likely to kill you than the bull. I'm not saying a bull can't kill. Some of the best riders have died in the arena. If it's your time, it's your time, I guess. But you can make it your time, if you panic. When you ride a bull, you have to trust your instincts and all that practice you did. It's just—you're there, the bull's there. Are you going to ride or not? If you are, you can't think. You just have to react."

Felicity listened and understood. She felt like that herself. She was here. Taggart was here. She'd spent two years thinking. Hibernating.

Now she just had to react.

She kissed him. She couldn't help it. She was sitting on his lap, snuggled in his arms, her lips bare inches—ten centimeters, she would have told her kids when they did the metric system—from his. The temptation was too great.

She had kissed him before and regretted it. She didn't regret it now.

Perhaps because he didn't seem stunned, only eager, as if the fires, long banked, had suddenly burst into full flame and he was as desperate for her touch as she was for his.

The first kiss had lasted less than a second. This one went on and on.

Lips only at first, then tongues, tasting, teasing. Teeth nibbling, nipping. Mouths that hungered, that sipped and savored. Until just the touch of their mouths wasn't enough anymore. Felicity rubbed her cheek against his, loving the soft-rough feel of the day's growth of whiskers. Men's skin was so different from women's. She lifted a hand and smoothed it along his jaw, traced the curve of his ear. Her fingers crept up to ease his hat off and stroke his hair.

Dirk's hair had been long enough to thread her fingers through. Taggart's was short, clipped close to the back of his head, trimmed above his ears. Long enough on top, though, to tousle. Felicity tousled it. She played in it, running her fingers over his scalp, brushing, combing, loving the soft silky feel of it.

She felt his hands burrow in her hair, too. Not only his hands. His face. He pressed his lips to her ear, nuzzled her with his nose. And all the while, his hands wove themselves in and out, smoothing and teasing, raking and caressing. The simple feel of his fingers was so wonderful that she felt a shiver run right down her spine.

"Not warm enough yet?" Taggart said. The ragged edge was still there, but she could hear a smile in his tone.

"Warm," she murmured against his cheek. "Very warm. How about you?"

"Hot. And you know it." She felt his jaw tighten and felt a moment's qualm. She didn't want to tease. She wanted to love. She kissed him again, tenderly at first, trying to set him at ease, to let him know how she felt. The response she got moved from tenderness to urgency in seconds. His tongue slipped between her lips, plunging into the heat of her mouth, delving, seeking. And Felicity met it with an urgency of her own. This, too, was a part of love, and if this was what he wanted...

She twisted further to come around to hold him. He moaned, his hips lifting to press against her bottom. She felt the heat of his arousal right through her wool trousers and his jeans. She eased away from him slightly and reached between them, her fingers finding the buckle of his belt.

He stilled suddenly, sucked in his breath. "Felicity." His eyes met hers, dark and desperate.

"I can help."

He gave a shaky half laugh. "I know you can. But—" he shook his head and let out a ragged sigh "—you shouldn't."

"No?" She should have been embarrassed at her wanton behavior. He was the father of one of her pupils, for goodness' sake. He could easily get her fired.

He wouldn't. She didn't know how she knew that, but she did. Taggart would never do anything to hurt her. She looked into his eyes.

"No, Taggart?" Her breath was a whisper against his mouth.

He shut his eyes and dragged in a ragged breath. "Isn't the shoe supposed to be on the other foot?" he asked, a tremor in his voice. He sounded halfway between pain and amusement.

"You mean, aren't you supposed to be seducing me?"

He opened his eyes to meet hers again. "Something like that."

She smiled. "Go ahead."

He groaned. Then his hands, which had been still against her back, very slowly began to move, coming forward, sliding along her rib cage, thumbs inward as they came up beneath her jacket and, through her sweater, cupped her breasts, then stroked across them, the pads of his thumbs caressing her nipples, making her shiver. She bit her lip. She saw him smile.

She bent her head, laying her forehead against his temple, letting her hair brush across his chin, his lips, his cheek. With her tongue she touched the curve of his ear. A shudder ran through him. She could feel it.

He shifted, and suddenly she had more access to his belt.

She didn't have a lot of experience with world championship belt buckles, but she couldn't think of a better time to get some. She fumbled with it, then fumbled some more, muttering and feeling a heat climb into her cheeks that had as much to do with embarrassment at her ineptitude as it did with arousal.

For the moment, anyway. But then the hook gave, the belt opened beneath her fingers, and her hand lay against the soft denim covering him.

His hands stilled against her breasts, each of her nipples caught between a thumb and forefinger. Slowly, carefully, not fumbling this time, Felicity undid the button and lowered his zipper, then slid her hand inside and touched him.

He sucked in a sharp breath. His thumbs and fingers drew on her nipples, sending a shaft of desire straight to the core of her. Felicity's fingers tightened around him, moving slowly against the rigid column of his flesh. He trembled. He pressed his head back hard against the window. His whole body stiffened.

"Felissssity!" Her name came out on a hiss of urgency. Taggart's hips surged, and then he shuddered and sank back down in the seat, his eyes closed, his jaw locked. Felicity pressed her lips against his cheek.

He quivered and let out a groan.

"Taggart?" She felt suddenly awkward, embarrassed. She didn't want to pull her hand away, not yet, but if she left it...

"God. I'm...sorry. I've never—" He pulled one of his hands away from her and pressed it against his eyes. "Hell."

"It's...all right." She hated the tremble in her voice. She wanted to sound calm, blasé, a woman of the world.

He made a ragged sound deep in his throat. "Yeah, sure." He opened his eyes and looked at her ruefully. "I should never have let you touch me. It's...it's been a long time. Too long, obviously.'' His gaze slid away. "It's no excuse, but—''

"It's a good excuse," she said softly. "The best."

He looked at her. "But—''

"I wouldn't like to think I'm just the next in a long line of women.''

He straightened. His brows drew down. "You're not."

She leaned forward and touched his cheek with her lips. "I'm glad."

"Yeah, well, I could've just told you. I didn't have to...to demonstrate." He gave her a rueful look.

Felicity smiled. "Did you really think we were going to be able to make love in here?'' Her gaze moved doubtfully around the narrow confines of the truck cab, then came back to him.

Taggart sighed. "I wasn't doing much thinking, if you want to know the truth." He leaned his forehead against hers, then reached down to adjust his jeans.

Felicity eased her hand away, but she didn't want to stop touching him entirely, so she slid her hand beneath his shirt to curve her fingers over his rib cage. Taggart zipped his jeans again and settled back against the door. Then, after a moment's hesitation, he slipped his arms around Felicity and drew her close.

She sighed, resting her head on his shoulder, settling in. Loving the closeness. Loving him.

She wasn't sure precisely when she realized this was love she was feeling. Maybe it was when she watched him teach the cowboys how to ride bulls. Maybe it was when she saw him ride one of his own. Maybe it was when he took her to dinner to tell her about Sam's parents even when he obviously didn't want to get involved. Maybe it was when he let him touch him, feel close to him, *give to him*. It didn't matter. It was enough that she knew. It was enough that she did. She sighed and turned her head into the curve of his neck and shoulder.

"Are you...all right?" Taggart asked worriedly. "If you...I mean, I'd like...if you want..." His voice trailed off, a note of chagrin lingering.

She touched her lips to the warm, slightly stubbly skin on his jaw. "It's fine. I'm fine. Better than fine. I haven't been so right in a very long time."

Go figure, Taggart thought.

A guy makes a fool of himself, behaves with all the savoir faire of a high school kid on his first hot date, and a girl acts like he's done good, like she's pleased with him!

Not all girls, he reminded himself. This girl.

Woman, he corrected himself. Holding her, sharing the warmth of her body as it pressed into his, reflecting on her words—her generosity—he knew she was no child. She was certainly nothing like Julie had been. He could just imagine what Julie would have said about what had just happened! It wouldn't have been complimentary, that was for sure.

"Taggart?"

"Hmm?" He lifted his hand and stroked her hair. She sighed and snuggled closer. The truck shuddered, buffeted by another gust of wind.

"Tell me about going down the road."

"Nothin' to tell. A whole lot of miles in trucks and cars. A little bit of being jerked around on the back of this bull and that bull."

"There's more to it than that."

Not according to Julie. But he shifted, settling Felicity more comfortably on his lap, and said, "Well, yeah, I guess."

She lifted her head, brushing her hair away from her face, turning so that her nose brushed against his cheek. "So tell me. Why do you love it? You must or you wouldn't do it."

He shrugged, feeling self-conscious. "It's hard to explain."

She drew a line along his jaw. "You explained lots of things to those cowboys in your school."

He shook his head. "Not the same thing." But she was looking at him expectantly, and he knew she wasn't going to let him off the hook.

"It's a challenge," he said slowly. "It's taking all you are—all your courage and your know-how and your desire—and putting them all on the line. It's focusing all your attention on one moment in time, demanding everything you've got. It's a risk. It's skill. It's—let's face it—partly luck. It's life. Life is skill and courage and know-how and desire—and luck—all rolled into one." He stared into the fogged-over, snow-covered windshield, trying to explain the sensation, the emotion, the essence of what those years of miles and seconds of rides had meant to him. "It's a distillation of what it means to do your best, to live your life to the fullest. Sometimes you win. Sometimes you lose. But you always try."

He turned his head back to look at her. The expression on her face, the way she was looking at him, made the heat crawl into his face. He gave an awkward shrug. "See, I told you I couldn't explain it. I'm no philosopher."

"I wouldn't trade you for Aristotle." Her finger traced once more along his jawline, then she threaded her fingers in his hair, leaned over, and, with exquisite gentleness, she kissed him. She kissed him first on the forehead, then on each of his eyelids, then the tip of his nose, and, finally—he thought he'd die waiting for her—on his mouth.

It was a tender kiss, a gentle kiss, and yet it spoke of hunger and yearning and a million things that Taggart knew were out there somewhere out of reach—both his and hers.

If it weren't for Julie, he thought, the ache inside him growing, billowing, filling every inch of his being... If he hadn't failed so miserably once, he thought as need seared him... Not sexual need; no, it was more than that. It was emotional need, personal need. The desire to share, to be part of something larger, to connect. To love.

He shut his eyes tightly. Inside his head he heard the word drumming over and over: If...if...if...

Finally, slowly, he drew back and forced himself to look at her squarely. "Tell me," he said, "more about Dirk."

It was the hardest thing he'd ever done.

They awoke to the sound of banging on the window of the truck.

Felicity groaned and stretched, stiff from the cold and from being cramped on Taggart's lap. She cracked open one eye. Someone was brushing snow off the glass. Embarrassed to have whoever it might be catch her in Taggart's arms, she hauled herself up, then struggled to push open the driver's side door. Through the cleared glass the early morning sunlight streamed in.

"S'at?" Taggart muttered. He was moving stiffly, too. Barely awake. Felicity didn't know how long they'd finally slept.

She fumbled with the door handle and felt it jerk out of her hand as the door opened and Noah peered in at them.

"Thank God. You all right?"

Felicity straightened and managed a smile, trying to run a hand through her mussed hair. She doubted it was helping. "We're fine," she said. Taggart didn't say anything. She could feel him moving behind her. "Taggart braked to miss a deer,'' she went on quickly, ''and we went off the road.''

''So I see. No chains?'' Noah looked over her at his buddy, an expression of disapproval on his face.

''He lent them to some hunters who went off the road below Clyde Park.'' Felicity gave Noah a bright smile and eased herself toward him, blocking his view of Taggart who was, she hoped—judging from the movements behind her—buckling his belt.

''You're out early,'' Taggart said gruffly now. He edged around and opened the passenger side door—belt buckled, Felicity was glad to see—and stepped down into a foot of snow.

''Becky was worried.''

Taggart ducked his head. ''You told her I was all right, didn't you?''

''I told her I figured you'd decided to sit out the storm somewhere. I didn't know you were all right.'' Noah gave him an accusing look. ''I wasn't saying something I had to go back on. You could have rung up.''

''Forgot to take the cellular with me.'' Taggart tugged his hat down on his head and met Noah's gaze defiantly.

Noah's brows lifted. ''Forgot?''

''Forgot.''

Felicity felt as though she was watching a duel—glares at ten paces. ''You've been known to forget things at times,'' he reminded Noah pointedly.

Neither spoke for a long moment. Then Noah kicked one of the tires. ''Yeah, I reckon so.'' The staring contest went on for a few more moments, then Noah cocked his head Felicity's way. ''You kept him in line, I hope.'' He gave her a wink that made her blush furiously. She hoped he'd think her heightened color was due to the still icy wind.

"Of course," she said in her best schoolteacher voice. "He was a perfect gentleman."

Noah laughed. "A perfect gentleman. Whoa! Wait'll I tell Mace and Jed!"

"Stow it," Taggart said gruffly. His face was red, too, and Felicity knew very well it wasn't just from the cold. "Did you come to harass us or are you gonna help get us out of here?"

Noah grinned and headed back to his own truck for chains. But even with the chains they were so far down the slope and at such an angle that they couldn't get out.

"Want me to call a tow truck?" Noah asked.

"No!" Taggart was adamant. "You think Felicity wants the world to know she spent the night in the truck with me?"

Felicity didn't actually care what the world knew, though she realized that was, perhaps, foolish of her. After yesterday evening's display on Apple Street, she knew this was a small town and not anonymous Southern California. "I don't mind."

"You do," Taggart said firmly. He looked her straight in the eye. "Sam Bacon's dad drives the tow truck."

"Oh."

Noah must have got the point, too, for he said, "I'll call Jed," and climbed the slope to his own truck to get his cellular phone.

"Tuck's uncle," Taggart told her. "He won't say a word."

Felicity could well believe that. "Fine."

While they were waiting for Jed, Noah called Tess and told her to get Becky. Then he handed the phone to Taggart.

"Hey, Pard. How you doin'?" There was a tenderness in his voice as he talked to his daughter that melted Felicity's heart. His smile broadened at the sound of her voice, then faded. "I know," he said after a moment. "I know I should've taken it with me. Then I could have called and you wouldn't have worried. I'm sorry."

Taggart's gaze flicked up to meet Felicity's. "She's fine, too." He hesitated, his eyes locking on Felicity's. "Yeah," he said a little hoarsely. "I...took good care of her." He looked away, his voice dropping. "Not long now. Jed's coming. I'll see you pretty soon. Promise." He smiled once more. "Love you, too, Pard."

Jed arrived an hour later in a heavy-duty truck with a winch on the back. For cattle as much as machinery, Noah told her.

Felicity smiled at Jed uncertainly, wondering if he, like Orrin Bacon, might look at her and Taggart with speculation in his eyes, but she could barely see them, shadowed as they were beneath the brim of his hat.

He gave her a faint nod, touched a finger to the brim of his hat and followed Noah and Taggart to study the lay of the land. In the end, it took forty-five minutes to get Taggart's truck out. Noah and Taggart discussed and theorized. Jed waited till they were done, then set to work. When they were once more on the road, he rolled down his window, touched his hat brim to her once more, then drove off.

"Talkative, isn't he," she said to Taggart when both Jed and Noah were gone.

Taggart shrugged. "That's Jed."

Once they got back on the road she could see that more than a foot of unseasonable snow blanketed the entire valley. The wind, still blowing, rearranged it in drifts. But the sun was strong and warm.

"It'll melt in two days or less," Taggart said as he drove her up Apple Street. Felicity was suddenly conscious of window curtains on either side. Was one twitching back just a bit? Was another being adjusted just now? She didn't care.

"Good. But I must say, I'm glad it happened." She turned to him and smiled.

He didn't. He looked grave as he parked in front of her house. She started to open the door, but he stopped her. "I'll carry you in."

"I thought you were worried about the neighbors."

His scowl surprised her. "You're right. Is your house unlocked? I'll go get you some better shoes." He came back a few minutes later with a pair of deck shoes. "If this is the best you can do, you'd better go to Bozeman and get prepared for winter."

Felicity slipped them on. "I will. I thought I'd have more time." She slid down out of the truck and followed him, stepping in his footsteps all the way to the door. "Will you come in?"

"Gotta pick up Becky." But he didn't immediately turn to go. He ducked his head, staring at the toe of his boot as he scuffed it through the snow on the porch. "I'm sorry...about last night. About getting stuck in the snow. About—" his color deepened "—everything."

"I'm not." She wanted to kiss him. She wanted to take that look of misery off his face and make him smile the way she knew he could smile.

She wanted to tell him she loved him. But if the rest of Elmer was ready and waiting to hear it, Taggart wasn't. Not yet.

Felicity wasn't positive that the residents of Apple Street were aware she had spent the night with Taggart Jones in his truck. If they were, they were discreet enough not to mention it—at least in her hearing. And if they passed on that little tidbit to anyone else, no one told Felicity. But even so, it took her three days to breathe a sigh of relief.

At last, though, when Monday's classes came and went and no one pointed a finger in her direction and tittered and giggled, she felt she had weathered the storm.

That storm. And the snowstorm which, as Taggart predicted, had all but melted away by Monday afternoon. In fact, the weather was almost balmy, making her feel that Friday night's experience might have been no more than a dream.

But another storm—also one Taggart had predicted—blew in Monday afternoon.

She had just settled down at her desk to go over some arithmetic assignments when a shadow from the doorway fell across the floor. She felt a leap in her heart—then she looked up and discovered it wasn't Taggart, but a man she didn't know.

He wasn't quite as tall as Taggart and not nearly as handsome. In fact, his features reminded Felicity of the pug dog that lived next door to her parents' home in Iowa.

She stood up. "Can I help you?"

"You're Ms. Albright?" His tone reminded her of the pug, too. There was a yappy belligerence in it that made her stay where she was, rather than go around the desk to shake his hand.

She nodded. "That's right. And you are…?"

"Orrin Bacon."

Felicity rubbed her palms surreptitiously against the sides of her skirt, drying them before offering her hand to Sam's father. "How nice of you to drop by. We missed you on Friday. I have the video if you'd like to—"

"Wouldn't," he said. "No time for foolishness." He gave her hand a quick, perfunctory shake. "It's what I came to talk to you about, Ms. Albright. That foolishness you had those kids doin' on Friday. Friday, hell—I mean, heck! They been doin' it for weeks! Waste of time.''

"I don't consider it foolishness, Mr. Bacon. Or a waste of time. It's simply another teaching method. One you may not be used to.''

"You can say that again! Stupid method. Playing when they oughta be learning.'' He scowled at her.

Felicity tried not to scowl at him. She drew a careful breath, reminding herself that she wasn't going to win any converts by battle. "Children learn in different ways, Mr. Bacon.''

"Nothin' wrong with the way I learned.''

"I'm sure there wasn't,'' Felicity said in as conciliatory a tone as she could manage. "And perhaps you learned well that way.''

"So can Sam if you stop coddling him.''

"I am not 'coddling' him, Mr. Bacon. Sam is working very hard.''

"Making toy guns.'' He snorted, nostrils flaring. "What the hell for?''

"So he gets a feel for the work that goes into making something. So that he has something to do with his hands while he listens to the tapes I've made of the history.''

Another snort. "Tapes! Why can't he just read the book and learn it?''

"He can,'' Felicity said. "But he hates it. It's a struggle.''

"It's work,'' Orrin Bacon agreed. "Nothin' wrong with work.''

"No. But there's nothing wrong with enjoying your work, either.''

He looked at her suspiciously, about to argue, then hesitating.

"Do you enjoy your work, Mr. Bacon?''

"Of course. Wouldn't do it if I didn't."

Felicity smiled. "I suspect Sam feels the same way."

"He's got to do it. He's a kid."

And where, Felicity wondered, was the logic in that? Kids shouldn't enjoy life; only adults had that right? "We all have to do things we don't like at times, Mr. Bacon," she agreed. "But when we can learn by doing something that feels right to us, don't you think it's better?"

Bacon clamped his jaw together, not speaking. The look he gave her was wary, suspicious.

"It's just that things are new," she said quietly.

They stared at each other. Bacon looked away first, and Felicity heard him mutter something under his breath about "furriners."

"I beg your pardon?"

His jaw jutted. "I said, I don't like all you hippy foreigners comin' in here tellin' us what to do. Go back to California where you're from."

"I'm from Iowa, Mr. Bacon," she told him. "I only lived in California. But some of my best friends are Californians." She smiled. He didn't. "Look, what it comes down to as far as I'm concerned, is, *is Sam learning?* And I think he is."

Bacon scowled. "You didn't learn that way, I bet."

"No, but I wish I had. I would," she said now, "if I was trying to learn something new."

"You're not a student now. You're a teacher."

"I still can learn. Can you?"

His eyes bugged at her direct challenge. "What? Of course I can. What are you playing at, Ms. Albright?"

"How about a deal?" She was making it up as she went along. "If I can learn something new, something hard, something that I would find challenging, you'll learn something, too?"

"What something?" Orrin Bacon asked suspiciously.

"To let me teach Sam my way."

He pondered that. "What are you going to learn?"

"I don't know yet. Something local. Quilting?" Alice could teach her that. "How to use Uncle Fred's printing press?" She'd love to do that. They could have a class newspaper. "What do you say, Mr. Bacon?"

For a full minute he didn't say anything. Then, at last, he nodded slowly. "But if you don't learn, then you start teaching Sam my way, right?"

"Right."

Orrin Bacon nodded. "All right, Ms. Albright. You got yourself a deal."

Ten

———

He owed her. Big time. But it was a debt Taggart wasn't at all reluctant to pay. Hell, if the truth were known, he'd been looking forward to it all week!

He was just glad he didn't have a school this weekend that would tie up all his time. Noah had a bunch of bronc riders in, and he would have to show up to do the video-taping, but other than that, he had no commitments.

Except making love to Felicity Albright.

When his parents had called to ask if Becky could come down and spend the weekend with them, well, it wasn't too hard to say yes.

"You won't be lonely, will you?" Becky asked worriedly Friday afternoon when her grandfather came to pick her up.

"I'll survive."

"You can go see Ms. Albright." Becky hadn't said too much about last Friday night. She knew he'd spent it stuck in his truck with Felicity Albright. Undoubtedly she had her own ideas of what transpired. Taggart was quite sure he was better off not knowing what they were.

"I could," he said vaguely. He wasn't going to deny it. Going to see her—making love to her—didn't mean he was going to marry her. Marriage wasn't an option, and he'd told her that. But a little loving—or a lot of loving—in a bed this time, would suit him just fine.

"I knew it!" Becky crowed.

Taggart scowled and pointed a finger at her. "You don't know nothin', young lady."

"I know that's a double negative!" She leapt, giggling, into his arms to kiss him good-bye.

Even though he fully intended to enjoy every moment of his weekend with Felicity Albright, he still felt a little nervous when he knocked on her front door an hour later. He hadn't called her all week—unsure, under the circumstances, what to say.

Now he didn't know, either. And he didn't know what she'd say to him.

The door opened. Her face lit up. "Taggart!"

"I brought dinner," he said, juggling the two small grocery sacks in his arms. "I hope you don't mind." It suddenly occurred to him that she might be going out. He stared at her, stricken.

But she only opened the door wider and smiled a welcome. "Come in."

She didn't step back, so he practically brushed against her as he passed. Certainly he was close enough to catch a whiff of lilacs again. He remembered it from last weekend when he'd held her in his arms, buried his face in her hair. A shaft of pure longing shot through him.

"What have you brought?" She followed him into the kitchen and watched as he unloaded the bags.

"Steak. Potatoes. Lettuce. Tomatoes. A bottle of salad dressing. Ice cream." He brandished each in turn. "Nothing fancy. I just—" He stopped, looking at her. God, she was beautiful. "I've been thinking about you all week," he said. *About touching you again. Loving you. Finishing what we'd only just begun.*

She dimpled. "And I've been thinking about you."

"You...don't have plans? I know I should've called first, but—" he shrugged "—I thought you might say no."

"No, I don't have plans?"

"No, you don't want to see me." He swallowed as their eyes locked.

"I want to see you, Taggart." Her voice was quiet, but firm. Her gaze seemed almost to devour him. "All week I've wanted to see you."

Me, too. He didn't say it, just sucked in a ragged breath. "Good." He cleared his throat. "That's good."

Still they stared at each other. Needing. Wanting. Hungering. And not for steak and potatoes. But since they were the excuse, Taggart felt obliged to try to get through them first.

"Do you want to do them on the grill?" Felicity asked him, unwrapping the meat.

"We can broil them."

"The grill would do a better job."

"But then we'd have to be outside." A grin quirked the corner of his mouth. "And Cloribel and company would be supervising."

"They'll know you're here, anyway," Felicity said. "They'll see your truck."

He shook his head. "I parked on Main Street," Taggart said. "In front of the bar."

"And you don't think they saw you coming up the street?"

"Maybe. But they won't think I'm still here hours from now."

"Are you going to be here hours from now?" she asked, raising her eyebrows. She leaned against one of the kitchen cabinets and crossed her arms over her breasts.

"I'd like to be."

A flush crept up Felicity's cheeks. She hugged herself tightly. She reminded Taggart of a doe, cornered, looking for a way to bolt. But then something inside her seemed to settle. She dropped her arms so that they hung loose at her sides. She pushed herself away from the counter and lifted her face to his.

"Good," she said.

It was all he needed. In two steps he was across the room and taking her in his arms. He folded her against him, kissing her with a week's—hell, months'!—worth of longing. The night they had spent in the truck had given him a brief, incomplete satisfaction. If for a few minutes his body had been sated, the rest of him had only grown to hunger for her more and more.

He needed her in every way he could think of. Mostly he needed to give her the loving she'd already given him. "I want you," he murmured against her lips. "I want to love you, Felicity."

She pulled back just far enough to look up at him with doelike eyes. "Yes," she whispered. "Oh, yes."

She took his hand and led him up the stairs into her bedroom. The furniture was old and heavy, dark and decidedly masculine. Fred's, no doubt. But the walls were cream-colored, and airy Irish lace curtains brought a contrasting feminine lightness to the room. Seascape watercolors hung on the walls, and on the table by her bed Taggart saw the photograph of a smiling young man. He tensed, knowing it was Dirk.

Felicity felt his tension and saw where he was looking. She reached over and picked up the photo, handing it to him. Taggart forced himself to look. Dirk was a combination of determination and gentleness. A kind man, Taggart thought. The sort of man Felicity deserved.

"He made you happy," he said, forcing the words through his too-tight throat.

Felicity brushed her fingers over Dirk's picture. "Yes," she said. And then she took it from his nerveless fingers and put it in her dresser drawer. Then she looped her hands around his neck and tugged his face down to hers. "And so will you."

He would, Taggart vowed, shutting his eyes. Or die trying. At least for tonight.

He threaded his fingers in her hair, luxuriating in the heavy silken tresses as he weighed them in his hands. He kissed her again. First her nose, then her eyes, then her mouth. He feathered kisses along her jaw and nuzzled her neck. Felicity made a sound almost like a purr.

He opened his eyes and smiled at her, then sat on the bed, drawing her into his arms. She came willingly. Eagerly. But there was a reserve about her, too. He had her. But he didn't have all of her. Yet.

His hands roved over her—arms, shoulders, breasts, hips. Learning her curves and contours. He remembered doing things like this to Felicity in his dreams and waking, hot and hungry and eminently unsatisfied. The reality was far better.

Now, smiling, he skimmed her scoop-necked shirt up and over her head in one quick movement and tossed it aside. And there she was, before him, creamy pale skin, narrow bones and a peach-colored bra that barely covered the fullness of her breasts. He cupped them in his hands, brushed his thumbs over them, making her tremble at his touch.

She reached for him, then, fingers fumbling with the front of his shirt.

"They're snaps," Taggart said. "Not buttons."

She laughed a little unsteadily. "You'd think I could see that." She undid them carefully, one by one, until his chest was exposed, and she ran her hands over it—over him—and it was his turn to tremble.

He lay back and she came with him, settling alongside him so that they lay knee to knee, nose to nose. They kissed, nipped, nibbled. He reached around and undid the clasp of her bra, then eased it off, and let the soft weight of her breasts spill into his hands. Then he bent his head and touched them each in turn with his tongue.

"Taggart!" Felicity wriggled against him, hooking an ankle over his calf and pressing against him.

"Mmm?" He didn't raise his head, but his hands kept working—though it didn't seem much like work, this caressing, touching, undoing the fastener of her slacks and sliding the zipper down. With care he hooked his thumbs in the waistband and eased them down over her hips, past her bottom. He did pull away long enough to tug them off and send them following the top she'd worn. And then he looked back at Felicity as she lay on the bed beside him.

She was everything a man could ask for. Warm and willing. Eager and waiting. Just for him.

She smiled and held out her arms to him. He shucked his boots and jeans and briefs, skinned off the scrap of peach-colored lace that was the last thing Felicity wore, and then he settled between her legs, trembling with anticipation.

Slow, he told himself. *Take it slow.* There might have

been an excuse for last time. There was none now. This time was for her. For both of them.

It was a dance of touch and taste. His fingers and hers. His lips and hers. Gentle brushing. Soft nibbling. Here. There. Everywhere. Circles and spirals, loops and lines. Focusing. Centering. Closer. Closer.

"Now," Felicity whispered. And she took him in. Loved him. Let him love her. The world splintered around them, and reality—and Felicity—brought him the satisfaction that dreams never had.

It was everything he wanted. It was more than he'd hoped. It was everything he feared. It was more than he dared.

He'd sought this once and thought he'd found it with Julie. He'd been wrong. Dead wrong. He'd consoled himself after she'd left him, telling himself it didn't matter because such joy didn't exist. For eight years he'd believed that.

Wrong again.

Eyes shut, he lay perfectly still. Felicity's fingers were gripping him hard, holding him close.

"I love you," she whispered.

Taggart felt his insides knot. Love you. Love you. The words echoed in his head. They were so easily spoken. So lightly said. Julie had said them. Then he'd believed. In the words. In Julie.

In himself.

And now?

Felicity isn't Julie, he told himself. But Felicity wasn't the problem. The problem, as Julie had been all too quick to point out, was him. A tight, painful sound filled the back of his throat.

Felicity's fingers stroked his back. Her lips teased the

curve of his ear. "Taggart?" she said. Her breath tickled his cheek.

He opened his eyes and slowly, very slowly, eased himself away from her, bracing above her on his hands, looking down into her face. She was smiling. An angel's smile. Something else he wasn't sure he believed in.

"Don't," he said, looking away, rolling off.

Her smile faded. "Don't? Don't what?"

"Don't love me." He shook his head, then turned his head to look over at her, to try to meet her gaze. It wasn't easy. She looked wounded. Eyes wide, hurt. No surprise. He was good at wounding people. The knowledge stiffened his faltering resolve.

"I don't want love," he told her raggedly.

Felicity didn't reply. She turned onto her side to face him, her expression serious, and she studied him with her big, wide eyes. She was close enough that he could feel her breath touch his cheek, but she didn't touch him.

"What *do* you want?" she asked slowly, almost gently.

He struggled to come up with the words. "Just…what we had. Closeness. A few hours— A little—" He broke off, unable to form them. It sounded crass when he tried to put it into words.

"A little sex?"

He scowled. "That's crude."

"You're the one who is saying it has nothing to do with love!" There was pain in her voice now, and the very sound of it hurt him, too.

Taggart moved away and sat on the side of the bed. "Hell." He rubbed his hands through his hair, then dragged them down his face. "I didn't want this. I never meant—I should never have come."

Felicity sat up, too, shoving herself against the headboard, grabbing the blanket and pulling it around her. "No, you shouldn't have! Not if that's all you're here for. What was tonight, Taggart? Payback time? A return engagement to make up for whatever inadequacies you thought you displayed last weekend in the truck?''

Her words knifed him. He felt the color rise in his cheeks. He didn't answer. He didn't have to. His silence was condemnation enough.

Felicity made a strangled sound and leapt off the bed. ''Well, thank you very much. Consider us even, then, won't you? Now, get dressed and get the hell out!'' She was scooping up his jeans and shirt and throwing them at him as she spoke.

He caught them. His boots came sailing, too, one after the other. He caught the first. The second narrowly missed his head. ''I didn't mean—I never intended—!'' But once more he couldn't find the right words.

''No,'' Felicity said bitterly. ''I can see that now. You never intended anything more than a roll in the sack, did you? Well, you got it. I trust you will keep the news of it to yourself,'' she said, her lips twisting as she spoke. ''Not only would it not do my professional reputation any good, it will prove better than anything that I'm a fool!''

She turned then and darted from the room. Taggart stared after her, feeling like he'd been gored. He heard the door to the bathroom slam. He stood irresolute, for a long moment, wanting to go after her, wanting to tell her it was all a mistake, wanting to say that he loved her, wanted to marry her and live happily ever after.

But this was reality. He got up and started to dress.

She hadn't come out by the time he'd finished. He hesitated outside the bathroom door, then tapped lightly. ''Felicity?''

The door opened. She was dressed, too, in jeans and a black shirt. It washed out her complexion, made her look pale and ashen. The glow of their lovemaking was already gone from her face. She didn't speak.

He pressed his lips together. "I wish..." he began, then shook his head. "Never mind. I'm sorry. I didn't want to hurt you. Really. And I'd only hurt you more if I—" He stopped again.

She stared at him, unblinking.

There was no point. "I'll go." He turned, then hesitated. "Thanks."

"For the sex?" Felicity said bitterly.

"No, damn it! Not the sex. Not...just the sex. For everything. Just...being you." He swallowed. "I'm sorry. I'll go. I just want... Oh, hell, if—if there's ever anything I can do for you..."

She gaped at him.

"Never mind." He shrugged awkwardly, then, crushing his hat in his hands, he stumbled down the stairs.

She was a fool.

She was mortified. Horrified.

At her gullibility. At the wanton way she'd behaved. Every time she thought about it, about him—about loving Taggart Jones—her cheeks flamed, her gut twisted, she felt ill.

She wanted to pack up and run back to California, Iowa, her mother's womb! Anywhere far enough to get away from the confusing, taunting memories that haunted her.

But there was nowhere she could go to run away from herself.

Or from the love she still felt.

Perverse as it was, she found that when the mortification began to fade, when the horror subsided, when the anger began to seep out of her bones, the love—heaven help her—was still there.

She didn't know what to do about it. About him. There was nothing she could do, she told herself. He'd made his decision; he'd shoved her—and her love—out of his life.

"Chicken," she called him fifty times a day. "Coward."

But she never had a chance to say it to his face.

And then five days after Taggart had turned her life upside down, Orrin Bacon called.

"Ms. Albright? Been waiting to hear from you," he drawled. "About our little deal."

"I'm sorry, Mr. Bacon. I've been...distracted."

"Maybe you'd rather not do it. Lot of pressure on you. I'd understand if you were to change your mind."

But he wouldn't change his, Felicity knew. "I haven't changed my mind, Mr. Bacon. I'll do it."

"Do what, Ms. Albright? What exactly is this new trick you're going to learn?" He was chuckling. She could hear him.

Another day she wouldn't have done it. Another minute and she might have been more level-headed. But right now Felicity was reckless with need and anger and sorrow and longing. "I'm going to learn to ride a bull."

"Don't talk nonsense."

Just hearing her voice on the phone had stunned him. For a moment the words made no sense. When they did, his anger flared. He'd spent the last few days—ever since he'd walked out of her house—trying to put her out of his mind, trying to convince himself he'd done the right thing getting her out of his life.

And now here she was back in it again.

And spouting garbage about wanting to ride a bull?

"You've had women in your classes before," she reminded him. He cursed the fact that he'd told her so.

"Cowgirls," he said dampeningly. "Women who knew one end of a horse from the other."

"I know one end rather well, thanks to my acquaintance with you. Besides, this isn't about horses. It's about bulls."

He swore under his breath. "What's all this about, Felicity?"

"Orrin Bacon. I made a deal with him." She sounded downright breezy as she babbled on about old dogs and new tricks and him agreeing to let her teach Sam her way if she'd learn to do something, too. "So I said I'd learn to ride a bull." She made it sound like she'd agreed to learn to knit!

"That's idiotic!" Taggart paced as far across his living room as the phone cord would allow, then stomped back the other way again.

"It's necessary," Felicity countered. "So when's your next school?"

"Saturday. It's full."

"You can make room. Becky says you often do."

"You asked Becky?"

He and his daughter weren't on the best of terms. Ever since he'd told her flat out that he wasn't interested in her teacher, that she needed to keep her mind on her schoolwork and out of his love life, she had been talking to him in monosyllables—if at all.

"I did not ask Becky. She volunteered the information some time ago," Felicity said stiffly. "She says you make room for friends. And while I may not qualify as a 'friend'"—her voice twisted both the word and his gut "—I think you might allow a mere acquaintance in, especially your daughter's teacher."

"Damn it, of course you're a friend!"

"Am I?" Her tone was cool. "And here I thought I was just a roll in the hay."

He gritted his teeth. "You were never...! Look, Felicity. There must be a thousand other things you could learn to do!"

"Of course there are, but this is the one I've agreed to. And I am not a chicken. What's the matter, Taggart? Are you?" she taunted.

"Damn you. No!"

"Well, then—?"

He raked a hand through his hair, then tugged it hard. "Oh, hell. All right."

She must have been out of her mind. That was all Felicity could think when she got up Saturday morning and realized that in an hour and a half she would have to turn up at bull-riding school.

She could call and back out, of course. It was what Orrin Bacon wanted. It was what Taggart wanted. In one sense, it was what *she* wanted. But she wouldn't do it.

Because more than she wanted to back out, she wanted to teach Sam the way he ought to be taught.

And because she wanted one last chance to see Taggart Jones—and make him see her. She'd felt this kind of determination only once before, when she had to convince her parents of her love for Dirk. It hadn't been easy. But she'd never regretted it.

She took Dirk's picture out of the drawer and looked at him. She hadn't been this scared since the day they got married. That had been a watershed moment, too. Everything in her life afterward had come as a result of that choice.

So it would—for better or worse—this weekend.

She brushed her thumb over Dirk's face. "Wish me luck," she whispered, and gave him a smile.

As always, he smiled back at her.

The cowboy hats were milling around when she got there. This time, though, she was one of them, wearing a new one she'd bought just yesterday. Tess Tanner had lent her some chaps, and old Mr. Eberhardt had come up with some spurs.

"Used to ride a few bulls myself in th'old days," he'd told her last night when he brought them over, folded inside the *Chronicle.*

Now she carried them to Taggart. The minute he looked up and saw her standing in front of him, all conversation in the room stopped. Did they all know? *What* did they all know? she wondered. Felicity ran her tongue along her upper lip, then held out the spurs. "Are these all right?"

Taggart took them from her. There was a low murmur of wonder that swept among the cowboys in the room. Taggart spun the rowels. He took his file and dulled one rowel, then another, carefully, deliberately. Then he handed them back to her.

Their eyes met. Felicity held herself very still.

"All right," Taggart said, eyes probing, querying, then finally sliding away. "Let's get started."

Eleven

He'd hoped she wouldn't show up. He'd known, of course, that she would.

It was the sort of woman Felicity Albright was. Stubborn, determined, committed. Crazy.

The same adjectives people had used to describe him when he resolved to keep Becky with him and take her down the road.

"A baby in a truck? You? By yourself?" He couldn't count the number of people who had gaped and shaken their heads at his foolishness. His own parents had told him he'd be better off to leave Becky with them. But he'd disagreed.

"A kid needs parents," he told them. "You were there for me when I was growing up. I'm gonna be there for Becky."

It hadn't been easy. Without Noah's and other cowboys' help at times, he couldn't have done it and he knew it. But he was glad he had. He had a relationship with his daughter that he never would have had if he'd left her with his folks.

She probably wouldn't have felt free to try to set him up with her teacher, for example. And he wouldn't be in the mess he was in right now.

How the hell was he going to teach Felicity—or anyone else, for that matter—how to ride a bull? He couldn't even think straight, let alone talk coherently.

The cowboys were shifting around restlessly in their chairs, waiting for him to get started. Felicity was watching him, too.

Just then, the door to the classroom opened and Becky poked her head in. "Daddy? You got a phone call at the house."

Taggart welcomed the reprieve. "Be right back," he said. With any luck she'd have come to her senses and left by the time he returned. He went up to the house.

"Taggart? Orrin here. She show up?" There was a note of mocking doubt in Orrin Bacon's tone.

No need to ask who he was talking about. Taggart straightened. His fingers tightened on the phone. "She showed up."

There was a second's surprised silence. Then, "With spurs on, no doubt." Orrin laughed.

"She has a pair, yes."

"Damn fool woman. You don't go lettin' her get hurt now."

"Injury is always a possibility in bull riding, Orrin. You know that."

"You ain't gonna let her on one, are you?"

"She has as much right to take my class as anyone else."

"But—but she's a *woman!*"

"I've noticed."

"She could get killed!"

"I hope not. I'll do my best to teach her how to be careful as well as how to ride. Why don't you come out and watch?"

"Watch? But what if—"

"I have to go, Orrin. I have a class waiting."

"But—!"

"Fish or cut bait, Orrin." Taggart banged down the phone and stalked back to the classroom, his mind whirling. He hadn't done much for Felicity Albright besides make her miserable since the day they'd met. He'd thought he owed her a night of loving. He'd been wrong. He didn't think he was wrong when he realized that he owed her this.

He walked straight over to her. "That was Orrin... checking up on you."

She looked nervous. "What'd you tell him?"

Taggart smiled grimly. "I told him to come out and watch you ride a bull."

It was the moment of truth.

Felicity stood on the metal rail of the chute and watched as the bulls were put in. In her mind she juggled a dozen thoughts, a thousand words. Put your feet even with the rope line when you start. Stay perpendicular to the back of the bull. Keep your body right over your feet. Angle your toes out. Pivot at the ankle, not the knee. Hug the bull with your calves. Keep your chin level. Don't drop your head. Be cool.

Only the last seemed to penetrate the fog swirling through her head. Cool, she told herself. Be cool. Be calm. Be collected. Don't think. Just react.

As if she'd be able to think, Felicity thought. The bull in the chute ahead of hers clanked loudly against the metal rails, blowing snot back over his shoulder and making the bell on his flank strap clatter as he kicked.

Tommy Hill, the high school boy slated for the ride, braced above the bull, hauled up on his rope once more, then lowered himself onto the bull's back. Half a dozen cowboys had already ridden—the advanced group, according to Taggart.

Now it was the beginners' turn.

Taggart, standing in the arena next to Jed McCall, who was going to pull the gate, was talking to Tommy as he eased down onto the bull's back. "Nice and slow," he was saying, his voice soothing. "Let him get used to you."

Felicity saw Tommy's hat bob once. The bull kicked against the metal. The railings clanged loudly once more. Tommy stood straight up again.

"It's okay. Go down again slow," Taggart said in the same calm, steady voice. "Good. Now, move up right into your hand. That's it."

Felicity could see Tommy wriggle forward cautiously.

The bull in the chute right below—*her* bull—snorted and kicked. She kept focused on Tommy.

"Ready," Taggart asked him.

Again Tommy nodded, one quick jerk. He let go of the rail and raised his arm, textbook perfect. Felicity could see the tension in his shoulders in the one moment of stillness before Jed pulled the gate and the bull exploded out of the chute.

It was over almost before it began. The bull spun sideways. Tommy slipped. His hand dropped. And he was on the ground and scrambling for the fence before Felicity could blink.

"Not bad for the first time," Taggart called. And then he looked at her.

She gulped.

"All right, Felicity," he said, his voice cool and professional. "Let's get you on this bull."

It was odd, she thought, how suddenly the world changed, shrank, and immediately everything around her became sharper, louder, clearer. The bull's back with its loose skin and rough hair. The pits in his one stubby horn. The smells of the resin on her rope and glove, of dirt and manure and chewing tobacco, of somebody's fruity bubble gum.

She was conscious of her knees wobbling. She sucked in a deep draught of air and hauled herself up to straddle the chute.

"Put on your glove," Taggart commanded.

She fished it out of her belt and pulled it on.

Taggart hauled himself up on the rail next to her. He was all business now. Steady. Firm. Dependable.

"Okay. Come on down." His voice had that same soothing tone he'd used with Tommy. Mindless, Felicity obeyed. She felt the loose warm hide of the bull spread beneath her. She felt the bite of the glove into the rope and instinctively rubbed it up and down, getting it warmer and tackier, the way real bull riders did. The way Dirk did with his cello bow.

Dirk.

You weren't supposed to think of anything irrelevant. You were supposed to stay focused, in tune. Taggart had said that. Felicity knew that.

And yet somehow the thought of Dirk gave her the edge she needed to clear everything else out of her head.

"I don't think about where to put my fingers," he'd said to her once when she was talking to him about a very difficult technical piece. "If I think about my fingers, I'll fumble all over the place. I'll hit the wrong notes altogether. I think about the music. I make music. I don't make notes."

"All set?" Taggart asked her. Her hand was wrapped. Her arm was up. Her calves clutched the sides of the bull.

I make music, Felicity thought. She smiled and drew in a breath. "Yes." Her voice was a whisper, but Jed heard her.

The gate swung open. Dirk fell away. Taggart fell away. Sam and Orrin Bacon and the rest of the world fell away.

It was just Felicity and the bull.

He gave a twist. A leap. A spin. She clung for one second. Two. Barely more. The world became a sea of color and motion, of power and thrust. Felicity clutched, meshed, balanced, swayed, flailed—was flung.

And then she had dirt in her mouth and her eyes, and felt the earth shaking beneath her as the bull's hooves barely missed her.

"Here!" Taggart yelled, and she scrambled toward him.

He hauled her up and onto the fence. "Okay?"

She lay half-over the fence, trembling, the world still spinning, all except the deep concern in his eyes just inches away.

"Okay," she said shakily. It had been like holding a tiger by the tail. Terrifying. Exhilarating. Awesome. She spat out a mouthful of dirt and grinned at him. "That's one." she said.

He admired her spirit, her determination, her grit.

He told his students he could teach them mechanics, but he couldn't teach them try. Felicity had try—in spades. She had everything he could ask for in a student—willingness, commitment, intensity.

He made up his mind to teach her the rest.

"That was a good move right there," he said when he critiqued her ride on the slow-motion video. "You were right where you were supposed to be." He forwarded the tape a few frames further. "See where your hand is here? You're starting to let it drop. When you do that, you pull yourself over to the side." He looked at Felicity.

She had a smudge of dirt on her cheek. Her braid was coming undone. She nodded, eyes intent on the video. He played the rest of the ride, including her spill face-first into the dirt. She grimaced, then laughed ruefully.

"You'll do better next time."

The smile she gave him nearly melted him in his boots. He steeled himself. "All right, guys...and girl—" he grinned at her "—let's go."

She did do better next time. They were using pretty mellow bulls by rodeo standards. But any bull could give you a thumping, and Felicity lasted almost four seconds on the brindle bull she got on later that afternoon.

"You kept your arm up this time. But there, see where you stopped gripping with your calves?" He pointed. She nodded. The tape rolled on, showing her flying off and landing hard on her shoulder in the dirt. "That's what happens," he said matter-of-factly. "Back to work."

He wouldn't have blamed her if she'd called it quits. But when the cowboys limped out of the room minutes later, headed for the barn, Felicity limped with them.

Becky was impressed. She'd scarcely believed it when Ms. Albright got out of the car that morning wearing jeans and boots and a hat.

Becky knew she had the expression on her face that her grandpa said would catch lots of flies. She couldn't help it.

She'd been tempted to run back into the house and call Susannah right then, but she didn't want to miss a moment. She'd stayed right by Ms. Albright all day long. She hadn't gone to play at Susannah's that afternoon. She hadn't even gone down to Bozeman to spend the day with her grandparents, though they came up to get her. "I can't," she said. "I gotta stay here."

And watch. Supervise. Pray.

She didn't even stop to think that God might not be listening to a troublemaker like her. He couldn't be leading her on. He couldn't! He wouldn't bring Ms. Albright all the way out here just to grind her into the dirt before Becky's and Taggart's very eyes.

Would He?

Not the God Becky was praying to.

She'd worried quite a bit this past week, because her dad hadn't been exactly easy to get along with. He'd even yelled at her about staying out of his love life and minding her p's and q's.

Susannah said that was normal, but it hadn't felt normal to Becky. Now she thought that maybe Susannah knew what she was talking about.

Except that her father and Ms. Albright didn't seem to be all that happy to see each other. Was that normal? Becky wasn't sure.

She was sure, though, that Ms. Albright would be an okay mom. She decided that after the second bull ride.

"You okay?" Becky asked worriedly when Ms. Albright came limping back to the bleachers where she sat. "You're bleeding." She pointed to a scrape on Ms. Albright's chin.

"Am I?" Ms. Albright dabbed at the cut with her finger, then opened the water jug Taggart had sitting on the bleachers, poured a little water onto a tissue and washed the scrape. Then she fished in her knapsack, rooted around, and pulled out a Band-Aid.

Becky stared.

Misinterpreting the look, Ms. Albright hesitated, "You think it's sissy to put on a Band-Aid?"

Becky shook her head. "I like Band-Aids."

"Will you put it on for me?"

Becky took the Band-Aid and peeled off the paper covering. Then gravely, carefully, she covered the scrape with the sterile pad and smoothed the ends of the Band-Aid down flat.

"There," she said, studying Ms. Albright's chin with satisfaction. She smiled and looked up into her teacher's eyes. Ms. Albright smiled right back.

"Do you like carrots?" Becky asked suddenly.

Ms. Albright blinked, then wrinkled her nose. "Hate 'em."

Becky beamed. It was like they were sharing a secret, Becky thought.

She hoped they were.

By the time they had ridden their third bull, had listened to Taggart critique every ride, and then had gone back over what they'd learned, Felicity thought she might never get up out of her chair.

Every muscle in her body hurt. Every bone. Every sinew. Every ligament. Every brain cell, too, she was sure—provided she had any left.

"That's it, then," Taggart said at last. "See you tomorrow morning. 8:30."

There was a slow scraping of chairs, a few muffled mutters and groans. She was comforted to see that she wasn't the only one easing herself stiffly out of her chair. She pulled on her jacket, picked up her knapsack and headed for the door.

"Felicity." Taggart's voice stopped her. She turned. "I'll call Orrin tonight and tell him you've done it."

"I haven't done it."

"You've done enough. You don't have to ride eight seconds. For God's sake, pros don't always ride the full eight seconds!''

"Pros don't ride bulls like the ones I've been on, either." Though God knew they were rank enough for her. "I have to do it once," she said firmly. "Just once."

If she did, there would be no question in anyone's mind that she had ridden a bull. If she didn't... No, that didn't bear thinking about. She wasn't going to have gone through this for nothing.

"You don't—"

"Good night, Taggart. I'll see you tomorrow."

When tomorrow came, Taggart was willing to bet, she'd hardly be able to move her eyeballs. He half expected that she wouldn't show up. After all, she wasn't really trying to learn to ride a bull; she was just there to prove a point, and as far as he was concerned, she'd proved it.

But when he came around the corner of the barn the next morning, there she was.

She still had a bandage on her chin, and when she moved, it looked as if she was giving it some thought beforehand. But she was there.

He said, "Back again?"

She said, "And ready to go."

He gave them a pep talk first thing, then reviewed fundamentals. He talked to them about role models and showed a couple of brief video clips of some of the best bull riders in the business today.

"Learn from them," he said. "Watch them. Remember, it isn't the style you want to imitate. It's the mechanics. And the try. Go on now. The bulls are ready. But remember what I told you. It not only works in bull riding, it works in life."

Felicity, sitting in the front row, muttered something under her breath.

Taggart frowned. "What?"

She didn't answer, just lifted her gaze and stared challengingly up at him. Everyone else got up and left.

Some of them rode better than yesterday. Some rode worse. Felicity hit the ground on the second spin. She stumbled getting to her feet and fell again. The bull kicked her in the back.

Taggart heard the sound on the protective vest she wore. He shut his eyes and felt the bottom of his stomach drop. Felicity made it to the fence and scrambled over. Taggart breathed again. He was sweating and it wasn't even hot.

At noon Orrin Bacon showed up. He pulled into the yard in his dark green truck and sat for a minute, looking over the group as they ate hot dogs and bratwursts that Taggart's mother and Tess had fixed. He looked smug and supremely pleased until his gaze fell on Felicity. Then the satisfied smile disappeared.

He got out of his truck and crossed the yard. Felicity, who had been eating with a couple of the college boys, saw him and stiffened. Taggart saw her excuse herself and go to meet Orrin Bacon. It didn't take a genius to guess at the content of the conversation. Orrin asked a question. Felicity answered. Orrin's satisfied smile reappeared.

Felicity turned and came toward him. "We're not done yet, are we?"

Taggart wished he dared say yes. She looked like a stiff wind would blow her away. He didn't see where she was getting the strength. But he owed her honesty. "Not quite. Though from here on out, it's up to you. We're done with the critiquing. We've only got the jackpot left to do."

"What's that?"

"Anybody who wants to enter throws five bucks in the

pot. We draw bulls and the guys ride. Just like a rodeo. Winner takes the pot. Two pots, actually, one for the beginners, one for the advanced. They don't have to be the full eight seconds. Just the best ride.''

''Guys?'' Felicity asked, eyes narrowing.

''Students,'' Taggart amended.

''So I can enter?''

''You could, but—''

''Good. I will.'' She gave Orrin a smile of her own.

''Who does the scoring?'' Orrin asked.

''Noah,'' Taggart said. ''And my dad.'' Sometimes he did it himself, but he didn't figure that would cut much ice with Orrin.

Orrin nodded. ''All right, little lady. One more chance.''

''Hey, Felicity drew Sunfish!''

''He ain't no beginner's bull!''

''Who put Sunfish in that round?''

''Whoa, wish I had 'im. That's half your points right there!''

''Gotta stick on 'im, though. Won't be easy.''

''I can do it,'' Felicity said in a voice so small that not one of them heard her. It didn't matter. Not as long as she heard herself. ''I can do it,'' she said again.

''You can do it,'' a small voice echoed beside her.

Felicity looked down. Becky stood looking up at her, eyes as green as Taggart's imploring and supporting her. Felicity smiled faintly. ''You think so?''

Becky nodded, then reached out a hand and squeezed Felicity's fingers hard. ''I know you can, Ms. Albright. If you want, I'll lend you my lucky spurs.''

A weight seemed to lift off Felicity's shoulders. She smiled again, this time inside as well as out. ''Thank you, Becky. I'd like that very much.''

* * *

Taggart wanted to punch Orrin Bacon in the face.

He sat there at the top of the bleachers, fat and complacent, like some smug toad about to eat a bug. And Felicity was down behind the chutes, preparing to be the bug.

"Sunfish! For God's sake, who put Sunfish's name in the beginner's draw?"

"Oh, dear. I'm afraid I did," his mother said. "I didn't know you had a bull called Sunfish. I thought you meant Sunbonnet. You know, that nice little Angus bull?"

Taggart knew. It didn't help. He couldn't change things now. Everybody knew about Sunfish. Half of the guys envied Felicity for drawing him. The other half were glad it had been her and not them.

Taggart went back behind the chutes, uncertain what to say. He didn't want to spook her any more than she undoubtedly already was. The first riders were already going. He didn't pay any attention. He looked around for Felicity.

She was standing off in a corner by herself, not looking at the bulls or at the cowboys riding. She was in the midst of mayhem and yet seemed totally by herself. In a zone. He understood. He'd been there himself, looking for that center somewhere deep inside to hang on to.

Just then, she seemed to snap back to the present and look around. Her face was pale, but composed. It was a strong face, he thought now. Her bones were fine, but not frail. There was nothing ethereal or insubstantial about her.

"Felicity?"

She looked at him, seeing him for the first time.

He gave her a grave smile. "You can do it. Knock 'em dead."

When Sunfish blew out of the chute, he nearly ripped her arm right off. She didn't know how she managed to stay aboard, but she did. Maybe it was providence. Maybe it was grace. Maybe it was the extra suicide wrap one of the boys showed her how to take around her hand.

Whatever it was, she didn't ride pretty, but she rode.

She was whipped and spun, snatched and flung. But her calves stayed hard against Sunfish's sides. Her fingers stayed wrapped in the rope, and her overhead hand stayed high. She made a ride that was full of the clashes of cymbals and the pounding of drums. But in the end, it was music, not notes.

She heard yells and exhortations, cheers and shouts. Then she heard the loud blare of a truck horn that went on and on.

The buzzer! she thought. The buzzer! I've made it.

And then she couldn't figure out how to get off.

Wasn't that always the way? Nine times out of ten you got thrown off without wanting to, without even trying. And now, when you wanted—*needed*—to, you were stuck!

She wiggled her hand, trying desperately to free it, to shake off that last wrap. It held fast. She dropped her other hand, wanting to use it to free herself. But just as Taggart had said it would, brought down low, it threw her off-balance, caused her to slip sideways into the well of the twisting bull.

Jerked and snapped, flung and plunged, she slipped, slid, fell—but still couldn't let go. The bull's hooves caught her legs. Her arm was whipped and yanked, her body trapped. She saw Mace Nichols, who'd been doing the bull fighting, trying to move in close enough to free her. Jed and Taggart appeared out of nowhere, running, yelling, trying to move in, too. Desperately Felicity tried once more to wriggle free of the rope.

Suddenly Mace was next to her, shouldering his way in, catching hold of the bull with one hand and sliding his arm beneath her trapped one, levering it up and breaking the press of her weight against her hand hold.

Free, Felicity thought, free at last!

She fell to the dirt, stunned. Taggart bent over her. His face was ashen. "Are you all right?"

She knew he didn't mean that literally. He meant, *Are you alive?*

She was. Barely. She managed a smile. "Tell Orrin I know how to ride a bull."

The EMTs said she had some pretty impressive bruises. They said she had whiplash and that she was lucky she hadn't dislocated her shoulder and it wouldn't hurt to have an X ray just to check on her head.

They might have meant to see if she was concussed, but Felicity suspected they thought she was nuts and that had simply been a polite way of saying so. Maybe she was, but she was satisfied, too.

She was sitting on the table at the back of the classroom where they had taken her on a stretcher to poke and prod and check her over while the rest of the bull riding was still going on. But the minute they finished with her and opened the door, Orrin came directly in to see her.

The bluster was gone. "I gotta hand it to you, little lady," he said, shaking his head. "You got guts." He pumped her hand, making her grimace. "Oops. Sorry."

Felicity smiled a pained smile, and eased her hand out of his grasp. "It's all right."

"And you? You're all right?"

"A little sore, but I'll be fine," she assured him.

"Good. Good. Wouldn't want you missing any school, would we?" He shot her a quick look, one that said she'd won and he knew it.

Felicity smiled. "No," she said. "We wouldn't." Then,

wanting it spelled out, she asked, "Does this mean you think you can trust me to know how to teach Sam now?"

Orrin Bacon smiled, too, a little self-consciously, then took a deep breath and nodded. "Said so, didn't I? I reckon I'll learn. I probably should say I'm sorry I pushed you to do this—" she opened her mouth to protest, but he held up a hand "—but I'm not. I admire you for it. You put your body where your mouth was, little lady. I'm proud to have you teach in our school. I'm proud to have you teach my son."

"Thank you," Felicity said faintly. "I'll do my best."

They shook hands again, more gently this time. Then Orrin Bacon left.

"I'm glad you're my teacher, too," Felicity heard Becky say soberly, and she realized that all this time the child had been sitting on a chair in the corner of the room. Now she came to stand next to the table where Felicity sat.

"You rode 'im good," she said. "Did my spurs help?"

"Oh, my, yes. Thank you."

"I'll lend 'em to you whenever you want."

"I…probably won't be riding any more bulls."

"Good. I don't want you to. I used to think I wanted to ride bulls like my dad, but after today, I don't think so." Becky still looked very worried.

"Not everyone gets hung up, Becky," Felicity said gently.

"But you did. You could've…you could've…" The little girl's lower lip quivered. Her green eyes were round and full of tears. "I'm glad you're not dead."

A faint smile lifted the corners of Felicity's mouth. "I'm glad, too."

"I wish…" Becky began, then her voice faded. She hugged her arms tightly across her chest. "I wish…" She tried again, then shook her head.

Felicity reached out and touched the little girl's cheek. They looked at each other. There were so many words, Felicity thought. None of which either of them dared to say.

Suddenly the room was filled with milling, whooping cowboys. "Hey, Felicity! Lookee here!" They crowded around her, beaming, and Becky got swallowed up in the throng. One of them handed Felicity a fistful of bills. "You won!"

She gaped at him. "Won? The jackpot?"

"You got a 65!"

"That's prob'ly 50 for Sunfish and 15 for you, but who cares?" Tommy Hill grinned at her.

"Not me." Felicity grinned, too. She felt giddy, disoriented, happy—and somehow desolate at the same time. Maybe she did have a concussion, after all.

"That'll teach ol' Orrin!" one of them crowed. "You better go out and celebrate! You deserve it."

"We all deserve it!" someone else yelled, and several more whooped their agreement.

"Of course," Felicity said, mustering what enthusiasm she could. "We will—with all this lovely money."

A general round of raucous cheers greeted that announcement. "Yea, Felicity!" And two of them made to hoist her onto their shoulders.

"Put her down!"

A sudden stunned silence filled the room. Taggart stood in the doorway, glaring at them, hands on his hips, green eyes flashing fire.

Slowly, with exquisite care, they put her down and stood staring at their boots.

"Back off," Taggart said tersely. "Give her some room. Better yet, get your carcasses out of here and let her rest."

Felicity had never heard him sound this way before—harsh and angry, ready to fight.

"I'm all right," she protested, trying to lever herself off the table.

He ignored her. "Out," he said to the men. "All of you. Now."

They shuffled. They mumbled. They grumbled. They left.

All but Taggart—and Becky.

"You, too," he said to his daughter. "Grandma and Grandpa are waiting for you up at the house."

"But—" Becky's gaze flickered from her father to Felicity and back again, worriedly, warily, as if she didn't know what was going on.

You're not the only one, Felicity thought.

"Go on now," Taggart said in a gentler tone. "I need to take Ms. Albright home."

"You don't—" Felicity began.

But Taggart was walking Becky toward the door. "Please, Pard."

She looked up at him. Their gazes met. Whatever passed between them, Felicity couldn't see.

Then Becky nodded once. She turned and looked back at her. "'Night, Ms. Albright."

"'Night, Becky."

Becky started down the steps, then stopped and looked back at her father. "She doesn't like carrots, either."

They rode the whole way to town in silence. Only when they reached the highway and Taggart had the choice of turning south toward Livingston or taking Main Street toward Apple Street, did he speak.

"You sure I can't take you to the hospital?"

"I don't want to go to the hospital." She hurt enough.

She didn't want any more poking and prodding of her body that night.

Taggart didn't argue. His lips set in a firm line, but he turned on Main, and the next thing Felicity knew, they were in front of her house. It was dark and she hadn't left a light on. Of course, Cloris had her porch light on. So did Alice. She just hoped they wouldn't come running out when they saw Taggart driving her home instead of her coming by herself.

"Thank you," she said tonelessly. She reached for the door handle, but he was out of the truck and coming around to open it for her almost before she'd moved.

Because he could hardly wait to be done with her, no doubt. Well, he could leave right now! She didn't know why he'd bothered to drive her home. Surely he didn't expect her gratitude to extend to a night in her bedroom! No, of course he wouldn't.

This was just some more stubborn Taggart Jones responsibility, she supposed. He needn't have bothered. She could get by just fine without his help. God knew in the long run she was going to have to. She'd accepted that over the past two days.

She couldn't control Taggart any more than she'd been able to control those bulls. He would do what he had to do, what he felt was right for him, and that was all she could ask. It hurt, but she knew that you survived hurt. She'd done it after Dirk's death. She'd do it again.

Taggart took her arm to help her down from the cab. She pulled away from him abruptly, hurting her shoulder as she did so. She sucked in a sharp breath. "I can move on my own!"

Taggart muttered something under his breath, but stepped back, stuffing his hands into the pockets of his jeans, and let her get down by herself. She was already stiffening up again, and she limped as she went up the walk. She thought perhaps he'd leave if she didn't acknowledge him, but instead he followed her up the walk.

She rounded on him. "You don't have to trail after me! I'm fine. Leave me alone!" She was perilously close to tears. Apparently knowing she'd survive and having to face it were two different things.

Was it the sudden depletion of adrenaline, maybe? The letdown after she survived her hang-up on the last bull ride? Or was it because she knew that for all Orrin Bacon would be singing her praises now and welcoming her into Elmer Elementary School, she also knew she couldn't stay.

It was like the old westerns always said—the town wasn't big enough for both her and Taggart Jones.

"I want to talk to you," Taggart said. He didn't come any farther, but he didn't leave, either. He stood at the foot of the steps, looking up at her.

"Now?"

He nodded.

Felicity gripped a porch pillar. "Fine. Talk."

He glanced around as if he could see the curtains twitching. "I'd like to come in."

Felicity gave her best imitation of an indifferent shrug. Whatever he had to say couldn't be any harder to listen to than everything he'd already said. "Suit yourself." She turned and opened the door, going in. Taggart followed her.

Felicity turned on the light, then turned to face him. "Forgive me if I don't offer you coffee, but I don't think you'll be staying that long."

"I'd like to," he said quietly.

She stared at him, jolted.

Was he expecting to go to her bedroom then? Her eyes narrowed suspiciously.

Taggart shifted from one foot to the other, looking less

remote now than ill at ease. He still didn't speak, though. Neither did Felicity. She couldn't think of a thing to say.

Finally he ran his tongue over his upper lip and swallowed. "I know it isn't worth much," he told her, "but I wanted to tell you...I was proud of you." Green eyes met hers, deep and intense.

Felicity knotted her fingers in front of her. "Thank you."

"You've got guts."

"Thank you again."

His mouth twisted. "So, after a fashion, does Orrin—being willing to trust you with his kid. Even though you proved yourself, he's still taking a risk."

She didn't know what to say to that, so she didn't say anything.

Taggart dug his toe into the faded rug underfoot. "Made me think," he said, "how everybody else has guts but me." He slanted her a quick glance.

Felicity stared at him, breath drawn in, mute.

He sighed. "I talk a good fight," he told her. "You heard me." Once more a corner of his mouth lifted self-deprecatingly. "All that stuff about determination and willingness to risk and try. And I can do it on a bull. But I don't do so good in real life."

Which meant...what? Felicity didn't say a word, only waited.

Taggart ducked his head and stared at the floor for a long moment, then raised his eyes once more to meet hers. "What happened with Julie scared me spitless. I felt I'd let her down bad, and maybe I did."

"You don't have to explain."

"Yes, I do, because it's what I used as an excuse not to try again. Like if you'd got thrown and never got on another bull."

"It's hardly the same thing."

"It's exactly the same thing. All that stuff I spouted about bull riding being like life. Well, it's true. Only I never managed the connection myself. You did. You got up and got on again. Didn't you?" His eyes bored into hers.

Felicity ran her tongue over her lips, then nodded slowly.

"You tried again," he said heavily. Then he gave her a look that was both hungry and wistful. "I'd like to try again, too."

Felicity felt like her tongue was welded to the roof of her mouth. Was he saying what she'd hoped for so long that he'd say? Or was she, in fact, concussed?

"Maybe I should have that X ray after all?" she said faintly, still disbelieving. Her knees wobbled and she gripped the back of the overstuffed chair.

Taggart closed the distance between them and put his hands on her arms, his grip gentle, but strong, supporting her. A rueful smile quirked the corner of his mouth. "You aren't concussed. Everything you're hearing is true. I love you, Felicity. I've loved you for a long time and it's scared me to death." He gave a shaky laugh. "I'm still scared, but I can't be any more scared than you were when you got on those bulls."

Lifting a hand, she touched his cheek. "I was terrified," she admitted.

"Yeah, well, so am I. And you ought to be to, 'cause I'm asking you to marry me."

Her eyes widened. Her heart leapt. She stared up into his gaze, hardly daring to believe his words. But she could see the truth there in his eyes. She saw his heart, his soul—his love— waiting just for her.

"Well," he said impatiently and more than a little apprehensively when she didn't reply at once. "What do you say?"

Felicity blinked. She sniffed. She managed a watery

smile and winced as she raised her arms to loop them around his neck and draw his head down for a kiss.

"Yes," she said. "Oh, yes."

"What *is* that smell?"

Taggart knelt naked straddling Felicity's equally naked thighs as he rubbed the soothing salve into her back. He rued the bruises he saw forming. He bent to kiss each one. "Horse liniment," he said. "Bag balm. Oil of wintergreen. Camphor. A little turpentine." He grinned. "I really don't know what it is. My sister dreamed it up. She's trustworthy."

"Do I get to meet your sister?"

"Not today. Today you're staying right here." He straightened up and began to knead her shoulders.

Felicity sighed. "Heaven," she mumbled and tried to roll over, but he kept her trapped between his legs. She was smiling. He was glad. He wanted her to keep smiling for the rest of her life. He leaned down and feathered a row of kisses along her spine.

She shivered. "Taggart," she protested.

"Hmm?" He nuzzled her neck.

"You're insatiable."

"Uh-huh."

He was—but not just for her touch. For all of her. Forever. Mind and body. Heart and soul.

He'd come so close to losing her. Not just to Sunfish—though the memory of her hung up on that bull would haunt him the rest of his days—but to his own reluctance to risk, to love again. After his divorce from Julie, it had seemed smarter—safer—not to.

Why bother to try when you might only get hurt? Why dare when you might just get shot down?

When was love worth the risk it would take?

The sight of Felicity's tense, white face as she'd settled down on Sunfish this morning had answered that question for him.

First it had made him want to stop her. *You don't need to do this!* he'd wanted to say.

But the look she had given him froze the words in his throat. There had been a steadiness in her gaze, a centerness that he'd seen in other bull riders. One he'd found, when he was riding, inside himself. He recognized it, understood it. But there had been something else, too. There had been a connection—a link between them, a trust that he didn't think he imagined.

It was as if she had been saying, *I can do this because you taught me how, because I know you believe in me.*

And sensing that trust, he'd answered with his eyes. *I do. I'll help you.*

Now he hoped to God that, when it came to love and marriage, Felicity would help him, too.

She tried once more to turn beneath him, and this time he let her. They looked at each other a long time. Touched. Smiled.

The connection—the trust, the love—was still there.

"Come to me, Taggart," Felicity whispered then, and held out her arms to him. "I must be insatiable, too."

He sighed and settled into the warmth of her embrace. He should have been sated, loving her the way he had. But he wasn't. He didn't think he ever would be. He ought to let her rest. She had to be stiff and sore.

But when he said so, she just shook her head. "I'm fine. Must be that miracle salve you're using."

"I love you."

"Show me."

He smiled, no proof against her touch and the flame of

love in her eyes. "Maybe I will," he murmured, feathering kisses in her hair, "just once more."

Felicity smiled. "Just once?"

"Well, maybe more than once." He kissed her mouth. And then, with exquisite care, he set about showing her how much she meant to him.

He drew her on top of him this time, then waited, letting her settle over him and take him deep inside. And then their gazes, their bodies, their very hearts and souls were locked together.

Two made one.

He still wasn't sure he deserved this love she was offering, but if it was his for the asking, he wasn't saying no.

He was saying yes, please, forever. And ever. Amen.

"When will you marry me?"

It was morning now. Late morning. His truck was still parked in front of her house. No doubt the neighbors would already have spread the news. If they didn't, the secretary at Elmer Elementary certainly would have, after Felicity had called at six-thirty to tell her she wouldn't be in that day, she was just a little too stiff and sore.

And not entirely from bull riding, either, though she didn't mention that.

"As soon as you want," Felicity said now, nibbling along the line of Taggart's jaw.

"Tomorrow?"

"In a hurry, are you?"

"Damn right. Besides, ol' Cloribel and company will want you to make an honest man out of me."

"I will," Felicity promised. "But maybe we should wait till the weekend. I have to teach tomorrow."

Taggart smiled thinking about how her students would react to the news. "Wonder what Becky will say."

"I don't," Felicity said dryly.

He laughed. "Neither do I. She'll say I told you so." He rolled over onto his back and pulled Felicity on top of him. "When we get married, you'll have your daughter in your class. Think you can handle that?"

Felicity smiled lazily. "I'm looking forward to it. But I'm looking forward to having her in my family even more."

"She's going to be thrilled." And Taggart, remembering Becky's imploring looks, her desperate intensity, knew that *thrilled* didn't even begin to cover it.

"She can be my bridesmaid," Felicity said. "I'll make our dresses."

"She'll like that." An understatement if there ever was one. Taggart smiled, imagining the two of them—the women in his life—walking down the aisle to meet him. Then a grin split his face. He laughed.

"What?" Felicity demanded.

Still grinning he rolled her in his arms. "I was just wondering if we'll be able to talk her out of wearing her spurs!"

* * * * *

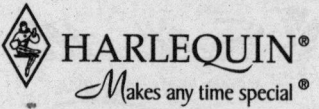

Silhouette® Desire is proud to present

SONS OF THE DESERT

THE SULTANS

Powerful sheikhs born to rule and destined to find love as eternal as the sands.

In three breathtakingly sensual new romances, Alexandra Sellers continues her bestselling series, Sons of the Desert. Love and adventure are the destiny of the three grandsons of the late Sultan of Bagestan, who must fight to overthrow a ruthless dictator and restore the sultanate.

Look for these exciting stories:

The Sultan's Heir
(Desire #1379—July 2001)

Undercover Sultan
(Desire #1385—August 2001)

Sleeping with the Sultan
(Desire #1391—September 2001)

Available at your favorite retail outlet.

Where love comes alive™